Cheryl Lanktree is a clinical psychologist who is on the faculty of the University of Southern California, and trains therapists on trauma treatment throughout the United States. She has co-authored two non-fiction books. *The Last Vanishing Point* is her first novel. She lives in southern California with her husband and their Labrador retriever.

For Flight Officer Bruce Graham Black, whose art, courage, love, and sense of wonder of all things beautiful live on.

Cheryl Lanktree

THE LAST VANISHING POINT

AUSTIN MACAULEY PUBLISHERS™

LONDON • CAMBRIDGE • NEW YORK • SHARJAH

Ordering Information
Quantity sales: Special discounts are available on quantity purchases by corporations, associations, and others. For details, contact the publisher at the address below.

Publisher's Cataloging-in-Publication Data
Lanktree, Cheryl
The Last Vanishing Point

ISBN 9781647507114 (Paperback)
ISBN 9781647507121 (Audiobook)
ISBN 9781647507138 (ePub e-book)

Library of Congress Control Number: 2021920865

www.austinmacauley.com/us

First Published 2023
Austin Macauley Publishers LLC
40 Wall Street, 33rd Floor, Suite 3302
New York, NY 10005
USA

mail-usa@austinmacauley.com
+1 (646) 5125767

The Last Vanishing Point would not have happened if not for the love and art that Bruce Black and Gloria Morgan shared, and inspired me to begin writing almost nine years ago.

I am especially grateful to Eve La Salle Caram, an accomplished novelist and award-winning teacher who mentored me with kindness, wisdom, and wit from my first fiction-writing class in the UCLA Extension Writer's Program to the subsequent Algonquin West writer's group, and through the following years of countless drafts. Your insight and encouragement to keep writing will always be appreciated. All beginning novelists should be so lucky!

I wish to extend my heartfelt gratitude to all those who read *The Last Vanishing Point* in varying degrees of completion, and in some cases, multiple installments and drafts, while enthusiastically encouraging me to keep writing. Your thoughtful feedback and belief in this story kept me going in ways you could never imagine. Thanks so much, dear friends and family—Carl Maida, Sarah Kenney, Anne Galbraith, Meghan Ingstad, Bruce Lanktree, Jean Lanktree, James Manson, and Lucy Berliner. I am also very grateful to Mark Cousins and Gillian Moreton who provided much inspiration and loving companionship while traveling together to many places that appear in this novel, as well as sharing thought-provoking feedback on the manuscript and invaluable advice in the pursuit of publication.

Special thanks to my sister, Lynda Manson. We have taken a monumental creative journey together and may there be many more. My gratitude is boundless to Roy Lanktree, for your legacy of curiosity, appreciation of unseen wonders, and unique sense of humor.

To wonderful friends near and far: Colleen Friend, Lorna Gallant, Rosland Gellatly, Mandy Habib, Naomi Halpern, Claire and Bill Hurst, Victor Labruna, Usha Raj, Ellen Ridgeway, and Susanne and Stirling Sublett, we have shared so happy times through the many years of writing this novel and before it all began. I am forever grateful to share this life with amazing people like all of you.

I am deeply indebted to Jennifer McKinley, Holly McKee, Norman Black, Dave Manson, Marcel Croteau, Laurie Morgan, Scott Morgan, Brenda Morgan, and Bruce Morgan who provided essential material used in writing The Last Vanishing Point.

To Jake, Molly, and Winston Blue—your steadfast devotion and joyful appreciation of road trips and beach walks reminded me always of what is most important. And finally, I am grateful most of all, to John Briere, my partner in life and creative adventures. Your love and support for so many years, continue to sustain and inspire me.

Vanishing Point

1. (Fine Arts and Visual Arts/Art Terms) The point to which parallel lines appear to converge in the rendering of perspective, usually on the horizon.
2. A point in space or time at or beyond which something disappears or ceases to exist.

Part I

Family Secrets

Toronto, Canada, 2013

Just when you think you have escaped the past, there it is. My sister and I had returned to the house where we grew up to help our father prepare for his next chapter. Mom had died a few months before. The last time I saw her, she would look at me with a puzzled expression then shake her head and say, "I should know you. Who are you again?"

She died clutching onto secrets that remained locked away but still affected our family deeply. The historian in me longed to know what had happened to her to cause the angry outbursts and impatient demands for perfection. When we were kids, she would sometimes be giddy with joy in family gatherings, then suddenly without warning, become silent and retreat into herself.

While we packed her antique Limoges china into boxes labeled 'Good Dishes,' in the dining room, Lauren and I talked in the ebb-and-flow rhythm of remembrance. The gleaming table was the scene of so many memories. I saw my younger self sitting there writing my master's thesis. Another time, home for the Christmas break, I sat talking on the phone late into the night to an intense graduate student who would later become my husband. Years later, Lauren and I served tea and strawberry cream layer cake for our parents' 50th wedding anniversary celebration.

I was living in San Francisco, working as a history professor and writer, teaching at a small college in nearby Oakland. I wasn't sure I wanted to face the memories and secrets of our family after so many years away. But I always had a strong sense of duty. No matter how long it had been since I left, invisible ropes pulled me back.

Lauren sat by the large paned windows overlooking the lawn rolling down to the lake, packing crystal goblets and the sterling silver tea service that had been passed down from our grandmother. She was dressed in a long, beige linen skirt and tangerine silk blouse. Her fingers sparkled with emeralds and diamonds catching the light and brightening the room in flashes of green and white. Her long, vivid red hair contrasted with the heaviness of the day. She had an artist's sense of color and design. Even before she started school, she had created tiny outfits for her dolls. Lately, she painted landscapes with pastel skies and beams of golden light filtering through billowing clouds that mingled with mist rising from blue-gray water.

That afternoon, we worked mostly in thoughtful silence, then suddenly would collapse into fits of giggles, with the discovery of more artifacts from our parents' life together—odd ceramic ornaments, garish pottery, and suggestively obscene wooden statues—wedding presents, and souvenirs from their trips to Hawaii, Europe, Africa, and Australia.

"Why would they keep these, Liv?" Lauren cried, as she held up a bowl in the avocado green of the 1970s, then a grimacing pottery troll, a souvenir from a Scandinavian cruise.

"Mom never liked to part with anything," I said with a catch in my voice.

"Yeah. Dad isn't so sentimental. He doesn't mind hurting someone's feelings if he feels they have wronged him," she said and then added, "Remember when he yelled at our neighbor, 'You just ran over my rose bush, Fred—you goddamn idiot!' and ran after him down the street?"

"Yes, he does have a strong sense of justice," I agreed with a smile. I felt especially grateful that we still had Dad. We were in this thing together.

At that moment, he was in his study sorting through papers and called out, "How's it going, girls?" He was having a good time shredding documents, always vigilant against identity theft.

The furniture movers arrived at the back door later that morning. The older, brawnier one who was clearly in charge—a large, cheerful, curly-haired man with warm brown eyes and muscular, tattoo-sleeved arms—greeted us with, "Hi, Olivia and Lauren, right? Nice to meet ya." Then he said with a friendly grin, "Name's Stu and this here is Pete." He gestured to a younger man with a pony tail and a gap-toothed grin. They shook our hands firmly. "Your father gave us the list. Okay, let's get this show on the road!" he said, then both men followed me up the stairs to the master bedroom where they quickly began dismantling and removing furniture—an eclectic collection of French provincial and mid-century dressers, chairs, mirrors, nightstands, headboard, and a floral, chintz reading chair. Somehow, Mom had made it all work.

Over the next few hours, pieces of our family's life were carried away. As they were finishing up, Stu paused when he walked back through the kitchen and gazed at Lauren who sat by the window wrapping dishes.

"You look just like a painting," he said in a quiet voice. It was an odd comment especially for a furniture mover, but then I noticed she was backlit in the soft glow of the morning light, like a forgotten Impressionist portrait. Other strange things would happen that day.

I felt the ghost of our mother following us as we worked in one room then another. It was a house of shadows, shards of memories, and creaking floors. I heard her voice, "I'm not ready for this. Why are you leaving my house? Where are you going? Don't leave me."

We found boxes moved to different rooms from where they had been left—the contents re-arranged. A coin suddenly appeared on the floor of an empty room that had been swept clean. As Lauren packed another box in the living room, a small cascade of more coins inexplicably dropped in front of her and she yelped, calling to me, "Liv, where are these coming from?" It felt like we were being watched.

In the damp, dimly lit basement, we found tall stacks of books revealing some of Mom's passions from her younger days—*Wuthering Heights*, *The Tenant of Wildfell Hall*, *Pride and Prejudice*, *A Tale of Two Cities*, *The Great Gatsby*, Europe guidebooks and maps, art history books, and a French dictionary. I thought about what she had given up to be a housewife and a mother. I shuddered at the resentment this decision might have caused her.

Then, an old cedar chest caught my eye sitting long forgotten in a corner of the musty darkness. I knelt down on the shag rug covering the concrete floor and lifted the heavy lid. Buried under layers of old blankets, crocheted table cloths, and hand-embroidered pillowcases was an antique tin box wrapped in delicate lace doilies. I held my breath as I slowly opened it. On the top was a collection of medals, pieces of costume jewelry, and a few Victorian-era photographs. As I dug deeper, a bundle of letters tied with a blue ribbon appeared.

I opened the first letter and then the next, each one addressed "Dear Auntie." I knew this was our Great-aunt Elizabeth—Mom's aunt—also known as Aunt Lizzie. She had been a successful clothing designer in Toronto many years before and had married four times. Auntie had a dry wit, sometimes used to conceal an air of sadness. She was also opinionated, elegant, and charming.

"Oh my God, Lauren," I said. "These are letters from Uncle William when he was stationed in England—from somewhere called 'The Manor.'"

William was an artist and our mother's younger brother. When I was a kid, I asked Mom questions about him when I noticed his photograph hanging in the hallway. Her answer was always curt, "He died. His wife Maddie was a concert pianist in New York City." Then her face would tighten and close down.

Portraits of beautiful plein air landscapes, Uncle William painted before he enlisted in the Royal Canadian Air Force (RCAF) in 1942, were hung in our house. They were signed CRAIG, his last name, in the bottom right-hand corner followed by the year—1940, 1941, 1942. He was Mom's 'Irish twin,' born eleven months after her in 1921.

I found out more as time went on. He was a graceful dancer, a boxer, and a long-distance runner. He listened to opera on the radio Saturday afternoons. He was a bombardier in the War, stationed in England, and disappeared just before D-Day—supposedly shot down near Paris—declared missing. But the navigator on his plane had returned safely and told my grandparents—William's parents—"William was right behind me."

But what exactly had happened to William remained a mystery.

I placed the tin box aside noticing the scene of smartly dressed Edwardian picnickers disembarking gaily from a Model-T Ford painted on it. The first letter, written in distinct black ink on thin ivory paper, reached out to me across the years in a script that swept dramatically across the pages. Lauren stood next to me, as I began to read aloud:

The Manor, Waverley, England
October 24, 1943

Dear Auntie,

Your letter arrived in just nine days after you posted it. I don't know how it happened to come so fast, but it was very welcome. It was very nice to receive such a long newsy letter; yours was just that.

The new car sounds very flashy. You're lucky our family is dispersed and can't use it when you're not looking. For my part, I now have a huge old bicycle to carry me around and it does very nicely. I generally take it with me on my days off, if I go up to the Manor—which I will tell you about. That way I can see the country firsthand.

It is beautiful here and I have been doing quite a bit of painting—the villagers as well as the surrounding countryside. This past week, I had a splurge of sketching and painting. The Manor is truly my home away from home when I am able to leave the base.

The letter went on but I couldn't continue. This didn't seem like the right time.

Why had these letters been hidden away for 70 years? Why had they never been mentioned yet kept in a safe place? Were there more letters that we didn't know about?

A door had opened but I wasn't sure that I wanted to walk through it.

I hesitated, then made my decision. "We can read these later," I said and put the letters back into the tin box. It would be some time before I would look at them again.

This day would lead to other days of unexpected discoveries: a photo album and the sketchbook that William had used when he was stationed in England, and meetings with people who had lived through the war and knew him. All that was to come later.

Chapter 1

The Cotswolds, England, October 1943

It had been a week since the last bombing mission over Occupied France. In October, the rolling hills of the English countryside were beginning to show the burnished golds and reds of early autumn. For the most part, this was a safer part of England although Luftwaffe aerial attacks had shattered villages nearby during the past several months.

After late summer, William welcomed the chilly evenings at the Manor and the crackling fire in the cavernous stone fireplace that extended the length of the combined library and sitting room. Leaning against a stone wall of the garage was the oversized, old relic of a bicycle that he'd found in the gardening shed, a noble steed that conveyed him on long rides around the countryside on the afternoons he spent sketching and painting.

Canadian, British, and Australian crew members remained at the nearby base shared by the RCAF and Royal Air Force (RAF) or spent their leaves in towns with the usual attractions of noisy pubs and female companions. Those who remained on the base tended to be senior officers who spent their so-called "free days" discussing the latest directives from the Home Office while they studied maps and prepared for the next bombing mission.

William preferred to spend his leaves at the Manor in Waverley, one of the most charming, tiny medieval villages of the Cotswold district of southern England, 30 minutes from Oxford and another hour and a half by train from London. In a few days, he would have to return to the base and resume his other life as an Air Force bombardier. He just wanted to stay at the Manor and forget about the war.

He painted when he could, away from the ribbing by the other members of his squadron.

He drew with a charcoal pencil in brisk strokes on the large, spiral-bound sketchbook that rested on his knees. Henry, an impish young boy from the village, with bright blue eyes and ginger hair, was his subject. He squirmed on the stool in front of William, in the spacious Manor library, barely muffling a giggle after he crossed his eyes and stuck out his tongue.

William stopped sketching and raised an eyebrow suggesting his mild disapproval. But he couldn't help but chuckle. "Okay, try a more natural expression if you please, young man. This is serious business!" he said with a wink, then bent over the sketch, his hand flying across the page.

Henry struck a more serious pose, quickly sitting up ramrod straight. He raised his chin and said in a sober voice, "Right then. Yes sir, Officer Craig!" and saluted, then burst into more laughter.

William knew his model was getting tired but wanted to please him. Henry was a mischievous ten-year-old boy and reminded William of how he had been when he was that age. He watched as Henry made more of an effort to sit still, his hands resting in his lap with just a hint of a crooked grin on his face. He felt a connection to the boy—probably also because he missed his brother, Teddy, who was only a few years older than Henry. Then he thought about his father, William Sr., who he had tried to please in his own way and who was a large part of why he was now in England, fighting in a war that was not likely to end anytime soon.

His father had never liked the fact that he wanted to be an artist. William recalled a scene when he was seven years old and his father found him in his bedroom painting on a large canvas resting on a child-sized easel. He shouted, his face contorted in rage, "Stop that foolishness! The next time I find you doing such nonsense, you will get a good thrashing!" then stormed out and slammed the door.

William had known all too well that this was not an empty threat. He smiled at how he had continued the "foolishness." Despite his father's objections and with the support of his mother and Aunt Lizzie, he had attended a specialized high school for the arts and then art college in Toronto. Eventually, his father had been forced to accept that he was a painter.

There were many things about him that he knew his father would have hated, had he known. That he had loved to listen to opera on the radio Saturday afternoons. That he secretly took voice lessons when he was a teenager. When Teddy found out, William threatened to skin him alive if he breathed a word to anyone.

Working on the charcoal study, he thought about how he wanted to be an artist as long as he could remember. He smiled as he remembered drawing lithesome female figures on the covers and pages of his textbooks during long, dull, French and Latin classes in high school.

Later, one of his teachers in art college had told him, "Your style has a slight resemblance to some of the Group of Seven artists, William. Maybe even Lawren Harris when he was young. And a bit of early Cezanne. But don't let it go to your head, young man! You have much to learn." She had smiled and said, "But who knows? If you keep at it, you could be famous one day." She pushed him to spend even longer hours in the studio as she saw more of his work.

William didn't dare believe he was really an artist until later when he started showing some of his paintings. All he knew was that he had to sketch and paint. Every chance he had, he biked to the woods and hills outside Toronto, whistling and carrying his portfolio under his arm.

He felt that same breathless excitement when he was painting at the Manor and could push the war out of his mind, even for just a few hours.

His father was on his mind because he was feeling increasingly uneasy with the bombing missions. And because he knew that he was here mostly due to his pressure. He thought back to that afternoon when his father was teaching him to box after he had been bullied walking home from school.

"Remember, my boy, our family is one of engineers and ship captains! We have to toughen you up and that's a fact. You have a good head for figures and science, William. Don't waste it all on making those silly pictures!" he said, jabbing William hard on the chin with his boxing glove, almost knocking him off his feet.

Without thinking and surprising himself almost as much as his father, William swung his gloved hand in the air and punched his father squarely in his stomach with such force that he flew back, landing on the floor, winded but laughing.

"Now that's more like it, lad! We'll make you into a man yet!" his dad shouted, gasping for air, and then jumped up and slapped William on the back.

If he was going to be a painter, he would need to be tough especially if his father was ever going to respect him. His father was bitter about losing his own father to art. Granddad had suddenly walked away from his job as a ship's captain on the Great Lakes to write and paint in Montreal, leaving William's father at fourteen to raise his four younger siblings with his frail, overworked mother.

His father loved to recall his brilliant record as a decorated aviator of the *Great War*—a misnomer, William thought, if there ever was one. He thought of one of his uncles who had returned from the trenches in France, debilitated by shell shock. He didn't know how his father had survived so many harrowing missions, piloting a biplane over Germany in World War I.

He had said, in disgust, after being refused active duty as a pilot in 1940, "They think I'm too old to fly a plane. What nitwits! We'll show them what stuff this family is made of!"

William understood that with World War II, the family business was to continue. He had enlisted almost two years before while attending the Ontario College of Art in Toronto. Although his father expected him to become a pilot, he was soon assigned to train as a bombardier after it was discovered that he had a depth perception problem. He completed all the requisite training, advancing easily through rigorous hours of practice flights and navigation classes. Even his mother who usually defended him against his father commented with pride in her voice as he stood before her in his newly minted First Officer Air Force uniform, on his wedding day, "Well, thank goodness, you will be married as a proper officer."

Others weren't so lucky, dying in crashes even before completing their training and departing for the European front. He knew that the majority of those who made it there would never return home—some said 60 or 70%, or even more. So many of the crews never came back to the base after bombing missions. And they were often barely adults—in their late teens and early 20s.

He was proud to be one of two Canadians on an elite bombing crew of the British RAF, stationed in southern England at a base not far from London. Only the English Channel separated them from the Germans who occupied most of Europe. The Nazis had even invaded Jersey and Guernsey, the Channel Islands so close to both England and France, without any resistance from the British. He had heard that Jews who had concealed their religion had been discovered there and rounded up, then transported to what they called "deportation" camps.

The nighttime bombing missions had become more frequent. He was having more and more difficulty not imagining the devastation below when the bombs exploded. He wondered how long he could keep going. At least, painting at the Manor gave him some relief.

Now there were rumors of an Allied invasion into France, although no one knew for sure where or when it might be. Churchill was orchestrating as much deception as possible as the war dragged on. There was the ever-present fear that Germany would invade Britain. U-boats surrounded the British Isles and lay in wait elsewhere in the Atlantic Ocean, the North Sea—seemingly everywhere. Various plans and strategies circulated among the aircrew with the intent of deceiving the Germans and distracting them from the real plan. He and the other airmen were only briefed on the approximate locations of the targets just before they left the base for more nightly bombings, usually by moonlight.

As he thought about the events leading to his current situation, he fought the anxiety and misgivings with his decision to enlist almost two years before. He also knew that he could not have lived with himself if he had stayed behind pretending that the war was not happening.

His hand moved quickly as he sketched with carefully hoarded charcoal pencils, not easily found during wartime in England, where severe shortages meant that even the basic necessities were rationed. Maddie, despite her anger at him for leaving so soon after their marriage began, as well as his mother and Auntie, sent him art supplies in packages when they could, along with socks, chocolates, homemade cookies, tea, photos, and the cherished letters.

Henry squirmed again on his stool, making more faces when he thought William wasn't looking, then mimicked a serious pose, prompting William to say, "There's a good lad. We won't be much longer."

The boy had been recruited by Lady Braithwaite-Smith, the owner of the Manor, with a promise of extra tea and sugar for his family. She was a widow of some apparent means, who remained secretive about her current life. All William knew about her was that she appreciated art and music. Her husband, Lord Braithwaite-Smith, had made his fortune in India then served as a Colonel in World War I and died soon after his return to England.

The estate where she lived was a large, gracious sixteenth-century house of golden Cotswold stone, enclosed by high matching walls. Ancient trees leaned into the house and guarded its secrets like stalwart sentinels. The stone glowed in the afternoon light in the same way the stately buildings of Oxford did when he had painted there. Tall yew and hornbeam hedges surrounded the back garden where Lady Braithwaite-Smith spent long hours pruning, mulching, weeding, and preparing the more tender plants for winter—like the large rose bushes now wrapped in burlap bags to protect them against the occasional frost.

She preferred to do the work herself saying, "It helps me to think," rather than hiring one of the village boys too young to enlist. William wasn't sure what she needed to think about. He had noticed people sometimes coming and going at odd hours but hadn't paid much attention as he immersed himself in sketching and painting.

"Can you at least stop fidgeting for five minutes?" William asked, adopting a stern tone but smiling slightly. Henry looked like he might make a dash for the door for a quick escape.

William was dressed in a brown tweed jacket, starched white shirt, and gray flannel pants saved for his visits at the Manor. He carried a similar suit on bombing missions in case they were shot down and had to disguise themselves as civilians. His straight blond hair was trimmed close to his head in military fashion, parted on the side, and combed back. One small lock escaped from a side part onto his forehead as he worked more vigorously.

Except for the stubborn stains of charcoal and paint that he never seemed to be able to completely remove from his hands, he was fastidious about his appearance when it was possible.

"It's almost time for tea, Officer Will and you know how my ma is," Henry wheedled with a grin.

"Okay, can't have you upsetting your mum," William said. "Just a few minutes more. Your painting could be hanging in the National Portrait Gallery someday, master Henry." They both laughed as Henry raised his chin again, then burst into another giggling fit trying out a range of comical expressions.

A short time later, William finally told the boy they were done for the day. Henry jumped up with a grin and a smart salute shouting, "See you later, Officer Will!" as he flew out the door.

William continued sketching in the library as the light faded in the afterglow of an autumn day in Waverley. It was a glorious escape—rolling hills, ancient walls of stone gathered from the fields they enclosed, and narrow winding roads lined with graceful trees that arched over them forming protective canopies—a world away from the frenetic, mind-numbing, all-night bombing missions.

He cherished his leaves at the Manor painting in the countryside, exploring the surrounding villages on his bicycle, carrying his pochade box of paints, watercolor paper, and sketchpad in a knapsack. Evenings were spent in the drawing room by a crackling fire as the nights grew chillier chatting with Lady Brathwaite-Smith about painting and art. Often, they listened in silence to Churchill delivering yet another stirring speech on the radio.

William remembered how the one ending with the words, "We shall never surrender!" had especially affected him back home in Toronto—spoken first to the British Parliament then broadcast on the BBC. Words that fired up a national optimism and furor to fight back against Fascism. No peace treaty with Hitler brokered by Mussolini, another Fascist dictator.

British optimism for victory surged when the Americans joined the war after the attack on Pearl Harbor. That day was seared into his memory, a Sunday morning almost two years before, a few days after his 20th birthday. He joined the RCAF soon after, in early 1942.

He sketched with confident, powerful strokes, trying to capture the angles of Henry's animated face shifting between boyish mischief and thoughtfulness as he pondered his next escapade. William was anxious to finish the sketch so he could begin the painting. He never knew how much time he had or when he would have another chance to return to his work.

He first met Lady Braithwaite-Smith at one of the get-togethers after the Sunday service, held at the crumbling yet still stately Gothic church in the village. He knew she had sought him out, ignoring the other officers.

She reminded him of Auntie, who had enthusiastically nurtured his painting and taken him to his first opera. He was dressed in white tie and tails for the first time. And on his arm, Auntie was a handsome woman with a commanding but warm presence in her long shimmering silver evening gown, white gloves that rose above her elbows, and a tiny velvet feathered hat.

The music, the costumes, the Art Deco theatre. What a thrilling night it had been. He missed her and wrote her often from England about his painting excursions, the Manor, and the concerts and exhibits he had seen in London—never about the war. He had told her about the paintings he was working on and especially the one that had captured his interest—a study for a landscape near the Manor that he had just begun. One that seemed to have a special magic.

Lady Braithwaite-Smith had a daughter who was about his age he guessed and was a Red Cross nurse at a nearby hospital for injured soldiers. He had cycled to Evesham to visit her on his last leave and had sketched the men sitting in wheelchairs in the sunroom, in varying degrees of pain and loss. Some sat with bandaged heads and were barely aware of him as he drew their somber faces and chatted with the nurses, until he had to leave before sunset to cycle back to the Manor. Others, despite their missing arms and legs, cracked jokes and teased him that he was wasting his time drawing their "ugly mugs."

He had noticed a young man sitting apart from the others in a wheelchair by the window, bandages wound around his head and covering his eyes, one arm missing, fingers gone from his other hand, and one leg amputated at the knee. He thought about what that would be like and tried to imagine the unimaginable—not ever being able to see the trees, the sky, the green hills— never being able to hold a paintbrush again. *How could I survive that?*

Flashes of sad faces and broken bodies intruded into his thoughts well into the night and shattered his sleep, merging with nightmares of explosions and flying body parts. He often woke in a cold sweat, imagining that his bombs had caused such carnage. He'd had to shake off those thoughts and remind himself that they were here to win the war.

Waverley felt so far removed from all that. It was a village where art and Bohemians were a large part of its history. He had been told by Trevor at the pub that in the 1920s, a wealthy female friend and neighbor of Lady Braithwaite-Smith drove through the countryside in a shiny, beige Rolls Royce convertible with a troupe of Isadora Duncan-style dancers and actors from London who performed at country inns and estates.

Competing with the fading light, he sketched more rapidly as music played on the phonograph next to his easel on a small pedestal table. It was Chopin's Piano Concerto No. 1, a piece that always reminded him of Maddie, especially the second part, the Romanz Larghetto.

She was known to others as Madeleine Craig nee Ainsworth, former child prodigy and virtuoso pianist, now studying at the Juilliard School under the tutelage of Madame Samaroff, a well-known and formidable music teacher. William had no doubt that Maddie would be performing someday soon at Carnegie Hall—maybe even in the prestigious Stern Auditorium.

He thought of what she might be doing now, five hours earlier in New York. His face flushed as he thought of Maddie's proud, dark beauty and how much he missed her.

Without wanting to, he remembered her fury the last night before he left for active duty. The image of her flashing brown eyes below thick bangs and perfectly arched eyebrows, her delicately featured but expressive face framed by long, shiny black hair curling on her shoulders, filled him with love but also reminded him of what had come between them.

Madeleine was barely 20 and he 21 when they were married in late February, eight months before. They had known each other for three years, spending idyllic, sunburned summers together swimming and canoeing on Kahshe Lake at the southernmost end of the Muskoka Lake District—just over two hours north of Toronto but much further removed from the world of art and music that preoccupied and captured them the rest of the year. Despite their deep understanding of each other, he knew she still couldn't accept the decision he had made.

The constant, pervasive fear at home of losing the war and knowing that lives were lost every day compounded his own desire to do what was right. He would not be one of those "zombies"—men who were resisting the recently instituted draft in Canada. Even at art school, where they immersed themselves in art history, painting, and sculpting classes, the men talked constantly about enlisting to fight the war.

He recalled the image of his father's angry red face and narrowed sharp blue eyes at that fateful dinner with his family at their Chestnut Avenue home in Toronto. In the midst of the meal marked by long uncomfortable silences, his father suddenly raised his voice and pounded his fist.

"No son of mine will ever be a pantywaist coward. Sit and paint here while our boys are getting blown up? That would be unforgivable. This is not up to you, young man!" he shouted as he shook his finger at William. His mother and sister Lily said nothing but stopped eating and looked at him, waiting for his response. The pressure had been too much. He enlisted a week later.

Maddie repeated in her last letter how upset she was with his decision. He knew she was afraid for him but he didn't know how to make her understand, especially now as he wondered whether he had done the right thing. Others managed to serve safely on bases in Canada, never seeing combat. William had been discovered in the first few months of training to have exceptional mathematical and navigational skills, which in combination apparently made him the perfect bombardier. He had also learned to fly because as an air bomber he often co-piloted, assisting with takeoffs and landings. But he hadn't really understood what he had committed to, until later. On bombing missions, night after night.

Maddie's words on their final evening together swept through him with such force that he felt unsteady on his small stool. He had been packing in the upstairs bedroom in his parents' house preparing to leave by ship for England early the next morning. Maddie, angrier than he had ever seen her, sat on their bed in a pale blue silk chiffon nightgown—the scene of such unbridled passion just a few hours before.

"You think you're being so brave and noble," she said her voice rising. "You're really just a coward! You're still trying to please your father—the tyrant that he is! Why can't you stand up to him? You don't have to do this!" She paused for air, gaining momentum for her next plea, her cheeks flushed with emotion. Her voice trembled with a barely controlled sob. "It's not fair!" she cried. "You are joining with the other fools who might never make it back! Bombing missions! Do you have a death wish, William? You could have done something here—been stationed somewhere safe like my brother, a medic on a ship in Halifax harbor. Charlie will be fine. Why do you have to go right into the bloody war! What if you don't come back? I couldn't live with that!" She clenched her fists, holding back the tears, her voice rising.

He felt her anguish that night, but there was nothing he could do.

Her dark eyes, usually warm and loving, pierced his heart as she fought back tears. "We have something to live for, William! Don't you ever think about that? You can't do this!" she cried, then her voice became muffled as he pulled her into a tight embrace and she sobbed even harder, beating his chest with her fists.

As he hugged her, then held her face in his hands, he could only say, "I have to do this, Maddie" and "I'll be back." He hoped he was right.

A sudden movement in the hallway interrupted his thoughts. Lady Brathwaite-Smith had returned from the garden. Her gloved hands carried traces of wet, pungent, peaty soil. Beads of sweat gathered on her barely lined brow, above a patrician nose and penetrating blue eyes. Her high cheekbones, dignified carriage, and aristocratic speech were exactly how William imagined a woman of her education and means would look and sound. She wore an eccentric ensemble of blue plaid wool-pleated skirt, cream silk blouse with lace at the cuffs, long black-and-white checked coat, and a small slightly brimmed felt hat. Her hands and forearms were enclosed in elbow-length sheepskin gloves. Her face wore an expression of inscrutable intelligence, devoid of emotion.

He watched as she carefully placed her gloves and hat on the small table in the hallway. It had been a quiet day, without any of the usual visitors furtively arriving at the Manor, then departing just as unceremoniously. Lady Braithwaite-Smith was often aloof and preoccupied. She could even be a bit imperious at times.

She had invited him into her home that summer. "It would be good for you to paint at the Manor when you have leaves, away from the base," she had told him at a church supper in the village for the officers and aircrews from the nearby base, one early summer evening not long after he had arrived in England. He had to admit that it was an offer he couldn't refuse. It seemed a bit odd that she had singled him out, but he didn't question it.

Suddenly, there was a loud knock at the kitchen door, at the back of the house.

"Mary, can you get that?" Lady Braithwaite-Smith called out to her housekeeper. "We should have our tea soon, as it's getting on."

She knew she sounded impatient but she was anxious to go through her mail, make some telephone calls, and plan the events for the coming day. There was much to do.

"Yes, Ma'am," Mary replied from the kitchen as she dropped her hands from the dough she had been kneading and wiped them briskly on her apron. She opened the door and welcomed Trevor who owned the pub that had sat a few houses down the lane for almost four centuries.

William could see Trevor through the open window squinting at the housekeeper as he removed his cap.

"I need to have a word with the Lady, if you please," he said quietly. "I've received a message." Mary led him into the small office.

"We'll have our tea when I'm done, William. I shan't be long," Lady Braithwaite-Smith said over her shoulder as she quickly left the library and moved past the sitting room where he sketched, then stepped into her office across the hall. She firmly closed the door behind her. He heard only faintly murmured conversation as he continued, absorbed in finishing the drawing of Henry that would later become a watercolor painting.

* * *

William set out as dawn was breaking with a warm, rosy glow over the serene landscape.

An early morning fog drifted over the hills partially obscuring the stone cottages and grazing sheep, creating a mystical scene that filled William with anticipation of what might lie ahead.

This particular time of day had lured him into painting the hills and woods near his home before the war, but he barely noticed the sunrises when he was at the base. Days there were filled with training and briefings, or he was collapsing exhausted into his bed after another night of lying in the glassed-in nose of the Halifax.

What a relief it was to be on a different kind of journey. He pedaled faster, feeling his leg muscles clenching more tightly as he climbed higher on the rough country road.

"Ya wouldna wanna take on Clifton Hill in the mornin' without a bit of breakfast in ya, Officer Will," Henry had said the day before when he gave him directions. "It's a long way up, for sure. And be sure to jump in the ditch if one of those lorries or even a nag comes along," Henry warned, then added, "Yes sir, that'd be a busy road for around here, but the best way to get to Chipping Campden."

William was glad he had followed Henry's advice, quickly drinking some hot tea while bolting down currant scones with Mary's gooseberry jam. He felt fatigued after a restless night and hoped that the ten mile—mostly uphill—trip, would end soon. Lady Braithwaite-Smith had given him only cursory instructions for where the meeting was to occur and what it was about.

As he passed rolling hills and valleys dotted with the ever-present sheep enjoying their own breakfast, he considered the enormity of his decision.

He had sensed for some time that the Manor was not what it appeared to be. But he had been so grateful for the relief from the bombings that he hadn't thought much about it. He had tried not to think about whether he was actually hitting the appointed targets and not innocent villagers or Resistance fighters who hid in the French countryside ready to rescue those who might be parachuting to safety after their planes were hit. At 12,000 feet or higher, to avoid anti-aircraft gunfire from the ground, the accuracy of his bombs was often questionable. Although he understood his fellow crew members' zeal to "bomb the fuckers," he knew he was not a part of their world.

One night after they had returned from a mission, he had rolled fitfully back and forth on the hard, narrow mattress, even more uncomfortable and preoccupied than usual, surrounded by the other men who slept peacefully. They had collapsed fully clothed on their beds in utter exhaustion. But sleep was not going to rescue him from the tightness in his chest or the bursts of deafening explosions that filled his head. He eventually rose, found the sketch pad and charcoal pencil stowed beneath his cot, and began to draw. Fragments of moonlight streamed through the narrow windows of the bunker as he gazed at the sleeping men and sketched with renewed energy. In that moment, he almost felt removed from the war.

Lady Braithwaite-Smith had finally told him what had been on her mind all along. After her meeting with Trevor, they sat by the fire drinking tea and talking about his paintings. She suddenly cleared her throat and placed her cup on the side table.

"William, it's time for you to know," she said, her eyes appraising him with a steady gaze. "There are other ways of fighting this war. I can help you. I've spoken with the Home Office." She paused. "I am what they call a handler, William, a recruiter for agents in the Special Operations Executive—the SOE—established by Churchill for especially audacious undercover missions. As he has instructed us, we are to 'set Europe ablaze,'" she said without emotion and watching him for any reaction. "In any case, we work with MI5, MI6, and the RAF – sometimes with a bit of difficulty, mind you. But nothing we can't manage," she said dryly. "We have fewer rules. And we are very effective." She met his gaze as she spoke, narrowing her eyes meaningfully.

William leaned forward and held his breath, wondering how all this would involve him.

"My code name is Bluebell." She paused, studying him intently. "We need your skills, William. Being an artist will be an excellent cover and you will have more time to paint. You must be sure you want to do this. It may be less predictable work than dropping bombs."

They talked late into the night about the new plan.

Now he was cycling on this road so far from his home, on the other side of the world, about to meet someone named Simon. A code name, no doubt. He wondered where this meeting would lead him. But he knew that it was better than dropping bombs—at least for a while.

Chapter 2

Upper West Side, New York City

Maddie sat at the grand piano in her darkened apartment on the seventh floor of the Art Deco brownstone on West 75th Street. It stood out even among the other pre-war and nineteenth-century architectural jewels in the neighborhood, with its neatly sculpted evergreen trees and colorful flowerbeds on both sides of the brass-trimmed glass entrance, protected by a cherry-red awning and an equally welcoming doorman. Sparse bronze leaves brushed against the panes of the tall French double doors. Gusts of wind stirred the potted rust and gold chrysanthemums on the narrow balcony while a light rain beat rhythmically against the ornate black iron railings with curlicue detailing and sharp spikes. A partially obscured view of Central Park was possible now, visible through linden trees holding just a few clusters of dying leaves that had resisted the onset of early autumn.

A crash of thunder signaled a shift from the rain's soothing melody to a dramatic downpour, as Maddie transitioned from a restful Chopin's Nocturne into Beethoven's rapidly accelerating Sonata, Op. 57, feeling the intense emotions of the aptly named *Appassionata*.

Although it was late October, the doors to the balcony were slightly ajar. The honking and screeching of passing cars from the street below interrupted by an occasional shout or peals of laughter, both comforted and reminded Maddie of the great distance from the apartment to the chaotic destruction of William's life in England. The war he had chosen over her.

A Tiffany floor lamp that her mother had brought from their Toronto home where her banker father remained illuminated Maddie and her piano in a pool of soft light. She had begun with Chopin and Schumann, interpretations that Madame had described most recently as "unbridled vanity and capricious childishness," and "a trifle too emotional." She smiled to herself thinking of the power struggles with her mother and Madame. Ones she usually won. Yet, as her hands flew over the keyboard, now producing the loud chords and rapid-fire movements of Beethoven and Rachmaninoff, she didn't feel the usual sense of calm that often paradoxically arose in her when she played this demanding and dramatic music. Instead, she wanted to throw something hard and sharp through the window or at anyone who happened to have the misfortune to be walking nearby.

Whirling images and words threatened to interrupt her practice. How she hated what William had done. Why couldn't he have found another way? Maybe a post in the Arctic out of harm's way. Or maybe not serve at all. He could have had flat feet. Or a heart condition. Or a debilitating illness that could be miraculously cured after the war. Or he could have been assigned to the repair depot on the distant prairies of western Canada, counting equipment parts, rehabilitating planes, and whatever else his father was doing there.

Other options involved members of her family in England and Scotland. Although that would be a last resort.

But no, he had to serve his country in the Air Force and replace his father who was too old to fly planes anymore. William had told her he didn't want to follow in his father's footsteps but he had done just that. She thought about Charlie. Her brother was safely stationed with the Royal Canadian Navy in Halifax. It wasn't fair.

Even Lily, William's older sister, seemed to have too much influence over him. She had contributed to the righteous cacophony that Maddie heard at family gatherings. "It's our family's legacy. We have a responsibility. You have a responsibility to this family, William. And to your country," Lily had said. Maddie had felt some anger from Lily once she and William became so close, then planned to marry. Maybe Lily had felt replaced. She didn't dare believe that this was why Lily so strongly encouraged him to enlist. In any event, the family pressure had led to his decision to be where he was now.

It felt like they had thrown him into the fire. She couldn't stop asking herself why he had to be a bombardier in one of the most dangerous places in the world right now. She didn't care that airmen were thought to be the most glamorous of all in the service. She couldn't imagine how as sensitive as he was—creating beautiful works of art—he could possibly participate in such a theater of death. She just wanted William back safely and in one piece.

Maddie had been immersed in her music in New York for eight long years, and their lives had become entwined in that world. What William was doing seemed inexplicable and a cold affront to her, and what they shared.

Her friends at Juilliard had expressed strong ambivalence toward making such a sacrifice, at least until the attack on Pearl Harbor. It was different for Canadians. As a Commonwealth country, they had been in the war since September 1939, soon after Britain declared war on Germany. And now, even men at Juilliard were enlisting.

They were all so young like her, 20 years old or a bit older, and some even younger. How sad it all was. Their entire generation was being sacrificed. And for a world war that should never have happened in the first place. Of course, she knew this war could not be lost. But why did William have to be in the middle of it? She wanted so much for their lives to return to the way it was before William enlisted—when they both had shared a passion for their art. This was a time of complicated feelings and difficult decisions, but she still felt angry at him. She knew she was being childish and self-indulgent, but at the moment, she didn't care. She just felt so lonely and sad. There had to be a way to get him back to safety.

As she continued to play, hoping her spirits would lift, she thought about their hastily prepared wedding eight months earlier in Toronto. The marriage ceremony was on a bright, crisp sunny February afternoon, in a stately church with walls of tall, multi-colored stained-glass windows depicting the nativity scene next to the sermon on the mount, Jesus in robes surrounded by children, the Last Supper, and finally, the Crucifixion—all dancing with light in broad beams of sunshine; the sweet notes of the soloist's *Ava Maria* echoing from the balcony high above them.

After the ceremony, the evening reception was held at the opulent King Edward Hotel. The King Eddy, as it was known in Toronto, was the setting for many a high-society occasion, even in these times. A sumptuous banquet was served by efficient white-gloved waiters dressed in black coat and tails who circulated gracefully throughout the immense candlelit Vanity Fair ballroom, amidst the glamor of huge, sparkling crystal chandeliers. A string quartet played Bach and Vivaldi unobtrusively in the corner. Everything had been planned quickly but focused on conveying the message that life must go on, despite the preoccupying gloom of war. For once, Maddie and her mother agreed on that point. Rachel, especially, had insisted on a grand celebration.

But their wedding day passed so quickly, followed by a weeklong honeymoon before William had to leave again. She knew that he had been selected for specialized, elite training, and their happiness had ended abruptly. And now, he was probably on the front line in great danger.

Fighting rising anxiety, she returned to memories of their wedding day. Arrangements of white calla lilies, blue hydrangea globes, and long-stemmed brilliant red roses, with garlands of rare white stephanotis blooms—also known as "bridal veil"—so apt Maddie thought—decorating the pews, filled the church with a heady fragrance and reminded her of the gardens in summer at their family home in Toronto. She had floated on a veritable cloud nine that day, in a happy dream that she never wanted to end.

Sometimes it didn't even seem real. Had they actually married? But then she remembered the gilded, mirrored ballroom where elegantly dressed family members and friends toasted the newlyweds, clinking glasses throughout the five-course dinner, then danced late into the evening, a world away from the war raging on other continents.

Maddie played on, seeing herself and William smiling at the table for the bridal party and holding hands—she in her antique ivory silk brocade gown, adorned with a Juliet cap of tiny pearls holding her fingertip veil of illusion, and William, in his freshly pressed khaki RCAF uniform with the military bars designating his newly acquired First Officer's status. Her grandmother's diamond heart locket and a large bridal bouquet of white gardenias and roses made her feel even more like a princess.

Nothing and nobody could take her beloved William from her. Or at least that was what she had wanted to believe. She had almost been able to forget that he would be shipping out to England for who knew how long. No one could predict.

"This is really too much when others are fighting for freedom and losing their lives. This is wrong, Maddie. Why do you need all this? Let's just do it quietly," William had said one afternoon. "Or we could elope!" he teased with a coy smile and twinkling eyes—a look she rarely could resist. But seeing the look of horror on her face, he quickly added, "Well, maybe at least a simple ceremony? The important thing is to be together."

She and her mother had prevailed. Rachel had reveled in the planning of the wedding. She looked so proud and regal that day—stunning in a midnight blue beaded gown, matching stylish turban, and sparkling diamond and sapphire jewelry. A little Hollywoodish Maddie thought, but it all suited Rachel so well. She wondered whether the wedding had helped to distract her mother from the war. It was hard to know since she never talked about it and especially not her family in Europe, or what might be happening to them.

The wedding had been a beautiful interlude in the midst of the constant, dismal news of more countries being invaded by Germany, more bombings, and the rising death toll. The disturbing movie reels of people being marched off to trains taking them to relocation camps.

And now since the attack on Pearl Harbor, war raged in the Pacific as well. It was all too much.

The fact was, despite her entreaties to William, he was in serious danger and she might never see him again. She was growing increasingly impatient to do something. She wasn't ready to tell anyone what she was planning—not yet.

She had tried so hard to reason with William. But in saner moments, she understood the meaning of the greater cause and his sense of duty. She desperately held onto the hope that he would not be lost. That he would return to her. But since he'd left for England that night in July, she had felt increasing panic. His letters had become less frequent and she hadn't heard from him in several weeks.

Maddie thought about the last letter she mailed to William. Her feelings overflowed into words she regretted later in some ways, but she was determined to express—

My darling William, maybe we are too different. You didn't have to leave. Isn't there some way that you can return to me? I miss you so much! You don't belong there. Can't you find a way back to me? I can't stand being so far from you. Maybe there is something I can do.

Bundled against the wind in her mid-calf red wool coat with its mink collar turned up to warm her neck, she thought, *you need to do this. It's right. Keep going*, as she walked to the nearby post office earlier that day to mail the letter. She hoped that her words would cause William to rethink everything and find a way to come home to her. She knew she was being foolish but she also knew she could be very persuasive.

Then, remembering the post office was closed, she had slipped the ivory envelope into the narrow slot of a nearby blue mailbox whispering, "I love you, darling. You will come back."

She heard William's gentle voice answering, "You are strong, Maddie. We will get through this."

She wasn't so sure. But she was not going to wallow any longer in this painful state of yearning and fear. She turned her attention back to the Rachmaninoff piece before her, fighting the familiar waves of loss and sadness as she thought about William's sweet smile and the memory of his loving caresses. She felt a sudden surge of confidence that she could do something to bring them back together—into their shared dream.

A plan was growing in her mind when she heard a key turn in the lock and the door opened. She braced herself for the return of her mother breaking the afternoon's reverie of music and memories.

Despite the cold chill in the air that day, Rachel wore only a light cashmere coat over a long-sleeved silk jersey dress. She shook out her umbrella and placed it in the stand near the door.

A small pillbox angled over her dark auburn hair, artfully arranged in a French chignon with a delicate net veil partially concealing her eyes. As she entered the apartment, she raised the veil with a gloved hand and set down her shopping bags, slowly removing her hat and gloves and placing them on the hallway table.

Rachel and Maddie had lived in the Upper West Side apartment since moving to New York when Maddie was 12 years old so that she could study piano more seriously. She began training with Jose Iturbi, the famous concert pianist and former movie star, then other acclaimed teachers. Even as a child, she knew that this was necessary.

But Maddie missed her father who lived in Toronto with her older brother, Charlie. They had occasional weekends and holidays together in New York and Toronto as well as summers on Kahshe Lake in the Muskoka region of Ontario, but her life was now mostly in New York. Her father could be quiet and immersed in his work as a prominent banker, but he always had time to joke with her, hugging her and saying with a laugh, "Maddie, my madness." He told her and her mother often how much he loved spending time with "my girls." His visits to New York were infrequent but Maddie always looked forward to their walks in Central Park and lunches at Sam's Deli in midtown—

a favorite of hers—a noisy place filled with shouting, joking customers, and huge pastrami sandwiches, where her mother would never think of going.

Even though Maddie was now married and studying at Juilliard had forced her to grow up fast, she felt that her mother could never quite relinquish control over her life. A life focused on practice and performances. Rachel could be so overprotective that Maddie fantasized about running away. She knew her mother wanted her to be successful and probably gained some vicarious satisfaction through her. But Maddie also felt her mother was attentive in loving ways that Rachel's mother, Ma-mere had not been able to be with Rachel—for reasons Maddie didn't fully understand because she adored her grandmother.

Life had been fairly comfortable before the war. But now, their maid came just three times a week to clean and prepare meals—rather than every day—and a driver took them wherever they needed to go, although only on Fridays and Sundays. It was considered *de rigueur*, in her mother's circle and among other wealthy New Yorkers, to make a necessary sacrifice for the war effort and reduce their staff's time. Many evenings upon her return from the studio across the Park on East 57th, they would just eat scrambled eggs and toast, Welsh rarebit, or tuna casserole—or sometimes meatloaf and mashed potatoes if they were feeling especially ambitious.

Rachel glanced at Maddie. "I should hope that you have been practicing this afternoon for the concert next week and not wasting your energy day-dreaming about how to get William back," she said with irritation in her voice. She approached Maddie who sat at the piano but had stopped playing and placed a hand on her shoulder aware of her impatience. "He is doing what he needs to do. You need to accept the situation," she said firmly.

Maddie turned to face her mother, her eyes shining with tears, "You don't understand. I can't just sit here and do nothing!" she said in a trembling voice. She abruptly swiveled back to the piano and placed her hands on the keyboard feeling its comfort under her fingers as she resumed playing.

Rachel understood the pain Maddie was feeling but she had to accept that there was nothing to do but wait. They had to go on living their lives in New York as best as they could. She knew she should be more patient, knowing how headstrong Maddie could be.

She chose her words carefully as she tried to rein in her own anxiety. "I know it's difficult, but there's a war going on, Maddie, for heaven's sake!"

Rachel's voice rose and she knew that she was also angry for other reasons. She took a deep breath then added, "You just need to concentrate on your music. And put the rest out of your mind." She straightened to her full height— a few inches taller than Maddie but appearing even taller in her heels and in the way she carried herself—regaining her composure.

Rachel unbuttoned and tossed her coat on the pale blue velvet reading chair then clasped her hands in front of her. She desperately wished for Maddie to think only of her music and just get through this horrible time. She just wanted Maddie and William to have a happy life. She loved William too. He was truly a gifted painter, especially for someone so young. She thought then about her son, Charlie and hoped he would remain in Halifax out of harm's way.

She spoke quietly but there was no mistaking the steely tone. "You need to understand why William is doing this and not just think of yourself. I know it's difficult but we all have to make sacrifices. You must be strong and focus on what you have to do here." She patted Maddie lightly and reassuringly on her back as her daughter resumed playing. "The war will eventually end, as it did the last time. And we will win. We have to believe that. We just have to go on, Maddie." Her firm statements belied her own doubts, however, as she tried to shake the painful memories that entered her mind. She couldn't give in to the growing distress gripping her body.

Rachel softened her tone as she walked toward the kitchen. "I will make us some tea and we can have it with salmon and cucumber sandwiches. There might even be some of those lovely French lemon tarts you like so much, from Chez André."

That was it. Maddie could take no more. She slammed down the keyboard cover of the Steinway and threw her sheet music across the room. Her vision blurred as she shouted, "I am not waiting for William to be blown up, Mother. I will find him and bring him home."

Chapter 3

The Cotswolds, England

William walked quickly to keep up with Lady Braithwaite-Smith as she strode to the stone garage behind the Manor. Inside rested the sleek black and gunmetal gray 1940 Bentley under its khaki canvas cover. An hour earlier, they had been sitting in the library with the fire softly crackling in the massive fireplace. He was working on a large watercolor painting of Waverley and the surrounding area, its stone walls, and small cottages set against the golden hills and black skeletal trees. A medieval tower rose high on the hill above the nearby village of Broadway, a powerful magnet drawing artists and mystics alike for hundreds of years.

The phone in Bluebell's office adjacent to the library rang earlier that morning, breaking the silence. She quickly answered it, speaking briskly, "Yes, we are ready. We will leave for the station straightaway. He will be at Paddington by midday, then on to the north."

William had been hoping for this day. To have an assignment that would free him for even a short time from the endless bombing missions and the scenes of death and carnage he imagined with each bomb he propelled toward its target. The thought of having more time to paint was truly intoxicating. He couldn't stop thinking about how much more he could do—more landscapes, and portraits—if he was away from the bombings and the base, at least for a short time. He often soothed himself into sleep at night by imagining his next painting. Missions with the SOE might actually provide more time to paint. A crazy thought but one he had to hold onto.

"It's time, William," Bluebell said after the call, gathering up the papers she had been reading. "We must go now. The train leaves for London in 45 minutes."

He quickly grabbed his box of paints, sheets of paper, sketch pads, and charcoal pencils, throwing them into the large haversack with his pistol and knife, then tossing it over his shoulder. In his other hand, he carried an RAF duffle bag containing a change of clothing, a bedroll, maps, anorak, tins of food, flares, and a kit bag.

They sat side by side in the Bentley, the white-walled tires crunching over the gravel lane as they drove away from the estate then glided onto the narrow, paved road leading off to the train station in Moreton-in-Marsh. The regal sedan still looking new despite a few splashes of mud on its otherwise spotless fenders was used to deliver many strangers to and from the Manor. William noticed the polished leather upholstery and how the glossy walnut dashboard with its impressive gauges imitated the finest planes he had flown during his training and on bombing missions over the English Channel to Occupied France. He could imagine another time driving into the country for a picnic in the countryside, a basket laden with a sumptuous feast and a bottle of wine, the salon-like car filled with excited partygoers.

William had many questions as they drove in silence on the narrow, winding country road, but he knew better than to press the resolute woman for more information or reassurance. Since she was now his handler, he would have to wait until she was ready to tell him more about the mission.

Bluebell was focused only on getting him to his destination. Driving calmed her and taking William to the train station took her mind off other matters, even though she knew she was sending him into danger. She had given her usual driver the day off so that she could spend this time with him. He was one of her favorites although she would never tell him that.

William watched her as she stared straight ahead, a determined expression on her face as she expertly negotiated the frequent hairpin curves and passed the occasional farmer driving a truck filled with sheep or bundles of hay, at an agonizingly ponderous pace as if the world was not on fire.

Bluebell was deep in thought. She hoped William trusted she knew what she was doing and that he believed he had made the right decision. She thought about all the young, brave people she had recruited and sent into danger. But she knew all too well how many more agents were needed. And especially, ones with William's abilities.

As they turned onto a straighter road and sped toward the train station, she finally spoke. "You will take the train to London, then directly to York. I will call you there with the next briefing. We need your skills sooner than expected—things are moving fast in the north. You will first go to the base then meet your contact. He will provide further instructions." She thought this was enough for him to know right now.

"I still don't know exactly what I will be doing," he said more sharply than he had intended. He couldn't help feeling impatient. Everything had happened so fast.

"I know, William. It all seems mysterious and strange. But that's the way it has to be," Bluebell answered firmly. Even she didn't know yet exactly what he would be doing. She looked at him quickly, pursing her lips and gripped the steering wheel even more firmly as the Bentley's motor purred, accelerating past another slow-moving truck. She honked lightly and waved at the local farmer she recognized, as she sped by. How she loved this car and the way it responded reliably without challenging her the way people often did. So much more efficient, she thought. She glanced at William with a slight smile, amused at this comparison, then turned back to the road.

As she turned sharply around another curve in the narrow road, she spoke confidently, wanting to reassure him, "You will be able to sketch and paint wherever they send you. The base will be informed that you are to serve elsewhere for now. Your commanding officer knows, of course. That's how it works between the SOE and the RAF. We work together, but right now we're calling the shots. Your crew will think you are getting more training. The less they know, the better."

William nodded and his fists and jaw unclenched as he began to feel a growing sense of purpose. He had trained constantly at the Manor over the past few weeks—hand-to-hand combat, coded radio transmission, saboteur strategies, and target practice with the Llama Mark pistol used by the SOE. He felt ready. All operatives were shown ways to defend themselves with or without weapons and how to kill silently—training he hoped he would never have to put into practice.

Excitement and hopeful anticipation surged through him. The mission planned for several weeks was finally happening. At least for now, it would take him away from the flights into darkness and the deafening explosions. He was heading toward something that would release him from the anguish he felt for the destruction he caused on each mission—even if only temporarily. And maybe, if he was lucky, get him out of this war and back to Maddie.

Chapter 4

Paddington Station, London

After the bombings of the previous night, Paddington Station was swarming with crowds of anxious Londoners, pushing toward trains that could take them to safer destinations well removed from the air raids bombarding their city. Trim young men and women in uniforms reflecting their military assignments gathered in groups, smoking and talking almost as if none of the horrors of the night before had occurred. But they were more subdued than usual, and William noticed there was less of the usual flirting and joking. He walked through the station feeling the urgency and distress of not only London but also all of England under siege.

He preferred to be away from the military tourists, as he thought of them. On past visits, he had ventured out to the small private galleries still showing exhibits of local artists.

Sometimes, he even made it to the few brave theaters in West London that held occasional performances of plays and musical shows, despite the blackouts and the air raids. But there was no time for that now. The trains were running late, but soon, he would be heading north to York.

As he walked toward Platform 3, he noticed a woman with long shiny dark hair curled over her shoulders like his Maddie, in a gray flannel suit, stylish pumps, and a wide-brimmed hat concealing her face. That determined walk, her eyes alert to admiring glances. He could imagine her laughing out loud at some amusing man attempting to engage her in conversation. "Was it possible that she had found a way to London?" He walked more quickly toward the Maddie-vision.

A newspaper boy yelled, "Get the news here from the front! Bombing kills 20 near Russell Square tube station! More air raids expected tonight!"

The woman turned and his fantasy evaporated. This Maddie imposter had blue eyes instead of flashing dark ones. She was without the vibrancy and glow of his magnificent Maddie.

William sighed as he walked to Platform 3, shifting his duffle bag to his other shoulder. In another 30 minutes, he would be jumping onto another train. The trip from the Moreton-in-Marsh station to Paddington Station in London had been restful, disrupted only by the occasional outburst by the other passengers. He thought about the random snippets of conversation he had overheard that had amused him, then lulled him into a brief nap.

"Ah, crikey, where's my pipe?" someone had yelled.

Another voice grumbled impatiently, "Bloody hell, Joe, move over! You're snoring in my ear. I'm trying to sleep here, you wanker."

And then, someone behind him had muttered in a low voice. "It was balls-up, mate. No mistake. Then Mac took off, went AWOL."

William tried to focus on his own more pleasant reveries on these journeys by train hoping to escape the fears that plagued his imagination. But the fragments of conversation, nonsensical and sometimes disturbing, still somehow comforted him and made him feel less alone, as he traveled between London, Oxford, Stratford-upon-Avon, Moreton-in-Marsh, Cambridge, and York. He became accustomed to the trance-like state he entered as he sat on one stiff, leather upholstered seat after another. Always by a window so he could absorb the passing scenes of tiny villages, horses clustered in yellow fields with their heads gently touching as if in a serious meeting of the minds, rows of hedges, and rivers winding through undulating hills.

He liked to imagine where he might go to do his next painting—perhaps that village by the woods, sage green hills surrounding a tall-spired ancient church and rolling away into the distance. Grave sites filled with the bodies of young and old. He imagined the lives and stories of those who laid there— some for centuries.

Then, the unmistakable whistle interrupted his thoughts, followed by the conductor announcing authoritatively in a loud voice, "Train to York, Platform 3! All aboard!"—the vowels of the last announcement stretching out to command attention—*aaaall aaabooooaaarrd!*

William's heart raced as he dashed toward the train—if it hadn't been for what he was traveling to, he might have felt the excitement he remembered when he took the train on weekends from Toronto to Auntie's summer home.

He could see the peaceful rural town in his mind, filled with wooded parks and lush green lawns invigorated by water sprinklers spraying water in pulsating fountains dazzling in the sunshine, by the quiet shores of Georgian Bay. A two-hour trip—a lifetime ago.

William quickened his pace as he approached the gleaming black train with its red and gold letters spelling out Great Western Railway and its small oblong windows with tiny opaque curtains. He couldn't help but feel the childlike anticipation of taking a journey to another place.

No matter how many times his train trips might take him into danger and intrigue, he thought he would never lose that sense of joy in approaching unknown wonders and places that could reveal more of the world around him. Trains fascinated him, even in the midst of war. And now he was an agent on the way to a mission he knew so little about.

He sat back resting his head against the seat, his haversack with sketching and painting materials next to him and his duffle bag at his feet, then closed his eyes. Beneath the heavy drowsiness that descended, he saw images of his kid brother, Edward—nine years younger.

William thought he looked like a fuzzy bear with his spiky head of hair when he was born—so he had become "Teddy." His brother was often a nuisance, following him around like a shadow but also loyal and willing to hide William's adventures from his father.

He thought about sunrise cycling trips to paint miles from their home and late-night trysts with Maddie by the lake in the summer.

His sister, Lily, fine-boned and cerebral, usually had a book in her hand, and yet, was playful and laughed with enjoyment when he coaxed her into jitterbugging to "Little Brown Jug"—dodging the mahogany furniture in the lamplit living room on Chestnut Street. She actually was a pretty good dancer, he thought. He missed her and his brother, too.

And then, he saw Maddie—facing him in the small boat as he rowed across the calm lake on a serene, sunlit afternoon—in her white halter-neck swimsuit and pink-flowered skirt that on her seemed more like an elegant evening gown. The dazzling sunshine illuminated her striking beauty against the blues and greens of the summer day.

"William, I think it's time we got to know each other more," she had suggested that afternoon with a slight smile.

He knew what she meant, but she was only 18 and he was thinking about enlisting.

Suddenly, he couldn't take any more of her sly hints of what might follow—the sensual glances, her coy smile, the playful way she lightly brushed against him. He leaned forward, dropped the oars and grabbed Maddie around the waist. Together, they fell laughing into the prow of the skiff. He kissed her longingly, his tongue probing deeply into her welcoming mouth as he began to lift her skirt and touch her thigh, then her breast. She sighed and grasped more of his lean body. He could feel his rising arousal as he embraced her with even more urgency.

Then, breaking the moment of passion, she pulled away gently, saying, "William, we have to stop. You know we do." He did not want to stop.

But he reluctantly released her and, despite his disappointment, felt a thrill course through his body at the awareness that she could be his. Maddie, the brilliant pianist, sometimes teasing and funny, other times serious and distracted, yet always self-assured, passionate, and strong-willed. She was complicated and sometimes unpredictable. And once she made up her mind about something, she went after it with single-minded tenacity. She could be impulsive, though.

As he remembered their first sexual encounter on the lake, he reminded himself of how lucky he was. Maddie was his wife. The breathtaking excitement of that day on the lake had finally led to their magical wedding day. What was he doing 3,500 miles away, fighting this war?

He could have painted and lived with Maddie in her cloistered, glorified world—safe in New York.

But that was just wishful thinking. He was abruptly pulled back to the present. He could do nothing else than what he was doing right now. As the train slowly approached the station at York, his spirits lifted. No need to think more about Maddie. He had to focus on the mission.

Chapter 5

> *We'll meet again*
> *Don't know where, don't know when*
> *But I know we'll meet again*
> *Some sunny day*
> *Keep smiling through*
> *Just like you always do—*

William smiled as the song played on the radio behind the bar. Vera Lynn's clear, melancholy voice accompanied by a band he thought was not nearly as good as Benny Goodman's Orchestra drifted through the Officers' Mess at the RAF base at Yorkshire.

Some sunny day. That was out of reach right now, but he hoped not too far away. Two signs hung above the bar: *Careless Talk Costs Lives* and *Keep Mum – She's Not So Dumb!*—the last one showed a seductive woman in an evening dress surrounded by male admirers. Like other similar signs seen throughout England, often in deceptively quiet places, they warned what could occur if a careless word was dropped here or there in an unguarded moment. The message was clear to William—he couldn't be too careful. He had seen the equivalent, *Loose Lips Sink Ships* posted in train stations and public buildings back home in Toronto and New York.

At the same time, the soothing patter of the rain outside and the accompanying fog that enveloped them in the gloom of Yorkshire in late fall, almost convinced him that war, violence, and danger did not exist.

"Officer Craig, you've never had more than one quick pint before, all the times you been here. What ya up to, lad? I hear you left a real looker back home. Is that it?" The barman chuckled and raised a bushy eyebrow.

William quickly shook his head, not wanting to encourage the otherwise accommodating barman. He barely tasted the Guinness that was rarely available and the fried haddock and chips set before him on a dingy white, chipped plate. Even a bit of mushy peas would have improved the meal. The greasy, bland taste of the ubiquitous wartime English fare—often served in crumpled day-old newspaper, if they could even get it—clung to his throat. He thought longingly of his mother's Sunday roast beef and Yorkshire pudding.

The phone suddenly jangled on the wall. "Yep, he's here," the barman said and handed the earpiece to William.

"Uh-huh. Yeah, okay," he said. "Edinburgh tomorrow. Got it."

He had spent the night before talking with the others at the base and writing letters. He never knew if they reached Maddie, Auntie, or his parents. Sometimes, letters weren't delivered for a fortnight or longer and other times, miraculously in a week. The last letter he'd received from Maddie had alarmed him. She had written, "I can't stand to be separated any longer."

What did she mean?

Her words came back to him, preoccupying his thoughts.

I miss you so much, my darling. I yearn for you every night. I listen to our song, Moonglow over and over again. It takes me back to our nights of dancing and making love with you. I want you so much, William. But how long can we stand this? How long will you be so far away? How long before we can be together? Will we ever be together again?

The aristocratic, calm voice continued to speak through the phone earpiece, interrupting his thoughts. "The plans have changed," Bluebell said without emotion. "You will be going straightaway to Edinburgh. You will stay with Maddie's Uncle Hugh. He's involved too. You may have heard about him from your wife."

"Yes, but not much," William answered in a low voice, not wanting the amiable bartender who was turned away cleaning glasses to overhear the conversation. "She may have mentioned him once or twice," he said, wondering where this was leading.

"Well, he's a barrister and his wife plays first violin for the Edinburgh Symphony. He will tell you more about the contacts in the North," her voice faded as the line crackled then became clear again. "Hugh is well-connected. That is all I can say."

William couldn't hold himself back. "Can't you tell me more about what to expect, Ma'am?"

Although she could be distant and formal at times, Bluebell allowed him to occasionally call her *Ma'am*. After all, even the Queen—married to King George VI and described by Hitler as *the most dangerous woman in Europe* because of her apparent assets to British morale—was sometimes referred to as *Ma'am*.

And it was easier than saying *Lady Braithwaite-Smith*, which she preferred in public encounters. Such a cumbersome name, he often thought. He sometimes amused himself with private jokes—*Ah yes, Lady B-S, how do you do? What can I do for you, Lady B-S?* He could hear his brother Teddy snickering. William thought that even now, he was still a bit of a kid as well, placed prematurely in life-threatening situations like so many others of his generation. But he respected Lady Braithwaite-Smith's courage and devotion to her country and the way in which she managed to encourage and support his art in the midst of all this madness.

With her regal bearing and manner, she commanded such respect that he had to bite his tongue to keep from saying *your majesty* on a few occasions.

And now, she was Bluebell, his SOE handler. It seemed fitting that her code name was taken from the brave blue flowers that dotted the English and Scottish countryside in early spring. It no doubt also had something to do with her preoccupation—maybe even obsession—with gardening.

"Your cover is that you are traveling as a painter and visiting your wife's family," she said after a pause. "They entertain a great deal—dinner parties, music recitals in their parlor, luncheons. That sort of thing. You will meet others and find out more once you're there. It's best not to know too much ahead of time." The line crackled and there was another long pause.

He knew what she meant. If he was caught by enemy agents, he could be tortured and forced to reveal information that could lead to the deaths of others. German spies and sympathizers were all over England and Scotland, especially now that there were rumors of a possible Allied invasion in Occupied Europe. Not that it was known where or when it might occur. Their officers' training had included gruesome re-enactments of possible Gestapo interrogations, although without the removal of fingernails or the use of electrocution.

Nonetheless, quite frightening and realistic.

He thought for a moment of another operative who wasn't careful enough and was found in Glasgow with his throat cut. His attention returned to Bluebell.

"Hugh will tell you more." Her voice was firm and matter-of-fact. "Then you will take the train to Oban. Maddie's Aunt Catherine lives there. She's one of us—in that part of Scotland. She paints too. She will tell you more about what's happening in the Hebrides and who your contact will be. That's it for now. Be careful, William." A click ended the call.

William considered all of this. He knew very little about Maddie's relatives, except from occasional remarks about the war, over cocktails at dinners in Toronto with her family—"there are other ways," and the odd comment made about Uncle Hugh. Maddie's parents did not talk much about their past, especially her mother who would become remote and secretive if the conversation turned to war—including anything about Europe during the last war.

He sipped his pint of beer and thought about the plan, feeling that he could trust what she had told him. But he didn't know exactly how Maddie's relatives fit into the picture. Would Maddie also try to use their help to *do something* as she had alluded to in her letters? There seemed to be so much secrecy in her family. So much unsaid. Not that he really knew all that much about his own family.

Maddie was usually so immersed in her music—hours of piano studies and tedious scale exercises, then as she described it, her *reward*—rapturous hours of Mozart, Bach, Chopin, Haydn, Schumann, Beethoven, and Rachmaninoff. He often sketched or painted next to her as she played in her apartment when he was able to visit her in New York. One weekend the previous fall, they slipped away and explored Manhattan, trying to see as much as possible in their short time together. Walking through Central Park, window shopping on 5th Avenue, visiting galleries at the Metropolitan Museum of Art, a night at the Metropolitan Opera, and strolling past the beautiful Victorian and Art Deco buildings on the Upper West Side where Maddie lived with her mother.

They had walked arm in arm, looking out at the Hudson River, deep in conversation. Maddie leaned in close to William and spoke quietly, "I'm hearing things from my family. There is so much that we can do to win this war that doesn't involve dropping bombs, William. Uncle Hugh has connections. You could do other things… I can't really say what. But it could be safer. Think about it."

He hadn't asked what she meant and hadn't thought more about it until now. Later, when he was about to leave for England, she pled with him to consider other options. Maybe now, he was finally making the right decision.

After all the secrecy, and the classified training that was taking him further away from the base, he was looking forward to meeting Hugh. All he knew was that there was a network of spies working in Scotland, and there might be a possibility of Britain invading Nazi-Occupied Norway and elsewhere. He was trained now for espionage and counterintelligence operations and might also be involved in misleading the Germans about the whereabouts and timing of Allied invasions. Maybe sabotaging their communications. He might have to remove Nazi agents he encountered. He hoped that wouldn't be necessary or at least that it could be done without bloodshed. He tried not to think about it.

William heard that Churchill loved conspiracy and intrigue and believed that deception might be the only way to win the war. *Set Europe ablaze!* he had entreated when establishing the SOE as soon as Britain declared war on Germany. But it was likely that even Churchill didn't know all the missions involving the SOE and the RAF.

William had just finished another week of training in York and briefings on how to work with the French Underground, especially if one parachuted into Occupied France. He had also been trained in evasion tactics if his plane was shot down. He expected he would eventually have to return to flying with his crew on bombing missions and maybe drop supplies and agents behind enemy lines.

For now though, Bluebell would continue to be his handler for the SOE, interfacing with both MI5 for domestic affairs and MI6 for international activities while she remained at the Manor recruiting agents, overseeing their training, and sending them on missions following direct orders from the Home Office.

He signaled to the barman for another pint just as some officers loudly burst into the Officers' Mess laughing and slapping each other on the back and shouting while striding toward the bar.

"We got some more Jerries today, mate! Bloody hell, to be sure! Bring us some pints there. That's a good chap. Maybe even Guinness if you please—if you have it. Jolly good, mate," as they clinked their glasses of beer with more back-slapping and raucous singing—

Don't sit under the apple tree with anyone else but me
Anyone else but me, anyone else but me
No! No! No!

Then unintelligible words and more hoots of laughter.

William was content to sit on his own at the end of the bar, unnoticed by the boisterous group that sequestered a table in the corner where they began to play a rousing game of gin rummy. He thought more about how agents and case officers were everywhere. The village postmaster could be an agent. The wealthy young woman who smoked and drank coffee for hours in the local café or the middle-aged eccentric aristocrat living on an estate in the Cotswolds could be an agent. Ordinary citizens were very much involved in the ongoing effort to win the war. But it wasn't always clear which side they were on. Double agents were everywhere so you never knew exactly who you could trust.

He looked forward to spending time in Edinburgh and maybe seeing some paintings at the National Gallery. They hadn't been taken away for safekeeping like the masterpieces removed from the major galleries and museums in London. He had heard of some newly discovered Scottish landscape and abstract artists who were being received with high praise. But mostly, he wondered what he would be doing and how long he would be on this mission.

Chapter 6

New York City

Maddie sat at her small desk in her bedroom, writing a letter to William as the autumn wind shook the window with such force that the relentless, pounding rain threatened to crash into her bedroom and drench her. Or at least that was how she imagined the maelstrom of danger and worry that dominated her life. She wore a silk dressing gown loosely tied at her waist and the delicate diamond necklace William gave her on their wedding night. In her mind, she felt him wrapping his arms around her, nuzzling her neck, and coaxing her back to bed.

As she composed her thoughts, she listened to *Moonglow* and *I'll Be Seeing You*, the sentimental strains of Big Band music, a welcome respite from the days and weeks of practicing alternatively moody and compelling Chopin's Nocturnes and Preludes for her next concert at Juilliard. She loved to listen to Glenn Miller and Benny Goodman. She often imagined herself singing in nightclubs. She smiled at the thought of how the child prodigy turned cabaret singer would shake up her proper family, especially her always appropriate and dignified mother.

The record on the phonograph offered solace while, at the same time, tormented her by reminding her of the previous fall in New York. The weekend that William had a leave from training and came to visit her. Dancing at the Stage Door Canteen with him. Her first glass of champagne. Laughing and talking with other officers he knew and friends of hers from Juilliard.

A late lunch with her mother and William at the Waldorf Astoria the next day—Manhattans followed by Waldorf salad and chicken *vol-au-vent*. Her mother had not even objected to her having a cocktail. For a while, they had almost forgotten about the war.

When the record stopped, she remembered Rachel's stern admonishments that day.

"Maddie, you really must concentrate on your studies. You have three important recitals in the next month!" Then she turned to William and said, "Of course, you have your training as well to focus on." Adjusting her fox stole and sipping a second Manhattan, she said abruptly, "When do you think you will be leaving for England?"

William answered in his usual polite but noncommittal way, "I don't know, Mrs. Ainsworth. I've been told there will be more training before I get shipped out. But it could be fairly soon."

Maddie had felt her heart sink. She knew he was doing well with his Air Force training. She thought about how he seemed to have a gift for mathematics and science even though painting was his passion. She understood that dichotomy since music was an art and a science as well.

She thought about her mother who was also a bit of a mystery. At times, she seemed impatient for something more than her somewhat superficial, stylish life of furs, gowns, expensive jewelry, luncheons, and intimate soirees. Maddie felt a twinge of understanding. Perhaps her mother might be gaining a sense of fulfillment through William's accomplishments and her own. She wondered if maybe Rachel wished to live a very different life. Her dark moods hinted at a deeper side. Maddie knew her mother was worried about her own mother and grandmother in Paris.

Then a jolt of distress shook her to her core as she remembered the conversation over lunch that day at the Waldorf. Had she or her mother contributed to William's decision to be on the front line? She remembered telling him that they had relatives in Europe who were imperiled and others who were involved in working undercover with the Resistance and the British Government.

She thought of the months before their magical wedding and before William was assigned to receive further specialized training as a bombardier—an air bomber, one of the most dangerous posts in the war.

One afternoon, the most special of all, they walked through Central Park holding hands and kissing by the duck pond. It was one of the few times they could be alone—away from her mother and from practicing at Juilliard under Madame's watchful eyes. They had stopped to have an early dinner under the trees at the Tavern on the Green. Maddie wore a cream flared skirt and peplum jacket that accentuated her narrow waist, with a wide-brimmed hat. William said how much he loved her in that suit and how well it contrasted with her dark hair and eyes.

After the tomato aspic, Oysters Rockefeller, and Steak Diane—such rare guilty pleasures in a time of war—William suddenly stood, then dropped onto one knee, ignoring the whispers and sideways glances of the other diners.

"Oh, Maddie, you are the one. You take my breath away. I love you to the moon and back, my glorious Maddie!" He smiled broadly as his bright blue eyes twinkled meeting her gaze, and he held her hand. "Please tell me right now that I am the one for you, my darling."

Butterflies danced in her stomach as he paused, teasing her, then became very serious.

"Will you marry me?" he asked holding his breath with an anxious look on his face. He pulled a small ring case out of his pocket and opened it solemnly.

Was he imagining she might reject his proposal? William might be a bombardier but he was sensitive too, she thought. His easy good humor hid an intense side. He was a true enigma.

Maddie couldn't help herself and laughed in her excitement then said quickly, "William, how could I love anyone else? There will never be anyone but you," tears filling her eyes.

"Does that mean 'yes,' Maddie?" William asked, still looking uncertain.

"Yes, yes, yes!" Maddie cried and he gently placed the ring on her finger. The other diners clapped and whistled, as only New Yorkers can. Some stood, waving their napkins and shouting, "Hooray!" "Well done!" "Splendid, young man!"

William jumped to his feet and lifted Maddie from her chair, swinging her high in the air in a wild, ecstatic circle—both of them laughing with joy. As he set her down, they held each other closely and kissed with breathless desire, nothing else existing outside their world.

Maddie felt the excitement of that day all over again. A summer sunset shimmering through the trees. She—who felt so confident performing on stage—suddenly felt dizzy and weak-kneed.

She returned to her letter, furiously dipping her fountain pen into a bottle of Indian ink.

Dear William,

I am so angry with you for putting yourself in such danger. I can only imagine what you are doing. Flying every night in those frightening planes! You said you had long leaves—at a place called The Manor. Where are you exactly? I wish you could tell me. I just need to know that you're safe.

Please come back to me. And if that can't happen, I want you to know that I have a plan to find you. Don't laugh. I have my ways too. You know that I have family members who may be in great jeopardy. And others who can help. I have to do something.

This war will be over, eventually, but who knows when that will be. In the meantime, there may be things I can do. And we can be together. I will find you.

My love always,

Maddie

Chapter 7

Edinburgh, Scotland

William and Maddie's Uncle Hugh walked along the *causey*, the Scottish word for the cobblestone road of the Royal Mile, toward Parliament Square then on to Edinburgh Castle; their upturned collars and tartan woolen scarves shielded them against the bitterly cold wind that seemed to blow directly from the Firth of Forth, the estuary of many Scottish rivers and not far beyond, the North Sea. The castle, a historic fortress dating back to the Middle Ages, loomed in the distance from its promontory of volcanic rock. The silvery light evolving into twilight surrounded them with the magic of early evening while a light drizzle mingled with the wind.

The usual clatter of horse hooves and wagons sharing the road with an occasional car was absent as the city prepared for night. Edinburgh was seemingly removed from the eye of the storm, yet wore the somber cloak of war.

William missed the warmth of his greatcoat. He needed to blend in as an ordinary citizen and wore a navy woolen pea jacket over corduroy pants, sweater vest, and flannel shirt. Hugh was dressed in a finely tailored Harris Tweed dress coat over his pin-striped suit. It seemed strange to William to not be in uniform and to be with someone dressed so impeccably. He was usually surrounded by a sea of RAF blue-gray clad officers.

He wore a tweed cap over his close-cropped blond hair while Hugh's charcoal fedora was angled forward over his slightly longish dark hair—so like Maddie's, but with a hint of gray at the temples. The tips of their noses, cheeks, and ears became a deeper red the longer they walked.

The air was filled with the stench of coal-burning fires. The stone walls of St. Giles' Cathedral, a haberdashery, banks, pubs, and whiskey shops along the Royal Mile were black with layers of soot that had collected over more than a century. The distinctive crown steeple and surrounding spires of the massive church covering a city block, a religious focal point of Edinburgh for 900 years, rose to a sky streaked with iridescent clouds colored by the pastel hues of the fading sunset. The glowing orb of an almost-full moon rose in the gathering darkness, adding to the aura of mystery.

William thought about how he would paint these scenes when he had the chance. He tried not to think about how bombing missions usually occurred with a full moon and his crew mates would be flying without him.

They had just finished Sunday dinner with a few guests at Hugh and his wife's Georgian town house in New Town—the eighteenth-century part of Edinburgh—and excused themselves after the strawberry cream trifle and brandy, saying they needed a stroll to clear their heads.

It was almost as if the war was forgotten that afternoon in the flat's gaslit drawing room when William in his strong tenor voice and Hugh in a rich baritone sang Schumann parlor songs in perfect harmony. They were accompanied by Hugh's attractive young wife, dressed in a long black velvet gown, who played her Stradivarius violin. William appreciated the brief respite from his war-preoccupied thoughts. The guests applauded appreciatively and toasted the performance with their glasses of sherry as if there was no war at all. Amazing, he thought, how we can ignore the death and carnage even for a few hours.

"Okay, the time has come, William. I can now tell you what you will be doing. There are operatives here in Edinburgh, and some in the Highlands as well," Hugh said as he waved a hand in that general direction and they walked further, bracing against the wind and picking up their pace. He inhaled deeply from his cigarette, the end glowing briefly in the darkness. Hugh had a self-assured, unflappable manner that matched the elegant way he dressed and reminded William of Maddie's mother, Rachel—his sister. All of that served him well as a barrister in Edinburgh and in social circles interconnected within the web of deception spreading throughout Scotland.

As Hugh talked, William felt more certain about his mission. Between Bluebell and Hugh, I am in good hands, he thought. Hugh appeared at ease in his comfortable life in Edinburgh, seemingly removed from the dangers that William was about to face. But then again, William didn't know much about what Hugh was actually doing behind that calm facade.

"Churchill has made it clear that we need to act fast," Hugh said as he adjusted the scarf around his neck. He exhaled slowly, his breath forming long smoky wisps of small perfect rings above his head as he gestured with his cigarette emphasizing each word. He spoke in a low voice as they passed the occasional figure huddled in a darkened doorway or a shadow suddenly rushing down a narrow staircase to a *close* below—the Scottish term for a gated alleyway.

William noticed that many of the alleys had weathered signs posted above their entrance announcing the names—*Advocate's Close, Fleshmarket Close*—suggesting the original activities that had occurred there. He wondered about the mysteries hidden behind the stone walls and in the occasional crumbling medieval cottage in the distance—a glimmer of a pale-yellow light shining faintly from a window on the upper floor. He thought how easy it would be to lose your way in the darkness of the lanes winding away from them into the black night with street lamps providing only small pools of light in the thick fog that was rapidly obscuring the buildings around them.

The ancient cobblestone road took them past a small whiskey shop now closed for the night—a single bulb brightened the dark wooden door and a few lights strung above the windows illuminated a colorful display of bottled spirits arranged in ascending rows.

Hugh spoke quickly and matter-of-factly, "You will travel by train to Oban and stay with my sister, Maddie's Aunt Cate. Bluebell knows the plan, of course. There you can paint and travel a bit in the countryside with her—with the sole intention of maintaining your cover as an artist visiting with family."

"Yes, I know that Cate is a painter too. How long am I likely to stay there, Hugh? And what will I be doing undercover? Is she in on this too?" William said with more impatience than he meant to reveal. He couldn't help it. He had so many questions and was anxious to know more about what he was getting into.

Hugh smiled and seemed amused by William's eager curiosity. "It's a good cover, Will. Cate is well known in Oban. She teaches and paints so it absolutely suits our needs. Don't worry, she is quite capable. You will get to know people in the village—go to pubs, village get-togethers, and such. And obtain information that will be important for others to know. You will see. Other more aggressive techniques may be in order, down the road. All in good time, old boy." He glanced at William as he flicked the end of his cigarette into the darkness. Hugh placed a gloved hand on William's shoulder and his expression grew more serious. His voice was barely audible as he leaned in closer to

William and said, "Contacts will make themselves available and lead you to the German agents—who may or may not be working for us. That is for you to sort out. And of course, the idea is to feed them information about a supposed invasion of Occupied Norway and elsewhere—*Pas de Calais* is one possibility." He paused as he took out another cigarette for his case and lit it with a silver lighter cupping his hand against the bitter wind. He quickly inhaled, then blew a stream of smoke that drifted away from them and vanished. "But you will need to be quite cautious. Of course, not everyone is who they appear to be," he warned, raising an eyebrow.

William nodded and glanced at Hugh, changing the subject as he felt a surge of anxiety. "I just received a letter from Maddie. She is saying that she might try to come here. Can that be true? I'm worried. She needs to stay in New York," he said as he rubbed his hands together, then blew vigorously on his fingers. He wondered what Hugh might know. *Maybe he could intervene to keep Maddie from traveling to Britain.*

"William, you know that no one can tell Maddie what to do. Not even you. That's who she is," Hugh said managing a smile but then his forehead furrowed with worry. He became silent for a few moments, deep in thought.

"I just can't think of Maddie putting herself in danger. We have to stop her, Hugh. There must be something you can do!" William's voice rose as he felt himself getting increasingly more agitated.

"I know how you must feel, Will," Hugh responded not unkindly. "Maddie probably thinks that if she finds you, she can take you back home," he sighed audibly then added, "As unrealistic as that is. She is used to getting what she wants. You ought to know, Will." He chuckled and patted William lightly on the back, then said, "Maddie is truly one of a kind."

William nodded and tried to calm himself knowing it didn't help to get impatient. But he was feeling increasingly distressed that Maddie might try to leave the safety of New York and look for him.

Hugh's tone became more serious, "Also, from what Rachel has told me, William, Maddie has the idea that she can come over here and help some of our family members." This confirmed William's worst fears. "Maybe even work with the Resistance in France or some such thing." Hugh then inhaled from his cigarette again and waved his gloved hand underscoring his concern. He exhaled slowly and said in an exasperated tone, "A romantic notion, indeed. But Maddie has always been very determined and disciplined in everything that she does. She is quite unusual, to be sure." Hugh shook his head with appreciation.

Despite his worries, William couldn't help but admire Maddie's single-mindedness and determination when she had an idea. "That she is," he said. "But I don't want her coming here, Hugh. It's far too dangerous. Surely, you can do something."

They continued striding uphill. Hugh's expression became more intense as he glanced at William.

"Maddie is very busy with her concerts and studies," he said reassuringly. "I truly doubt that she could arrange a crossing right now. And especially with all the increased tightening of security. Her background is also a concern—she could be quite unsafe if she actually went to France. Things are becoming even more dangerous there, especially for people like us," Hugh said with emphasis.

William knew what Hugh meant—that the family secret could cause her harm. Being a Jew meant she could be in real danger if she came to Europe. He just wanted Maddie to stay where she was and not try to do anything crazy.

"I know Rachel will do everything to keep her in New York. My sister is also a force to be reckoned with, believe me."

William nodded. He hoped that Hugh was right.

As they kept walking toward a pub where they could escape from the cold wind, William felt somewhat reassured. Then he glanced at Hugh, trying to detect if he was keeping anything from him. *Should I be even more worried? Can I trust that Maddie won't be able to find a way to England?*

"We all should hope that she stays where she is," Hugh said. "Our intel isn't always reliable—especially out of France. So we can't even be sure that relatives working for the Resistance are still alive. Messages are intercepted all the time, radio operators arrested…" his voice trailed off and his tone became more ominous. "You know that others in our family—cousins in France and Germany—have disappeared, maybe even to the camps that we are hearing more about. You probably know there have been roundups of Jews by the Nazis all over Europe. And we haven't heard from Ma-mere and Grand-mere in Paris for some time." Hugh looked intently at William and pounded a gloved fist into his other palm as he spoke, "We need to win this war, Will. And soon. Too many people are dying." His tone was clipped and calm but unmistakably angry. Hugh stopped under a street lamp for a moment and cupped his hands to shield the flame of his lighter against the wind and lit another cigarette.

The two of them walked on, silent and lost in their own thoughts. William knew that Maddie and her family had emigrated by ship from England in the 1930s after the economic crash when business opportunities for her father had brought them to Canada. He also knew that Maddie's grandmother and her children, Rachel, Hugh, and Cate were Jews but converted to High Anglican when they arrived in England from Europe after the end of World War I. He didn't know much more. Maddie told him about the terrible nightmares her mother still had.

Maddie had become an unusually gifted pianist of rare talent. When she was only 12, she had been discovered at the Royal Conservatory near the limestone colleges of the University of Toronto and was swept away to study first with a famed Canadian tutor and then the acclaimed José Iturbi in New York. Maddie played at a dinner party hosted by her parents when he was in Toronto to give a concert. This was after Iturbi's career in movies as MGM's idea of a classical pianist had ended. William felt in awe sometimes of her accomplishments and her talent. She was capable of great things and could be quite brave.

Maddie auditioned when she was 16-years-old before the formidable panel of faculty judges at Juilliard. She soon became one of their most-prized piano students. As a fellowship student, she kept long hours perfecting her own particular style that Madame attempted unsuccessfully to rein in.

Maddie described colorfully how Madame would sigh and re-direct her to the metronome with a curt, "My dear Madeleine, this isn't the opera. Such histrionics, for goodness' sake! The piano deserves respect. Remember your timing, Cherie," then wave a slim baton in brisk, precise strokes while humming with obvious enjoyment despite her disapproving tone. According to Maddie, even Madame couldn't completely maintain her stern demeanor. She would suddenly erupt with, "Ah ha! That's more like it," and purse her Coco Chanel red lips into an appreciative mew. Maddie had a certain way of winning over even her harshest critics.

William could not imagine how someone like Maddie, cosseted in a world of privilege, structured days of practice and performances, and admiring concert audiences could leave all that. *To risk her life.* He was shocked that she could even consider leaving New York when so many Jews were trying desperately to escape Europe. Although she didn't really think of herself as Jewish and her true background was not known to most, he knew that the

Germans were obsessed with identifying and persecuting anyone who might have Jewish roots.

He understood her restlessness and impatience; her passion and spirit were what he loved most about her. But he also knew about her tendency to confront frightening situations head-on. As their separation continued interminably without an end in sight, who knew what she might try to do? He had heard that musicians occasionally traveled to England from abroad to lift the spirits of armed forces. William hoped with all his heart that Maddie would not plan such a reckless venture.

As he and Hugh walked past the Princes Street Gardens and the Mound below, he could see the National Gallery of Scotland in the distance. How he wanted to paint Holyrood Castle where Mary Queen of Scots lived for such a short time and witnessed the murder in her bedchamber of her secretary—her favorite and most-trusted advisor—instigated by her jealous husband, Lord Darnley, who was found dead in the garden after a mysterious explosion destroyed the house where he had lived apart from his wife. William thought of the legendary bloodstain on the floor of Holyrood Castle that supposedly remained there, centuries later.

Betrayal, murder, vengeance, and violence endured through the centuries. Unavoidable and pervasive.

But he loved the sixteenth-century beauty of Old Town. The cobblestone streets, the confusing maze of masonry, closes, narrow alleys, steep stairways, and mysterious vaults. Edinburgh was an intriguing city of bloody history, bone-chilling mist, furtive shadows, and whispered voices.

He felt drawn to bleak churchyards filled with ancient headstones—the inscriptions barely visible, "here lies Claire Mu…, may she… in… 1845–1847…" An aura of sadness hung in the air. Some plots were guarded by a large granite statue of a long-haired androgynous angel or dimpled cherub. He imagined the lives of those lying beneath the ground—the joys and tragedies, and some cut short by violence or illness.

The odd burst of color introjected stubbornly by perennial shrubs provided some relief from the slate grays of the approaching winter. The spires of medieval churches against the somber night sky were intermittently obscured by billowing clouds drifting in the wind across the almost full moon. An expanse of cottages with brightly lit windows dotted the darkness in the distance. All of this captured his artist's soul.

While they walked leaning into the frigid wind, Hugh warned William, "As difficult as this may be, you must focus on your work here. We have much to do. We don't know how long you will be in the field or when you might return to the bombing missions. Things are escalating on both sides. We need to win this war. The future of the world depends on it." His face turned grim.

William didn't think this was an overstatement, now that Japan had also entered into a violent pact with Hitler.

"I know, Hugh. And I have to do everything I possibly can to help." He took a deep breath, fighting rising anxiety. "I just don't know if Maddie can be stopped. Once she decides something, she can be a true force of nature."

He thought of the night she tried to stop him from shipping out to England. He hoped that Rachel was as strong as Hugh thought and could keep Maddie in New York.

Hugh nodded and smiled, "You are so right. Maddie is headstrong but with any luck, she will stay where she is—where she belongs. No matter how tough and strong she is, it would be very difficult if not impossible for her to get here... now. And the war may be over soon, William. We will win. We must win," he said firmly. "Churchill has plans."

They entered the tiny pub in the shadow of the magnificent Edinburgh Castle through the narrow doorway lowering their heads below the timbered ceiling designed for those of much smaller stature from previous centuries. The walls of whitewashed stone were supported with pine beams in the Tudor style so common in this part of the world. Once inside, they sat down by the fire facing each other, their faces beginning to relax in the genial mood of the pub.

Three British servicemen sat in a corner laughing and drinking frothy mugs of dark beer. They seemed to be debating recent escapades real or imagined with an American nurse and who had attracted her the most.

"You sods, she was begging me to get into her knickers."

"She gave me a jolly good once-over, ya know, Jackie-boy."

"Fuck yous both, she was ready to run away with me, you wankers," a tall, lanky airman wearing a crooked grin, said with a loud guffaw and slapped his knee.

One of them snorted. Another whistled then argued further in favor of certain body parts belonging to him that "any gal would want to know better." Satisfied that he had won this round, he leaned toward his companions, speaking quietly, barely above a whisper.

"You heard right. Bob was found shot in the back. Sittin' in a pub as ya please. Seems his wife had another fella when Bob was at the front. Then what about the crews shot by fuckin' Jerries on the ground after'n they bail? Or'n the air comin' down, thinkin' they're in the clear! I'm gettin' damn sick of this, mates."

Then, one of the servicemen wagged his finger at the others and said with swaggering bravado, "Ya know what Churchill says, *KBO. Keep buggerin' on.* That's what we're meant to do, lads. Carry on and show those damn Jerries what for! Then Bob's your uncle. There you go, mates." He raised his mug with a grin and said, "Cheers, mates!"

The others followed suit, with a collective shout, "To us—and to victory!"—their shared camaraderie providing a modicum of protection against the fear of whatever would come next.

William shook his head and wiped his hand across his mouth after taking a long sip of the warm beer. He lowered his gaze toward Hugh's intense dark eyes and said, "Hugh, I'm ready for this. I've left the base. I need to make good."

"No worries there, William. You will be on your way to Oban and the Hebrides tomorrow. Then your mission will begin."

Chapter 8

The Highlands, Scotland

William and Maddie's Aunt Cate hiked across the craggy, windswept hills of the wild and remote Scottish Highlands climbing over rocks aided by their walking sticks and chatting companionably. They gazed ahead at the majestic landscape, searching for the perfect location protected from the wind with views suitable for painting.

After driving Cate's vintage Vauxhall coupe from Oban, they had been ferried in a small open boat equipped with a sputtering outboard motor, by a weather-beaten sailor smoking prodigiously on his pipe, over the rough waters of Loch Etive that mimicked the wild seas of the nearby Atlantic Ocean. In the high winds, waves broke every few minutes over the low prow of the skiff barely large enough for the three travelers, splashing them with frigid water and jolting the boat sideways while the seaman with a fierce look of determination turned it back on course. A lone seal bobbed in the whitecaps accompanying them to the other side of the mid-sized lake as a graceful white crane swooped downward and plummeted into the water with a loud splash. It rose triumphantly holding a large twitching prize in its beak—one of the many salmon found in Scottish lochs—and flew away.

When a wave suddenly hit William squarely in the face, he laughed as he shouted to Cate, "Well, that was quite refreshing! Let's hope we don't go overboard!" He couldn't help but enjoy himself. He loved being on the water in any kind of weather.

Cate shook her head with amusement and shouted back, "We'll be to the other side soon enough, and we can dry off."

The seaman just kept staring in the direction of the opposite shore, grimly shaking his head and muttering unintelligibly, something about "what fools are these—"

Once they arrived at the shore on the other side of the lake and disembarked, Cate said to the crusty old skipper, "Could you come back for us around 4 pm, before nightfall?"

He just grunted and answered, "Aye, lassie." Then without another word as smoke curled upward from his pipe into the wind, he steered the skiff away from the shore.

They hiked on for a while, then found a spot in the lee of a hill overlooking Loch Etive where they could paint and eat a lunch of tea and meat pies. Sheltered from the wind, William opened his pochade box that contained tubes of paints and brushes. He squeezed the chosen colors into depressions of his palette, periodically dipping the brush into a wide-mouthed flask holding water that he carried in his haversack. He mixed the colors and thoughtfully applied them onto his watercolor paper after making a rough sketch of fine lines with a charcoal pencil.

As William painted, he said, "You wouldn't believe some of the art galleries in London, Cate. Even though most of the good stuff has been taken away for safekeeping. Hitler's not about to get his hands on those. It's a tragedy that all that art has to be hidden for who knows how long." He frowned for a moment and felt his face flush with anger, then recovered his good humor and said, "But the shows in Edinburgh! Have you been there lately?" he asked, feeling the excitement all over again of seeing other artists' work.

Cate looked up from her sketch on the easel facing her and glanced at William briefly with a slight smile but said nothing.

Not waiting for an answer, William said, "There are still wonderful works at the National Gallery in Edinburgh, you know—even a few of the masters— so wonderful to see after so much has been taken away from the big galleries in London." He returned to his painting with swift, dramatic brushstrokes. "I love the Scottish painters. But I'm not so sure about the two Roberts. They're showing in London now. You know—Robert Colquhoun and Robert MacBryde. Colquhoun especially has plunged headfirst into the Expressionist style—a bit austere but probably reflecting the mood of the war. A little too much like Francis Bacon, I think. Bacon is all the rage in London. Too dark for me, I'm afraid," he paused. "Then there's Lucian Freud," he spoke more quickly as he applied more paint. "His portraits are so unusual. And he's just my age. Quite revolutionary!" He shook his head and whistled with appreciation.

Then he thought about how he heard that Freud was *invalided out* of serving in the war. What would that have meant for me if I hadn't been able to serve, he wondered. William quickly shifted from thinking about what he was missing and said with a laugh, "Oh well, I guess I'll stick to my boring old landscapes, Cate."

She glanced at him and smiled.

"But who knows what I might do someday!" William said with a grin, trying to feel more than a thread of hope. It was more of a statement than a question.

He knew SOE and Resistance agents were dying every day, not to mention all the airmen who never returned to their bases. But he never tired of talking about painting or art.

William's face darkened briefly as another thought crossed his mind. How was it that these British artists were able to work on their art and weren't on the battlefield or in the air, fighting Germans? Some like Lucian Freud had legitimate medical conditions but what about others? He shook off a feeling he could only identify as envy.

But didn't they have the right to pursue their art without death and violence? Duty versus love. That was always the question. Art and beauty versus destruction.

Well, he would have to keep doing his duty but not lose sight of love or his art. He couldn't allow himself to feel the fear that often nagged at him—that his sense of duty could end up killing him. He would enjoy the beauty around him as long as he could. Images of the art he had recently seen returned to his mind.

Unable to contain his enthusiasm, he said with awe, "And then, there are Henry Moore's sculptures—so calming and unique." He waved his hands recreating the forms in the air that he had seen in London. "Very modern and elegant. Such clean lines. Yes, I intend to do more sculpting when I get back home. I can't wait!" He made another rapid flourish in the air and laughed.

Then he noticed that Cate still hadn't responded and looked thoughtful. She had smiled at William's last comment and continued to apply paint on the small canvas resting on a portable easel in front of her.

She finally spoke, with quiet authority, "I've heard that there are still some small exhibits, even in the midst of bombings. But I don't have much time for that, I'm afraid." She paused. "I haven't been to Edinburgh or London in ages.

I've been lucky and had a few commissions for portraits. You know how the rich and famous can be, William. Can't get enough of themselves." Cate snorted and laughed then added more seriously, looking off into the distance, "With the teaching too, it keeps me busy. And then we have the other business… a lot to do right here, I'm afraid." Her voice trailed off as she turned back toward William.

"So tonight is the night, William. We will make contact in Oban with Heather. Not her real name, of course, but quite appropriate given where we are. She will lead us to the German agent who is also working for us. We're not too sure about him but he's all we have right now. And we have to keep the information moving." She returned to the landscape she was painting of the rugged Highlands.

Cate was fortyish, the older sister of Maddie's mother, Rachel and younger than Hugh, Maddie's uncle in Edinburgh. She was tall and lean like them but more angular, wore no makeup, and was dressed in wide-legged tailored trousers, cable knit sweater, and a long tweed coat. She had removed her lambskin gloves to paint and occasionally rubbed her hands and blew on them briskly, warming them up. Her boyish appearance was softened by a mop of somewhat unruly, short, wavy reddish-brown hair that reminded William of Amelia Earhart. Cate had the same air of no-nonsense competence he had seen in newsreels at the movies when he was a kid, showing Earhart in the cockpit of her plane before her disappearance in 1937. William thought Cate was attractive in a self-assured way. She had a dignified presence like her siblings but was more reserved. Although she maintained a tough exterior, he thought there was also sadness in her manner.

Like the rest of her family, Cate had an air of mystery. Her eyes were an unusual shade of deep greenish-blue much like the turbulent waters they had just crossed. William also noted the sharp intelligence in them every time she spoke. She was quite different from her sister Rachel who was beautiful and self-confident as well, but more feminine, he thought. Rachel was always stylishly dressed and charming but a bit controlling, especially with Maddie. Cate was more like Hugh in her manner but they all seemed to have secrets. And they all communicated a deep, quiet strength, William thought. Whatever had brought them to England had formed them and given them a certain, indomitable power.

As with other handlers like Bluebell, Cate was calm and matter-of-fact in her briefings but she could also be cool and somewhat abrupt. Her voice became gentler and more relaxed when they talked about painting and art. He liked her despite her sometimes brusque, aloof manner.

Maybe her confidence and self-assured intensity also reminded him a bit of Maddie. He thought about how female agents and handlers had to be tougher than their male counterparts in so many ways because they were going against gender-related expectations that had existed until this war forced some changes. And they were frequently underestimated. He also knew that the Germans despised the British and French for using female agents.

Cate glanced up at the dark, foreboding clouds gathering momentum in the distance for a certain storm and said, "We might want to finish up so we can get back before we get drenched. It looks like the fog might roll in as well."

They had brought rubberized ponchos, essential in blustery, wet Scottish weather, and wore Wellies – the tall English rubber boots that were so useful for hiking in the Highlands.

Cate shivered and put down her brush then hugged herself. She added in a serious tone, "We are under orders to keep expanding the subterfuge. Even Churchill doesn't know everything that's going on, despite his love of mystery and conspiracies." Cate looked at William more intently as she straightened her back and stretched, then said, "There are many agents in this area—on both sides. You need to be careful, William."

William felt a chill down his spine but said nothing.

"Your cover is a good one—a painter who happens to be traveling in Scotland, visiting relatives. After a pint or two, you might find out more from the locals. Bluebell has arranged for you to work closely with another agent here. No matter who you are working with, remember that he or she could also be working for the Germans. Even those agents who have turned for us may be reporting to the Nazis. So it can't be avoided. You may be contacting agents who are doubles. One, in particular, to watch out for is called 'Magpie'— probably a very appropriate name from what I understand. You know, the intelligent black-and-white bird considered evil in English folklore, who steals other birds' eggs from their nests."

"Yep, I heard about him. A particularly nasty bloke."

Cate sighed then added, "This is all very cloak and dagger, to be sure, William. Wheels within wheels."

William nodded but his thoughts drifted elsewhere—to what he might have to do if he encountered an enemy agent.

"My brother and sister are counting on me to keep you safe. You must be careful. And of course, there is that wonderful niece of mine to consider. She most surely wants to see you safe and sound, after this is all over," Cate said in the reserved way that William had grown to appreciate. Then with her trademark confidence, she told him, "But I know you've been trained well. You know what to do."

Cate's last comments brought William back to the present. He thought about all the training back at the Manor and felt prepared.

He didn't want to think about jumping from the frying pan into the fire. That's how it now seemed. Instead, he thought about what an extraordinary day it had been—particularly the long hike through the Highlands and painting the distant hills and the quixotic sky—alternatively granite gray, then when the sun broke through the clouds, patches of azure blue appeared. He had sung earlier in the day to the sheep grazing on the hills as they hiked past them, their heads turning curiously toward the strange sound. He loved to sing, especially outdoors where his voice seemed to resonate with the landscape—the more rugged and remote, the better.

He remembered canoeing one spring evening back home with Charlie, Maddie's brother, on a lake that narrowed between two high cliffs. As their paddles dipped quietly in the darkness, they laughed at how his voice echoed and bounced off the cliffs. He couldn't believe how far away he was from all that now.

He thought about Charlie stationed with the Royal Canadian Navy in Halifax as a medic caring for the returning injured—not in harm's way, thank goodness. He hoped he would stay safe.

Cate's words were still hanging in the air between them but William couldn't avoid the reality any longer—of what he was here to do. He wasn't on holiday, although he wanted to think he was.

His eyes narrowed as he said, "Cate, if this is who I think it is, he may have killed a number of our agents. We're not sure. Bluebell warned me about him. I've heard that Magpie is fond of daggers and pistols that he conceals inside well-tailored suits."

Cate answered cryptically, "Right then," and quickly gathered up the remnants of their lunch, placing them in a wicker basket she had brought, with her paints, brushes, canvas, and folded easel. She showed no emotion. "Well, you know the dangers," she said as she glanced at him, her brow furrowed. "It's the time we live in, unfortunately. To be sure," she said grimly.

Despite himself, William wanted to linger in the wild beauty of the Highlands. Just to have a brief respite from all the violence and death.

Then, more gently, Cate said, "It's time to go, William. We can talk more on the drive back. You will be able to travel where others may not because of that innocent, young face of yours." She smiled with a hint of fondness.

William could see that behind her stern facade, she cared what happened to him.

"Your cover is a good one, William," Cate repeated almost as if to reassure herself as well. She added, "I don't think anyone will be the wiser. You will pass on misleading information to those who matter. There may be other things that you will need to do. We think there could be a turning point soon in this wretched war—in our favor." A flash of a hopeful expression crossed Cate's face, then she resumed her usual inscrutable demeanor.

As they packed up the rest of their things, he fought against rising anxiety. He knew there was probably more that she wasn't telling him. But he was about to do something important that wouldn't involve killing hundreds of people with a single bomb, not to mention the unseen damage he imagined with the cascade of more bombs that followed. Maybe he could feel redeemed for leaving his crew even if it was for a short time. And he reassured himself that he had been recruited into the SOE with the RAF's cooperation.

Nonetheless, he was not naïve to the dangers ahead and the possibility that he may have to kill to protect himself and others. He could also be called back at any time to resume the bombing missions, especially as the Allied forces' attacks escalated. He thought about how too many of the crews were not returning from their missions. Experienced airmen were becoming more scarce.

William and Cate hiked over the hills toward the shore of Loch Etive to meet the seaman for their trip back. Streaks of lightning in the distance accompanied by loud thunder claps warned them of the approaching storm that with any luck and a changing wind, could roll away from them. As they quickened their pace, they noticed a large dark object in the distance that could not be mistaken for a flock of sheep, roaming stags, or Highland cows. They kept walking toward it.

Whatever it was, it wasn't moving.

As they got closer to the thing sprawled on the ground, it became all too clear what it was. A well-dressed man in what remained of a tweed suit with a bloody mess above a crisp white collar where his head should have been. Fragments of bone, grey matter, flesh, and tufts of sandy hair were scattered around him in a macabre montage.

Chapter 9

Fear and desire—two sides of the same coin.
Chinese fortune cookie

Islay, Scotland

After William and Aunt Cate's encounter with the dead German agent on the Highlands, there was a change in plans, and it was decided after a call with Bluebell that William should move to another location.

"We don't know exactly what happened," Cate told William that morning as they shared a breakfast of tea and toast in her small, bright kitchen in the gray stone house on McCalley Lane in the deceptively quiet village of Oban. She poured more tea for William as she told him, "Herman was sent here by the Germans. Then he was recruited and worked for us. He got caught. It means that German agents or those working for them are in the area. You can't stay here, William. Islay is another point of contact and not far. We can't risk you blowing your cover."

Cate stood up from the table and began to collect and clean the dishes. Her face was grim as she packed some bread, tea, and tinned meat for William's trip later that evening. Like Hugh and Bluebell, she seemed sure of herself in every action and word she spoke.

William supposed that this was how one survived a war that had gone on now for nearly four years—*the Good War*—because of the supposed righteousness of the fight against Fascism. He thought about how the previous so-called *Great War* had nearly killed his father and brutally removed millions from the face of the earth. It had been believed that it would be the last war of its kind. Humans seem to be compelled to kill each other.

Later that morning, Cate covered her painting of William in his Air Force uniform with a white sheet and set it off to the side of her dining room that served as a makeshift studio. It had been her idea to do his portrait, like so many others she had been commissioned to paint for the King, members of the

74

Royal family, and others with titles or a great need to fill the halls of their mansions with their visages, or simply as she chided, "had more money than brains."

He had no idea if she was intending to finish his portrait or where it might end up, especially if he was gone. He shook off a feeling of foreboding that stubbornly nudged him when he allowed himself to think about what he was doing. He had to focus on the mission.

As he sat in Cate's kitchen drinking another cup of tea, looking out on her garden now brown with the oncoming winter, he felt restless and impatient for action. With enemy agents and double agents operating throughout London and Scotland, time was running out.

Misinformation and deception were needed to ensure the success of Churchill's invasion—the possible location was still a well-kept secret. *Would the invasion be into Occupied Norway or France? Or somewhere else?* He knew what he was about to do was part of the plan.

He had been told to rendezvous with another operative and then travel to the Orkney Islands off the far northern coast of Scotland – the birthplace of his favorite Scottish painter, the landscape artist, Stanley Cursiter, who was now the Director of the National Gallery in Edinburgh. That seemed like a good omen. He expected that he would re-unite with his crew in another fortnight or maybe longer, for more intensive training and bombings from aircraft in communication with Royal Navy ships offshore.

He thought about the lives lost every day or missing—not only those killed in the air and on the ground but those that disappeared, some sent to *re-location* camps. Reports by journalists and war correspondents were starting to surface. Agents who had escaped from behind enemy lines told stories of massive roundups and trains taking thousands of people away, never to be seen again. Agents were also sent to these camps.

After an afternoon of reviewing maps and sketching, William and Cate shared a quiet supper of lentil soup and fresh crusty bread that Cate had bought in the village. William left for the meet a few hours before sunrise from Cate's house in Oban, preferring to travel under a cover of darkness.

He traveled by train for a few hours south then by ferry to the Isle of Islay in the Inner Hebrides. Another wind-blown world so far away from Maddie and the life he had left behind.

He still felt rattled by the sight of the dead double on the Highlands but he had to do what he could to end this bloody war.

William planned to sketch and paint, then meet the other agent assigned by Bluebell, who would give him the intel for the next mission and work with him for some unknown period of time—probably at least for the next week or longer. He carried a pistol, a long-bladed Bowie knife, and a steel-bladed dagger in his haversack.

He could no longer pretend that he was just a painter on vacation. He felt fear of being found out even as he continued this double-life—digging increasingly deeper into a world of intrigue and danger—that still felt foreign. What he now faced had a more intimate and human face than the barrage of German fighter planes and flak they dodged each night his crew took flight. He hoped he could do what had to be done. He would know more after the meet.

As he stepped off the ferry, he walked toward the small village of Port Ellen on Islay, known for its whiskey distilleries. A local villager soon appeared, puffing on a battered corncob pipe. He squinted and nodded at William in greeting, then drove him to the village of Bowmore in a 1934 Studebaker truck that rattled and shook over the potholed road.

The driver dropped him in the village with a mumbled, "There you be," and drove off, spewing smoke that almost obscured a fan of stones shooting out behind it. William sat with a cup of tea at a small table in a shabby coffee shop adjacent to the only hotel, although he thought he might prefer a wee dram of whiskey or maybe a pint instead, if it hadn't been so early in the morning. He gazed out the window at the narrow street lined with identical, attached whitewashed houses. A few were adorned with vibrant red or blue painted doors and matching trim bordering small, curtained windows in an attempt to distinguish them from the others.

He left soon after and walked to the top of the hill away from the harbor to the round white church with the black roof, described in a church leaflet as built in a circular fashion to prevent the devil from hiding in corners. He only hoped that he wouldn't be confronting the devil himself.

He knew about the bunkers on the island and the seaplane base established there for the Catalinas and Sunderland Flying Boats that provided anti-submarine cover for convoys sailing to the Clyde River ports of Glasgow. This area was a central location for many undercover activities to defend the Hebrides and the rest of Scotland and England.

As he walked further into the hills above Port Ellen, he pulled out of his pocket, the neatly folded letter that had been delivered to Cate's house and sat on a rock to read it. The writing with all its flourishes reminded him of Maddie's strong, passionate personality that had captivated him on an idyllic summer day several years before.

Dearest William,

How I miss you! Where are you anyway? Your letters arrive weeks after you've written them. It's been over a month since the last letter and I don't know what you are doing or where you are. And the last one was impossible. Every other line was blacked out! It is so frustrating!

It seems that you are able to travel around some. How can that be? Are you training more? You also mentioned a Manor and painting there. I'm glad for that at least.

Are you still on bombing missions? I know you can't tell me much. I'm worried that you are in even greater danger, if that is possible. And that's why I'm not hearing from you.

I can't just sit here in my apartment playing the damn piano—and my mother watches me every moment! Madame hounds me, of course, to practice more—especially with the upcoming concerts next month.

It all seems somewhat futile when you are so far away and maybe not even alive. But I feel like you are—I never really know until another letter arrives in the post. It is too much. I can't go on like this.

I know that you are going to be very cross with me. But I have decided to do something. I have a chance to leave here and maybe even break away to do something important. I have decided to travel to London with the other musicians from our performance group. We will leave soon and sail to Southampton, then on to London.

You can't stop me. I will find you. I know that you may still be stationed near London.

There are people who can help. We will see each other soon. I have to believe that.

Yours always,

Maddie

He folded the letter carefully and put it back in his pocket. He waited another 30 minutes before the designated time. Then as he had been instructed, he walked to the meeting point, Strachan Castle. He carefully made his way on a narrow path that wound through scattered woods and over some hills dotted with grazing cattle. He passed a lone farmer guiding his sheep, poking at them with a crooked stick, and following a very single-minded black-and-white Border Collie. The dog's intelligent eyes barely registered William's presence while the farmer nodded curtly as they passed.

Eventually, he found the rendezvous point next to a tree on a grassy knoll overlooking the castle ruins and began to sketch in his small book that he carried everywhere. He opened the leather charcoal pencil case that also contained a small cluster of long, glossy black strands of Maddie's hair. She had cut a piece of her hair with miniature silver scissors the night before he took the train from Toronto to Montreal then Halifax, to ship out to England. It seemed like such a long time ago. She had also inserted a small oval photo of herself at the bottom of the case.

While he sketched, he was acutely aware of his surroundings, glancing away from his sketchbook when he heard a twig snapping, only to see a small rabbit scamper through the grass.

He returned to his drawing and waited.

Chapter 10

New York City

Maddie's heels clicked rhythmically on the polished oak floor as she walked away from the practice room where she had just spent two hours playing tiresome scales and studies, then eventually, Chopin etudes, Mozart waltzes, and Bach concertos. Fortunately, no one else was up so early on a Sunday morning, and she had the main practice studio of Juilliard to herself.

After a night of dancing at Café Jolie in Soho to raucous swing and jazz with some of the other students, it was comforting to retreat to her familiar classical pieces. Playing the music often carried her into a trance state that brought William back to her—even if only in her mind.

Playing in solitude also eased a terrific headache after a few too many gin gimlets. Thank God, she thought, at least it wasn't that dreadful rum they tried to pass off as gin left over from bootleg days.

A cup of Earl Grey tea and dry toast at her apartment that morning had alleviated the nausea so that she felt almost normal, whatever that was. Since William left for England, she had grown accustomed to the nagging stomach pains and nausea plaguing her each day. Nobody knew that behind the facade she kept up most days, she pondered possible catastrophes on a regular basis.

But this felt different. She hadn't had her period in a while. She didn't keep track since she was never on schedule with all the stress of performing.

The Royal Academy of Music in London had devised a plan to have American and British musicians perform together at the National Gallery. A collaborative effort to uplift English spirits was something that even the stuffy administrators of Juilliard could support—especially now with the United States in Britain's war against Nazi Germany. Collective American patriotism was reaching a new high, and the ties to Britain had been fortified. A series of concerts could boost morale for London citizens who had survived even more horrendous air attacks by the Germans since the Blitz of 1941.

She thought about all the carnage and devastation of war—the deaths and the disappeared. But she couldn't dwell on these thoughts. Although she wanted to make the journey for her own reasons, it felt like something she could actually do to help. Even with the nighttime bombings in London and potential dangers crossing the Atlantic, she felt more determined.

There would be a U.S. military escort accompanying them on the ocean voyage to Southampton, as well as during their stay in England with the other performers from Juilliard.

Uncle Hugh in Scotland might help her to leave London and search for William. She had a thrilling thought—Uncle Hugh might even know where he is! She knew that cousins in France were working with the French Underground—if they were even still alive. Conditions in Paris were no doubt worsening as the Occupation choked the City of Light.

Maddie worried about her grandmother, Ma-mere, who had left England to take care of her own ailing mother in Paris. That was nearly three years ago, and she hadn't received any letters from her in the past year. She had a wild thought that maybe she could find them and somehow bring them back to America where they would be safe.

Despite her reputation for being temperamental and a challenge for her teachers, Maddie had been chosen by Madame, her primary tutor and also the liaison with the Royal Academy of Music, to travel to England. A bit of good fortune, she thought. Madame said that her glamor and theatrical presence on stage, as well as her ability to perform well under pressure, made her a perfect choice for the morale-boosting London concerts. She had also been told by other teachers that she was one of the most-accomplished concert pianists the school had seen in the nearly 20 years since the inception of the Juilliard Graduate School in 1924. She felt the pressure of living up to her reputation and knew that some of the other students sometimes resented her. Only she knew how hard she drove herself.

Lunchtime piano recitals that started in 1940, even though the Blitz, were still being held at the National Gallery in London. Now that the nightly bombings had become less frequent, late afternoon and early evening concerts were also held occasionally. Maddie knew from Madame, who received letters from her London colleagues, that performers and concert-goers often made their way through the dust and debris strewn through the city after the bombings the night before.

Workers wearing masks, coveralls, and gloves dug through the piles of broken bricks, beams, pieces of shattered furniture, broken dishes, and tattered clothing buried among smoking embers. They gathered disembodied limbs scattered in the gutters and unearthed whatever other human remains they could salvage, then carried them away in wheelbarrows to waiting trucks for a more respectful burial elsewhere, but one rarely attached to any name. Sometimes bodies lay in makeshift morgues never to be claimed.

She had heard that as incredible as it seemed, Prime Minister Churchill held strategic planning meetings at all hours of the day and night in the map room of the underground bunker adjacent to the Mall in the Westminster neighborhood of London, near Buckingham Palace and 10 Downing Street. It was thought that he and his staff would be protected there. Despite all the dangers, Maddie yearned to leave for England to be close to William.

She had not received a letter from him in almost a month. Her last package had been returned unopened. She knew that as a bombardier, he was most likely still on the front line, but she also knew from the letters that managed to get through to her in New York and family in Toronto that he seemed to be traveling around England and Scotland even in the midst of the bombing missions. He had mentioned having frequent and lengthy leaves that he spent in the Cotswolds, painting and staying with an older woman named *Lady Braithwaite-Smith* at what he referred to as *the Manor*. Although she knew aircrews were sometimes allowed ten-day leaves at most, she had also heard that such extensive travel was only possible if one was a journalist, a diplomat, or a spy. *And William is not a journalist or a diplomat.*

The waiting had become unbearable. She needed to do something. Juilliard had provided the perfect opportunity for her to travel to London. Because she spoke fluent French and had family in Scotland and France, she imagined she could travel elsewhere and make a contribution beyond raising morale. She couldn't bear to be apart from William any longer, especially now that she suspected why she was so nauseous in the morning. It wasn't just the usual performance jitters she had before a concert. Her plan had to work.

Although she had been married for almost a year, she still wanted her mother's approval for what she was about to do. But she had made up her mind. She would go anyway, whether she got it or not.

And so, she and her mother were meeting for afternoon tea at The Plaza Hotel on a sunny November afternoon. Even though they shared an apartment close to Juilliard, they seldom saw each other. When they did, their conversations frequently degenerated into arguments that ended with one of them storming out of the room. Disagreements always focused on Maddie's studies, her performance schedule, and inevitably, how she wasn't diligent enough in her practice sessions, thereby disappointing Madame and, of course, her mother. She was tired of it all.

As Maddie walked briskly through the lobby of The Plaza in her new gray flannel suit, white silk blouse, wide-brimmed black hat shadowing her eyes, and ruby red pumps, she noticed the hotel's effort to counteract the gloom and doom of an endless war that pervaded everyday life. The huge gilded framed mirrors in the lobby reflected the oversized, hand-painted ceramic vases containing red and white roses, variegated pink stargazer lilies, and tall elegant stalks of exotic red ginger set on a pair of large round mahogany tables that contrasted against the sparkling marble floors. The dramatic arrangements appeared to rise up and shout in triumph against the war. Each time she had been at The Plaza, there was always at least one large bouquet of fresh flowers greeting the privileged, no matter what was going on outside the hotel doors in the Depression, or now, during another world war. She both appreciated this effort to carry on in the midst of war and resented the attempt at cheerful luxury. She couldn't help but feel the misery and suffering of those whose lives had already been lost and those who like her, were left behind.

Maddie and her family had stayed here when they first arrived from England, then after she had been recruited to study in New York before they moved to the apartment. She hoped her mother would remember those happy times and be more receptive to what she had to say. She dreaded having this conversation but maybe the family connections in England and Scotland could help. She even allowed herself to feel a little hope that her mother might support her plans.

As Maddie entered the Palm Court, she saw that her mother was already seated on a pale gold and cream flowered brocade banquette in the middle of the opulent room with its huge potted palms, expansive yellow and green glass-domed cupola ceiling, mirrored French doors, and *fleur-de-peche* marble columns.

Rachel wore a small navy pillbox hat with a peacock feather angled forward over her auburn hair arranged in a French twist. Her plum and navy, checked wool suit was expertly tailored and hugged her tall, slim figure. Her elbow-length matching kid leather gloves rested on the white linen tablecloth, next to her small handbag. As she raised a cigarette to her lips, it was clear from the expression on her face that she had been waiting a while for Maddie's arrival. And Rachel did not like to be kept waiting.

Maddie walked quickly to Rachel's table, coaching herself to remain calm. Her grandmother's small string of cultured pearls that rested in the hollow of her neck reminded her that she was loved and that her grandmother was with her.

She knew very little of what Ma-mere, her mother, and the rest of the family had endured during World War I. She had overheard fragments of hushed trans-Atlantic telephone calls late at night, followed by her mother locking herself in her bedroom. When Maddie was a child in England before they left for Canada, she heard snippets that never made sense but were just enough for her to wonder what had happened to her mother. She knew her grandmother insisted her children abandon their Jewish heritage and convert to the Anglican faith once they arrived in England from France. She also knew her mother and her family lived in Germany when World War I broke out. And that her grandfather had died there. Both her mother and grandmother refused to say any more.

She thought, no matter what, I have to convince her what I need to do. Although Rachel often appeared imperious and impermeable, Maddie thought it was likely her mother had her own pain. In that moment, despite Maddie's own worries and determination to get to England, she felt love and a sense of connection to her mother. Maybe she would understand after all.

"So, Maddie, what is going on?" Rachel asked as Maddie approached, in a low voice that barely concealed her irritation.

Maddie knew her mother would do anything to avoid a public scene. She kissed her mother's cheek then sat down on the Queen Anne chair across from her, trying to slow down her breathing.

"What is so pressing that we needed to meet in the middle of the day when I know you have classes and should be practicing for the holiday concerts? They are very important for your future, as you very well know," her voice was low but her exasperation was unmistakable. She waved her hand impatiently then removed another cigarette from a silver case in her small handbag and raised it to her lips. A waiter suddenly appeared, pulled a lighter from his pocket and with a flash of his hand, lit her cigarette. Rachel nodded a thank you with a gracious smile and turned back to Maddie.

"Really, Maddie, as much as I love afternoon tea at The Plaza, I know you are up to something. And it's unlikely that I will like whatever it is," she tapped the fingers of one hand while she smoked with the other.

Maddie could see that her mother was not going to be easily persuaded.

She took a deep breath. Despite her pounding heart, she spoke with confidence, "And hello to you too, Mother. Have you been waiting long? Of course, you have. You know how Madame gets before concerts. Practice, practice, practice." She forced a smile and placed her handbag on the table, reminding herself of her resolve. And what she had to do. She folded her hands in her lap and unwaveringly met her mother's implacable gaze.

Maddie knew her best strategy was to keep talking before her mother could say anything more. Aware she was trembling, she straightened in her chair and said firmly, "I know you're not going to want to hear what I have to say, Mother. Madame and Sir Austen Price at the Royal Academy of Music in London have organized a series of concerts at the National Gallery. I have been asked to be one of the American pianists." Maddie paused for effect as her mother raised one eyebrow. "The joint American/British performances are to raise morale and fortify Allied relations," she said quickly, then even more persuasively, "It is quite an honor, as I'm sure you know. I can't refuse. Madame says I'm ready." She stopped speaking and raised her chin, defiantly challenging her mother to disagree.

Cucumber and watercress sandwiches, currant tea biscuits, lemon tarts, macarons, petit fours, napoleons, miniature cream puffs, chocolate eclairs, and other ornately decorated pastries and dainties were presented on a three-tier cake stand with a gold filigree handle, by a white-gloved waiter wearing a black suit, crisp white shirt, and jewel-toned, striped bow tie.

He uttered a barely audible, "Madames, please enjoy," as he gently set the cake stand on the center of the crisp white linen tablecloth and backed away from the two attractive women glaring at each other. Fine gold-trimmed china and sparkling silverware had been placed at their seats awaiting their arrival. The waiter continued to watch attentively at a safe distance from their table.

Another waiter briskly wheeled a cart toward their table, with a silver tea service, clotted cream, and preserves. He opened a mahogany box so that they could select teas which he then placed into two pots and carefully added hot water from a silver pitcher. After a few moments, he poured their steaming tea into delicate china cups and offered cream and sugar. Then both waiters retreated quickly to serve the other guests in the full dining room.

Rachel glanced upward at the intricately paned and filigreed stained glass-domed laylight ceiling high above that illuminated the elegant dining room, then sighed, feeling another wave of impatience with her daughter. She knew she could be overly involved in Maddie's life and her daughter probably thought she didn't understand her—her single-mindedness, even stubbornness, especially in relation to William. She considered the tragic losses in her own life and how she didn't want to experience any more. Rachel also thought about how she knew so little about parenting—her son Charlie had been born when she was only 17 and Maddie, a year later.

After some moments of stony silence, Rachel spoke impatiently, "You can't possibly be planning to do this, Maddie. Our family has been through so much. We are safe here. And you have your studies. We have come so far. William is doing his part to fight this horrible war. You have to accept the situation," she said, then lit another cigarette and inhaled deeply with a long sigh.

Maddie's heart pounded as her words came in a rush. Her voice rose and tears filled her eyes as she said, "I can't stay here and just wait. This is my way to do something. It's all arranged. And *none* of us will be safe if we lose this war!" She spoke faster as she tried to rein in her emotions and steady herself. "There will be a military escort, and in fact, troops will be on the ship. All very above board. Churchill himself has traveled across the Atlantic several times. Cruise ships are now made to outrun U-boats. I need to do this!" Then more quietly, Maddie said, "Why are you so afraid, Mother?" She studied her mother's face, trying to understand more of what might be going on with her. Despite her own fears, she raised her chin defiantly. "They know what they're doing. I will be fine," she continued, trying to be convincing. Then, still with tears in her eyes, she said with all the strength she was feeling at that moment, "You can't stop me!"

Rachel reached out to grasp her daughter's hands placed on the table as if they were resting on the piano keyboard, preparing to play. She felt a sense of urgency to convince Maddie she couldn't help William.

"Maddie," she said, "I know how much you love William and miss him. And how much you want him to return. The waiting is terrible. I know that.

85

But there is nothing you can do. This war will be over. We have to believe that. You can't put yourself in danger." Her voice trembled as she pled with her daughter and gently squeezed her hands.

Maddie felt misunderstood as she had so many times before. Her mother did not understand her or her passion, even in relation to her music. Yet, she knew that Uncle Hugh, her mother's brother in Edinburgh, was a gifted musician as well as a successful barrister. And although she didn't know for sure, probably more. She could see that her mother wanted to hold onto some control over her life. *But that isn't going to happen.*

Rachel said, leaning closer toward Maddie, "There were things that happened before and during the last war. People do terrible things to each other. Things so unspeakable that they can never be spoken." She remembered an argument with Maddie not long ago. She had shouted, "You have no idea what I've been through. You take everything for granted, Madeleine. You are so spoiled!" before abruptly leaving the room and slamming the door. She had regretted those words but sometimes couldn't help herself after everything that had happened when she was so young.

Maddie wished her mother would tell her what made her so angry, instead of erupting so unpredictably and with such rage. As she grew up and saw photos of relatives she had never met, she tried to ask her mother what had happened.

Rachel's eyes would darken with anger and she would just say, "It was a long time ago. There is nothing more to say. We will never speak of this again."

"You know I've been thinking of ways that I can be with William. God only knows when this terrible war will be over. These concerts are important." Maddie kept talking, hoping she could persuade her mother. "The uncertainty and waiting are just too much. This is my way to get to England and maybe even find William. Don't you understand? I have a way to go there with ample protection. I haven't heard from William in almost a month. I can't just sit by and wait. Maybe others can do that. But I can't!"

Her voice rose as she felt herself flushing and impatiently swept her dark bangs away from her eyes. She kept her hands resting on the table after pulling them away from her mother's grasp as if she were grounding herself at the familiar keyboard—the black-and-white keys that comforted her and gave her strength. She took another deep breath, then raised her cup and sipped her tea. She looked around the dining room for a moment then calmly met her mother's angry eyes. Her decision had been made—with or without her mother's blessing. She signaled for the waiter, wanting her tea to be replenished and much hotter than before to match her mood and her resolve.

Rachel met Maddie's gaze and spoke more gently, "But darling, be sensible…"

Maddie interrupted, "You can't stop me, Mother. Madame has made the arrangements with the Royal Academy and they have already done all the publicity. This is happening. I am leaving next week," she said as she raised her chin again and met her mother's eyes.

Then, knowing how the teachers at Juilliard would have the ultimate authority where her mother was concerned, Maddie smiled and turned to the waiter and sweetly said, "A little more of the Earl Grey, please. And as hot as you can make it. Thank you very much."

Rachel straightened her back against the banquette and focused her deep blue-grey eyes on her daughter. Beginning to lose her temper, she raised her voice and said, "And just how will you find him? This is outrageous!" Her elegantly arched eyebrows rose as she spoke more quietly, noticing nervous glances from other patrons in the dining room.

Maddie sipped her tea and avoided her mother's eyes.

"You can't do this, Maddie. You know the dangers and what our family is facing." Then her eyes teared up, and she felt her throat beginning to tighten and her heart pounding as if it might explode.

Maddie leaned forward, ignoring her mother's statements and the fear on her face. "Uncle Hugh has been in contact with William. That much I know. Uncle Hugh has his ways. I think you know that. I intend to send him a telegram tomorrow. He can make things happen."

"And I intend to stop you, Maddie," her mother said with an intensity that Maddie had not often seen before, one hand clenched on the table, as her eyes darkened. "You could end up in one of those horrible camps or worse, Maddie! I won't let you go. It is quite impossible." Rachel felt herself drifting away. The panic and anxiety were becoming overwhelming, like the terror she had felt long ago.

For a moment, Maddie thought about her mother's often protective and controlling reactions and wondered again about what had happened to her. She suspected that these secrets haunted the entire family.

More cucumber sandwiches, scones, pastries, and tea were brought to their table but both Maddie and Rachel fell silent and ignored the food. Maddie knew she would get her way.

Her mother was no match for her. Not after all those years of study and single-minded discipline.

Chapter 11

Islay, Scotland

William felt the hard, blunt edge of a gun's barrel pressing into his back.

His sketching had transported him for a short time away from the world of spies and war. Until this moment.

He had been sitting on the knoll overlooking the castle, then stood to stretch. Without warning, the gun seemed to come out of nowhere. He felt like a fool.

"You're not much of a spy, mate. You didn't even hear me, you sod," the low voice said in disgust with a slight foreign accent William couldn't identify. "Don't turn around just yet. I hope for your sake, you haven't been followed. Keep your hands above your head and don't move." The voice paused. "I've killed for less."

There was a slight movement as the stranger seemed to be turning to check behind them although he couldn't know for sure. William thought this was odd but he wasn't about to challenge the man with the gun. He knew Britain was crawling with agents including double agents who played both sides, often with catastrophic consequences. This was the part that he hated the most. You could never be sure who you were dealing with.

That's why this remote place was chosen for a meet.

Whoever it was seemed to be affecting an English accent or even a slight Scottish lilt but not very successfully. William had been trained to listen for particular speech patterns and intonations. He detected Germanic or Nordic tones in the stranger's speech. He hoped he was hearing the latter. But even if he was from Scandinavia, he could also be working with the enemy.

Sweat dripped down William's neck as he held his hands flexed into fists, ready to take action given the chance. Then he was filled with relief as the gun shifted slightly away from the lowest point on his spine. But he couldn't ignore the next thoughts that bombarded him. *This is it. My God, after everything that's happened. All those dropped bombs. It could all end here. In this place.*

William heard his father's voice, "Don't be a ninny, William. Think!"

He quickly calculated how fast he could grab his knife from his trousers and throw the agent to the ground. He had a pistol and another knife in his knapsack but it was impossible to think about getting to either of those. He felt a rush of adrenalin as a flash of Maddie's face appeared suddenly before him. Was he going to die? He couldn't bear the thought of never seeing Maddie's smile or hearing her voice again. His life couldn't end here. Not like this.

He was about to make a fast turn and twist the gun out of the stranger's hand as he had learned in training exercises when the voice said, "Well, I just needed to be sure. And I had to keep you under control, mate. Now show me your papers." The man's fake British accent was still unconvincing and only worried William more.

William hesitated for a moment, thinking it would be a bad idea to make any sudden movement. But he was on alert and ready to pull out his knife that was strapped to his ankle.

Without turning around, he slowly pulled out his travel papers from his knapsack lying beside him next to his charcoal pencils and sketchpad and handed them to the agent.

He felt the gun's barrel shift away from him and began to breathe more easily. He turned around to see a slim, light brown-haired man about his age, with an intense, steady gray-eyed gaze, the gun still in his hand but now pointed away from him. The stranger looked jittery and maybe nervous with the situation, but he also had a cold, hard look.

He quickly looked over William's papers, then shoved them back with an off-handed gesture and said with a grunt, "Looks all right. So, William, is it?"

William stared him down and said, "Yeah well, the code name is Eagle. Bluebell's idea." He felt a bit embarrassed and a need to explain. "Maybe she thought I needed to remember that I fly too," he added.

The other agent looked him over and snorted. "So we're going to be working together. Simon told me about you and the artist thing is your cover. Bit of a panty-waist, are you?" He smirked. "Well, no matter. You know there are German agents all over trying to figure out what we're up to. A lot of dead bodies are showing up—but then you know that too."

He narrowed his eyes and William felt him sizing him up. The still-unnamed agent no longer looked quite as threatening but he wasn't warming up either. He sneered, then said sharply, "You should be more careful, bloke—and not get so carried away with those drawings of yours—or whatever it is you were doing. You didn't even notice me comin' up behind ya," he said with disgust.

William couldn't nail the accent but he wondered if this man might be one of the operatives parachuting into Scotland from Occupied Norway for training with MI6 and SOE. The Scandinavians were known for their audacity and courage. Bluebell hadn't told him much—just when to go for the meet on Islay.

William tried to sound more authoritative than he felt, "I was told to be here and that I would meet another agent who would brief me on the mission."

The other agent nodded almost imperceptibly.

"This is not the friendliest way to make contact, I must say. Perhaps I should see your papers as well," William said with an equal level of suspicion.

The operative passed him a folded paper. William looked it over and handed it back. "So, it's Sven?"

"Yes, Sven—not my real name, of course. I guess you know where I've come from. Norway as an occupied country has its intrigues as well, and I'm here to help the cause. There have been a lot of shootings and captures even here on Islay, believe it or not. You can't tell who's a German agent these days—they come in all sorts of packages. Best to keep your wits 'bout ya. So we're going to be workin' together." He narrowed his eyes and William felt a chill in his gaze.

William knew Islay was a prime location for covert operations both protecting the British shoreline from the Nazis and preparing for an Allied invasion somewhere in coastal Europe. U-boats lay in wait for Royal Navy warships—just offshore. A constant, ominous presence.

British and Allied forces practiced training exercises—mostly beach landings—on the western shore of the island.

Despite an increased awareness that he was playing a deadly game, William couldn't help but notice the neat, whitewashed cottages and well-tended farms scattered sparingly in small, lonely clusters on the rugged, windswept coastline. He wished he could stop and paint the beautiful landscape. Narrow paths wound snake-like along the edge of the precarious cliffs past remote graveyards and crumbling ruins of stone chapels assembled by Celtic clansmen for the reigning lords, centuries before. So much conflict and bloodshed, amidst all the beauty. The air was heavy with the mysteries and violence of long-forgotten battles and probably, more to come.

"Could you put that away?" William said, pointing at the gun in the other agent's hand. "You're making me nervous. We're supposed to be on the same side, mate," he said hoping he sounded more sure of himself than he felt. Sven seemed a little shaky in the spy business and probably was just as inexperienced as William was, although he had handled his gun with confidence.

"Uff da," the Norwegian spy muttered impatiently as he shook his head as if to say, *not by my choice*. After another moment, Sven reluctantly shoved the pistol into the waistband of his khakis and said, "We need to go," as he motioned William to follow him on the nearby path.

He didn't seem any friendlier, but at least William was no longer afraid of being shot and left for dead. The Scandinavians were known to be a serious lot. He didn't expect there would be much joking around with this new contact.

Sven kept his voice low despite the unlikelihood of anyone overhearing them talking. "We're heading to the bunkers west of here. We'll meet the others and work out the plan—then make contact with one of the German agents who works for us—a radio operator who will transmit information about an invasion. That is not going to happen. At least not right now. We will get more intel," he said in clipped tones without elaborating further.

William began to pick up his things and together they walked away from the hill overlooking the castle ruins.

A mud-spattered, battered jeep was waiting by a small grove of tall, thin ash trees grasping onto a few remaining leaves. They walked silently, the tension still lingering in the air. They hadn't been off to the best start but William hoped things would improve. He thought, at least I feel more like an agent and I'm not just taking trains and ferries to who knows where all over the UK—I'll know more soon about what this mission will involve.

He had to believe that he was doing something meaningful. Especially since, for now, he wasn't flying on bombing missions. He suddenly missed Hank, the pilot, his aircrew mates, and the camaraderie and trust they had for each other.

* * *

The jeep lurched and swerved as they rode over one narrow potholed path to another, eventually driving up to one of the bunkers situated in a desolate, windswept field not far from the steep cliffs overlooking the wild seas below and the German submarines lurking there, ready to strike. A lethal game of cat and mouse, he thought. *And the rules keep changing.*

As they pulled up to the low structure built into a mound of earth covered with scattered patches of grass and tall weeds, Sven and William jumped out of the jeep and lowered their heads as they entered through a narrow opening concealed by a rough-hewn wooden door protecting the occupants from the fierce wind blowing in from the Atlantic Ocean.

A group of men played cards in one corner of the large main room erupting loudly at times with, "You bugger, you got the lot!" Then another voice shouted, "Don't get your knickers in a twist, lad. I won fair and square!" Somebody else yelled, "That's a quid I owe so far. Put it on my tab!" followed by loud guffaws and hoots.

Others huddled in another corner with their heads together in quiet, earnest conversation, smoking and drinking from tin cups. Off to the side, away from the others, a heavy-set soldier also in uniform with slicked-back, reddish hair, and a flushed face stood hunched over an Aladdin paraffin stove. A dirty gray shirt that once might have been white was tied haphazardly around his waist as a makeshift apron. He was ponderously stirring a large pot, steam rising in invitation for what, no doubt, would be another undefinable, tasteless meal—maybe a combination of oatmeal, beans, carrots, potatoes—or something else. Low voices drifted from other rooms in the rabbit-warren-like structure but William couldn't make any meaning of the snatches of conversations he heard as they walked through the cold, bleak bunker.

Someone had attempted to brighten the dismal, cavernous surroundings by painting one wall a cheerful turquoise that made William think of how he imagined the sparkling Mediterranean Sea or the brilliant cloudless skies of the South of France—places he hoped he would see one day. It was amazing to him that in the midst of all the darkness of this war, there were those who also thought of and hoped for happier times. He smiled, feeling less alone.

Sven motioned to him and signaled with a curt nod of his head that he should join him where he was standing at a small table. He pulled out a map, pointed to their present location, then swept his hand to the uppermost corner off the northern coast of Scotland and poked a finger at the Orkney Islands. He glanced at William and then back at the map and said, "We'll be heading this way. It'll take us most of a day by train to get there. There's a radio in the other room here. We'll set up the meet." He waved William away as he muttered, "I'll take care of the other business." William knew he meant he would radio the information about a fake invasion.

Subterfuge and sabotage. He wondered again if he had made the right decision. And what it was going to be like working with someone he didn't trust.

William held his breath as he prepared for another journey.

Chapter 12

The Princess Sofia, Atlantic Ocean

Maddie focused her eyes on the blurry line of the horizon as the ship rose high above the waves, then dipped sharply, sinking into the turbulent, roaring darkness and the mountainous walls of churning white foam. The huge ship rode the 30-foot swells at precarious angles, then suddenly with the grace of the beautiful, dignified lady that she was, rearranged herself for a brief instant of stability and righted herself just when Maddie thought the entire ship was surely going to keel over. She knew she had an overactive imagination sometimes but she hadn't expected such a raging storm even if it was November. She hugged herself more tightly in the long wool coat she wore over her thin evening gown.

Ocean crossings were meant to involve romantic nights of dancing under the stars in glamorous gowns and afternoons spent reading a potboiler—maybe the latest Raymond Chandler. Or playing backgammon and writing letters on a reclining deck chair. With a nice cocktail or a cup of tea served by a handsome waiter in tails and white gloves.

Maddie brought Virginia Woolf's last novel before her death in 1941, *Between the Acts*, set at an English country house, to read on the voyage thinking that it might bring her closer to William and *the Manor* where he spent his leaves. She still couldn't understand how someone as talented as Virginia Woolf could have drowned herself. No matter how dire the circumstances, she could never imagine giving up like that. Her mother had met her at the University of London in Bloomsbury when she had taken a writing class before she married. Maddie loved Woolf's writing and her feminist spirit.

This crossing was a disappointing, stripped-down version of what she remembered as a child leaving England, sailing from Liverpool on their way to settling in Canada. She thought of the sparkling ocean, afternoons of running and playing on the deck, and dancing with her father in pretty party dresses and black patent leather shoes to a lively orchestra in the ballroom.

She reminded herself that there was now a war going on and she was on her way to finding William. *The Princess Sofia* was also transporting troops to Europe as well as occasional civilians who passed all the security clearances. The performances at the National Gallery of Art in London were the reason she was able to take this voyage. The ship had been upgraded from a strictly military transport carrier to accommodate special passengers like the musicians traveling from New York to London. The grand ballroom and elegant dining room had been restored to nearly their original glamor. Only the officers were allowed to mingle with the passengers. The staterooms, however, were quite modest.

Rachel had persisted in arguing adamantly with Maddie against leaving for war-beleaguered England and the air raids that still occurred there—right up until the day she was scheduled to sail from New York. Rachel had become so furious that Maddie was afraid she might throw something or even slap her. Her sudden outbursts of anger could be frightening. At those times, she seemed to be fueled by her own traumatic memories—although Maddie didn't know exactly what they were—and a desire to protect her from dangers like those she had experienced.

Maddie thought her mother would be even more upset and determined to stop her if she knew her secret and why now she was so especially intent on finding William. She had just found out from her doctor what she had suspected for a while. She felt an almost irrational need to find William and share her joy with him. She didn't think her mother would understand.

"This is insane, Maddie! I can't allow it! You have no idea what you are doing!" Rachel had shouted. Then, as if she knew was about to say things she might regret, her mother had calmed down and said only, "You don't understand what is going on and what our people have suffered. I can't bear to see you hurt. That would be more than I could live with." She had started to cry which almost broke Maddie's will.

Maddie gathered up all her strength and said firmly with tears in her eyes, "I know what I'm doing. I have to do this!" then walked away from her mother. She couldn't be derailed.

In preparation for the trip, she had packed her steamer trunk with her daytime suits and hats, evening dresses for the concerts, sweaters, trousers, a few sensible tweed skirts, silk and cotton blouses, a warm woolen coat and scarf, the practical cotton stockings she detested, a few precious pairs of silk stockings, and then the leather satchel filled with her sheet music. She hoped there would be a decent piano on board for practicing while they crossed the Atlantic.

Rachel had finally stormed into Maddie's room where she was packing and announced, "Well, there is no point in you doing this on your own. I am going with you and that's that. If we get sunk by the Germans, at least we'll be together." She had used her influence to ensure her passage as well on *The Princess Sofia*. The family's financial gifts to Juilliard no doubt had played a part, Maddie thought.

Maddie hadn't quite worked out how she was going to escape from her mother to the Manor in the Cotswolds after her performances in London. But she told herself she would find a way. William's letters had told her enough for her to know where the mysterious Lady Brathwaite-Smith lived—where he had spent so many of his leaves. She might even be able to get information about where she could find him. It was worth a try. She planned to leave London as soon as she could and take a train to Moreton-in-Marsh and then find her way to the Manor.

Maybe Uncle Hugh could help.

She carefully walked along the slippery deck clutching onto the railing whenever she could, balancing herself against the roiling seas. She had left her cabin after dinner thinking that maybe the night air would ease her nausea and clear her head.

Rachel was in the upper deck salon having a cup of tea and writing letters that would be posted from Southampton once they docked. Although Maddie had hoped for a calm crossing to England, she now welcomed the bracing cold wind and the frequent shock of salty waves crashing over the ship's railing and slapping her face. She laughed at the sheer excitement and beauty of the storm's drama.

It felt good to be alive. The ocean is a force to contend with—like me, she thought with a smile. She didn't care how her carefully applied makeup for the evening dinner might now be smeared. She could finally think, away from the nervous chatter of her fellow performers and the constant hovering presence of her mother.

Just as she was taking comfort from her plans for what was ahead once she arrived in England, she was suddenly interrupted. Robert, the US naval officer assigned to accompany the musicians to London and the subsequent concerts, burst out of a door adjacent to stairs leading down from the deck where Maddie and the others were staying.

"Good heavens, Maddie!" Robert shouted to her over the roar of the wind and the ocean. "What are you doing out here? You must go inside before you are washed overboard!"

She had felt his eyes on her from the moment they were embarking onto the ship at the pier in New York with all the others. In addition to the group of about 20 performers and a few family members, there were over 4,000 US military troops being transported to the front lines on the continent. It was mostly a secret that civilian musicians were also on the ship—part of the British–US alliance that Churchill and Roosevelt were so keen to reinforce, despite the potential dangers of crossing the U-boat-infested waters where many ships had been attacked and sunk before them.

But Maddie had to believe they would be safely delivered to Southampton on the southern coast of England. The majestic ship was known to easily outrun the German submarines. And although they could not see any escort ships even during daylight hours—destroyers prepared to defend them—she knew there was at least one accompanying them, that could fight the Germans if necessary and keep them safe.

Ever since the sinking of the *Lusitania* and countless other passenger and freight ships by U-boats during World War I, the Allies were much more prepared for transporting troops to the front. Even Churchill had traveled on the Queen Mary between England and New York during the current war.

Amid the noisy mayhem at the launching in New York while bidding a tearful farewell to her father who had come from Toronto to see them off, Maddie had been introduced to Robert. He seemed to be eyeing her from head to toe. He was handsome in a pretty boy sort of way, with cropped curly dark blond hair, a small rosebud mouth accented by a perfectly groomed mustache, and pale blue eyes that narrowed as he stared at her. He smiled but his eyes revealed no sense of a soul or human connection as he said, "I am so pleased to meet you, Madeleine. I have heard so much about you." She felt uneasy from the moment she met him.

Now he was standing before her, yelling against the wind, "Let me help you to a safer place, Madeleine."

She shook her head and said, "I am quite fine. I needed some fresh air. It was stifling in there. But thank you, all the same." She did not like the way he was looking at her.

Suddenly, he grabbed her arm and pulled her into a sheltered area off the deck. His breath was hot against her neck as he leaned into her, pulling her closer, and mumbled, "I've been wanting to do this for days. You know you want it too." He held her tighter and began kissing her, forcing his tongue between her pressed lips.

She thought she would gag and tried to pull herself away, shouting, "Stop this right now! I'm going to scream! How dare you!" Then she began screaming and looked frantically around her, hoping that someone would miraculously appear.

"No one will hear you in this storm, Maddie. Just enjoy yourself," he sneered as he then held his hand over her mouth. His breath was hot and foul, a strong odor of cheap whiskey making her feel dizzy and sick. He pushed her against the wall and pulled up the long skirt of her evening dress as he quickly unzipped his fly. She struggled against his hold on her as he pulled her panties down her thighs. She could feel him pushing her legs apart and inserting himself into her. *This is not happening.* The horror that swept over her gave her the strength to pull his hand away from her mouth even as he held her more tightly against the hard wall and began thrusting.

"No!" she screamed as she felt behind her for anything that she could throw at his head. She knew that there were some tools hanging on the wall to fight shipboard fires. Her hand scrabbled on the wall behind her, searching desperately for any sharp object.

Suddenly, there was shouting and laughter as two men in crumpled white sailor uniforms appeared. They were drunkenly navigating their way on the slippery deck as huge waves swept over the side of the ship threatening to throw them overboard. The storm was gaining momentum.

"Whoa, Jack, that nearly got you! Ha! Ha! You're gonna join the sharks!" the man yelled to his companion then quickly grabbed his arm as they lurched sideways. They managed to steady themselves, then turned and stared in the direction of the sheltered stairway.

Robert suddenly stopped, distracted by the noise, giving Maddie enough time to break free and adjust her dress and her panties.

William's face flashed in front of her and a tidal wave of anger rushed over her. All the rage she felt at this war, losing William to it and now this unspeakable attack rose within her with so much force that her heart pounded in her chest and she gasped for air, then shouted in his face, "How dare you! You disgust me!" With strength she didn't know she had, she slapped Robert across his face so hard that it shocked them both. He looked at her with such fury that she was afraid he would hit her back.

Before she could run away from him, he grabbed her arm roughly.

Then, she heard, "Hey there, mate! What's going on? A lover's quarrel, yous two? We can help!" And more loud, raucous laughter.

This was her chance to escape. She pulled her arm away from his grasp and looked directly into Robert's bloodshot eyes. "You will never get away with this," she spat the words at him.

Robert looked stunned and outraged that she would fight back but she thought his eyes seemed more focused. He might have finally realized where he was and what he had done. He pulled away, adjusting his uniform and straightening his hat. Then he leaned over her and stared into her face with unbridled hostility.

"No one will believe you," he said. "Everyone knows how dramatic you can be. Don't even think of telling anyone or I will come after you. You're no match for me, Madeleine. I always get what I want, one way or the other." His mouth turned up at the corners exuding false warmth, his cold blue eyes piercing through her.

An unpleasant chill washed over her.

"Your precious William is a long way from here. For all we know, he's been blown up already." He laughed mirthlessly and tossed his head arrogantly, throwing his words over his shoulder as he walked away with a noticeable limp.

So that's why he was stuck with us rather than serving in active duty, she thought. *Or is he faking it because he's a coward? Whatever his story is, he needs to pay.*

The drunken men heaved and swayed as they walked unsteadily toward her, their sailor hats and ties askew and arms flung over each other's shoulders. "We are here to help, little missus!" they called out then laughed giddily before launching into a very loud off-key rendition of *What shall we do with a drunken sailor? What shall we do with a drunken sailor? Early in the morning!* followed by more laughter and mangled lyrics.

She could see they would be of no help. She found her voice again and called back to them, "I'm fine. Thanks anyway." She considered what would happen if she tried to tell them anything now or even went to someone later. She had heard how women who tried to report assaults by officers were seldom believed and, more often than not, humiliated in the process.

She turned and ran to the safety of her cabin.

* * *

An hour later she heard the key in the lock, then the door opened slowly. It was Rachel quietly returning to their cabin. Maddie was on the floor by her bed. A pool of blood was forming under the skirt of her cream silk evening dress that she had worn to dinner. She had tried to lurch toward the tiny bathroom adjacent to their shared bedroom but had felt too weak and collapsed where she now lay on the rough wooden floor.

The small area rug had not softened her fall. But fortunately, she wasn't hurt anywhere else. Oh no, I'm ruining my best gown, she thought. *How ridiculous. I could be dying. This is it. What have I done? This can't be happening.* She felt as if sharp knives were slashing through her abdomen, cutting her in half.

"Maddie, what happened?" her mother cried with fear in her voice, as she crouched down next to her daughter.

Maddie murmured, "It hurts so much." She could barely breathe through the pain. She began to feel even more dizzy and nauseous as she slowly drifted away down a dark tunnel.

In the distance, she heard her mother trying to stay calm and saying firmly, "I'm getting the doctor right now."

She felt herself falling into darkness. *I can't lose our baby.*

Part II

Toronto

Fall 2013

The letters that Uncle William wrote to Aunt Lizzie in the middle of World War II from the Manor, his refuge in the Cotswolds, had remained unread for 70 years until I discovered them buried underneath lace tablecloths and hand-knit sweaters in the cedar chest forgotten in my father's basement. I wondered how it was that Aunt Lizzie had been the only member of the family who had kept his letters. But she had always been unusual in a family that held onto its secrets. A successful clothing designer in Toronto from the 1920s until the 1970s, she had married and been widowed four times. As she became older, well into her 80s and less able to manage her business, she moved in with our family. Auntie was feisty, witty, well-read, and full of lively anecdotes.

When I was in high school, I would spend time with her in the upstairs apartment where she lived in my parents' home, most days after school. We talked about fashion, music, art, books we had read, what was going on in the world and, of course, history—a passion for both of us.

But she always steered clear of any conversation about William and Maddie. I was hungry to know more about them but this subject was off-limits—just as it was with my mother.

Now, while I was attempting to piece together William and Maddie's story or what I imagined it to be, my sister was re-discovering her love of painting. She had been vehemently discouraged by our mother to become an artist like her lost brother. But we never knew why. We only knew that Uncle William was a painter with much promise and had a wife who was a concert pianist.

The family story was that he had been declared missing a few days before D-Day, then presumed dead a year later. But the circumstances and reports were contradictory and confusing—as they were for so many others who had disappeared.

I was back in Toronto helping Dad unpack more of the boxes stacked in a corner of his crowded apartment and organizing closets after his move from our family home. I sorted through box after box of old photographs, long-forgotten Kodak slides, and reels of home movies. Then, at the back of the guest room closet, in a large box, I found an old, battered, photo album—filled with pages of black-and-white photos lovingly mounted and labeled in my grandmother's writing.

A smiling, trim, handsome, athletic-looking, blond-haired young man stood beside an elegant, stern-looking, older woman. *William at the Manor in England* was the caption. There were photos of elaborate, well-tended gardens, and a large stone house. Behind the album was a large, now sepia-toned photo of a wedding party—William, handsome and erect in his RCAF uniform, and his beautiful, dark-haired Maddie smiling faintly beside him, resplendent in a long, softly draped, white wedding gown and veil. They were surrounded by formally dressed members of the wedding party—all with intensely serious expressions. Why had I never seen these photos before?

My father was reading the newspaper in his leather recliner in the spacious living room of his modern apartment with afternoon sunlight streaming in through the windows overlooking the park and the river below. He liked to keep up with the major events in the world, so he was also watching the late afternoon news.

"Can you believe that?" he asked as he shook his head with great disgust. "Those clowns on Wall Street are at it again." Then, a short time later, when watching another news program about refugees escaping from yet another war-torn country, he muttered audibly, "I wish I could do more for this world." He paused then chuckled, "Oh well, I'm not dead yet!" And we both laughed.

Despite his occasional cynical diatribes—I thought that were exaggerated sometimes for shock value—he would suddenly burst forth with youthful excitement and curiosity, questioning younger family members about how the Internet worked or what Facebook or Twitter was, or whether gay marriage was a good idea. Caring for my mother for 10 years as she succumbed progressively to Alzheimer's hadn't destroyed his sense of humor or joy of life.

I continued the task of going through my parents' things trying to determine what should be delivered to Goodwill and what should be kept. I hadn't felt ready before to take a closer look at my mother's chest of drawers. But on this day, I thought, okay, it's time. Better now than never.

I pulled out drawer after drawer, discovering a jewelry box filled with brooches; mismatched costume jewelry earrings; a gold chain with faith, hope, and charity charms; her favorite string of cultured pearls; and diamond stud earrings in a velvet-lined box.

Then, I reached into the back of what appeared to be an empty drawer lined with fragile paper imprinted with faded pink antique roses. I felt a thicker sheet of paper and pulled out a small unframed watercolor—of a golden country road surrounded by rolling green hills and a tree that dominated the scene with broad strokes of abundant, vivid burnt orange foliage. It was unsigned, and I had never seen it before, but I knew who had painted it. The date "1943" was written on the back.

It appeared to be a study, much like ones I had seen in galleries hung next to their much larger and more elaborate replicas on canvas—finished paintings that were usually much more detailed and polished.

A small book filled with page after page of pencil sketches drawn with bold strokes had also surfaced. Castles, village streets, countryside scenes, sleeping men—many drawings labeled with names of villages in England and Scotland. But this small painting seemed to carry a different magic.

And then, as if waiting for discovery, was another letter folded and enclosed with a narrow, blue ribbon. I opened it and read:

Dear Auntie,

I hope you are doing well and the clothing business continues to thrive. Women still need nice dresses—and especially in wartime.

I have been to London and Oxford since the last time I wrote. London is filled with the military tourists I've mentioned in other letters. I like the cities less than the villages but I have been to some wonderful concerts in London and Edinburgh which of course remind me of dear Maddie. There are a few smaller galleries that haven't been bombed, showing art that never fails to take my breath away. It has been some time since I heard from Maddie but I know how unreliable the mail can be. Her last package contained some photos of her recent concert. How I wish I could be there.

For now, I am able to travel a bit and will be seeing more of the northern areas before I have to return to the base. I am sending some photos of the

Manor where I spend some of my leaves and do a fair bit of painting. I hope that the letters reach you without the censor's hand since I can mail them from places away from the base.

I have a sketchbook that also comes in handy when I am on a train for any length of time.

It is wonderful to see so much of the beautiful countryside. I must sign off now but I will write again soon. Be assured that no matter what is happening here, I will be all right.

With all my love to you and the family,

William

Chapter 13

The Atlantic Ocean, November 1943

Maddie struggled to raise her head from the hard mattress, but it felt unbearably heavy. She felt the ship rising and falling over the waves, as the wind whistled outside the small cabin. Her jar of face cream and glass of water slid precariously on the nightstand by her bed.

But it no longer felt like this was going to be the last night of her life. She felt light-headed and drowsy but the sharp pains stabbing like knives in her abdomen were mostly subsiding into a single throbbing ache. She fought with all her strength against sliding into unconsciousness. She wanted to know what was happening to her and whether there was any hope.

She heard lowered voices and could see two shadowy figures. The doctor had come to the cabin after her mother raced away to find and bring him to help her. She knew he had examined her and gave her a shot of something that made her drowsy while her mother had waited outside their cabin, pacing on the deck. She could barely hear the murmured conversation not far from where she lay in bed and suddenly felt sharp surges of pain again.

"I can't imagine what she was thinking, doctor. Here we are, miles from home in the middle of the Atlantic Ocean. And pregnant!" she shook her head in dismay. "I had no idea that my daughter could be so foolish. No concert is worth this. I would never have let her come had I known." As she spoke, Rachel folded her arms across her chest. She was still in her long silver satin evening dress and matching jacket from dinner. Maddie could hear her mother's voice shaking.

The doctor's shoulders were stooped as he stood next to Rachel with his head bent toward her. He answered in a calm, quiet voice, "I understand how upsetting this all is. We couldn't save the baby. Your daughter is weak now and should sleep for a while. I've given her a sedative and something for the bleeding which should also help with the pain. I will check back on her in the morning to make sure she is out of the woods. But for now, things seem to be under control." He slowly pulled his stethoscope from around his neck, rolling it up neatly and leaned down as he briskly placed it back in his small black leather bag.

Maddie gasped and almost cried out, then stifled a sob with her shaking hand, desperate to not believe what she just heard. She pulled the covers over her face to muffle her scream, "No!"

She heard Rachel speaking in a tremulous voice, "Can she travel? Although I'm not sure why I'm asking that—since we are in the middle of the damn Atlantic Ocean!" Her voice rose with anger. Then, more quietly, she asked, "Do you know why she miscarried?"

The doctor carefully replaced bottles of medicine and a syringe to be sterilized and used again in his bag, then said impassively, "Sometimes extreme stress can precipitate such an event." There was a pause, then he added, "But we don't really know. Sometimes it just happens." He stood up, cleared his throat and faced Rachel as he told her, "I am guessing, of course, but she was probably around 14 to 16 weeks or so. Can't be sure." Then sounding more confident, "She is young. I'm sure she and her husband will have many more babies."

As Maddie heard this, more tears came to her eyes and she felt as if her throat was closing. She knew the doctor was trying to reassure her mother but he was speaking in an almost casual, distant way—no doubt because her little tragedy was only one of many that he had seen in his wartime practice and probably those other tragedies were much worse. *Well, I haven't lost an arm or a hand. I'm not dead.* But this felt like the end of something wonderful. She turned away from them and faced the wall as she cried quietly.

"Don't be too sure about that, Doctor," Rachel said with tightness in her voice. "Maddie's husband is a bombardier in the RAF, stationed in England. We haven't heard from him in over a month. This terrible war is killing our boys every day. My daughter may be young, but who knows what lies ahead for any of us." As she spoke, Rachel hugged herself even closer in the cold, dark cabin feeling naked in her anger and her fear.

The doctor looked more intently at Rachel and asked cautiously, "Your daughter kept shouting, 'You will pay for this, Robert!' Is Robert her husband's name? What do you think she meant?"

There was a long pause. Then Maddie heard her mother respond curtly in a low voice, "No, that is not her husband's name. I have no idea who she was talking about. She was probably confused." Rachel thought, what was the doctor implying? What was there between Maddie and this man, Robert—whoever he was?

Maddie couldn't bear to hear anymore. She could feel herself begin to sink back into the darkness. She couldn't hear the Chopin Nocturnes and Beethoven Sonatas that usually calmed her into sleep. She had always been able to imagine a keyboard that she played in her mind as she heard each note. Until now. And she could no longer see William's kind, smiling face that sometimes soothed her into sleep. Especially when she thought she might go mad from worrying about whether he would ever return to her. As tears burned against her eyelids, his tall, straight figure walked slowly away from her.

* * *

The Scottish Highlands

At the very moment that Maddie was trying to envision William's face filled with love to comfort her in her sadness, he was traveling in Scotland and picturing Maddie's beautiful face. He was on another train traveling through the Highlands from Oban to Inverness, then onto the most northerly end of Scotland—the remote Orkney Islands. With the new orders, he had left Islay with a sense of regret for losing the distraction of its isolated beauty.

As the train passed over the rugged and increasingly more steep hills that would be considered mountains anywhere else, William thought of his day of painting with Maddie's Aunt Cate not so long ago. He wished that he could be painting again.

He could see out the train window some of Scotland's mystical sights while others he remembered in his mind. He closed his eyes briefly to see some of the scenes more vividly. The dramatic, rushing, and roiling brown streams so crucial in the making of that rich, smoky, and peaty Highland scotch whiskey he had tasted his last night in Edinburgh. The jagged dark hills dotted with white stone, patches of moss, and odd fans of long grass waving in the relentless wind. The gray mist rising from the hills into the dark ominous sky threatening a sudden downpour. The majestic stags that seemed to appear out of nowhere strolling across single-lane roads, sometimes even stopping to stand in the middle of the road without concern, since cars were seldom seen. The reddish-brown Highland cows in their fenced pastures that slowly blinked their eyes through shaggy mops of long-fringed hair badly in need of a trim. William thought they were the clowns of the Highlands—often standing knee-deep in mud, impervious to sharp branches of trees and brambles perilously close to entangling their hair, but still impassively and almost robotically following any passing human with solemn eyes. Dark, gloomy days cloaked in fog and driving rain, suddenly and unpredictably glowed with magical rainbows that arched over the hills when glimmers of sparkling sunshine escaped through breaks in the gray clouds.

As he gazed out the window, he gasped at what suddenly appeared and quickly reached into his duffle bag and pulled out his sketchpad and charcoal. He began to draw the deserted medieval stone castle that appeared below. The train labored upward over more hills past the castle that stood alone on a tiny island barely large enough for it, a small rowboat tied to a battered dock at the lake's edge. He wondered about who might be there now and the lives that had been contained within its walls—centuries ago. The castle's reflection in the glass-like stillness of the lake surrounding it, made it appear twice its size as if it were part of a grand fairy tale. It was a flash of sudden unexpected beauty that he had to capture.

Sven, William's Norwegian companion, shifted a little on his stiff leather seat across from him. Although Sven's eyes were closed, William knew he wasn't dozing and that he was probably aware of his every move. Sven's long legs were stretched out in front of him, his arms crossed. His dark green canvas haversack lay beside him on the seat. William knew it contained the gun that only a short time before had been pointed in his back.

Chapter 14

Southampton and London, England

Maddie and Rachel left the Southampton dock, their trunks accompanying them on the rolling cart being pulled by the amiable porter who followed close behind. They barely spoke after a tense breakfast together and now were disembarking from the ship. Rachel had attempted to ask more about what had happened the night of the miscarriage, but her insistent questions seemed to Maddie more like judgment and criticism than support. She had stayed in their cabin to rest for a few days and tried not to think about what had happened. She felt that familiar sense of responsibility and that once again, she had done something wrong.

She was miserable enough without having to discuss what had happened that night. For now, she told herself she had to focus on what was ahead of her—the afternoon and evening concerts the next day at the National Gallery of Art and then plan her escape to the Manor and meet Lady Braithwaite-Smith. She felt anxious about how to make this happen but she had to try. She had to find out where William was. He had spent so much time at the Manor on leaves. She was sure she could find out something there that could lead her to him. She would find a way to leave London.

Earlier that morning, they had eaten breakfast together—a light meal of tea, toast, and for each of them, a single, precious soft-boiled egg, in the ship's salon reserved for the special civilian passengers and Naval and Air Force officers.

Rachel had tried to start a conversation. "We need to talk about the other night. Did something happen before you miscarried? I know there is more. You have been so quiet. So unlike you, Maddie," she smiled encouragingly. "I know you have suffered a terrible shock. You gave me quite a scare. But is there something else you want to tell me?" She paused while she scrutinized her daughter. Maddie sipped her tea and avoided her mother's eyes.

"I am quite worried about you. Why didn't you tell me that you were pregnant?" Rachel asked with an edge in her voice, as she added milk to her tea and stirred it with a tiny spoon. She tried not to say what she was really feeling—that they shouldn't be where they were. That none of this might have happened if they had stayed in New York. She was worried about Maddie and her state of mind. She was far too quiet. Rachel wanted to turn around and go back—even forget about the concerts. Especially now. But she didn't want to upset Maddie any more than she was already. Despite her desire to see Maddie play in London in such important concerts, she had a strong sense of foreboding for their arrival in England in the midst of war.

On the other hand, Rachel knew how Maddie could uplift and inspire others with her remarkable performances. And it might also help her—to play again before an appreciative audience. The concerts had been planned as a way to remind the British of their indomitable spirit despite the bombings and the pall of death hanging over them. The haunting air raid sirens, the senseless deaths, and the rubble that was all that remained of those who had lived, in so many neighborhoods in London. The concerts were also meant to instill a sense of camaraderie with the Americans and boost morale in a city she loved.

She thought about all the tragedies that were occurring in this war and the ones that still haunted her from the previous war. She was no longer Jewish after her family's conversion and marrying her Anglican husband, but she still felt a strong visceral connection to her real cultural background. She felt fear for her Jewish family—especially relatives in France and Germany, as well as countless others who were being persecuted and murdered throughout Europe. She worried about her mother who had left England for Paris to take care of her own ailing mother, a few years before. She hadn't heard from her in several months.

Rachel was still angry with Maddie for taking such risks but she also felt pride for her strength and determination. She thought that in some ways, they were cut from the same cloth.

Maddie shook her head and met Rachel's gaze, noticing the tears in her eyes. She said firmly, even as her body trembled, "You know that I couldn't have told you. You would have kept me from leaving. I have to find William. That's all that matters. And I *will* find him. I can't let what happened on the ship interfere. I will be all right." She sighed and looked away, feeling shaky and sad but even more determined.

Rachel responded just as adamantly, "You can't look for William, Maddie. You know that can't happen. I know you are upset. It is a terrible thing that you went through. But the doctor said there can be other babies. We have to believe that William will come back. And anyway, how could you possibly find him?" She paused for a moment to brush a few crumbs from her lap, then pressed her napkin to her lips and looked more intently at her daughter. She said with increased concern, "You seem especially upset. Is there something else I should know?"

Maddie felt rising emotion again as she fought to hold back the tears. She wiped her eyes quickly with a handkerchief from her leather clutch purse and said, "You know as well as I do that William may never come back. If I can find him, I can persuade him there are other ways to fight this war and besides, there are other artists who have managed to stay by the sidelines—he could too!" She took a deep breath to steady herself. She didn't know exactly how this could happen but thought about times she had accomplished things even with overwhelming obstacles. She felt sure she could find him. She had made it this far. There had to be ways. She had to believe that. *Maybe Uncle Hugh can help?* She knew he had connections.

Rachel interrupted her thoughts placing her hand on Maddie's and said firmly but with love, "Now you know that would be impossible. William can't leave the war. Remember your concerts this week, darling. And why we are here. Are you sure you can still perform?" Her voice softened and she squeezed her daughter's hand more tightly.

Maddie's thoughts wandered again, to what might be possible.

Maybe she could perform at more concerts and stay longer in England. She had to find a way to get to the Manor in the Cotswolds. She was sure she could find out more there.

"Yes, I can do it," Maddie said, not wanting her mother to notice her mind was elsewhere. "I haven't forgotten anything, believe me. And besides, the concerts will be good for me." Maddie took a few deep breaths as she spoke, to keep from snapping at her mother. Even after what had happened on *The Princess Sofia*, she was not about to give up. With more determination than ever, she said, "I have to go through with the concerts. What choice do I have? And anyway, I know I can do it. I'm ready, Mother." She knew she couldn't let anyone down, especially not Madame.

"Well then, we will soon arrive in Southampton and then on to London," Rachel told her, emphasizing her words with more strength than she felt.

As if nothing distressing had happened on the ship a few days before, Rachel was dressed in a finely-tailored grey and brown checked wool suit, a cream silk blouse with an antique emerald, sapphire, and pearl peacock brooch on her lapel, matching earrings, and a small dark brown velvet hat angled slightly over her neatly coiffed auburn hair arranged in a tight chignon at the nape of her neck, with a delicate net covering her high forehead. She had carefully placed her long camel hair coat and leather gloves on the chair between them, as they would be leaving soon after the ship was docked in the harbor. She dressed the part of the mother of a famous Juilliard piano student already well-known on the concert circuit.

Rachel felt anxious about what her headstrong daughter might try to do next. But she had learned from her own mother that it was best to conceal whatever you were feeling behind a facade of dignity and good taste. She could see that Maddie was pale and exhausted after the traumatic events of the past few days. Rachel was still bothered by what the doctor had said. She leaned toward Maddie and asked in a low voice, "Is there something more you need to tell me? Who is this 'Robert' the doctor mentioned? Isn't that the name of our military escort? Why ever would you be angry with him?" Maddie looked away, not responding.

Rachel persisted, "I don't understand. Did something else happen? Talk to me, Maddie. I am your mother, after all." Maddie was keeping something from her. She had been quiet and distant ever since the night she lost the baby.

Maddie knew her mother loved her and was worried about her. *But I can't tell her what really happened.* She had to find a way to make sure Robert didn't get away with what he had done. But her mother was not going to be a part of it. She just shook her head and sighed, "I don't really want to talk right now. There's nothing more to say. I'm just so tired."

As Maddie sipped more of the lukewarm weak drink which only barely passed for tea, she felt cold eyes on her. She glanced up from her untouched toast and egg.

It was Robert—seated across the small dining room, staring at her with obvious malice and a self-satisfied smirk on his handsome face. Her mother was seated with her back to him and unaware that he was watching them.

Without anyone else apparently noticing as if they were the only ones in the dining room, he narrowed his gaze and placed his forefinger on his lips. He then dropped his hand, looked away and nonchalantly continued with the conversation he was having with his breakfast companion, also dressed in a Naval uniform.

Maddie gasped slightly but managed to suppress the overwhelming urge to rush over to his table and slap his smug face. This wasn't the time. She only hoped she would have another opportunity. Although she wanted to flee at that moment, she sat with her mother a little while longer. She didn't want Robert to think she was afraid of him. *He is not going to have that satisfaction.*

Just then, he glanced at her again, his face filled with menacing arrogance and an unmistakable threat. She stared back at him with an equally icy glare.

* * *

Later, after disembarking from the ship, they stood at the end of the dock waiting with a small gathering of other passengers, for a taxi to take them to the Southampton train station.

Maddie had no desire to continue a conversation with her mother or anyone else. She felt lightheaded and nervous—her mind preoccupied with possible plans. She hadn't slept much the night before and was still sore all through her body. She winced slightly at the occasional sharp pain lingering deep in her core. At least the bleeding had stopped, thank goodness. She fought the sadness that washed over her.

She had to stop thinking about what happened and just focus on the concerts. She was scheduled to be the solo pianist for the British-American concerts the next day. She loved the Rachmaninoff Piano Concerto No. 2 in C Minor—a demanding piece that always lifted her spirits to the highest balcony of the largest concert hall no matter what was going on in her life.

She would perform with the other Juilliard musicians and the London Philharmonic Orchestra or at least what was left of it, after so many had been killed in the bombings, were now fighting or worked with the War Office. She trembled in anticipation of what might come after the concert. Maddie was used to performing under pressure, but the assault and losing the dream of the baby that would keep her connected to William, threatened to overtake her in ways she had never thought possible.

117

She still considered reporting Robert or making sure he suffered some consequence for the attack. But she knew if she did report him, there would be a very unpleasant investigation during which she would most likely be blamed by the authorities. It was the time they lived in. Those in the military—especially officers—were always put on a pedestal, no matter what. And neither she nor her mother would benefit in any way from the public scandal that would follow.

There might be another way to make sure he didn't do it again to another woman. She just didn't know how. For now, she had to put it all away on a shelf so that she could go on.

She would get through the concerts then leave London afterward—as soon as possible. She felt a sense of urgency as if something was about to happen to William and only she could stop it. Maybe one of the British musicians could help her?

A black cab with mud splattered on its fenders and an illuminated roof-top sign indicating its availability, pulled up to the edge of the curb then drove them to the nearby train station.

Soon after, they left for London.

* * *

Rachel had chosen Claridge's, the opulent Art Deco hotel on Brook Street in Mayfair for their stay in London. She associated it with her previous life before she and her husband had emigrated to Canada in 1930. She loved the hotel and its history—that it had been founded in 1812 then expanded into neighboring town houses before becoming a hotel. It was known for its elegance and royal guests. She remembered intimate candlelit dinners in the formal dining room with her husband. Even their honeymoon weekend in 1922 was spent there.

In 1943, it was considered the "*American Club*" because the hotel drew those, in particular, who had been displaced from the United States. Rachel felt comforted surrounded by men and women speaking with a familiar Yankee accent—especially in the midst of her fear about being back in Europe and in a beleaguered city that was struggling to survive.

The other Juilliard musicians were staying at The Savoy. It had been bombed in the Blitz of 1940, then rebuilt, and now was frequented by journalists and British war leaders. It was even possible to catch a glimpse there of Winston Churchill arriving for lunch with his cabinet. Rachel thought Claridge's, with its close proximity to Hyde Park, would have fewer reminders of the war even with the wall of sandbags stacked at the formidable entrance.

With Madame's assistance, they had arranged for the Grand Piano Suite at the hotel so that Maddie could practice in privacy. In a brief telephone conversation with Madame, Rachel had alluded to Maddie having had a *very stressful* ocean crossing and needing time on her own to practice. So the suite was swiftly arranged. Although Madame could easily match Rachel's authoritative manner, she deferred to her when it came to Maddie's emotional states.

Rachel and Maddie swept into the luxurious hotel lobby with its marble columns, pale yellow walls, ornate ivory crown molding, black and white tiled floors, sparkling chandeliers, leather club chairs, and large portraits of famous Lords and Ladies hanging over fireplaces glowing with welcoming fires. Hushed voices rose from high-backed Queen Anne chairs and a sofa arranged in a cluster to one side where tea was being served. Rachel felt immediately that they had found a quiet sanctuary away from the war and her own painful memories.

Once they were checked in, Rachel said to Maddie, "Why don't you go on up to the room and start practicing so you will be ready for tomorrow? The bellhop will bring the bags." She then turned back to the desk clerk and requested that cheerful flowers and tea be brought to their room as soon as possible.

Maddie was starting to feel faint and thought she might collapse right there in the elegant lobby. She turned on her heel and held her head high as she walked toward the shiny brass elevators.

I may feel like screaming right now but I will get through this.

Then I can plan my escape.

Chapter 15

The bombers who fly and do not return threaten our need for stories because they thwart the possibility of an ending. The bombers who kill civilians in foreign cities threaten our demand for goodness in our heroes, and it is for both of these reasons that the poetry is theirs.

> *Daniel Swift*
> *Bomber County: The Poetry of a Lost Pilot's War*

The Highlands

The train rumbled through the mountains and valleys of the Highlands heading toward Inverness where the next meet would be. William was glad they weren't going directly to the Orkney Islands, off the remote northern coastline of Scotland. They would be given more intel to be passed to another agent, before their final destination. With all the radio traffic in the area, it was believed that the message was so important, they couldn't afford to have it intercepted.

William looked forward to seeing Inverness, considered to be the capital of the Highlands. It was also a bit of a fairy-tale town and mystical, given its proximity to Loch Ness and the fabled Loch Ness monster. He thought, there might be more ancient castles to sketch and colorful streets filled with scenes of everyday life to explore.

His Scottish heritage also made him feel at home here. He smiled despite himself thinking of his otherwise usually stern father who, when he was in a jovial mood after Sunday lunch, would pull his harmonica out of his pocket and expertly render Scottish ditties while dancing a jig. His father also liked to play ear-splitting bagpipe music on the record player—loud honking and whining groans that drove him and the rest of his family into other parts of their house.

At least it wasn't Country and Western music, thank God. How he loathed the sound of the "fiddle," the twangy voices, and the slide guitar. *Ugh.* He shuddered at the thought.

It was the sound of classical music—Maddie playing Chopin and Beethoven, Saturday opera on the radio—and Big Band ensembles with their clever jazz rhythms led by Glenn Miller and Artie Shaw that he longed for.

He never forgot his Scottish roots. Once on a trip to see Maddie in New York, he wrote without thinking, *Scottish* on the immigration form when he was crossing through Buffalo from Canada into the United States. It felt familiar here as it had at the Manor. As if ancestors were reaching out to him and whispering in his ear. Painting in the countryside and in Edinburgh and Glasgow had helped him to feel an eerie closeness and kinship to this land.

He thought how his father's unrelenting pressure had brought him here, taking him away from Maddie and into a war that had killed so many. It made him angry. The war. His father—the decorated Lieutenant Colonel. How his father made him feel that being an artist wasn't good enough. That he had to follow in his footsteps. Not something he wanted to do, at all.

But he loved the feeling of rising gracefully from the ground. Flying, he had to admit, was exhilarating.

It was the sound of the guns and the bombs dropping from the Halifax then exploding violently that kept him awake in the officers' quarters the nights he wasn't flying. Imagining the destruction below. It was all so mixed up. He felt himself hating his father and hating what he was doing. He knew what they were fighting for but he worried about the lasting effects of these bombing missions and what he might become.

In the midst of these feelings of rage and confusion, he cherished the moments when he could paint and not worry about the dangerous missions ahead. He reminded himself that his training at the Manor—hand-to-hand combat exercises, target practice, sabotage strategies, and briefings on working undercover—had prepared him well.

William sketched some of the fleeting scene of the magical castle on the small lake of glass that he had glimpsed from the train, before rolling it up with the others and placing it back in his knapsack. Sven sat across from him with his eyes half-closed. There was no easy conversation or even companionable silence between them. He still wondered about Sven threatening him with a gun and why that would have been necessary if they were supposed to be on the same side.

He wasn't sure whether he was going to be using his navigational and mathematical skills as a bombardier or whether his cover as an artist would be more important as he passed misinformation to others thought to be German operatives. Or maybe, all of it would be needed.

Sabotage was also a possibility, as they were heading for northern Scotland near where Germans had attacked and taken Norwegian fishing boats. German U-boats were lurking not far from the Scottish northern shore. They could be preparing for an invasion. That's why the SOE was increasing activities in the Highlands. He might even be in the air again, once they arrived in the Orkneys.

There had been a particularly harrowing bombing mission soon after he was stationed in England when they barely missed a mid-air collision with another Allied plane. He and his crew could be shot down at any time. Visions of how he was causing innocent deaths on the ground with each bomb he dropped, plagued him most at night after they returned from another mission.

Not long after, he met Lady Braithwaite-Smith who invited him to stay at the Manor and paint on his leaves. Her plan for him to become an agent relieved him of the destruction of the bombing missions that led to his violent nightmares and sleepless nights.

William was born in 1921 at the beginning of the Jazz Age. He thought of the times his father would take him and his older sister to the Amusement Park at Sunnyside Beach on Lake Ontario. They would ride the merry-go-round and when he was a bit older, some of the roller coasters. He loved the height and speed as they whizzed through the air. Maybe that's what got me hooked on flying, he wondered, not for the first time. There were no more Saturday outings with his father once Wall Street crashed and triggered the grim years of the Great Depression. His father who was a Civil Engineer working for the city of Toronto found himself without a job for several months in 1929.

Around the same time, he became obsessed with sketching with whatever he could find—even once, his father's fountain pen and bottle of ink—which ended in a thrashing that only caused him to be more careful about when and how he would draw or paint.

William learned how to be resourceful and use whatever he could find to draw—pencils, bits of charcoal, childhood crayons, and discarded, nearly empty tubes of paints he found in his art classroom at school. Biology and history textbooks with the odd half-empty page and seductively plain covers, wax paper his mother used for baking, and brown paper grocery bags all worked well for his constant sketching and painting.

One of his teachers at the special arts high school told him, "Just keep drawing, William. On whatever you can find. It doesn't matter what you draw or paint—just keep doing it. You've got what it takes. And don't be afraid to break some rules!" She had laughed with a playful pat on his shoulder. She was the one who had convinced his parents he should keep studying to be a painter. By the time he was a teenager in the mid-1930s, he had learned that his art gave him great joy. Every chance he had, he drew and painted small watercolor studies in a sketchbook he always carried.

Despite loving the speed and height of the roller coaster in his childhood and being captivated as a child by his father's exciting World War I stories of flying a biplane, he could not imagine a career after the war in any way associated with flying. Especially not now, after all the mid-air explosions and the tragedies on the ground below that he visualized each time he expelled yet another bomb as he lay on the floor of the glassed-in nose of the Halifax. He thought more about the millions of people who died on both sides of this war, not only here in Great Britain but elsewhere in the world, bombed by people like him. And the thousands of aircrew men and women who had been killed in the line of duty.

He didn't know what he had expected. Probably not countless missions dodging enemy aircraft, sometimes successfully hitting their target and other times not knowing exactly what they hit. The constant presence of death never left him. He never forgot the threat of being hit from the ground or in the air, and always felt dread—along with the relief of having survived another mission—when they returned to the base, knowing that some planes would not return.

He thought of the other crews he had eggs and bacon with, in the mess hall filled with an air of bravado and joking, sharing stories and forced laughter before taking off across the English Channel to Germany or Occupied France. So many of those crews vanished. And so many of the airmen were—like him—just starting out in life.

But he knew he could not have stayed at home while others risked their lives.

He imagined returning to his life as an artist with Maddie in New York when the war was over. He had finally begun to admit to himself, though, that enlisting in the RCAF had not only been out of duty and carrying on the *family business*. It had also been partially due to that aspect of him that loved danger and taking heart-stopping risks. Just not ones that involved killing innocent people.

William never revealed to Maddie this part of himself—of loving speed and living on the edge. That was not something he could admit to her. She loved to tease him by saying he was her "dreamy artist*"*—carrying his sketchbook and pulling it out on country walks or at cafés with her in New York. With swift flourishes, his charcoal pencil would capture scenes of people strolling by or peering longingly into shop windows, canopies of trees laden with fragrant lilac blooms, a noisy market filled with overflowing stands of fruits and vegetables in dazzling jewel tones of reds, purples, oranges, and yellows contrasting with variegated shades of leafy greens.

Sometimes, he would wait until later when he had his paints and by that time, his mind would be so crowded with vivid swirling images of light and color that he felt his head might explode.

One of these times, Maddie sat across from him in Frankie's Diner on Broadway in New York while they drank coffee and shared a piece of pie after one of their walks. He didn't have anything to sketch with and was deep in thought, pondering scenes he would paint later.

She said with a sigh, "Oh William, where are you now? What am I going to do with you? Am I not captivating enough?" Then she tossed her head and laughed good-naturedly.

He knew she understood the need to create beauty and his excitement—the same thrill he was sure she felt when she sat down at a grand piano in a crowded concert hall.

William thought about how friends often laughed at him and didn't understand why he needed to draw and paint every day. Even his best friend, Charlie, would complain when they rode their bikes together to a spot in the country so William could paint *en plein air*. He'd laugh and say good-naturedly, "For the love of God, man. Time for a break! You're obsessed!"

Maddie often had to lock herself in the music room at Juilliard for hours on end or not answer the phone for days—sometimes practicing the same piece over and over again. He had to do the same when he painted. They both knew from childhood what they wanted to do with their lives. It made them seem much older than others their age.

But he also felt an intoxicating exhilaration whenever he put himself in danger—not unlike how it felt being with Maddie. The way she fearlessly challenged those who tried to control her, made him anxious about where this strength might take her.

He loved to push himself beyond the point of exhaustion or fear—hours of hiking and climbing up and down steep cliffs, racing in a kayak through rapids churning with life-threatening torrents of icy white water, skiing at breakneck speed down treacherous icy mountains, careening around curves down steep hills one-handed on his bicycle while bellowing *Chattanooga Choo-Choo* and holding onto his portfolio under his other arm. He smiled thinking about these escapades before leaving Canada. A part of him relished the world he had just entered. Spying fit his temperament in many ways.

His thoughts were interrupted by the train's whistle and the conductor moving through the aisle of the train calling out, "Next stop—Inverness!"

Sven stirred, his eyelids suddenly fluttered open and he fixed his cold gray eyes, the color of a stormy Scottish sky, on William. He muttered more to himself than anyone else, "Well, that's it then. Time to get off."

William wondered if Sven's lack of communication was due to his limited English or if he was hiding something. He had no choice but to grab his duffle bag and haversack and follow Sven off the train.

* * *

A little while later as the sun was beginning to set, they entered a smoky pub that was down a narrow alley removed from the streets filled with tea rooms, food markets, whiskey shops, and the odd general store owned by a purveyor of local woolens and millinery.

William thought the lowered voices could be discussing anything from the market prices for the local sheep farmers, to details of a covert mission—or maybe both. A few women sat together sipping drinks and cups of tea, smoking, and chatting quietly. But most of the patrons were men dressed in civilian suits or country overalls and heavy jackets. After pausing briefly to glance at the two strangers entering the pub, they returned to their drinks and murmured conversations punctuated with the odd laugh.

Except for a pair of serious-looking men, well-dressed in suits and ties who kept their eyes on them, their fedoras placed next to pints of beer—the signal for the meet.

They nodded in unison at William and Sven who then sat down with them at the small table in a darkened corner. William thought these agents didn't exactly blend in. They were probably from the Home Office and most likely, not accustomed to being in the field. They looked like MI5 or MI6—professionals. Not the young risk-takers typically recruited by the SOE.

The taller one with flat, expressionless eyes, spoke first in such a low voice that William and Sven had to lean in to hear him. His smooth accent betrayed an upper-crust education, "All right, then, we're here to brief you for your mission. Not our choice to work with you bloody lot. Amateurs." His lip curled slightly as he spoke, eyeing them with disdain. "No names are necessary. We know who you are. You will meet Elsa tonight, which of course, is not her real name and pass on the intel. She's a double working for us. They think she's one of theirs." A small smile crossed his face briefly as he passed a folded piece of paper to William.

The other agent with a dark mustache and furrowed brow above deep-set brown eyes took a sip from his pint and then spoke in the same hushed voice, "She's a student at the local art school and has the connections we need. She will radio the people who need to be told. Don't worry, she only carries a knife and has been known to use it once or twice. But we have her family. So she will cooperate."

William understood that things like this were happening all the time but it still shocked him to hear statements about lives endangered, spoken in such a cavalier fashion. There were some things he just couldn't get used to—even in war.

"After that, we need your bombardier and flying skills—and a few other things," the agent with the dark moustache added, meeting William's eyes but making it clear he was not going to elaborate further. "You'll go further north to the Orkney Islands. We will be in touch." He turned toward Sven and said, "Of course, you will stay at the same safe house, as before. You can take him there," and gestured with his head at William. Then, with a tone of finality in his voice, "The fewer people who know where you are, the better." He turned back to his beer and spoke in a low voice to his companion.

William saw that the meet was over. There was no time for tea, a pint, or social niceties. He would pick up bread and cheese at one of the grocers on the way to the art school.

"Nice meeting you fellas. Seems straightforward. And thanks for the tip. I'll keep an eye out for the knife," William said as he stood up and headed toward the door, Sven following behind. It felt good to know what he had to do.

Chapter 16

Mayfair, London, England

Rachel sat at the small Chippendale writing desk in the bedroom of the sumptuous suite she shared with Maddie at Claridge's. Ornate gold-filigree wall sconces cast triangles of pale light on the cream and buttercup yellow striped wallpaper. A pair of recently polished brass lamps with amber and turquoise glass Tiffany shades on the nightstands by each of the single beds illuminated the room with patches of glowing optimism in the fading darkness of the early morning. She wore an ivory silk dressing gown and her auburn hair was arranged in an uncharacteristic loose Edwardian top-knot in preparation for a hot, relaxing bath before the afternoon concert—a true luxury in wartime London.

As she wrote a letter to her husband, she looked out the tall, paned French doors fitted with heavy blackout curtains and streaked with the steady morning rain so typical of London, toward the street several floors below. This smaller room of the suite was chilly as there was only a small gas radiator, but she felt a gathering warmth in her body—almost as if a very hot fire had been lit within her while she tried to sort out her thoughts. She felt a headache beginning to infiltrate her temples—brought on, she knew, from the ocean voyage. It seemed or so she imagined they had been constantly dodging U-boats and the raging storm of the last few nights at sea had threatened to drown them all.

She was haunted by the horrible sight of her daughter collapsed and bleeding on the small hooked rug on their cabin floor. She knew what it was like to long for children and suddenly lose them before they were even born. She thought again of her two pregnancies after Maddie that had ended suddenly and tragically. And she understood Maddie's fear that William might not return and her desperate need to do something. But her daughter's stubborn silence after they left *The Princess Sofia* and later, on the train to London added to Rachel's distress. She felt so helpless. Unbidden and unwanted memories were stirring within her. Her own demons had been awakened.

Rachel felt strongly that something else—maybe as terrible as the miscarriage—happened to Maddie that night. She still wondered how Robert, the military escort was involved.

She knew her daughter's moods well. She was going to find out somehow.

She returned to writing her letter and felt grateful that at least for now, they were safe.

There was less damage from the bombings here in Mayfair than in other parts of London. That was partially why she had chosen Claridge's. It was also because she had such happy memories of the hotel when she was newly married and beginning to enjoy the benefits of being a member of a socially prominent family. There had been gay evenings of elegant cocktail parties, dinners, and dancing in the ballroom, as well as black-tie dinners in homes in nearby Belgravia—before the market crashed and things changed. She had been so young then—not quite Maddie's age. She had never seen anything like it before in her life.

Now, looking out the tall, rain-spattered windows, she could almost imagine being back in that world and that a war was not happening outside this room. She tried not to worry about Maddie's performances as she listened to her practicing Rachmaninoff and Chopin pieces in the adjacent sitting-room—crashing chords played with even more emotion than usual. The music ended and she heard the scraping of the piano bench on the oak floor followed by footsteps pacing back and forth, softened intermittently by the plush Oriental rugs scattered throughout the spacious room. Rachel knew that it was best to stay out of Maddie's way. And she was having her own struggle, pushing away old memories.

She tried to stay calm and concentrate on describing to her husband some of the more mundane events of the journey to England. As she wrote the letter to Richard, she struggled to find the right words—wanting him to know that they were managing well enough. She did not want to worry him more than she knew he already was, now that they were in London. She thought it was best to spare him the distressing details of the last few days and Maddie's current emotional state which seemed precariously balanced at best.

Richard was ten years older than Rachel and a successful banker who had re-built his career through the financial upheaval of the Stock Market crash of

1929 and then the Great Depression. Even now in wartime, he was calm, decisive, and unwavering in the face of any disaster—and always with an English stiff upper lip. Richard rode each storm soothing her anxieties with, "Now dear, we will get through this too."

She secretly found his unflappable demeanor sometimes annoying but she had never told him how she felt. It was best not to bother him with her tedious emotions. She had learned to compartmentalize and so far, it had worked for her.

Their childhoods and upbringing were so different. His—so privileged and stable. Hers—so chaotic and filled with trauma—her childhood in Germany then France, and finally arriving in England after World War I with what was left of her family—refugees from war and violence. He had grown up on an estate in York and attended an exclusive boarding school then Cambridge University while she had been uprooted repeatedly. She just wanted to forget what she had been through. He had provided a safe place for her and their children. And for that, she would be forever grateful.

When it came to his daughter, his distant and sometimes brusque manner melted away and his eyes shone with pride. He wouldn't be able to tolerate knowing Maddie was so upset.

Their children were the center of their lives. He had remained in Toronto, building a successful banking career and taking care of their son, Charlie while she and Maddie moved to New York so their talented daughter could study piano with the best. They returned to Toronto periodically during the year, for visits whenever social occasions required that she be there and to spend Christmas and summer vacations. The arrangement had worked well for them.

As she wrote her letter, she also thought it was best not to tell him how she was fighting reminders of her own childhood tragedy in Hamburg, Germany. Her family—mother, brother Hugh, sister Cate, and she—had barely managed to escape to France to be with her grandmother, just before World War I broke out.

Fragments of the scene that haunted her dreams many nights, intruded into the silence of the bedroom where Rachel sat gazing out the window at the rain and fighting the memory.

She heard the German soldiers loudly crashing into their house on Schramsberg Avenue, into the kitchen where her mother stood making bread.

They yelled, "You Jew bitch!" She saw herself, a frightened child, hugging her mother desperately and crying, "Mama! Mama!"

She saw the red-faced man who loomed over them like a giant, throw her mother to the floor while another man grabbed Rachel and tossed her aside as if she was a useless rag doll.

She ran back to her mother then saw herself being pulled away from her. Her mother lay on the kitchen floor screaming and crying "Run, Rachel! Run!" She could see her mother's legs forced apart by the giant as she was pushed by another uniformed man through the door into the dining room. She collapsed in a corner sobbing for her mother. Her eight-year-old self didn't understand what was happening but she knew her mother was being hurt in a horrible way.

She saw herself crawl under the table where her family had enjoyed such happy meals together before the persecution that began as a constant dull roar, inflicted their lives with escalating violence. Neighbors disappeared and her family stopped going to the local synagogue. They had been targeted not only because they were Jewish but because her father was a successful tailor with political leanings not in sync with the local authorities.

She heard her mother's screams, "No! No!" then saw the tall angry figure of her father burst through the front door of the house. She saw a flash of movement from under the table where she was curled up frozen in place, as he ran to the kitchen following her mother's screams.

Then, the gunshots and her mother screaming even more. Then silence.

Rachel shook her head, rubbed her neck, and straightened her back as she finished her letter.

She slowly rose from the desk with the grace she had learned from her mother and left the room to prepare for her bath.

Chapter 17

Inverness, Scotland

William walked along a narrow street in the rosy light of early evening just before darkness descended. He felt the brisk, damp wind from the River Ness on his face as he passed a couple walking arm in arm. Before long, he noticed a creaking sound. He looked up to see a sign swaying rhythmically in the gusty, cold wind, from a steel rod inserted above a doorway. The words, *Inverness Fine Art School* in faded red letters were visible enough for him to know that he was in the right place.

He took off his hat, checked his pockets to make sure his commando knife and pistol were still there and walked into a small, dimly lit room with a few bare lightbulbs drifting down haphazardly from a low ceiling. The stark room was crowded with easels where students stood in loose smocks splattered with paint, holding brushes and curved palettes. A few young female models lounged languorously on stools in various still poses wearing slightly dingy sheets loosely draped across their nude bodies at angles revealing only portions of bare shoulders, hands, feet, and the occasional curve of a slender back. Their faces were turned sideways with eyes dreamily gazing elsewhere into unknown places. He felt the excitement of being in the midst of a group of artists and almost forgot why he was there. He didn't want to interrupt the class.

An older, gray-haired man with a craggy face suggesting a life lived to the fullest, stood to the side, watching the artists intently then broke the silence in a strong voice gently cajoling in an authoritative yet encouraging tone, "Ach, dinnae fash yersel about gettin' it parfect. Jus' fel yer brush, the strokes, and keep yersel goin'. There, lassie, that'd be it!" as he stepped closer to a pink-cheeked, earnest-looking young woman with golden plaits wrapped around her head. "Aye, that's better. Dinnae hold yersel back there. Yer felin' it more, girl, I ken see!" he said with an impish grin, in an accent that placed him as a likely native of Inverness.

William nodded to the instructor who kept up his patter while the students diligently painted at their easels. "Ye ken do it. Yer doin' fine there," he said as he leaned over one middle-aged woman pursing her lips as she carefully sketched an outline of a figure, a few steps behind the rest of the class.

"Dinnae forget t' fel yer strokes. Dinnae yous be shy nigh," the instructor invoked, then stepped away to the side of the room where William stood. He leaned forward and said, "So ye visitin' our wee class?"

William answered in a low voice, "So sorry to interrupt, sir. But I need to speak to a student of yours—her name is Elsa. I've come to see her but we never actually met before. I am also a painter and I was told she might be here. Just for a moment or two, if you don't mind."

The older man squinted with bright blue eyes peeking out between a multitude of wrinkles and graced William with a crooked, bemused smile. "Aye ye, she be n' bonny lassie. I'll hav'er stop what she's doin'. I'm Angus, young fella." He reached out and shook William's hand firmly as he studied his face closely.

William thought he might clarify that he wasn't interested in a date but then decided against it. He wanted the old gentleman to think that he might be a randy bloke or maybe, a long-lost cousin. He chose the latter – to make sure he didn't guess the real reason he was there.

"I was traveling in the area doing my own bit of painting and thought I would stop by and see the cousin my mum told me so much about. I guess you can tell I'm not from here."

Angus chuckled and said, "Aye, I ken see that, chappie. American are ye now?"

"Close enough, sir," William answered with a quick nod.

Angus stepped away from William and tapped the young golden-haired woman lightly on the shoulder. She slowly turned from her easel where she had been working. William thought her painting showed signs of Toulouse Lautrec's sweeping broad-stroke style and especially, his portraits of Moulin Rouge dancers but with more inhibitions. Her face showed no emotion and her startling, icy pale blue eyes pierced right through him. He could only imagine what she might be thinking. From the sharpness of her gaze, it was likely she knew why he was there. And how what she would do next could determine whether, along with her family, she would live or die.

William motioned to her to leave the room and he followed her into the darkened alley. He could feel the palpable anger that surrounded her.

Conceding her position because she knew she had no choice, she leaned against the wall with a frown and spoke with obvious hostility, "Okay then, get it over with."

He looked at her intently, wondering if she thought this was where it would end. Trying hard not to show any emotion or any sympathy for her, he said, "This is what you must pass on to your sources. And it needs to be soon. Or you know what will happen. You are being watched. Radio the intel to your contacts tonight."

He leaned toward her and held out the piece of paper that said, *Allied invasion Norway coast from Orkney Islands. Attacks may be sooner. More details later.*

Without a word, she grabbed the paper from him clenching it in her fist and walked away. He had accomplished what he was there to do.

Suddenly, a familiar figure stepped out of the shadows. It was Sven. Even in the darkness, William could see the commando knife in his hand.

* * *

Paddington Station, London

Rachel stood on the platform waving then blew a kiss to Maddie who smiled and waved back at her from the window of her compartment, then turned away to settle in for her journey on the Great Western Railway train departing soon for Cardiff. She had accompanied Maddie to Paddington Station, feeling more at ease with the plan for her daughter to recuperate from the concerts with a fellow performer's family in northern Wales. Rachel began to walk away as the train spewed clouds of billowing gray smoke and steam, in preparation for its departure.

Suddenly, Robert, the military escort on their ocean voyage appeared— pushing his way through the crowd. Despite an obvious limp, he moved quickly toward the train that was now about to leave the station, roughly shoving people who were embracing loved ones in tearful farewells. It looked like he was about to leap onto the stairs leading up to one of the carriages in the middle of the train where Maddie was traveling on her way to a much-needed rest.

It was too much. Without thinking, Rachel stepped out in front of him, looked briefly into his arrogant face and registered his eyes meeting hers in an angry challenge. She pushed her hand lightly but firmly against his chest—just to let him know that whatever he had done he wasn't going to get away with it. She had to protect Maddie.

But her slight push and the element of surprise were just enough to throw him off balance. He had no time to react. His eyes widened in shock as he lost his balance, tripping into another traveler. Then with his arms flailing uselessly in the air, he stumbled from the platform onto the tracks below and into the path of the oncoming train.

Chapter 18

The Manor, The Cotswolds

Maddie sat on a chintz-covered chair in the drawing room that also served as a library at the country estate of the woman known as Lady Braithwaite-Smith—the Manor House that William had written about in his letters. She fidgeted as she looked out the lead-paned casement windows at the gardens now cloaked in subdued shades of brown and gray clusters of hydrangea and rose bushes forlorn in their skeletal remains of the past summer. She could imagine how beautiful the gardens had been only a few months before. A bench by a pond at an outer edge of the garden suggested quiet conversations in the midst of lush blooming plants when the weather turned warmer. She still felt guilty that she had left London. But she reassured herself, *I've done the right thing.* She touched the necklace at her throat that William had given her on their wedding night and felt strong.

She couldn't believe her good fortune. She had successfully escaped from London, more performances at the National Gallery, and her mother. She smiled to herself at how easy it had been as she waited anxiously for the meeting to begin.

A pale-complexioned and courteous but business-like young woman opened the door when Maddie arrived earlier and greeted her with a chirpy, "Hello. Do come in. I trust your journey was satisfactory." She had dark brown hair with a few premature streaks of gray pulled away from her delicately featured face in a tight, unflattering bun and peered at her through wire-rimmed glasses perched gingerly on an upturned nose. Maddie noticed she took great pains to look unattractive even though she could be quite pretty without the glasses and the bun. She also had an air of mystery and Maddie thought her tight-lipped smile might be concealing a secret that amused her. She wore a trim brown tweed suit with a thistle pin on her lapel and practical brown oxfords. Probably from Scotland. But in these times, no one knew for sure where anyone was from. This is quite a strange place, Maddie thought.

Maddie said with a voice that she hoped sounded confident, "I'm here to meet with Lady Braithwaite-Smith. I'm William Craig's wife."

The other woman nodded curtly and showed Maddie into the drawing room. With a voice colored by a faint brogue, she said formally, "Madam will be with you momentarily. She is detained just now," and left the room.

Maddie wondered what this woman's actual role might be. She didn't seem at all like the usual secretary or housekeeper. And why would someone like this be needed at a country estate, in these times, with everyone cutting back on staff? She felt impatient with all the intrigue. But then she reminded herself, I have not lived with what they are living with in this horrible war. Things are definitely more secretive here, she thought. And probably need to be.

Shortly after, another woman, plump and wearing an apron, brought a tray with tea, cream and sugar, warm biscuits, clotted cream, and a tiny, square divided dish with a dab of wartime margarine on one side and precious marmalade on the other. Without a word, she set everything down on a small side table next to Maddie. She straightened more in the chair and pressed her palms firmly on her woolen skirt, anxiously waiting for the meeting.

She thought about the concerts and the conversation with her mother before she boarded the train in London. The last concert at The National Gallery had been held in the early evening as the sky glowed a brilliant and fiery red-orange almost as if the entire city was aflame, then reluctantly receded into the darkness created by the inevitable blackout of war.

She analyzed every aspect of her performance. Had she rushed the opening? Had she expressed the correct level of feeling—without overdoing it? She got through the concert somehow, despite a bone-weary sadness and rage after the traumatic events on *The Princess Sofia*. It gave her hope that she still had the strength to perform. Probably something she had learned from her parents.

She thought of how the curtain rose slowly over the darkened stage with only a single row of bright footlights separating her from the audience. She had looked out at the faces lifted with hope and expectation, despite the horrors outside the theatre. She was moved by their courage. Beauty is still around us.

As she crossed the stage, she felt a surge of anxiety. Could she do this or would she make a complete fool of herself? As she sat down on the piano bench before the beautiful glossy black Steinway and lifted her hands to the keyboard, she felt the music rise within her and she was swept away—her fingers transporting her to that other world. The drama and passion of Rachmaninoff. She no longer felt the pain of William so far from her—only the music. The sadness, the anger, the lost promise of their child. She had learned a long time ago how to separate anything that was upsetting in her life from her performances.

That was how she was able to push away thoughts of the assault, Robert's arrogant smirking face, the shock and pain of the miscarriage, and immerse herself completely in the music and give the audience what they had come to hear.

She didn't remember much about what happened after the music ended. Only that the audience rose to their feet, applauding a long time and shouting, "Bravo! Encore!" She acquiesced with a quiet but melodic Chopin Nocturne, then left the stage without much awareness of what happened next.

All she knew was that her mother took her back to the hotel soon after and put her promptly to bed. Her last thought before drifting off into a deep sleep had been *tomorrow's the day*.

The sounds of the sirens came back to her, signaling *All is clear*—a welcome respite from the nighttime bombings. Although they had become less of a regular occurrence since the Blitz ended in 1941, London was still a city under attack. Bombings continued, especially in East London. Even Winston Churchill had been forced to direct the British armed forces from the underground barracks below the Parliament buildings not currently in use, in Westminster. It was rumored that he cherished his maps so much that every room of the command center was dominated by enlarged, detailed renditions of the entire British Isles with black markings indicating areas in England and Scotland that were dangerous for tanks and others at risk for German invasions. Ever since Britain almost fell to the Germans early in the war, Londoners fled to the Underground at the first sign of sirens. If they had time, they grabbed blankets and pillows while their children clutched threadbare teddy bears.

Maddie woke the day after the concert, in the suite she shared with her mother and began to work her persuasive abilities on Rachel over breakfast.

"I just have to get away, Mother and recuperate from everything." Her eyes had teared up and her lips quivered as she spoke with true emotion. "Then I'll be ready to go home," she said convincingly.

Rachel argued, "But Maddie, you know we need to travel together. There is a war going on, darling. And you have had a terrible shock. A bit of a break might do you good. I want to take care of you." She paused and grasped Maddie's hands.

Maddie felt pulled but she was not going to be deterred from her plan.

"I am so proud of you!" Rachel said with a smile, changing the subject and her eyes filled with tears. "Everyone loved your performances, darling. Last night was one of your best concerts! But, now, I think you need some rest. Then, you will be able to play again. And I will be there the whole time and take care of you," she repeated and squeezed Maddie's hand.

Maddie saw the tension on her mother's face. She struggled with an urge to do what Rachel wanted, against what she was here to do. She was not to be dissuaded.

"I promise I will get back to my studying with Madame and do all the concerts scheduled back in New York for the Holiday season," Maddie said with renewed alacrity. "I know last night could have been better. I just don't think I'm up to the next concerts at Royal Albert Hall. I'm quite exhausted, Mother. I'm not myself. I need to get away." She sighed and raised the teacup to her lips, avoiding her mother's eyes.

"Maddie, don't you remember the audience shouting for an encore? You were wonderful!" Rachel smiled and patted Maddie's hand, studying her face. "But all right," she said with concern in her voice. "Yes, I agree. You need to rest. Maybe we can arrange something. Can't you take a break in Scotland with Hugh and Cate and then return to London? We could take the train and stay there a fortnight or longer. It would be good for you, Maddie. You have been through a terrible thing," Rachel said and squeezed her hand again.

Maddie felt her mother looking at her sharply as they continued to share a pot of morning tea and toast. She would have to work harder if her plan was going to be successful. She knew how stubborn her mother could be. She would try to go with her and that couldn't happen.

"You remember Priscilla who played the first violin yesterday?" Maddie spoke quickly before she lost her resolve. "Well, she has invited me to stay with her family in northern Wales. They have a country home outside a small seaside village near Llandudno. Quite a lovely spot, I understand. And as safe as a place can be, away from everything. I can stay there for the next week or two," feeling stronger as she spoke.

Rachel interrupted, "I don't think this is a good idea, you…"

Maddie continued with more determination, "I can take the train to Cardiff. Priscilla's parents will meet me there and drive me to their house. It is a good plan. I promise. It will give me a chance to rest as you have been telling me I need to do. They even have a piano so I can practice," she smiled as she met her mother's eyes.

"But, Maddie, I must go with you." Rachel's blue-gray eyes darkened as she searched her face.

Maddie thought she look tired. She was probably also in need of a good rest. She said, even more firmly, "Mother, you know it would be good for you to see Uncle Hugh in Edinburgh and then spend time with Aunt Cate in Oban. You could get some rest too. Don't worry. Priscilla's family will be there to take care of me. And I will be safe. Then we can meet in Edinburgh before we take the voyage home. Or maybe I could perform again in London before we leave."

In the end, Rachel was persuaded and Maddie left on the Cardiff-bound train from Paddington Station. But she had taken it only as far as Moreton-in-Marsh in the Cotswolds. She sat by the window on the two-hour trip thinking about what she would say to persuade Lady Braithwaite-Smith that she had to see William.

Once she arrived at the train station in the village, she rang the Manor. After sending a telegram from London to Uncle Hugh in Edinburgh who apparently knew Lady Braithwaite-Smith, arrangements had been made for the meeting. A young earnest man not much older than Maddie picked her up at the train station. He drove her in an aged but still regal sedan to the imposing estate. It was surrounded by high walls of the same golden stone as the glorious Christopher Wren-designed colleges at Oxford—known as the "city of dreaming spires" she had glimpsed in the distance from the train window.

Then, at that moment, interrupting Maddie's thoughts, a tall, middle-aged woman entered the room. She had no more time to worry about meeting Lady Braithwaite-Smith who sat down on the silver velvet wing-backed chair facing Maddie.

"So, you have come to find out about William. I have been expecting you, Maddie," the woman said, with a touch of irony in her voice.

* * *

The Flying Scotsman to Edinburgh

While events were beginning to unfold in the Cotswolds that could take Maddie closer to William, Rachel was on a train traveling to Edinburgh. She pulled a silver pen and small leather-bound journal from her handbag and began to write. Her train case and suitcase were stored on the shelf above her. She had started writing—more than letters—when they were on *The Princess Sofia* crossing the Atlantic. It helped to sort out her feelings. She pushed away her worries, hoping that Maddie was safe and resting in Wales far away from danger. And she was on her way to be with Hugh.

Suddenly, vivid images of the violent scene at Paddington Station flashed in her mind.

Her hand shook as she put the pen down on the table in front of her and closed her eyes. She couldn't escape the horror that she had caused someone's death. But she had acted on instinct.

There was definitely something malevolent about Robert trying to board Maddie's train.

She saw him stumble from the platform onto the tracks as the oncoming train rolled over his once-imposing body. As the train left the station with accelerating speed, his head was crushed and bloody but his cold blue eyes were open and staring accusingly. As she remembered the horrible sight, she gasped and covered her mouth to keep from crying out—thoughts racing through her mind. *What have I done? But it was an accident! I didn't mean for this to happen. I just wanted to protect Maddie.*

She had stood immobilized on the platform until people started shouting around her but she thought they hadn't noticed her in the confusion. Then she turned up her wide fur collar of her long cashmere coat to shield her face as she hurried away.

Suddenly, the horrifying memory was interrupted by footsteps approaching from behind and she jumped in her seat. She turned and saw it was only the conductor collecting tickets from the passengers. "Tickets, please, thank you very much!" he called in a cheery voice. She took a deep breath and gave him her ticket as he punched and returned it to her then walked away down the aisle of the car to the next passenger.

Rachel couldn't shake the feeling that she was being followed or that a police officer might appear and arrest her. She looked out the window and hoped she was doing the right thing by traveling to Edinburgh.

Chapter 19

Inverness, Scotland

"I wasn't sure if you could handle the situation there, mate. You're a bit unreliable with all your sketching and painting," Sven chortled then continued with an air of superiority, facing William in the dark alley behind the art school. "Anyway, I thought I should be there, just in case. She might have used her knife. She's been known to try such things."

William let it go although he felt himself fuming and wanting to prove to Sven that he knew what he was doing. He was incensed that Sven continued to underestimate him. He didn't think Elsa was a dangerous killer. And she had been warned her family would be hurt if she didn't cooperate. She had been caught collaborating in Scotland with the Germans and her family was in Occupied Norway now divided into Nazi-collaborators and Resistance fighters.

And like so many other countries in Europe invaded by the Nazis, your neighbor, friend, or family member could betray you to the enemy. Even the King of Norway had fled to London.

William was ready. He always carried his knife and pistol. He would use them if he had to.

Sven returned his long-bladed commando knife, similar to the one William carried, to his pocket.

William knew he needed to be careful with what he told Sven and not let down his guard but also appear to trust him so they could work together. Sven could very well be a double agent and Bluebell didn't know it. William would have to play along. He had no choice but to follow her orders and keep working with him.

"I can take care of myself," William said feeling irritated but staying calm. "You need to stop showing up with a gun or a knife. Have some trust, mate. We're supposed to be partners."

Sven grunted and narrowed his gray eyes which had darkened to the color of a night sky in the Hebrides. "All right," he said. "Let's go back to the safe house. We can't do anything more here tonight. And we're leaving early in the morning for the Orkneys."

They left the dark alley and walked through the village streets to the small cottage on a quiet, isolated lane bordered by tall hedges, their silence broken by a lone dog howling in the distance.

* * *

The next morning, William sat in the kitchen with a cup of Earl Grey—a rare luxury in these times. Bluebell gave him a tin filled with the precious tea on his last visit to the Manor and said, "This may come in handy."

Rations had tightened even more by 1943, after four years of war but Bluebell always seemed to have a plentiful supply of food and drink at the Manor. He suspected that the SOE or MI6 had something to do with that. Bluebell also seemed to be a woman of considerable means. The Manor was filled with valuable antiques and Oriental rugs. An unusual-looking and probably, rare Steinway grand piano dominated one end of the combined library-drawing room.

Sven had left earlier from the safe house in Inverness. William was reviewing the maps and mathematical calculations for the mission in the Orkney Islands, north of the Scottish mainland and in strategic proximity to Occupied Norway. The goal was to keep the Germans from invading this island that continued to be a focus of the Wehrmacht. If Britain was invaded, the war would be lost.

The operation required William's navigational and flying skills to not only intercept enemy invasions from nearby Norway but also sabotage fishing boats that had been snatched by the Germans. U-boats and probably, a battleship could be lurking in the waters off the northern coast of Scotland. He would know more after the briefing.

Bluebell had telephoned the night before, after the encounter with Elsa and gave him his orders in her usual curt, succinct manner. He wondered how things were back at the Manor. He knew Bluebell continued to recruit more agents who were trained there and at other estates in northern England and Scotland. Agents were being captured, killed, or disappeared with alarming frequency. Undercover operations were increasing as both sides became even more desperate to win the war. There was an urgency to place more agents in the field all over the United Kingdom and abroad, behind enemy lines.

William thought more about Maddie and how she might be putting herself in danger to find him. He had not received a letter from her in some time, not since the last one saying she had found a way to travel to Europe. How he hoped she would stay where she was—safe in New York. But she had a mind of her own and he knew he couldn't stop her.

Danger was everywhere. This small island comprised of England, Scotland, and Wales was vulnerable to invasion from the enemy on all sides. As he pored over the maps in the gloomy kitchen and considered the directions for the mission, he was startled by a sharp knock at the back door.

William pushed away from the table and stood up as he pulled his pistol out of his pocket then peered out the small window at the top of the door. He quickly grabbed the iron knob and flung open the door, holding his pistol behind his back in his other hand.

It was Angus, the instructor he had met at the art school the night before.

"Guid mornin', young lad. I thought I'd come by and give ye a bit of a tip. I saw yer partner in the pub before ye show'd up at our wee art class. He was talkin' to some other fellas. Take my advice and keep yer eye on tha' un. We dinnae knae who's to be trusted these days. Aye, strange times." As he spoke, his bushy gray eyebrows gathered in an inverted V, almost obscuring his worried eyes.

William responded, feeling suspicious, "How did you know where to find me?"

Angus laughed and said with a wink, "Ach, we're watching all the time, ye knae." He continued with a hint of pride in his voice, "Ye may think we be fools out here far from London and Mr. Churchill hissel'. Ye cannae be sure. We're watchin' just the same and we're doin' things too. We're nae about to be invaded by Hitler and his Jerries." Then he narrowed his eyes more at William and shook his head, saying with emphatic disgust, "Gonnae no' dae that!"

William nodded in agreement and motioned for Angus to enter.

He shook his head and said "Nah, I must be goin'. I know ye have questions. Ah dinnae keen. An' I know ye cannae talk but there's much going on here. Yer mate there may nae be who he says he is. Ach, be careful, laddie."

Then, he said with a wry smile, "Lang may yer lum reek," which William knew from his Scottish grandmother translated into "long may your chimney smoke" and meant *may you live long and stay well.*

Angus then doffed his cap with another wink, turned and disappeared down the lane.

After Angus departed, William wondered even more about this mission, but his orders were that he should keep traveling with Sven to the next point of contact—the Orkneys—and maybe beyond. Or even stay there for a while. Military activity was heavy in the north because of the proximity to Norway.

Angus had confirmed William's doubts about Sven. He would just have to be careful.

He was to meet Sven at the Inverness train station in an hour. He gathered up his haversack with his pochade box of paints, charcoal, pencils, sketchbook, watercolor paper, and small rolled-up paintings, then placed his pistol in his ditty bag beneath his clean socks and underwear packed in his duffle bag and left the house. His commando knife remained safely strapped to his thigh.

Soon after, he and Sven boarded another train. But this time, he couldn't escape into himself with imagined paintings of the sights they passed as they traveled further into the more remote part of Scotland. He sat facing Sven who despite his half-lidded eyes, kept a close watch on him.

After the conversation with Angus in Inverness, William had more questions. Was Sven really there in the alley the night before to protect him? Or for another reason? Had he intended to do him harm but missed his opportunity? Was he reporting every move to German contacts?

But he had to trust Bluebell. She had to know what she was doing. And Hugh trusted her. It wasn't for him to question the mission.

Survival could depend on knowing who was spying for the other side. Part of William's training had included what to do if a German agent or even a British Nazi sympathizer was revealed. Just as he and his fellow aircrew men were also trained to evade the enemy if their plane went down in Germany or anywhere in Occupied Europe and, if captured, how to survive the Gestapo interrogators.

But if captured, death was likely. He knew from briefings at the base and his training at the Manor that Hitler had issued an order that "all opponents engaged in so-called 'commando operations' and 'sabotage troops' are to be exterminated, without exception… the chance of their escaping with their lives is nil."

As the train rumbled rhythmically toward whatever was waiting for them, he bent over his mathematical calculations and maps with a pencil plotting the movements for the mission in the Orkneys—anticipated altitude and speed of the incoming enemy planes and the possible position of Norwegian fishing boats, most of which were now controlled by the Germans. The mission would involve reconnaissance flights in the Orkneys to communicate intel to waiting Royal Navy destroyers and prevent an enemy invasion. He might return afterward to the base for more air raids over France and Germany or to deliver agents and supplies. Orders constantly changed and anything could happen. He was getting used to the uncertainty.

But William hoped that soon he would be able to go back to the Manor. He thought about the paintings he had been working on there.

Then he surprised himself with the thought that whatever he had to do, he was not afraid to kill if that was necessary. Never before had he believed this possible. But this was different than the night bombings over Occupied France with the inevitable innocent casualties. Things had changed with the events of the past few weeks which included the dead agent on the Highlands.

* * *

The Cotswolds, England

While William was traveling further away from Maddie—to the Orkneys and to unknown dangers close to Occupied Norway, she had been working on her own plans. Maddie was even more committed. She felt exhilarated with what she had done.

Before arriving at the Manor, she had phoned her mother from the train station in Moreton-in-Marsh, saying she had reached Cardiff and that Priscilla's parents were there to take her to their country house in northern Wales. She felt guilty that she had lied. But she had no choice and she didn't want to be distracted with worrying about her mother who was now on a train to Edinburgh to spend some time with her brother Hugh. She was glad she hadn't told her about what had happened with Robert that night on the ship. It was best that she did not know.

In the drawing room with a fire glowing in the immense stone fireplace, Maddie and Lady Braithwaite-Smith sipped their tea and eyed each other quietly. Neither of them paid any attention to the plate of golden tea biscuits that had been brought earlier by the woman who seemed to be the housekeeper for the Manor. Maddie hadn't eaten anything since before leaving London that morning but she was too nervous to be tempted.

After all these months, Maddie could not believe she was finally meeting the mysterious woman William had mentioned in his letters.

The older woman sitting before her was dressed in a mid-calf wool skirt, crisp white high-collared blouse, gray Harris Tweed jacket, pearl earrings, and dark green rubber gardening boots that somehow put together looked quite elegant on her. She had removed her brown leather gardening gloves and placed them on the small antique rosewood table inlaid with mother-of-pearl, next to her chair. She spoke in an educated, upper-class accent.

"Madeleine, is it? Such a lovely name. French, is it?"

Maddie nodded and said, "Yes, on my mother's side."

"Excuse my appearance, my dear," Lady Braithwaite-Smith said with a gracious smile. "I have just come in from the garden. I knew you were here and didn't want to take the time to remove the Wellies," she laughed, almost girlishly, making Maddie feel a bit more at ease.

Her face became serious and her penetrating gaze told Maddie that she was not likely to miss much, despite her almost chatty tone.

"Still much to do preparing for winter—covering the rose bushes with burlap bags and such," she said as she looked out the window. "You know it can get frightfully cold here in the winter. Well, at least for a few weeks. But it's not inclined to be nearly as blustery and snowy as New York," she paused, her sharp blue eyes catching Maddie's look of surprise. With only a slight hint of warmth, she added, "I know a great deal about you."

Maddie held her breath waiting for more.

"I understand from Hugh—of course, that would be your Uncle Hugh in Edinburgh," Lady Braithwaite-Smith eyed her closely as she spoke, "that you were determined to leave your studies in New York and try to find your husband William who is in the RAF. I know you are quite an accomplished pianist and have come to England to perform at a number of concerts."

She bent down to remove the green gardening boots briskly, then put them aside and eased her stockinged feet into expensive-looking but worn leather pumps next to her chair. Maddie thought they had probably been placed there by one of the Manor's staff who moved about quietly behind the scenes.

Lady Braithwaite-Smith then re-crossed her legs with a sigh. Every movement was measured and careful, and yet she seemed unconcerned with her appearance. Maddie noticed a smudge of dirt on one of her cheeks.

Lady Braithwaite-Smith gazed at Maddie thoughtfully then said with what seemed to Maddie as possible consideration for her feelings, "But of course, I can't reveal anything about William's whereabouts or what he might be doing. I know you have come a very long way, indeed. And in such dangerous times. However, I'm really not sure how I can help you."

She appeared genuinely concerned but quite firm in her reticence to offer any assistance. *Or was something else on her mind?*

Lady Braithwaite-Smith slowly sipped from her forget-me-not flowered china teacup, continuing to watch Maddie closely. She noticed the battle of conflicting feelings that crossed the younger woman's lovely face.

Maddie felt angry and anxious that she might not be able to find out anything about William's whereabouts but she knew she had to keep pushing. She had confronted strong women before—Madame and her mother, in particular. She could be a force to contend with and she was not going to give up now. She felt a flush in her cheeks and a sudden bristling of fine hair rising on the back of her neck. She had not traveled halfway around the world to be thwarted—to find out nothing about William. It was quite impossible.

Maddie's heart pounded and her stomach tightened but she spoke confidently, "I will do whatever is necessary to find William."

Lady Braithwaite-Smith considered this and hesitated a moment before she responded, "Well, Maddie, I can see that you are quite determined. All I can say is that William is on a mission. There may be a way for you to help us though. And then it might be possible for you to see each other."

Maddie gasped quietly but didn't respond, not wanting to reveal her rising excitement.

Maybe her plan would work after all.

Then Lady Braithwaite-Smith said, "But first, you must call me Bluebell."

Part III

San Francisco, California

Spring 2014

I sat at a bistro table shaded by a red Parisian café-style umbrella in the small courtyard behind our Victorian house in Pacific Heights in San Francisco. A heart-shaped koi pond with a miniature waterfall and two gurgling pedestal fountains where yellow-crowned finches splashed and dipped their tiny wings provided welcome relief from the unseasonable heat of an early Spring day.

My marine biologist husband had designed and installed the garden and pond a few years before. A light breeze from the bay in the distance occasionally lifted the fans of palm fronds surrounding the pond. Periwinkle blue, white, and pink hydrangeas, as well as rose bushes heavy with *Julia Child* buttery yellow, *French Perfume* cream and fuchsia, and *Scarlett O'Hara* vibrant crimson blooms, flanked the gray flagstone patio. High stucco walls espaliered with magenta bougainvillea and fragrant night-blooming jasmine blocked out the sirens and steady hum of traffic from the streets nearby.

Since returning home to California from Toronto, I had more time to think about Uncle William's letters and other clues that might help to uncover how he had disappeared. I had found my grandmother's photo album hidden away in the back of my father's closet in his new apartment where he moved after my mother died. Some of the small black and white pictures were faded, sepia-toned, and shadowy—especially old pictures of grim-faced family gatherings.

Others were still crisp, clear, and ageless—especially those of William and Maddie. They were smiling broadly, arm in arm at a train station and in another photo—walking on a city street—Maddie in a wide-brimmed hat, pleated skirt, and fitted short tweed jacket, laughing as she looked at William with adoring eyes. There was another photo of Maddie smiling coyly as she sat on a lush lawn, her slim legs hidden under an elegant off-the-shoulders long full-skirted gown. Her dark hair curled over her shoulders and her dress spread out around her like a beautiful flower.

The last letter I had that was written by William was dated February 1944. Although he had apparently been a prolific letter writer while stationed in England, I had only a few of his letters—all written to Auntie. Where were the rest of the letters? They were poetic and filled with descriptions of what he was painting and where he was traveling—the Highlands, Edinburgh, Glasgow, and London—and how he was visiting galleries and cathedrals and attending concerts but never with any mention of war. He wrote of the beauty of the English and Scottish countryside, tea at the Manor, evenings spent writing letters by the fireplace, and his paintings—as if he were on vacation. It seemed to me that this was unusual for a bombardier.

A former World War II gunner who had walked into my sister's art gallery a few months before had shared his experiences during missions over France in the days leading up to D-Day, one afternoon with us at her seaside house on the Sunshine Coast of British Columbia. He confirmed that RCAF and RAF aircrew during the war did not have lengthy leaves or travel around the way William described in his letters.

Something else surfaced that made me wonder. Evelyn Waugh's novel, *Brideshead Revisited* became a piece of the puzzle. When I was in high school and looking for extra linen napkins for my mother's dinner party, I discovered an old, dog-eared copy inscribed with Nana's name, tucked away in a stack of neatly folded embroidered pillowcases, delicately crocheted ivory tablecloths, and a few piano and opera vinyl records. I held onto it through all my moves across the country for college and teaching jobs. I recently re-discovered it again buried in my collection of novels and books covering my interests in art, European history, philosophy, and psychology.

Nana was William's mother, as well as my grandmother. My mother said she died from a "broken heart," nine years after William disappeared. I never knew her. According to William's younger brother, Uncle Teddy, Nana believed William had survived the war but had somehow vanished. She thought he may have been injured so badly that he had lost his memory and wandered around Europe not knowing who he was. She checked the newspaper at her neighborhood store in Toronto every day, desperately searching for his name in the list of survivors returning home.

I was re-reading *Brideshead Revisited* in my backyard, thinking there might be a connection to William. Why did my mother keep this book of my grandmother's and no others? Brideshead, an estate not unlike William's

Manor but in Oxford not far from the Cotswolds where William spent most of his leaves, had a central role in the novel. The narrator of the story left his studies to be a painter.

William was apparently stationed at York at least some of the time – 160 miles from the Manor in the Cotswolds – yet was able to frequently spend time there. There was no obvious explanation for why he traveled so freely when he was supposed to be on bombing missions.

Had my grandmother been drawn to this novel because the story centered on an estate in the English countryside, one like the Manor in William's letters and photographs? And it was published in 1943—the year that William was stationed in England. The narrator in the story returned to Brideshead, a beautiful country estate, when it was used for World War II operations just as the Manor in the Cotswolds might have been used.

I began to wonder if the Manor that William wrote about might have been used to train agents. I knew many other manors throughout the UK had been used for such purposes during the war.

In Nana's photo album, there were many pictures of William with an older woman, labeled in my grandmother's handwriting, *Lady Braithwaite-Smith at the Manor*. She never smiled and was dressed elegantly but eccentrically in old-fashioned hats, gloves, suits, and long coats. Many of the photos showed only her profile as if she wished to avoid the camera.

I also wondered about Maddie. What had happened to her? All I knew was that she was a concert pianist and had traveled to England during the war.

Besides long-forgotten family artifacts surfacing, other strange things had started to happen.

My sister Lauren had started to paint dreamy Turneresque landscapes. She hadn't painted much since she was in her 20s. She wasn't sure why she had become so preoccupied with painting landscapes in the style of an early nineteenth-century pre-Impressionist English painter. At the same time, I discovered William's letters.

Later, while painting a scene from Uncle William's sketchbook from when he was stationed in England during the war, Lauren noticed two parallel smudges as if two fingers had scraped diagonally on the canvas in front of her—disappearing into a dark doorway in a foggy landscape of a village. Another painting she was working on, of her young son playing at the shore of a lake had instead become a child who looked like William. He was looking over his shoulder at the viewer while a dark, foreboding storm gathered behind him. As much as she tried to re-paint her son's face, William's reappeared.

On a trip to research the Juilliard School of Music in New York, I had lunch at the Palm Court at The Plaza. A long, black hair appeared (unlike my own which is reddish-blond) on the immaculate white tablecloth not once but twice and then, later that evening, in the white porcelain sink in the bathroom of my hotel room. Maddie had long black hair.

I started noticing 1940s era cars with small porthole back windows, huge round headlights, running boards, and curved fenders that appeared on city streets and freeways, with uncanny frequency. One day, a gleaming ivory vintage sedan with a license plate proclaiming "1941" cruised by. Another night, I went to a restaurant to have dinner with friends where the parking spaces were numbered so that payment could be made at the machine nearby. When I peered down in the darkness to the pavement, there was the number— "1943."

I put down the book and began to read one of William's letters again—sent from the Manor rather than the base, so it had arrived uncensored.

Dear Auntie,

I have Chopin's piano concerto #1 playing beside me on our gramophone. This is what Maddie was learning when I left. Where did we get a gramophone? Well, that's quite a story. I was invited to our pilot Hank Wiley's place—his family's actually—in Shrewsbury this last weekend. Three days. It was quite wonderful. We brought it back with us, as well as some very good records to play—classical music and swing.

Thank you so much for sending the paints, charcoal pencils, and sketchpads. I seem to be going through it all very quickly! There is so much to paint here.

I think being in New York helps Maddie to be less lonely. Most of her friends are there and she is busy. I believe Madame is pleased with her progress. Her music does make her happy.

I want her to be as successful as she has always been. I still worry about her trying to travel to England. That would be such a bad idea.

Any leave I get, I go to the Manor where Lady Braithwaite-Smith lives. I paint as much as possible when I'm there. It is only two hours journey by train from the base. I have made a good friend in her cook too, which is very important!

Many people here have to keep up their homes on their own—country estates that once were quite grand. I spent one afternoon painting on the grounds of friends of Lady Braithwaite-Smith, an older couple, who live nearby. He looks after acres of grounds. She carries on, keeping up their rather rambling old mansion and cooking for the two of them. I had tea with them one day last week while I painted. The splendor of the old days around us was rather sad. One can see the unbeatable spirit of the English. I have also painted in Chipping Campden, a beautiful medieval village near the Manor— especially a magnificent cathedral there.

I will have some leave in a couple of weeks. I plan to go back to Scotland then spend the rest of the time at the Manor. I have started a large watercolor of the village and surrounding countryside. I am anxious to finish it. There's so much to sketch and paint, the country being rich in old Tudor villages and churches and color. I've done some awful stuff but I think I'm improving.

It is nice to have a roaring fire to sit by in the evening. You would love the fireplaces here at the Manor. There is one in the kitchen, but the one across one wall of the drawing room library is absolutely immense. Lady Braithwaite-Smith sometimes reads and we discuss art or listen to music. My home away from home. No nightlife but exactly what I need.

The gardens were quite beautiful this summer. They surround the big stone house and there is even a large lily pond, a rock garden, and a gazebo. Until a month or so ago, Lady Braithwaite-Smith would work in the garden and cut flowers for the house while I painted. As the days grow colder, she is often in the greenhouse tending to her orchids.

I'm so sleepy, I'm afraid this is becoming incoherent. Coming back from Shrewsbury, the other night by train, a dense fog held us up and the trip took all night. I'm not fully recovered. I swear I didn't sleep a minute but I'm told I did.

Hope you and the rest of the family are well. I write to Mother, Dad, and sister Lily but I don't hear from them very often. I expect they're all very busy. I know I shall be when I am home with my dear Maddie. How far away that seems, right now.

Until the next time. With all my love,

William

William's words called to me from a distant place and time. The letters were hidden for 70 years and discovered only when my great-aunt's cedar chest was finally opened. Pandora's box.

The small unsigned painting I had found in my mother's chest of drawers—in the same distinctive style of other work by William I had seen in my parents' house was hung with a cream, linen matte and dark, cherry wooden frame in my bedroom. It was the first thing I saw when I woke up each morning. Was it a study for the large painting he referred to in his letter? A large tree with a broad dark-colored trunk and vibrant burnt orange foliage leaned toward a golden road winding off into the hills. The road disappearing into the distance reminded me of how war makes people disappear.

An estimated 60 million people died or vanished during World War II. The violence and trauma of war had impacted millions more, through thousands of years and countless wars. World War II was only 20 years after the war that was supposed to *end all wars*. I thought about the effects on the generations after the conflicts ended and how it must have changed them—just as our family had been forever changed by the war and the tragic loss of a shining spirit.

Tears burned in my eyes as I thought of all the girlfriends, wives, husbands, fathers, mothers, sisters, brothers, daughters, and sons left behind. And war still continues in so many parts of the world. So much suffering.

I hoped that I would discover how William had vanished. More and more of his art might be discovered. I decided I needed to travel to the Cotswolds and see if I could find the Manor.

Suddenly, my cell phone rang, interrupting my thoughts. A Toronto phone number appeared on the screen. I picked it up, thinking that there might be a family emergency and answered with some trepidation. An unfamiliar voice at the other end—trembling yet strong, said, "I received your letter and I would love to meet with you."

It was Charlie, William's best friend and Maddie's older brother who was now in his 90s.

I had found him on the internet. Just about anything could be found there. Maddie was no longer alive. But I had discovered a Toronto newspaper article of an interview with Charlie and his wife on their 70th wedding anniversary. My sister found his address in an old court document involving a break-in at a neighbor's house and Charlie had been a witness. He and his wife still lived in the house where they had spent the last 60 years. I sent Charlie a letter, proposing that we meet on my next trip to Toronto. And now he was calling.

He said with palpable warmth in his voice, "I am so glad that you are trying to find out more about what happened to William. I may be able to help you."

Chapter 20

Thurso, The Northern Highlands, Scotland, December 1943

The train trip from Inverness was uneventful. William managed to doze for only a few minutes since he had to keep an eye on Sven. The visit from Angus was on his mind and added to his worry that he and Sven might not be on the same side. He reviewed mentally where his weapons were and how easily he could get to them. His commando knife in the metal-tipped leather sheath was strapped on his thigh, within easy reach. His pistol was in his duffle bag but he could quickly get to it, if necessary.

A radio and other SOE equipment would be waiting at the room arranged for them. He met Sven at the station in Inverness before boarding the train for Thurso, the most northerly point of the Scottish mainland and the closest point to the Orkney Islands. Sven thrust a wireless telegram in William's face, muttering, "It's from Bluebell." He would read it on the train.

They had been told that the mission was less likely to be discovered with them traveling by train rather than flying from the base at York or the one near the Manor. German agents were closely monitoring flight activity but not the trains—as far as they knew. The rhythm of the train and constantly changing scenes of the rugged beauty of the Scottish Highlands drifting by as he looked out the fogged-up, rain-splattered window, distracted him from worrying about the op or where Maddie might be.

William wanted to believe that she was still in New York and that her letters suggesting dangerous plans were just wild fantasies. He hadn't heard from her since her last letter that arrived at the Manor shortly before he left. But it had been written several weeks before. His letters to her were uncensored as long as they were sent from the Manor. If sent from the base, words would be crossed out with a thick black pen or cut out so the letter resembled a piece of paper lace. He hadn't been in the Cotswolds since leaving for Islay. Bluebell had instructed him to not send letters home when he was on the mission.

It was strange and disturbing to not have contact for so long. He tried hard each day to communicate to Maddie with his thoughts—*I'm alive and I will return. I love you with all my heart. You must wait where you are. I will come back to you. Stay strong.* But he had to stay focused on where he was and what he was doing or he could end up dead.

He unfolded the telegram Sven had given him and quickly read the latest order from the Manor:

Must move quickly. stop. Enemies everywhere. stop. Immediate action needed. stop. See Iona at Pie Shop Main Street Thurso. Full stop.

As always, Bluebell was a woman of few words.

* * *

The train station in Thurso was modest but welcoming with two long wooden benches in the small waiting area that looked to William like they had been there for 100 years. It was empty except for a lone ticket agent wearing a small green plastic visor that shaded his eyes. He was holding the earpiece of an old-fashioned phone and speaking in a gravelly voice that had probably been made more so by local whiskey.

He said to the caller, "Aye. The next train fer Inverness be at 9:05 in the mornin'. That is if it be on time. Cannae tell fer sure. Ye never know, these days. None more 'night, chappie."

William knew trains could be unreliable, especially in this part of Scotland. It reminded him how isolated they were and how difficult it might be if they had to leave in a hurry. Luckily, there were several airfields in the Orkneys where they could get a plane and he could fly one if necessary. But right now, they had to find the pie shop.

A train station attendant wearily swept the platform as they left the station. They walked past a few other passengers—mostly workmen who were roughly dressed, carrying lunch pails and looking like they had arrived for jobs in the nearby shipyard.

Two young mothers who seemed to know each other, held their tousled, drowsy children by their hands as they disembarked and pulled them along the path away from the station. As they hurried by, the women spoke urgently to the children, "We best be quick or we will miss our tea. Aye, ye know how yer grannie is about havin' her tea on time."

William thought as they walked on toward the town, how lovely it would be if he could have tea right now with Maddie as she played the piano.

He remembered a night together in her apartment in New York before he had to leave for more training. He sat near her sketching while she practiced scales and tedious studies then transitioned into a sensuous Chopin prelude and Liszt concerto. Her profile was serious as her slender but powerful hands rose above the keyboard and stretched across octaves, playing flawlessly with single-minded concentration as the music filled the room. She then played a particularly difficult Prokofiev concerto ending with a loud bang and winked at him playfully, smiling the way he could never resist. She rose from the piano bench and leaning over him, took his hand that had been holding his sketchpad in place and gently coaxed him toward the bedroom, closing the door behind them.

She began to slowly undress and put a record on the phonograph, the words of the song coming back to him—*let's get lost… celebrate this night we found each other… let's get lost in each other's arms. Let's get lost.*

They made love as if it were their last night together. Streams of golden moonlight through the paned French doors leading out to the terrace illuminated the length of their entangled bodies. As if they were on a stage performing an act of love, but only for themselves.

They lay nude on the flowered coverlet, glistening with sweat as their tongues met in a rhythmic dance of intense passion. They caressed each other with rising desire, William's mouth on Maddie's breasts as she held him firmly against her, stroking his hair. He arched over her, loving all the angles of her face and all its expressions. They moved together in unison—slowly at first, taking joy in each other and then with increasing urgency.

Maddie moaned, "Don't stop, William. Please, don't stop," until they finally reached an ecstatic release.

He had thought, how can I leave Maddie? What am I doing? He had wanted the night to never end.

Sven coughed, breaking the silence between them and dissolving William's bittersweet memory. He reluctantly returned to the present and northernmost Scotland as they walked toward the village of Thurso.

The memory also reminded him of how he had given in to his father's pressure to enlist in the RCAF. He could have stayed in Canada and served in some other way like Maddie's brother or his father. But then he thought, I have made the right choice—to become a Special Ops agent.

Even if it means returning eventually to bombing missions. Bluebell had not given him any idea of when this mission might end.

Remembering that night with Maddie filled him with sadness and longing. But he was even more resolved to do what he could to end this horrible war so he could return to her.

With artist eyes, he took in the narrow two-story stone houses rising up on both sides of the narrow, curving road. The afternoon was unusually warm for late fall and had brought a few people out to enjoy the rare sunshine. A woman in a green polka-dot dress and bright yellow cardigan pushed a pram on large, thin white wheels, steering carefully over the stone-cobbled road then disappeared down an alley. A bearded man carrying a basket filled with potatoes and turnips, walked briskly past a grandmotherly-looking gray-haired woman with stooped shoulders, who held the hand of a small girl and clutched a bulging burlap bag close to her chest.

Life seemed to be going on without perceptible interruption by the war or suggestion of the clandestine activities of the Royal Navy supposedly taking place on the nearby Orkney Islands.

He thought that regardless of what he was here to do, he would have to find a way to sketch the picturesque village streets of Thurso and then the ancient Earl Patrick's Palace near Kirkwall in the Orkney Islands—ruins of a Renaissance castle built almost 400 years before—by a royal scoundrel who was an illegitimate and unrecognized son of King James V. He had engaged in a reign of terror but created a beautiful estate in this remote part of Scotland.

As they walked on, William saw a small shop attached to other stone buildings, with a weathered sign over the doorway revealing the barely legible words, *Robertson's Pie Shop*. As they entered, a tiny bell tinkled a greeting quietly above them. Enticing aromas rose from the warmth inside reminding him that he hadn't eaten anything since before they left Inverness.

A plump, rosy-cheeked woman with lively green eyes stood behind the counter wearing a white apron and a loose net over her tightly curled bright red hair surrounding a wide strip of gray roots at her crown, betraying her wish to look younger with the help of hair dye. She handed a white pie box tied with string to a young man wearing a cap lowered over his face. He avoided eye contact with any of them and muttered, "Thank you" under his breath before he quickly left the shop.

She glanced at William and Sven, raising her eyebrows slightly and smiled; showing a few missing teeth.

William said, "Iona?"

She nodded and said, "What took you so long, laddies?" She beckoned to them to follow her to a room in the back of the bakery, saying over her shoulder, "I have something I think yous may want. Then ye'll be off to the Orkneys."

Chapter 21

Edinburgh, Scotland

The sky was a brilliant coral streaked with wispy ribbons of vivid orange and pale-yellow clouds over the towers and spires of the stately Balmoral Hotel. Some darkening clouds in the distance threatened an evening storm—a regular occurrence in Edinburgh. Rachel glanced up from her writing as the train slowly pulled into Waverley station. She gained comfort in knowing she was far from London.

The horrible scene played over and over in her mind. Robert falling onto the tracks, his head crushed. Accusing eyes staring at her. She told herself again, *I was only trying to protect Maddie.* Not to kill him, no matter what he may have done.

Rachel knew her daughter well enough to know that something had happened to Maddie involving Robert, but she wasn't sure what it was. She had acted instinctively with dire consequences. She wondered if she really was so damaged by her childhood that she could kill someone. *Are those feelings dormant within me, just waiting to erupt if my loved ones are endangered?* She shivered and tried to shake off the guilt she felt. *No, I'm not a murderess.* It was an accident. But she still wondered.

While she wrote in her notebook on the trip from London, she half-expected that at any one of the many station-stops, a uniformed policeman would enter her car and announce, "Madame, you are arrested for the murder of Sergeant Robert Horton of the Royal Navy. Come with me now. It will do no good to resist." But amazingly that hadn't happened. Writing calmed her and helped her make sense of her feelings without having to share them with anyone else.

After the train crushed Robert's head, the crowd around her seemed to be moving in slow motion—oblivious to what had just happened. Then suddenly, a woman began screaming. Had she seen Rachel before she rushed away?

Several men began shouting, "Police, police! Over here! There's a man on the tracks!" A station officer ran past her, blowing a whistle but not noticing her. As she looked back, a crowd of concerned citizens not yet so weary of the war as to ignore another sudden violent death gathered at the edge of the platform.

Rachel tried to push the scene out of her mind. A constant sense of approaching disaster had often accompanied her through each day for most of her life. Then she would remind herself of her comfortable life, her two beautiful children, and a loving husband. Her son Charlie who had just turned 21, was a Naval Officer with the Royal Canadian Navy and for now, safely stationed in Halifax. She thought, maybe someday after this terrible war is over, he might fulfill his ambition to become a physician. He always had a passion to help sick people. She never really understood that. The sight of blood made her nauseous and dizzy.

And then she thought of Maddie. Her headstrong, talented daughter who caused her so much trouble but often reminded her of herself. The sight of her bleeding and in pain on the ship crossing the Atlantic still haunted her. She knew how much Maddie had wanted that child.

Art and music were things she understood. She felt awe for those who could create beautiful things. She knew how dedicated Maddie and William were to their art. It wasn't common in these times. She had painted earlier in her life before she married and for a while after she had children, when not much more than a child herself. She had always longed to be an artist like her sister Cate but she knew she didn't have the talent for it.

Secretly, she shared Maddie's rage that William was fighting in this horrible war instead of safely working as an artist in New York. She thought of the beautiful sculpture William had made of Maddie and him—their faces side by side, cheeks caressing – before he left for England. There had been other sculptures—graceful figures of naked men and women in various poses and also, busts that were often ironic and clever in their subtly humorous resemblance to family members. She hoped he kept sketching and painting his watercolors no matter where he was.

Rachel doubted that any of them—Maddie, Charlie, or William—knew how much she loved them. She knew how difficult she could be but she had her reasons. Despite the frequent joys of her life, there were demons and memories that she fought with every day, especially now.

She thought of the nightmare that regularly tormented her. Her mother, then her brother Hugh, then her sister Cate, then her husband, then her children—their heads blown apart by a gun or a bomb. It always ended with her trying to put their exploded brains back into their skulls. As she awoke from this reoccurring dream in a cold sweat and tried to shake its terrifying grip, she would relive the horrors from her childhood—her mother's brutal rape, her father's anguished cries, the explosion of guns, her mother screaming, and finally, silence.

Then she remembered splashing at the shore of some lake on a summer's day, with her brother, Hugh and sister, Cate—the sun glistening on the waves that gently rose and fell, eventually ending on the shoreline. Hugh patiently taught her to swim, showing her how to hold her breath and leap into the waves. A playful black-and-white spaniel barked happily, darting in circles around them and nipping at their heels as they tossed a large red-and-white beach ball. Cate sat on the beach sketching on a pad of drawing paper, her brow furrowed, curly hair unruly and wild, and long legs crossed underneath her.

Those were happy times despite her father being gone. Her mother always seemed shadowy in these scenes—present but often sitting apart, reading a book and glancing up occasionally to make sure they were safe. These fond memories often came to her late at night or when she thought about family as she was now, thinking about seeing Hugh.

As the train entered Waverley station with its vast domed glass ceiling built in the 1870s and covering 12 adjacent tracks, next to the majestic Edwardian Balmoral Hotel, she glimpsed her tall, handsome, dark-haired brother smiling and waving from the platform. She felt immediately uplifted, seeing him there waiting for her. She could almost believe she had just arrived on holiday and not that a devastating war was raging on. She thought of cousins, aunts, and uncles in France and Germany who may have been sent to relocation camps, never to be heard from again. She wanted to do whatever she could to help—short of knitting socks—since she was here and Maddie was safe in Wales.

"Look at you, Sis! I say, you are a sight for sore eyes!" Hugh shouted over the clamor of the other passengers reuniting with loved ones. The train released a loud hiss and a huge burst of swirling steam engulfed them as she flew down the steps from the car to the platform. They rushed toward each other—Hugh with outstretched arms and Rachel balancing her handbag, train case, and matching brown leather-trimmed suitcase. She was expecting this to be a short visit and had left her steamer trunk at the hotel in London. Despite Hugh's steady, serious gaze, he laughed with delight as he swept her into his arms.

She thought, how lucky I am to have this strong, smart older brother. Maybe now, things will be right.

* * *

A few hours later, they were sitting in Hugh's bright, spacious kitchen in his flat in the Georgian New Town area of Edinburgh, having tea, oatcakes, rare Devonshire cheese, and potted meat arranged on plates by Hugh's wife. She was an accomplished violinist who had left earlier to rehearse with her string quartet for a concert later that evening. Neither of them ate much. They were too engrossed in talking about Maddie's concert in London, the war, rations, and the spare details of Rachel and Maddie's ocean voyage from New York.

Rachel thought about her daughter's sudden miscarriage and how worried she was about her. Then she saw Robert fall onto the railroad tracks and felt herself starting to panic. She told herself again that his death had been accidental. She forced herself back to the present, knowing she couldn't share any of these thoughts with Hugh.

She studied her brother's face as he sipped his tea slowly and seemed to ponder something. Hugh's dark hair with slightly graying temples was still as thick as ever but the lines around his eyes and frequent lapses into silence suggested that more was going on with him than what he was willing to share. He looked older than the last time she had seen him in 1941, a few years before. He had been in Washington and took the train to New York to see her and Maddie. Britain was seemingly on the brink of losing the war. He was involved in some official business with the American government that he was not free to discuss.

Hugh said with some hesitation, "I'm not sure how to tell you this, but I think you should know. Maddie is not in Wales, Rachel." His gaze met hers and he frowned as he spoke, then took her hand knowing how the news would upset her.

Rachel looked at him with alarm. "What do you mean, she's not in Wales?" she asked, not believing her ears. "That can't be, Hugh. I saw her off to Cardiff!" She stared at Hugh with disbelief.

Hugh took a deep breath and sat upright as he swept his hair back from his forehead. He rose to fill the tea kettle with water and placed it on the stove to make a fresh pot of tea, then sat back down facing Rachel. He repeated more firmly, "Maddie is not in Wales. I can't tell you much more. But I can say this, she is still in England. In the Cotswolds. She thinks she will find out where William is and convince him to go home. She could be—," his voice trailed off.

Before he could say anything more, Rachel interrupted, "Hugh, that is ridiculous. You must be wrong. How could you know this?" She studied her brother's face more closely and understood he was holding many secrets. What he had told her already may have been a violation of some sort. "Why would Maddie go to the Cotswolds—of all places? Why would she lie to me?"

Rachel put her hands over her eyes as if to block it all out. She felt herself fighting competing emotions—anger, sadness, fear—all mixed-up and battling within her. And probably another Maddie-induced pounding headache would soon begin to infiltrate her being. She was starting to feel dizzy as if she might faint.

"Hugh, please tell me what is going on," she whispered as she searched his face.

"Rachel, Maddie may be getting herself into some trouble. I can't tell you how I know this." He took his sister's hand then said carefully as he met Rachel's eyes. "I'm sorry, Sis. I shouldn't be telling you this much." He paused, then added quietly, "Maddie may have found a way to try and find William. But she could also be putting herself in great danger. It might not be possible to stop her. It may already be too late."

Part IV

Like water through your fingers,
All the best things in your life.
Are you waiting for a little break in the clouds,
Praying for sunlight?

Saying, oh, how long will it take till it doesn't hurt?…

Even when the sun goes down on,
All the things you thought would last so long,
It's alright, life is still beautiful.

Life Is Still Beautiful
The Orange Lights

Spring 2014

I was flying to London on a 787 floating soundlessly on carpets of cotton-ball clouds and listening to a song that reminded me that despite pain and loss invading our lives at an agonizing rate, there is joy and beauty all around us. I loved these times of drifting stress-free 35,000 feet above the ground – thinking, imagining, and often writing for hours. I flew frequently so I had developed a routine of installing my headphones immediately after settling into my seat, sometimes listening to music while I wrote. Other times, I enjoyed the noise-canceling silence. I seldom watched movies shown on tiny screens that just put me to sleep. Long flights took me away from the steady stream of emails, incoming texts, and phone calls and at home, the jubilant *I'm-so-glad-to-be-on-duty* barking from our obstreperous, adolescent Labrador retriever.

A writer-filmmaker friend in Edinburgh who embraced life with boyish excitement had shared the music I was listening to, by an English group that had the gift of Lennon-McCartney lyricism buoyed by U2 rhythms and harmonies, on a road trip through the Scottish Highlands.

He thought nothing of walking 15 miles of busy city streets from Beverly Hills to Venice Beach on a hot July afternoon and swimming nude in icy streams of Scotland in the pouring rain.

We can find love and joy wherever we are, if we just open ourselves to the experiences that are all around us. Life is still beautiful. Even in the face of destruction, cruelty, and loss.

William's letters had appeared when I most needed to be reminded of this.

I continued alternating between journal notes, research, and thinking about William and Maddie. Two glasses of California Pinot Noir with dinner had long worn off. I had no interest in sleeping and signaled the flight attendant approaching in the aisle, for a cup of black coffee. I listened to my playlist of Chopin, Massive Attack, Red Hot Chili Peppers, Gotan Project, Bruce Springsteen, The Cranberries, XX, Rachmaninoff, and Lady Gaga while I wrote and read. Beethoven's Emperor Concerto was also a favorite when I needed to feel a connection to the piano keyboard while I typed on my iPad.

The other passengers seated around me slept on, huddled under their blankets as I read the *World War II Secret Operations Handbook* co-written by two senior lecturers at the Royal Military Academy Sandhurst. I studied the maps and drawings of covert operation strategies—how to land safely after a parachute jump, how to feign an illness or *throw a tail*, how to conceal a knife in the sole of your shoe, how to alter your appearance with various disguises such as dressing like a farmer or darkening your hair with charcoal powder, how to forge documents or attack a sentry, the contents of a railway sabotage kit, combat techniques, and other clever tactics. Agents 70 years ago didn't have the advantages of all the technology of the twenty-first century but they certainly didn't lack ingenuity.

I had such mixed feelings after meeting with Maddie's brother, Charlie, in Toronto, who told me more about William and Maddie. How I wished I had known them both. I also had to admit to myself the sense of injustice I felt that Charlie had survived the war and lived a long life but William had not—or so we believed.

Charlie was elderly and frail, confined to a wheelchair by the window in his stately red brick house on the lake. I thought about our conversation that afternoon. His mind was sharp and he was generous with his time, saying with disappointment when I finally had to leave for the airport for my flight to London, "Do you have to leave already?"

He told me how devastating it was when William vanished.

"He never wanted to be like his father," Charlie said quietly after we hugged tightly like long-lost relatives. I held back the tears as I prepared to leave. His bright blue eyes followed me with a sharp intelligence as I clumsily packed up my notebook, photos, and William's letters, not wanting to leave this gracious man who had loved William and was so eager to talk about him.

"You know, he was quite an artist," he said as if he really wanted me to understand something important. He struggled with the words as his eyes filled with tears. "Sensitive and spiritual, you can be sure. How I miss him." And then his tone changed but still held deep affection. "He was tough too. When Wills was mad at you, you knew it." His eyes twinkled.

I sat down again on the chair in front of him, feeling the urgency in his voice to tell me more.

He said with a wry smile, "Once, William stopped talking to me for a week when I teased him a little too much about his crush on my sister, Madeleine, after they met at the lake." Charlie slapped his knee and laughed with a wide smile, his face lighting up with pure joy. I laughed with him, enjoying the moment, grateful for a glimpse into the person my uncle had been.

Charlie also told me how talented and headstrong his sister had been. "Yes, she was quite the handful for my parents. But my mother was certainly a match for her," he chuckled. "Boy, did they have some rows!" he said as he smiled at the memory.

He wasn't able to tell me much about how William might have disappeared. He just said, "We never knew for sure what happened. There were different theories. But it was the French Resistance who told his family that he had vanished." His face became serious and sad at the memory. I hadn't heard this before.

As I was leaving, he gave me a small book with a faded, worn cover, saying, "This was sent back to Maddie with William's other effects when he disappeared." I had put it aside as I packed and left Toronto for England.

I thought now about all the demands in my life and how grateful I was to have a break from teaching, the research lab, and the endless, dreary faculty meetings of academic life. Even my book editor who was hounding me for revisions of my latest writing project couldn't ruin this trip. I was traveling back in time to another part of the world to learn more about my lost uncle and maybe discover more of his story.

A life-size painting of William in his RAF uniform dominated the wall of the main staircase in Charlie's house. I hadn't noticed it when I arrived. But as I was leaving, it literally stopped me in my tracks and I couldn't move. He looked so alive. I suddenly felt overcome with emotion and grabbed onto a railing to steady myself as my eyes met his.

I knew that the portrait had been painted in 1943 by Charlie and Maddie's Aunt Cate who had lived in Scotland. The background was a rich deep crimson. She had painted many portraits including those for royalty but never before with a red background. William sat for the portrait when he traveled to Oban and painted with her but then left suddenly. She told her family she felt something terrible was going to happen to him. When she finished the portrait after he left, she had been unable to avoid painting the color of blood behind him.

For nearly 70 years, this painting had hung on a wall of the main staircase leading to the upstairs bedrooms of Charlie's house, where he passed it numerous times a day and Maddie saw it whenever she visited her brother. As I thought about how much William had impacted Maddie's family and mine, I felt the almost tangible pressure of a gentle hand on my shoulder— encouraging me to keep going. I shivered a little with the sense of being watched.

I felt a surge of excitement thinking about my plan to take the same journey by train that William had taken to the Cotswolds—to the village where he had spent so many of his leaves. Would I find the Manor? Would it look like the photos? Would I learn more about William and what might have happened to him? And what about all the paintings that he described in his letters from the Manor? Where were they?

As the plane began descending toward Heathrow, beams of light appeared in the rosy glow of the sunrise—reminding me of the possibility of more discoveries.

Then I reached into my carry-on bag and pulled out the small book that Charlie had given me. I had carefully placed it inside a plastic bag then wrapped a cashmere shawl around it. The words, *Royal Canadian Air Force FLYING LOG BOOK for Aircrew other than Pilot* were written on the faded cover. I slowly opened it and turned the fragile pages. I read the entries still clear in black and blue ink and signed in William's distinctive handwriting. I was overwhelmed with the honor of holding this part of William in my hands. I thought about how far this book had traveled.

It was his log of training flights and bombing missions. I held my breath as I absorbed what had been recorded on the now yellowed pages. It began with certificates showing that William had qualified as an "Air Bomber" (Bombardier)—"high level" on April 20, 1943. All his training courses were recorded—free beam tests, gunner, bomber, and navigation—with 58 bombs dropped during the day and 37 at night. I wondered what he was thinking as he completed the training and prepared to go to England—knowing that there was no turning back. And he might never return.

Entries of "ship recco" (ship reconnaissance) for 13 hours and bombings 6 hours in late July 1943 somewhere in Europe, then a gap—no missions recorded again until September. October entries included a 4-hour night cross-country flight, several 6-hour and 5-hour cross-country day flights and bombings noted but not specific locations—34 hours of flying at night that month. Numerous specialized trainings were recorded; all graded with high marks. Charlie told me that he had been part of an elite aircrew.

I turned the next page and couldn't believe what I saw. There were no further entries of bombing missions until February and March 1944—72 hours of night flights, 164-day flights. *A gap of almost four months between October and his next entry? Where was he and what was he doing in those months?* I knew this meant that for whatever reason, he had not been on bombing missions because if he had been, they would have been recorded in the logbook. He had written about many leaves in his letters during this time. I could only guess that he had been involved in something else—not bombings.

April 20 – *ops* to Terngier, April 22 – *ops* to Ottignies, April 24 – *ops* to Dusseldorf, April 25 – *ops* to Karsruhe, April 26 – *ops* to Villeneuve, then more *ops* to Finniere, Aulnoye, Acheres, Marsalines, Lens, and Bourg-Leopold. I knew from my research that 'ops' meant *operations*, but they could also be special operations flying at low altitudes to drop agents and supplies for agents behind enemy lines. What were these missions and did they relate to his disappearance?

I started googling—thanks to the plane's wi-fi—the locations of the places I didn't recognize and noting the distances William would have flown for each mission. All the flights were in Belgium, Germany, and France before D-Day.

The last entry was written and signed in red ink by Officer Spencer and dated June 2, 1944—*Missing O-(*over) *Trappes, France*, which according to the map I studied was 16 miles from Paris.

Chapter 22

The Manor, The Cotswolds, England, November 1943

Maddie opened her eyes, yawned, and stretched across the four-poster bed in an upstairs guest room at the Manor. She had slept soundly which surprised her. But then, she thought, it is because I am finally getting closer to finding William. She knew bombings were occurring nearby in the surrounding countryside. One of the most disastrous sites had been at Coventry, a mere 50 kilometers from the Manor. The cathedral was partially destroyed and from the conversations she had overheard on the train, she knew many lives had been lost. There had also been reports of German planes being shot down even in this deceptively quiet part of England.

London was frequently under attack, while coastal areas throughout England and Scotland were also threatened with possible invasion. It seemed that nowhere was safe, but strangely, she felt reassured here as if unseen forces protected her.

There were a few stubborn embers glowing in the stone fireplace leftover from the walnut logs that had burned through the night filling the large bedroom with a woodsy scent and keeping her warm while she slept. She could scarcely believe that she was here—finally. With Lady Braithwaite-Smith who had taken William in. She now knew her by the code name, *Bluebell*.

Maddie felt breathless at the thought of finally seeing William. Some people might think she was crazy for what she was doing. She knew differently. She had made the impossible a reality. Besides, she had come so far.

Was this the room where William slept when he was here? The thought of him sleeping in this same bed thrilled her. She felt herself becoming aroused at the thought of his slim, muscular body wrapped around her. She could easily imagine him here in this room. That made her skin tingle and sent shivers through her body. She felt his fingers gently caressing her body. The familiar yearning swept over her as she imagined their bodies intertwined, finally together sharing their love.

She reluctantly left this luxurious dream-state, feeling that if she allowed herself to stay there, she might not ever be able to pull herself away to face whatever Bluebell might propose. She rose from the bed pulling a plaid flannel robe from a nearby chair and put it on, then opened the door to find a tray with tea and toast. She thought about the previous evening as she sipped her tea.

After a somewhat unsatisfying conversation with Bluebell in the drawing room, she had pressed her more over dinner. She had gazed longingly at the beautiful grand piano in the far corner of an adjacent room, facing a window overlooking the garden. They sat at a long, candlelit cherry dining room table, undoubtedly used in the past for large dinner parties, over shepherd's pie and dry sherry—the latter giving her more courage to ask what she needed to know.

Shepherd's pie was a dish that she had always thought of as a wretched concoction not even worth its name. But now she understood it was a typical British dish in wartime, like soggy fish and chips or overcooked boiled potatoes and mushy peas. This one was especially unpleasant with more watery mashed potatoes than stringy meat and a layer of what, no doubt, was corn from a tin, all immersed in a tasteless gravy. But she was too anxious to feel very hungry. The fresh warm home-baked bread accompanying dinner was delicious. She could imagine eating a loaf of it with a wedge of English cheddar cheese. But not with that horrible greasy, petroleum-tasting margarine that masqueraded poorly as butter. Another reminder of the war. For a moment, she fantasized about how wonderful a large piece of warm cherry pie à la mode would be right now. Like the pie that she and William had often shared at Frankie's Diner, a favorite spot of theirs on Broadway in New York.

The conversation over dinner hadn't been as focused on what the plan might be, as she had hoped. Nothing the older woman said was clear or straightforward. Maddie was impatient to find out more about what she could do to find William. Bluebell seemed to be intentionally trying to distract her—alternatively formal and a bit mysterious then telling her detailed stories of country life before the war while also alluding to times in London—maybe a childhood and possibly adolescence spent there. Bluebell spoke with a dry wit, sometimes leaning forward, studying Maddie's reactions.

Over raisin and cinnamon bread pudding, Bluebell commented, "You are such a contained young woman. I'm sure that comes from performing on stage." She continued with another story, then abruptly interrupted herself, "And it will be so pleasant finding out more about you," she said enigmatically. Bluebell seemed to look right through her then added, "We will get to know each other very well, indeed."

A chill crawled slowly up Maddie's spine to the base of her neck. She also noted that as Bluebell spoke, she kept an eye on the shotgun propped up in one corner of the dining room.

It was obvious that unlike many women of her generation, Bluebell had the benefit of an extensive education. Through the remainder of their candlelit supper, she digressed into lengthy discussions of literature revealing a wide-ranging depth of knowledge of Chaucer, James Joyce, T.S. Eliot, Dylan Thomas, Virginia Woolf, and others. Maddie guessed she had attended nearby Oxford University or, possibly, Cambridge University since she seemed to know many of the literary figures she mentioned who had studied at Cambridge. She knew women had become full members of Oxford in the early 1920s after women's colleges were first established in the late nineteenth century. Maddie was engrossed in Bluebell's stories and impressed by her sharp intelligence.

Maddie was unsure of what she might be agreeing to but she was not going to turn back from her goal. Despite the possibility that she might see William soon and knowing she would agree to just about anything if it would bring her to him, her chest tightened and she felt the familiar knot in her stomach that was often there before a concert. Her hands started to feel cold. She shifted her weight in her tweed travel suit that was scratchy against her skin as she became increasingly more nervous. And still there was no mention of William.

Maddie had wanted so much to make a good impression. She tried to think of her conversation with Bluebell as another performance requiring her to remain calm and sure of herself. But a second glass of sherry had left her light-headed.

Finally, at the end of dinner, Bluebell said, "Let's have our tea in the drawing room."

They sat by the crackling fire in the immense, cavernous stone fireplace that extended the entire width of the room. The same fireplace that William had written about in his letters. According to Bluebell, it had been built with the newer part of the house that had been added in the 1700s to the original sixteenth-century farmhouse—a somewhat smaller but still stately structure with its timber and stone walls and low ceilings. She glimpsed the beautiful gardens and sweeping lawns from the library where she sat earlier.

There was a grand piano at the other end of this room, one that Maddie had recognized as a rare model of circa 1870s burl wood Rococo style Steinway. It appeared to be in perfect condition—gleaming in the candlelight. How she would have loved to play it right then!

She knew that it had probably been built in Hamburg, Germany, if not in the factory in New York City. How ironic that this beautiful instrument could have originated from one of the very centers of violence and cruelty that had turned the entire world into destructive chaos. She could barely keep herself from approaching it and playing some Schumann or Chopin to calm herself and return to a place where she felt most at home.

She had made a decision back in New York. But she was starting to have second thoughts. *Was there another way? This is crazy, I'm twenty years old. What do I know about spies? What am I getting into?*

She wondered about Uncle Hugh and how he had arranged for her to meet Bluebell. She was willing to do whatever was necessary if it meant seeing William. She could manage her fear. She had before—many times. She had survived Robert's assault on the ship and the miscarriage. Both events had changed her and made her more determined. She could do something to fight back in a different way—help others and, at the same time, not feel like a victim.

She thought about all the strong people in her family including her mother and grandmother, and great-grandmother who had provided refuge to her mother and her family in Paris at the beginning of World War I when they had escaped from Germany. She knew Jews were being targeted by the Nazis. But since her family had converted to High Anglican after World War I, she hoped her secret would be safe. Maybe she could become an agent and that could bring her closer to William. She had heard of spies being recruited in unusual places and in unlikely ways.

She knew she was out of her depth with this smart, intimidating older woman who seemed to have plans for her. Yet, Bluebell continued to obfuscate. She hadn't revealed anything about how Maddie might be involved.

Maddie became increasingly more impatient and uncertain as Bluebell continued to speak in code and sipped her tea, "There are things going on now that will help us win the war but not necessarily in ways you would imagine.

You could find yourself in some very difficult situations. Are you ready for that?"

At that moment, Maddie wanted to jump up and shout, "Please, Bluebell, tell me where William is! I don't care what I have to do to see him!"

But she remained on the soft, floral sofa facing the fireplace and took a deep breath. It wouldn't help to lose her temper right now. Maybe she could both find William and do something worthwhile—more meaningful than giving morale-raising concerts. The thought had crossed her mind before. She had heard of female spies being able to do things men couldn't. What a frightening but thrilling thought!

"Maddie," Bluebell said interrupting her musings, "I know you must be wondering what I might suggest that could bring you closer to William. He is on a mission right now but you might be able to help—and also see him. There would be training involved, of course. And you must know there is likely to be a great deal of danger."

Bluebell paused as if waiting for her to object then went on, "There are German agents and Nazi sympathizers everywhere, even here in Britain. William is working with the SOE—the Special Operations Executive – in connection with the RAF. When he returns, you might be able to see him. Although, we're not exactly sure when that might be." She said this without emotion then paused to give Maddie an opportunity to comment.

"I will do anything if it means seeing William," she said firmly while fighting back tears. The sherry was fortifying her. "I haven't seen him in almost five months." Maddie's tremulous voice rose as she spoke more forcefully, "What is he doing? I want to take him home! He doesn't belong here."

She knew she had said more than she intended. She tried to calm herself. With great effort, she kept her hands clasped in her lap although she wanted to stand up and do something—confront Bluebell or stride over to the piano and play something loud and dramatic.

Bluebell just looked at her with her piercing agate-blue eyes and said, "You will have answers to your questions. All in good time. For now, we must retire for the evening. Tea and toast will be brought to your room in the morning, promptly at eight o'clock. We will talk again after that."

Maddie was then shown to the room where she had spent the night and was now trying to gather her thoughts. She re-played the previous evening again in her mind as she bathed in the claw-footed tub in the adjoining room, then dressed in wide-legged, grey-flannel trousers, and a long-sleeved cream silk shirt with a narrow black leather belt accentuating her small waist. She hoped that she exuded Katharine Hepburn-esque confidence and grace. She would have to convince Bluebell she knew what she was doing. She was ready for whatever Bluebell had planned for her.

* * *

Thurso, Northern Scotland

William and Sven spent the night in a quaint inn after picking up the package from Iona at Robertson's Pie Shop. They shared a meal of meat pies, chips, and warm beer in the small lamplit room, exchanging only a few words about the plans for the next day.

After the long train trip from Inverness, William hadn't minded the long periods of silence. Sven still bothered him—he was sullen most of the time, and when he spoke, there was usually an undertone of malice.

But William was too preoccupied worrying about Maddie to think much about Sven. From what Hugh had told him, she might have found a way to follow him to England. She could even be at the Manor. He worried about what this might mean.

Sven made tea after their supper and studied a map in the dim light. They had then opened the box they had picked up at the pie shop. William wasn't surprised to see the plastic explosives, detonator, and other equipment they would be using. They examined everything until they were satisfied that they could go ahead with the plan.

Then Sven grunted and announced curtly, "We'll be up early to plan the job. Then we'll be on our way." Without another word, he turned out the light, stretched out on his cot and turned toward the wall.

Still sitting at the table on the other side of the room, William wanted to sketch to calm his nerves. But he knew that would only invite ridicule from Sven. He wondered why Bluebell had arranged for them to work together. Hopefully, after this mission was over, he would never have to see Sven again.

Chapter 23

Orkney Islands, Northern Scotland

Someday, when I'm awfully low
When the world is cold
I will feel a glow just thinking of you
And the way you look tonight...

> Yes you're lovely, never ever change
> Keep that breathless charm
> Won't you please arrange it?
> 'Cause I love you
> Just the way you look tonight

As the ferry chugged slowly toward Stromness in the Orkney Islands from Scrabster on Thurso Bay at the northernmost point of the Scottish mainland, William sang some of the words of the 1936 song, *The Way You Look Tonight* along with Fred Astaire and whistled the rest. It was playing from a loudspeaker above the deck where he stood against the railing, keeping an eye on Sven who stood on the other side of the boat staring at the water below, smoking a cigarette.

William remembered the warm summer evening he and Maddie had danced to this song at the Pavilion on the lake where they first met. The night sky was filled with brilliant stars competing with the sparkling lights strung above the outdoor dance floor. They held each other at first tentatively then more closely as they raised their heads together and gazed upward at the sudden periodic gifts of celebratory shooting stars.

Maddie wore a long navy-blue jersey dress—the fabric gathered at her waist in gentle folds descending over her slight body, suggesting her budding curves and contrasting against her golden skin tanned from leisurely afternoons on the lake.

He knew then that he was falling in love with this brilliant, beautiful girl. They both had been staying with family and friends at cottages on Kahshe Lake for a blissful month of swimming and canoeing. Even the famous Jose Iturbi who had nurtured Maddie's precocious and rare talent had spent time there with her and her family. She often told William that these times on the lake were an idyllic escape from all the intense studying and concerts in New York. But he also knew how much she loved the excitement of the city.

He thought of the afternoon when he first met Maddie. William and her brother, Charlie, a friend from school who coincidentally spent summers there, were diving off one of the cottage docks and racing to rocky islands across the lake. He was stunned at the first sight of her.

Glamorous in a wide-brimmed straw hat and sunglasses, she waved to them as she sat on the edge of the dock in the dazzling sunshine. She wore a turquoise crop top and white shorts that showed off her tanned midriff and slim legs as she swung them back and forth over the shimmering water. Despite her long, shiny dark hair curling on her shoulders, and red lipstick, he could tell how young she was.

She called to her brother, "Charlie, it's time for lunch! Daddy will be leaving soon for the city. Mother says you must come now!" Her insistent, cheery cries across the water suggested a young woman with a strong personality.

As they raced each other back to the dock laughing and splashing, Charlie yelled to his friend, "Don't get any ideas, Wills! I saw that look on your face. She's just a kid!"

Three years later, he and Maddie were married and Charlie was his best man and almost as happy that day as they were. The sunny wintry afternoon in February was darkened only by the shadow of his frequent trainings that took him away from Maddie and his inevitable departure to the front line in Europe.

As the boat approached the port of Stromness on the windswept rugged coastline of the island with its jagged rocky cliffs, he gazed up at the ominous dark clouds gathering on the horizon and threatening a sudden downpour. A jeep arranged by the joint commanders of the Royal Navy and RAF units stationed in the Orkneys was waiting for them at the dock. As soon as the boat reached it, they were met by two young men who didn't identify themselves but were also SOE agents. He and Sven jumped into the back of the jeep and drove off as rain started to fall, and they pulled out rain gear from their haversacks.

* * *

The Cotswolds, England

Maddie narrowed her eyes as she stood in a field near the Manor and squeezed the trigger—the bullet hitting the target but wide from the center. She sighed with frustration and pushed her bangs impatiently from her eyes.

"*C'est non mauvais, ma chérie , Mademoiselle. Pour cette une jeune fille.*" The thin, dark-haired man encouraged her as he stood to the side of the target of a human figure nailed to a tree then walked back to Maddie and demonstrated with his own pistol. Switching to heavily accented English, he smiled and said, "You just need to, you know—" and paused. With a Gallic shrug, he said, "*Jusque pense il est un très mauvais homme*—you know someone not good—you not like very much."

That was not difficult for Maddie. The tall French agent was called Serge, which probably was not his real name. He had been assigned to teach her how to use the weapons of the SOE for work with the French Resistance and other underground movements in Occupied Europe.

He commented as he demonstrated a better stance, "This is the way you do it, Madeleine."

"Oh, for God's sake," Maddie muttered to herself. Feeling more and more frustrated, she thought, how am I ever going to be an agent? *I'm just not good at this.* Then she sighed and adjusted her position, holding the Ballester–Molina .45 more firmly with both hands. She pictured Robert and the night he assaulted her on *The Princess Sofia.* That helped—as she aimed again and shot—hitting the crotch area of the figure on the target.

"Good shot!" Serge laughed. "And you will get better, *ma cherie.* Believe me, you'll need to make *amis* with that one as soon as possible," he said, gesturing at her gun.

Maddie knew very little about Serge except that she was to complete the weapons and parachute training with him. She wasn't about to correct him for addressing her as *Mademoiselle* and tell him she was a married woman. She had learned already that the less the agents knew about each other, the better. She squeezed off another shot, this time a little closer to the head of the target.

"That's it, *chérie!* Take another shot. Then we'll work on some hand-to-hand combat. *Merde.* You learn *rapidement, mademoiselle,*" Serge said and shook his head appreciatively.

Maddie shot the pistol again and smiled as she felt herself improving. But it was frightening to think of the possibility that pistol practice and shooting a gun in a real situation could injure her hands. She had always taken great pains to protect her hands and wasn't about to be careless with a gun or handling explosives. As she prepared herself for the next exercise, she tried to put that worry aside.

"You have the… how do you say? The knack! You've—*Je ne sais quoi*—you 'nailed it,' ha! *N'est-ce pas? Bien sur!*" Serge chuckled gleefully, looking pleased with himself at his use of English slang. Then he said more seriously, with admiration, "*Vous avez un talent naturel—merveilleux.* We will do more practice *demain. Maintenant, plus de travail, mademoiselle.*" He nodded toward the barn where she would learn more about how to protect herself and practice hand-to-hand combat with the enemy.

* * *

Maddie sat at the grand piano in the drawing room and played Chopin's Piano Concerto #1. She had practiced it every day when she was still in New York. That seemed so long ago.

She even missed Madame tapping her mother-of-pearl cigarette holder on the edge of the piano to correct her timing as she played. The metronome was never enough for Madame. Then she played Beethoven's Moonlight Sonata. Both pieces matched her melancholy mood and apprehension for what she would be facing soon. The sun began to set as the pale rosy November light filtering through the paned windows faded over the monochromatically gray and brown gardens. Their abundant dry blossoms suggested the promise of another season of vivid color in a few months.

She wondered where she would be by springtime. Lost in her thoughts as she played, she quickly transitioned into modern swing songs and ballads, then sang *Wait Till You See Him.*

As her fingers danced dramatically over the keys, she imagined that her voice was rich and redolent of heartfelt emotion like Ella Fitzgerald's. She remembered the evening in a smoky Greenwich Village jazz club where she,

William, and some of her Juilliard friends had heard her for the first time. Their laughter and lively conversation had ended with Ella's first perfect notes. None of them could believe what they were hearing. Maddie imagined herself in a long, slinky gown singing at a piano in a noisy, smoke-filled cabaret. The thought made her smile.

Suddenly, she felt a quiet presence in the doorway leading to the dining room and looked up to see Bluebell.

"That is beautiful, Madeleine," Bluebell said with approval in her voice. "I understand the training is going well. I think you will be ready soon for your first mission. You have quite a nice voice. That may be helpful."

Maddie stopped playing, wondering what she meant.

"Another week and William may be able to return here—if all goes well. We will have a better idea shortly. We will know more tomorrow." A small enigmatic smile emerged on Bluebell's patrician face then disappeared just as quickly as she turned and walked away.

* * *

The Orkneys, Scotland

William and Sven ran in the darkness toward the fishing boat as it was approaching in the harbor at Kirkwall.

William had crept out earlier before Sven woke and sketched the Earl's Palace near there as the sun rose over the abandoned though magnificent ruins. He had to get away from Sven even for a short time. When he returned, there had been a telephone call from Bluebell.

She hinted that there might be a possibility of him seeing Maddie soon. But how could that be? He knew that Maddie was capable of all sorts of things. *Is she at the Manor? That's impossible.* He didn't dare hope that she could have pulled off such a feat. It was too dangerous.

But a part of him longed for it to be true. As much as he could imagine sweeping Maddie into his arms, he wouldn't be distracted from the mission.

The large Norwegian boat that they knew from their intel had been sequestered by Germans and was being used to transport enemy agents, began the docking process with ship hands tossing ropes to waiting dock crew. He and Sven hurried around the side of the ship out of sight from the other men and quickly jumped across the narrowing gap onto the slippery deck of the boat's stern, then ran toward the metal stairs leading down into the hold where they were to plant the explosives.

They were there to prevent Nazi agents from coordinating an invasion into Scotland. British agents in Thurso and Inverness had given them information about this ship and its intentions—to ultimately orchestrate the arrival of enemy troops from the remote Orkneys to the Scottish mainland and on to England. This could not happen.

As soon as this mission was completed, they were to join other RAF crews and fly from the Orkneys over the North Sea to bomb German carriers heading toward Scotland from Norway, as well as any U-boats in the area. What they had been ordered to do here—blow up the boat and kill enemy agents—was only one step in a series of carefully orchestrated plans by SOE agents and the RAF. Churchill was intent on both intercepting any potential invasions by enemy forces and convincing the Germans the Allies were going to invade Occupied Norway.

William followed Sven toward the bow where they would find the electrical control panel of the carrier and set the bomb.

Then Sven suddenly turned and pointed a pistol at William, "There is more to this, mate, than meets the eye. Come with me now and maybe you won't get hurt." He gestured with his gun for William to move ahead of him.

Chapter 24

Edinburgh, Scotland

Rachel walked along the Royal Mile in Old Town toward the Canongate Kirk, the parish church of the nearby Edinburgh Castle built in the seventeenth century for the Church of Scotland. The heels of her leather pumps clicked on the cobblestone road with the same determination that she hoped would help her to make a plan. She had to do something to get Maddie back and then return to New York.

A large, weathered gray stone structure with a churchyard filled with eminent dead Scots, Canongate Kirk stood on the central square above the Mound by the National Gallery, not far from Mary Queen of Scots' palace, Holyrood Castle. It was a cold, late November morning that began with a few courageous glimmers of sunshine. She could now see dark clouds gathering in the distance, no doubt bringing one of those sudden Scottish torrential downpours with raging winds that whipped right through one's body and chilled your bones for days afterward.

Earlier that morning, Rachel had decided to take a walk so she could think more clearly. She had dressed in a black wool sheath and a camelhair coat with a mink stole wrapped around her for extra warmth. A black cashmere turban covered her auburn hair that was pulled back into a tight chignon. She always felt better if she took care of her appearance. It was something she had learned from her French grandmother.

Rachel had felt agitated when she woke from yet another restless night of tossing and turning between terrifying violent nightmares. Hugh had already left for work and she wasn't keen to make small talk with his reserved, much younger wife. As she approached the church with its uniquely clear paned windows and Doric-columned portico over the arched heavy wooden doors with handles of iron rings, she felt compelled to enter. At this time of day, it would be quiet and empty—and might even calm her.

Her head was filled with anxious thoughts of what was happening to Maddie and the dangerous path she might be taking. She couldn't imagine how her daughter could forget the horrors facing those in Europe with any Jewish heritage, regardless of how they might have tried to conceal it as her family had done. She had heard of Jews who tried to hide their background and nevertheless were transported to German camps from the island of Jersey near the northern coast of France after the Nazis had invaded. Churchill had decided the small British island did not warrant the use of any military resistance.

Rachel thought about her conversation with Hugh when he took her hand in his and said, "Maddie is in the Cotswolds. She is trying to find William. He often takes leaves there. But she might be doing more."

What did he mean? Could Maddie already have been recruited? Maddie— an agent? *I have to stop her.* Her daughter had a strong sense of justice and hated this terrible war that separated her from William. *But Maddie could be killed!* She looked around the church feeling even more anxious.

And her mother was still in Paris—as far as she knew. She had left England to take care of her own ailing mother there in 1940 just before the German occupation. They hadn't received any letters from her for some time, even though she knew Grand-mere, her grandmother at a still-spry 82 years of age had connections and money stashed away for bribes. Even more useful, she had a wily mind that Rachel hoped was keeping her safe from the Gestapo.

She knew Maddie was worried about her adored grandmother, Ma-mere and her great-grandmother, Grand-mere, who had visited them a few times when they lived in London. Maddie might even try to find them.

Maddie had changed since the Atlantic crossing on *The Princess Sofia*— she was more quiet and pensive. As if she was planning something. She was never one to back down from anything, regardless of how much fear she felt. Even if she was so nervous before a concert that she would rush to the bathroom covering her mouth before going on stage, she would always emerge with a determined smile and say, "So that's done. I'm ready."

Richard always said she was the gutsy one in the family. She suddenly wished her husband was here. He would know what to do.

Rachel had wanted to leave immediately for the Cotswolds after Hugh told her Maddie was there to find William. But he had insisted that it would be safer for her to stay where she was—in Edinburgh. He would try to get Maddie back to London, he told her. Then they could leave by ship for New York. She wasn't convinced.

Hugh's words hadn't reassured her. He said, "I will try to reach Maddie at the Manor and do my best to persuade her that it will do no good for her to stay. She must not go any further with this, Rachel. It could be very dangerous."

As they talked longer, she pressed Hugh more. He had finally warned her as a worried look crossed his face, "You should know something. Agents are being recruited more than ever. And of course, they are volunteering—" he stopped. She knew he couldn't tell her more and was probably thinking about all the agents that had been lost.

She met Hugh's gaze and said with more urgency, "But Maddie is a concert pianist for God's sake, Hugh!"

Hugh sighed as he impatiently pushed back a stray lock of hair from his forehead and quickly massaged his temples, "I know, I know. But if we want to win this war, we need more agents. We need them even more now. But I will see what I can do." He abruptly got up and left the room. A little while later, she heard the phone ring in his library and his voice speaking in hushed tones before he left the flat.

Rachel had some idea what he meant. She heard from friends in New York and only fragments of details since she arrived in England—of the Resistance network in Occupied Europe—espionage of railways and bridges, and agents passing misinformation and decoding enemy messages. She now knew about the Manor. And that Bluebell who Maddie had gone to meet was part of the network of SOE handlers recruiting and managing operatives in the field. She guessed that the RAF was involved because William had been recruited.

She needed to stop Maddie from becoming a part of this. It was one thing for her to try and see William. It was another thing for her to become an agent. She was becoming more frightened for her daughter.

At the same time, she couldn't stop feeling responsible for Robert's death even if he had tripped onto the train tracks into the path of the oncoming train. The gruesome scene of his twisted body kept flashing before her, mixed together with images of Maddie's bleeding body on the ship cabin's floor. She felt horror—as if it was happening all over again. Then she was reminded of hiding under her family's dining room table and hearing her mother's ear-splitting screams, then the gunshots and more screams.

As she entered the majestic foyer of the church, she wondered what her Jewish relatives in Occupied France and Germany would think of her being here.

Rachel shuddered as she thought about how she and what remained of her family had fled from Germany after her father's murder and her mother's violent rape, at the beginning of World War I in 1914. Her parents were targeted because they had organized protests against the local politicians. Paid thugs persecuted Jews—including their family—smashing their shop windows, refusing them goods when they tried to buy food at the local grocer. They arrived in France, starving and filthy, staying first with family members in the countryside near Aix-en-Provence then in Paris with her grandmother through the remainder of the war.

Grand-mere had been so much gentler and more loving than her mother who was often distracted and detached. Rachel understood her mother's trauma. She had her own.

Anti-German sentiment in France after the war ended in 1918, pushed them on to England where her mother's wealthy great-aunt had welcomed them into her home—an Edwardian town house near Russell Square in the heart of literary Bloomsbury not far from where Charles Dickens had lived and the British Museum.

Rachel, her brother Hugh, and sister Cate had been able to finish school there in relative peace. It had been easy for them to pick up English since Great-aunt Charlotte hired a tutor. They adopted a refined upper-crust accent which enabled them to be more accepted into their new life.

Because of her fluency in French and continental flair with fashion—a colorful scarf artfully arranged around her neck and a beret angled over her long, wavy hair—Rachel was assumed by her English schoolmates to be French, much better than to be German in 1918. Her friends at school had been curious but she was able to easily deflect probing questions with stories of walks with her grandmother to the Luxembourg gardens, the Eiffel Tower, and the legendary Notre Dame Cathedral. She smiled at the thought of how they had been enthralled with her tales of warm croissants and *chocolat chaud* in Left Bank cafés.

Her mother said to her three children one day after they settled in London, "You will never suffer again because you are Jews. We need to blend in here."

After months of catechism classes, they became Anglicans—members of the Church of England—spending Sunday mornings at services at the Victorian stone church near their great-aunt's town house. Their mother insisted her brother change his name from Hans to the more English *Hugh* and Rachel's sister, Caterina became *Cate*. Rachel was only 13 by then and didn't fully understand her mother's decisions but she was glad to finally be safe. She understood now—the desire to protect her children.

As she sat in a pew in the center of the empty centuries-old church, she thought about cousins, aunts, and uncles still in Germany and France. More reports were surfacing of Jews being "re-located" in trains to "camps"—tens of thousands and probably more—never to be seen again. She hadn't heard from her family in Germany in a few years and worried they may not have survived. Ships of refugees had been turned back from the United States— passengers denied entry and returned to Europe to certain death. Nowhere in Europe was safe.

And what about her mother who had left London for Paris? Would her papers keep her secret from being revealed? Was she even still alive? She feared the worst.

Rachel knew what it felt like to be hated. She remembered the name-calling and the attacks before her father was killed when they were still in Germany. Jews in their neighborhood sometimes arrived home beaten and bloody.

Once when she and her family were walking home from the synagogue, red-faced, angry men and women in a park with their children playing nearby, began jeering and shouting at them as they tried to pass as quickly as possible—"*Schmutzig der Judes!*" then "*Go back to your promised land!*" translated in her mind from the German. Then loud laughter and rude gestures.

She had forgotten the harsh, guttural words but she remembered the meaning—in a language she still hated. The venom in those voices had stayed with her all these years. The adults and children followed them, shouting and throwing sticks then suddenly ran up to them and spit in their faces. Her parents said as they wiped their faces and walked faster, "Don't show fear. We are better than that" and gently pushed Rachel and her siblings toward home. Her parents kept walking with their heads held high, scolding her and her brother and sister when they wanted to shout something back—especially Hugh who was Hans then.

Later in Paris, children threw rocks at her as she walked to school during the four years they lived there during World War I. After witnessing her mother's rape and her father's murder in their house in Hamburg, she had finally lost her temper. She chased after a boy who taunted and yelled at her in French, "*Sale Kraut fille d'une pute!*" punching him in the face and throwing him to the ground. He fled with a bloody nose. He never came after her again.

She wasn't sure if she was attacked in Paris mostly because she was German or because she was a Jew or because she was both. It didn't matter. Life improved in London after the war.

Rachel met Richard in England when she was 15. He was 10 years older and worked at the same bank in London as her great-uncle. She hadn't intended to fall in love—or what she thought was love—a year later. He seemed like the knight in shining armor she had hoped to find—a kind and protective older man who could keep her safe.

They were married when she was 17 and two babies followed soon after—Charlie and Maddie, in quick succession. Then two more pregnancies ended in sudden and sad miscarriages.

Afterward, her doctor said it wouldn't be safe for her to get pregnant again. She hadn't really enjoyed being intimate with Richard after that. She loved him but the memory of seeing her mother being so brutally raped had stayed with her. She felt a sense of relief in the increasing distance between them and was happy to move to New York to guide Maddie's studies to become a concert pianist. Rachel loved to paint and play the piano when she was younger so when Maddie began to show signs of becoming a gifted pianist, she happily embraced the role of a very involved and enthusiastic stage mother.

After Rachel, Richard, and their children left England for Toronto in 1932, it hadn't been difficult for her to leave again three years later for New York City to spend ten months of the year. She appreciated the comforts of her life with Richard, thanks to an inheritance from his family and his hard work. But she was restless. She never felt completely at home anywhere but could adjust to living in any place. It was an odd way to be but she was used to it after all these years.

Rachel wondered how life would have been if Maddie hadn't been a talented pianist and a star student at Juilliard. If they hadn't left New York for the concerts in London. And now Maddie was in the Cotswolds to find William. A crazy, reckless scheme if ever there was one. She had to stop her.

Although Rachel was angry at Maddie, she blamed herself. She knew she could be controlling and sometimes demanded too much. Her mother had been hard on her at times, especially after all the trauma in Germany. Even if well-meaning, a mother like that could push you to do things that you might not otherwise consider.

Rachel started to feel more agitated, overwhelmed by guilt and anxiety. She was glad to be alone with her thoughts in the darkened, damp church. A few slivers of light shone through the immense clear paned windows—so unusual and austere for a place of worship associated with royalty. She wished the two candelabras lit only for services, on the massive altar facing the rows of empty mahogany pews, could now illuminate and lift her spirit.

The familiar suffocating tightness returned to her chest. Then she felt the trembling throughout her body that often accompanied the flashbacks and waves of anxiety. She was becoming unbearably warm in her heavy coat and fur stole. She started to rise from the pew, thinking *I have to get out of here and get some air.*

Suddenly, a hand with stubby fingers roughly gripped her shoulder and she jumped in alarm.

A low threatening voice in a Cockney accent growled, "Come w'me, girlie. Y' weren't too easy to find, were ya. Ha! And no yellin' 'cause we're in a church, y' know," he cackled, his words dripping with gleeful sarcasm.

She turned around to look into a face she hoped she would never see again.

Chapter 25

The Orkneys, Scotland

William raised his head from the cold metal floor of the Norwegian fishing boat and touched the large bump on his forehead. He felt rough edges of a deep, painful cut that was oozing something wet. As he held fingers in front of his eyes, he squinted through blurred vision and saw they were covered in bright red blood. He wondered if he was going to die right there. He felt dazed and light-headed and was having difficulty remembering what had happened after they jumped onto the boat.

Then it came back to him—Sven pointing his gun—followed by a sudden painful crack against his forehead, from what he figured was the butt of the pistol.

Sven's face appeared above him, his narrowed gray eyes, mean and penetrating.

"So you're coming around then, mate?" Sven sneered as he kicked William hard in his thigh. "Can't have you dying. But I had to do something to stop you. I wasn't going to have you ruin our plan." He paused then said with a smirk in his voice, "As much as I wanted to finish you off… No wonder you lot are losing the war. Well, we need a pilot." Sven's words slid from the pseudo-British accent he had adopted previously, into speaking with greater ease—more Norwegian-sounding with a Germanic edge.

I've been working with a double-agent, William thought. *What a fool I've been! Was I set up?*

There was no time to ponder any of this. He had to do something.

"What plan?" William asked through gritted teeth as he felt another surge of throbbing pain and the beginning of a pounding headache.

Did Sven think he could pilot a plane? He had sometimes co-piloted, especially on bombing missions when they were landing or taking off. He could fly—but landings were another story due to his depth perception problems. Maybe Bluebell hadn't told Sven this? And where was she in all of this? There had been signs that Sven could be a double agent—he had his suspicions but hadn't wanted to believe them.

"I thought we were supposed to be working together," he said, hearing how childish this sounded as he tried to figure out how he could either reach for his knife strapped to his leg or the gun he carried in his trouser pocket.

Sven continued to point his pistol at him and gestured for William to stand up. "Get up or I'll slug you again," Sven threatened, glowering at William, his eyes glittering with malice. "And I need you—so I'd rather not."

William struggled to his feet. Now he understood that it had been a ruse. Sven had no intention of blowing up enemy agents—especially agents he was working with. Or to blow up a boat that could be used to transport more Nazis for an enemy invasion. Sven had come here for another purpose.

William had heard of enemy agents stealing RAF planes in northern Scotland with the intent of bombing the British carriers in the North Sea—some that were attempting to keep Germans from invading Scotland and others on their way to Occupied Norway. He knew the Nazis couldn't keep up with their need to replace planes lost in air battles and had lost staggering numbers of young men, like the Allies. There were high costs to fulfilling a megalomaniac's insane vision.

Some Frenchmen had even been enticed to leave for Germany with the promise of work in factories building weapons and a better life than their dismal one with increasingly more dire shortages, interminable lines for food vouchers, and all the other bleak accoutrements of living in a country occupied by the enemy.

Sven was planning to use him to take one of the RAF planes and bomb their own carriers. William felt a surge of rage—like nothing he had felt before.

As Sven pushed the gun into his back again, something exploded within him. He thought of boxing with Charlie when they were trying to keep warm in frosty winter mornings so he could keep painting near the Don Valley Brickyards outside Toronto. But this wasn't a lighthearted contest with fake punches.

He suddenly turned out of Sven's reach then pulled back his fist as far as he could and smashed it into his face. Sven spun away with a loud groan, dropping the gun, and ducked away from William's next blow almost losing his balance. Sven quickly recovered and turned back to face William and charged with an ear-splitting yell, butting his head hard into William's chest.

William gasped and choked, the wind knocked out of him and suddenly aware that his head was throbbing with excruciating pain.

Then, energized with rage – and fear-fueled adrenalin, William reared up for another blow and ducked when Sven lunged at him. William pulled back his arm, ready to swing a powerful fist into Sven's bleeding face now ugly and distorted with violent anger. I have to keep standing, he thought. *And fight for my life.* He swung again, landing another punch that sent Sven off-balance and swinging uselessly—for the moment.

They had both trained in the same hand-to-hand combat maneuvers at the Manor—to hurt others as much as possible and protect themselves, especially if captured. One of them would have to die—if not now, then later. Agents didn't usually survive once they were captured and tortured. Especially in the hands of the Gestapo.

He wanted to live. More pent-up anger from the last few weeks of working with someone he didn't trust and rage with the war itself, propelled him toward Sven. He punched him hard in the stomach. Sven lost his balance and staggered toward him and the gun that was lying on the floor.

He lunged for it, sputtering and swearing in Norwegian.

William knew this was his only chance. He dived to the floor, landing on Sven as they struggled for control of the long-barreled and lethal Llama Mark V pistol. Their bodies twisted together in a horrible embrace as they wrestled on the floor—both of them gripping the gun.

As one writhing organism, they jumped to a standing position, still clutching each other in a deathly dance without music.

William struggled to push the barrel away from his chest. He could feel that Sven had been weakened by all the punches he had landed. But William knew Sven still had the strength to shoot him. Then suddenly, there was a loud burst of two gunshots. And the dance ended.

* * *

The Manor, The Cotswolds

Maddie stood by the Victorian stove of the kitchen built in the sixteenth century, still rock solid with its low-beamed ceiling and ancient white stone walls. She was boiling water to make a pot of fragrant, restorative Earl Grey tea—so precious in wartime. There was a crackling fire burning in the fireplace darkened by years of smoke, on the wall adjacent to the drawing room that offered only a little warmth in the chill of early winter. No one else was up at this hour as the sun was just beginning to rise and filtered through the trees, then struck the paned windows in streaks of glimmering rays.

Maddie thought over Bluebell's plan. She was to spend time later that morning on target practice and parachute training with Serge, then have another briefing for the mission in Paris. After that, she would pack her things in a large rucksack and be ready to fly from one of the nearby airfields for France, in a day or two when the weather permitted.

But she had come all this way to see William and try to persuade him to go home or, if not, find some way to get him into a less dangerous part of the war.

The tea kettle on the stove whistled. How odd, Maddie thought, it's the same whistle of my kettle back in New York, as she lifted it and carefully poured the boiling water into the china teapot. Then she thought of her grandmother, Ma-mere who had adopted the endearment from her French roots while rejecting the years of living in Hamburg. She was back in Ma-mere's cheery kitchen in her London flat on a rainy day—when she was six or seven years old—before she and her family left for Toronto.

"You must roll out the shortbread like this, Maddie," Ma-mere had said as she carefully handled the thick buttery dough with slow, precise movements. "Never too hard. Always with a gentle touch. Just like in life—gentle but firm is better," she said in her soothing French accent—unaffected by her time in Germany. Then with the edge of a linen tea cloth, she wiped some flour from Maddie's nose. Memories of her grandmother's kitchen, warm and fragrant with the enticing aroma of baking cookies filled her with joy.

Maybe I can find Ma-mere. She might still be in Paris. As she poured her tea, she felt a glimmer of hope and was confident that she was doing the right thing.

Her thoughts turned back to William. *Could this mission bring me closer to him? Will he return to the Manor, before I leave for France?* If she couldn't persuade William to go somewhere safe, maybe they could work together. *What a wild idea!* On the other hand, she knew that strange things were happening. And Bluebell had suggested as much. All the training of the past few weeks had been to prepare her to parachute into France and work with the resistance movement in Paris.

If only she could see William—touch him, share a bed with him. She would do whatever she could to make that possible.

She finished her tea and left the warmth of the kitchen for her room to study more French vocabulary and practice her Parisian pronunciation for the cover she would need.

Then Serge would be waiting at the barn to practice the parachute landing fall and other maneuvers that could save her life.

Chapter 26

Edinburgh, Scotland

"Come with me 'n' no messin' about," the scruffy man in a dingy trench coat, threadbare tweed jacket, and baggy plaid pants growled as he grabbed Rachel roughly by the arm, pulling her from the pew and pushing her toward the large wooden doors leading out of the empty church.

"What are you doing? Let go of me immediately or I will scream for the police," she said brusquely, pulling herself away and speaking with more dignity and confidence than she felt. *Who is this man? What does he want?*

She remembered looking around after Robert had tripped onto the train tracks and seeing this short-statured, stocky man staring at her, wearing the same drab tan trench coat, a five o'clock shadow, and a battered brown fedora. He was smoking a pipe and squinted at her through rimless glasses, his dark weasel eyes boring holes right through her. She had rushed away, hoping he only accidentally noticed her and hadn't seen what had happened.

"Hah! Nicely said, ma'am. But you 'n I know that y'll not be stupi'. Y're gonna pay dearly. Yep. Just hand over the bees 'n I'll forget what I saw. An' I know y're good for it." He coughed and grasped his pipe between yellowed teeth, sputtering, "I hav'n come this far for nothin'."

His cockney accent suited his rough appearance, she thought. *How could I have been so foolish to not realize there might be this man or someone else who might have seen what happened and now wants something?* She sighed and slowly pulled on her black lambskin gloves. Then she turned up the comforting fur collar of her coat to warm her face against the wind as they left the church.

"I have no intention of paying you anything, *sir*," she said with disgust and glared down at him. "You have no idea who you are dealing with." Rachel took a cigarette out of her silver case, managing to still her shaking hands then lit it with an engraved lighter and inhaled deeply. "This is not going to go well for you. I'm warning you, little man."

"We'll see about that, missus high an' mighty. Y're gonna pay. Or else I report to the Cozzer's what y' did to that poor heap of coke. An' I know about y'. Yep, transportin' off y' know where, huh? Yep. I got more' n you, girlie."

Rachel looked at him trying to hide her alarm and realized he knew something about her past and her family—*but how?* He might be bluffing. Jews were deported to relocation camps from all over Europe. She had heard about Ravensbrück, a camp in Germany for only female prisoners—especially those caught working with the Resistance. He could be an informer or a collaborator. She had felt relatively safe in England. She had been far too naïve.

Trying to reassure herself, she thought, Hugh can do something. *I'm sure he has SOE connections all the way to Churchill.*

"You are going to regret this, I assure you. You have no idea who you're dealing with," she repeated. Her mind raced through ways she could get rid of him. For now, she would have to go along with the nasty little man.

As they began walking on the Royal Mile in the morning mist of another cold, damp day in Edinburgh, she tried to calm herself and sound stronger than she felt. Only a few people were out—strolling by on the cobblestone streets while others swept doorways of shops opening for the day. No one seemed to take notice of them—just another odd pair, she thought.

"Haha. Y'know y're gonna pay some bees and honey. And more'n a few ponies. See that pub up yon," he said as he jabbed his finger in the direction of a small stone building with a sign over the doorway indicating it was *The Nag's Head.* "That's where we will do the arrangin', as nice as y' please. The right Royal Navy'd be very interested', I reckon, in what I have to say." He cackled as his eyes darted in the direction of a nearby alley they passed that led to a close below. Despite his words, she could see he was nervous too.

They entered the small, dimly lit pub looking like it had been built in Mary Queen of Scots' time. Rachel glanced around the room.

She couldn't believe her eyes. Hugh was sitting in the corner with a pot of tea and three cups on the table in front of him. He smiled at her startled look and gave her a knowing nod as he extended a hand in invitation to the two empty chairs.

"Well, Mr. Swift. I've been expecting you," he said. "I see you found my sister."

Mr. Swift shrank into his ill-fitting coat, his eyes shifting back and forth around the room then focusing on the door. A fleeting look of fear passed over his scowling face, then was replaced by a stubbornly defiant expression as he sat down slowly with a grunt on one of the proffered chairs, not meeting Hugh's eyes. He put his hat on the table, his face turning a beet red as he took out a bedraggled, stained handkerchief and wiped his brow.

* * *

The Orkneys, Scotland

William pulled away from the immobile body and saw the growing puddle of blood on the metal floor of the ship spreading underneath it. What have I done? But there was no doubt Sven would have killed him after forcing him to fly a plane and attack Royal Navy ships. *Thank God that didn't happen.*

Then he suddenly realized what this meant. He had to find Maddie and warn her that Bluebell might be working for the enemy.

He turned Sven over. He was bleeding from a wound in his abdomen and his breathing was shallow and faint. *He is probably going to bleed to death here, if he's not dying already. I have to leave him and get to Maddie.*

William rushed out of the hold and grabbed the sabotage equipment that he had dropped and ran to the engine room where he attached it and set the timer. He raced up the narrow stairs of the ship leading to the deck and jumped onto the wharf. As he ran for the street, he looked back to make sure no one saw him just as the boat exploded.

He saw an approaching truck and waved at the driver to hitch a ride to the nearby airfield. The truck suddenly screeched to a halt and the driver leaned over to open the passenger door.

William quickly swung himself into the cab and slid onto the seat, hoping he didn't have any telltale bloodstains on his clothes. But he knew he looked beat up.

"Stromness Air Force Base, thank you very much," he managed to say as he tried to slow down his breathing from the run and not appear too desperate. "I've just been separated from my crew. You know, it was one of those nights. A little too much of the grog—and friendly women. A bit of a scrap…" he said with a laugh. Then adding a little local color, "Everyone was up to high doh," he said with a laugh and shook his head hoping he was convincing.

"Ach, yes, mate. I've had a few of those meself," the driver told him and laughed. "Dinnae fesh yerself. We'll get ye there in a jiff, laddie."

They drove off, careening around corners until the airfield finally appeared before them.

William quietly sighed with relief and thanked the driver as he jumped from the truck. He hoped that he remembered how to fly.

Chapter 27

Chipping Campden, The Cotswolds

Maddie jumped onto the big bicycle leaning against the shed behind the Manor where the regal Bentley rested. She thought about how this was the same bicycle that William rode through the English countryside, carrying his paints and spending hours creating his watercolors.

She had seen a few of his paintings in the drawing room on two easels. One was large and dominated the library. She felt drawn to it every time she played the piano. It was partially finished in an almost surreal Turner-esque style—luminous yet dream-like with subdued colors depicting a scene of the village, surrounding hills studded with cottages, a winding golden road, a large tree with contrasting vibrant orange foliage, and a church spire rising above it all. The sky was dominated by billowing pale bluish-gray clouds permeated by narrow beams of radiant, bright light.

This was the painting that William wrote about in his letters. He said he couldn't seem to finish it but he also couldn't stop working on it. He hoped he could finally be done with it. He told her he felt so obsessed with this landscape that he had difficulty working on his other paintings. He kept getting pulled into this one. *As if I could disappear into it*, he had said.

As she began cycling to Chipping Campden, she still couldn't believe William would be there.

Bluebell had interrupted her while she was studying maps and practicing French in her room earlier that morning. She stood in the doorway and spoke quietly, "Maddie, things have changed. William is flying here today. He will meet you at the old Market Hall in Chipping Campden."

Market Hall was the crumbling stone building now vacant but its enduring medieval arches nevertheless made it a remarkable landmark in the center of the village near the Church of St. James also built in the sixteenth century. Bluebell told her William had frequently painted there, so it seemed fitting that this would be where they reunited after almost five months of agonizing separation. But she wondered why they couldn't meet at the Manor.

Her skirt was hiked up to her knees to more comfortably and quickly pedal up the many hills to Chipping Campden. It was not as cold as it had been, although the wintry morning was still chilly. Her breath curled in smoky clouds in front of her as she cycled faster to keep warm.

When she rose that morning, she had wanted to look her best, putting on a long-sleeved cotton white blouse with a lace-edged collar under a lamb's wool cardigan, pleated skirt to allow movement, knee-length Harris Tweed coat, and a red plaid scarf wound around her neck for extra warmth. She had become accustomed to wearing the thick cotton English stockings which she now put on most days for warmth—she never would have thought that possible when she was living in New York. So many things had changed in her life.

She gripped the bicycle handles tightly with her hands protected in soft kid leather gloves as she rode. She was always conscious of her hands—whether they were cold or numb or aching from practice and how she must always keep them safe. Almost as if they were a separate part of herself. She thought about how hard it had been to put her fear of hurting her hands aside when Serge was teaching her to use a gun and a knife. She didn't worry about being hurt anywhere else—just her hands. But she had to be prepared to defend herself. She knew how to kill—if she had to.

The cultured pearl necklace that her grandmother had given her rested in the hollow of her slim neck. She also wore the heart-shaped gold locket on a thin chain that William gave her. It made her feel close to him and now, that thought was about to become a reality. She had taken great care with her makeup—a little mascara on her dark lashes and the Dior *Femme Fatale* red lipstick that always gave her more confidence. She had even sprayed on some *Je Reviens* perfume—how appropriate, she thought—translated as *I return, I come back.*

I am returning to you, William, and you to me, she whispered as she continued to pump her legs with the vigorous muscular strength she had gained with weeks of training—running each day and self-defense hand-to-hand combat sessions with Serge at the Manor. Every day she felt stronger and more prepared. Finally, she was doing something more than just performing for others.

She climbed the long, steep Dover's Hill, anxious to reach Chipping Campden. The narrow country road was lined with tall, skeletal trees that she imagined at other times of the year would provide graceful green canopies. As she approached the top of the hill, a woman a few years younger than herself and dressed in a formal riding habit suddenly appeared, trotting briskly on a haughty young chestnut mare. What a beautiful sight, she thought as they passed each other and nodded in greeting—each of them smiling as if they shared an amusing secret.

This was a pleasant, incongruous encounter for wartime. It had to be a good omen.

As the horse's hooves rhythmically clomped into the distance, she wondered if this other woman was also riding to a rendezvous with her lover. She watched her disappear around a curve in the road, feeling a brief twinge of loneliness then resumed pedaling with increased excitement, anticipating the indescribable joy she was about to experience.

As she passed the now gray hills of early winter, miles of ancient stone fences bordering the rolling fields and sheep closely huddled in small gatherings, she began to feel increasingly breathless and anxious to reach the quiet village which was also the entrance to the three-day walk of the northern Cotswolds. Bluebell gave her an estimated time of late morning for William's arrival. She knew he was flying alone. She tried not to think about how dangerous that could be since he wasn't a trained pilot. He would land near Coventry then take a jeep from the airfield to Chipping Campden.

She pedaled faster, wondering if he would still think her beautiful. She was feeling nervous about seeing him after all these months and what they both had been through. *Will he be different?* She knew she had changed.

Worried thoughts raced through her mind. *Can I tell him anything about what happened on the ship? Should I tell him I was going to have our baby then lost it after I was assaulted?* But they were going to be together for only a short time.

I can't tell him. I just want to hold him and be with him.

Maddie breathed faster and thought about how she would be leaving soon for France. *My first mission.* She had committed to working with the SOE and the French Resistance but she had come here because of William.

She kept cycling with increasing excitement, her legs beginning to feel the effects of the steep hills as she passed thatched cottages and the road leveled off leading into the village.

* * *

Edinburgh, Scotland

Rachel sat across from Hugh and the man she now knew as Mr. Swift, who had brought her to the pub from the church. The man, who was just a short time before so cocky and threatening, cringed as Hugh discreetly held one arm in front of him to restrain him from escaping. She had taken off her coat and gloves since their table was close to the fireplace in the cozy, medieval pub. She held her breath and studied her brother's face. *What is going on? How did Hugh know where to find me? What else does he know?*

"Rachel, I know what happened in London. I had this *gentleman*—" Hugh met her eyes and grimaced slightly at the misnomer as he glanced at the disheveled man sitting across from him—"followed by my people."

In contrast, Hugh was dashing as usual—a gray flannel fedora matching his finely tailored suit, resting on the table in front of him. He had an implacable expression on his face as he said matter-of-factly, "They rang me up when they saw where he was going. We've known about him for some time. He has met others here for similar purposes."

Mr. Swift frowned and muttered something unintelligible.

Hugh truly is good at the spying game, Rachel thought. And what is he planning? She started to tremble despite trying to contain herself and felt her attention drifting away from the scene in front of her. *Stay focused. This is your brother. He can help you.*

"What are you saying? What do you mean *what happened in London?*" she repeated. She wanted to pretend nothing had happened, and she had almost convinced herself that this was true. Robert fell onto the train track. That was for sure. But he had stumbled. She had to believe that—and not that she had pushed him to his death. No matter what he may have done to Maddie.

"No need to pretend, Rachel. It's okay. We had you and Maddie followed once you arrived in London, for your own protection. German agents have been known to kidnap rich Jews in England and demand a large ransom," he frowned with distaste. "I can guess what might have happened on the ship since we now know something about this Robert fellow. He had assaulted women before. His injured leg kept him out of active duty but not out of harm's way when it came to women. There may be others besides Mr. Swift here who know about you," he said, waving a hand at the man now cowering with downcast eyes. "We suspect he's working with enemy agents. They may have followed you."

Mr. Swift remained mute and appeared visibly shaken. He mopped his brow with a forlorn-looking, dirty gray handkerchief.

Hugh turned to her and said firmly but with love, "We need to get you out of the UK. And back to New York. And as soon as possible. And as for this poor sod," he nodded at the increasingly agitated man next to him. "He will be taken care of in short order," Hugh said soberly as he met Rachel's gaze.

"What do you mean, Hugh?" Rachel asked with alarm. "There have been too many deaths in this war already. I can't have one more on my conscience." *And how can I leave, when Maddie is still in England?* She had to find Maddie and maybe with some help from Hugh, even find her mother and grandmother in France.

Hugh spoke quietly, "It will be all right, Rachel," then grabbed Mr. Swift's arm and abruptly pulled him to his feet.

The would-be blackmailer grimaced and squeaked a weak protest—"Don't be grabbin' me, sir! I have rights!" then reluctantly surrendered to Hugh's firm grasp.

Hugh's face was angry and determined as he put on his hat. He patted Rachel's shoulder reassuringly. "Don't worry, he won't bother you anymore," Hugh said to her and pushed Mr. Swift ahead of him toward the door. As they left the pub, he scanned the room to make sure they hadn't attracted any attention.

Chapter 28

Near Coventry, The Cotswolds

William peered through the narrow windshield of the Supermarine Spitfire fighter plane, opaque with fog and offering only a limited view of the winter landscape of rolling brownish-green hills, bare trees, fields of sheep, and rugged stone walls. He rubbed his gloved hand across the window of the cockpit with little effect. He was completely reliant on the panel of four gauges in front of him—fuel, oil pressure, RPMs, and altimeter. He focused particularly intently on the last one, due to his depth perception problem—to keep him from a sudden and fiery landing. He was grateful he had handled the takeoff without a problem.

Landings for any pilots but especially for him were the most dangerous part of flying. He had left the Orkneys early that morning and according to his charts, after flying the length of Scotland, would be landing soon in England. He impatiently wiped away the beads of sweat collecting over crusted blood on his brow where Sven had hit him. This was no time for nerves.

Through a brief opening in the clouds, the outlines of the familiar hills and farms of the Cotswolds appeared. He would soon see narrow lines painted on a meadow below—not really a landing strip but one of the many hastily created airfields scattered throughout the English countryside. He had never flown alone and would have to recall everything he had learned from watching Hank pilot the Halifax. He would be lucky if he could safely land anywhere, much less in the middle of a field without a clear landing strip.

William could barely see through the mist that hung over the airfield near Coventry—20-some miles from the Manor. He had watched for German ground attack planes and jet bombers throughout the trip over the Highlands and into England from the Stromness RAF base. He knew they were frequently sharing airspace and bombing this part of the countryside.

Despite having no more than a few hours of sleep in the last few days, he couldn't afford to lose his concentration. He imagined his father sitting next to him, encouraging him, and saying, "You can do it, William. Just stay steady. Don't rush your landing. Don't let me down, boy." He gripped the joystick more firmly and told himself that maybe, he was like his father after all.

Bluebell had notified the base in the Orkneys that William needed a plane. He knew how dangerous it was flying like this on his own and he might not survive. But he had no choice. He had to get away from the Germans and Norwegian enemy agents swarming in the Orkney Islands. And he was willing to take any risk necessary to see Maddie.

Since he had shot Sven the night before and blew up the boat, all bets were off. He didn't know who to trust. His life was at risk every time they left the base but what happened with Sven had shaken him. To kill someone he knew. Even if it had been life or death—and it could have been him instead.

It felt like he had jumped from the frying pan into the fire. He knew he had changed. No longer could he pretend he was on holiday—painting and touring the Highlands. German agents were probably pursuing him. His time with Maddie would have to be brief.

He forced his attention back to the panel in front of him. He had memorized the altitude and other critical readings for landings and how the needles should be pointed on the gauges in training exercises. Hank was skilled and taught William well when he had co-piloted. They had enough landings together that he had to believe he could do it. He studied the gauges in front of him, knowing his life depended on it.

Other unbidden thoughts interrupted his concentration on the altimeter as he pulled on the joystick. He couldn't help but worry about whether he could trust Bluebell. And Maddie had gone to the Manor while he was in Scotland. Bluebell could be persuasive and Maddie was often fearless but she could be reckless too.

He told Bluebell that he wanted to meet Maddie in the nearby village of Chipping Campden since Sven had turned out to be a double agent and Bluebell was his handler as well as William's. He couldn't be sure that she wasn't also working for the Germans. *If she was, what did this mean for Maddie?* He had trusted Bluebell. She had been so interested in his paintings and shared his love of music and art when she welcomed him into her home back in late summer.

But it hadn't taken long for her to recruit him to become an SOE agent.

Could he trust anything that Bluebell had told him? He knew he might have to report his suspicions about her to his commanding officer at the base if he hadn't already heard about Sven. He might be re-assigned to other Special Ops missions behind enemy lines in Belgium, France, or Germany.

He thought about the numerous enemy planes shot down in the past few months in this same area after the Germans had brazenly strafed Coventry killing hundreds of people. Both sides were becoming more aggressive and taking more chances. The fate of the western European front of the war was probably going to be settled in Britain or France in the near future. But there was so much secrecy. No one really knew. Especially those on the front and in the fight. They only knew what their next mission was and where it would be, not what was going on elsewhere. He couldn't even think about the magnitude of what they were facing.

And it was getting even more dangerous.

The image of Sven's immobile form bleeding onto the floor of the Norwegian fishing boat flashed briefly in front of him. He suddenly felt cold at the thought of what he had done.

But it could have been him who died on that floor. And this was the bargain he had made. *Kill or be killed* rang in his ears. He had to keep his cover and maybe even kill others if he was going to survive. He hated what he had become. But the war had to be won and over. Then he thought, if I can actually land this plane without crashing, I will be holding my darling Maddie. I can do this, cheering himself on while fighting his fears. He smiled at the memory of their last lovemaking. His cheeks began to burn despite the cold air in the cockpit and his heart pounded with the thought of her and the dangers ahead for both of them.

When he rang up Bluebell the night before to tell her he was coming back and Sven was dead, she had told him that a jeep would be at the airfield. He would drive to Chipping Campden where Maddie would be waiting.

He was getting closer to the airfield so he focused his attention on landing the Supermarine Spitfire, trying to stay calm. *Let's see what you can do, pal.* He held his breath, hoping his calculations had been correct. The plane began to shift more in the strong crosswind as he tried to gradually lower it toward the field below.

Then, the wind suddenly pulled the plane even more downward and sideways, making it increasingly more difficult to hold it steady. He watched the gauges on the small panel, especially the altimeter. The needle suddenly swung more to the left indicating that he was losing altitude too quickly. Approaching the ground much too fast, the plane was being buffeted in the strong headwind—first leaning to one side, then the other. The nose began to point down as the plane pitched and yawed—jerking it straight into the wind and dangerously downward.

William pulled up the throttle again with all his strength while holding onto the joystick as hard as he could to keep up the power, desperately trying to bring up the plane's nose before the wind caught it more and he crashed to the ground. He struggled to pull up the throttle more as he used his feet to manage the rudder to control the sideways angle of the plane and bring it up straight as he fought the crosswind threatening to push the plane over.

He felt his hands cramping as he held on tightly to the joystick, knowing this was his best hope. *Come on, you fucker!* William shouted into the air. Then he muttered a brief prayer. Swearing on missions was often followed with an urgent request to whomever was listening. He needed to increase the power as he tried to keep the plane's nose from being pulled and heading downward too fast. Finally, he felt the aircraft steadying. The nose rose up as he brought the plane higher and circled around the airfield. He slowly released his breath. This had been another close call.

As he circled around this time, he approached the landing strip from a different direction to get the nose of the plane more into the wind rather than being caught sideways. This time, he could see someone on the ground waving flags on the landing strip. One wheel touched down first and then the plane tipped at a precarious angle. He pressed one foot on the rudder as he eased up on the joystick and the other wheel miraculously touched the ground. Too warm in his aviator's leather jacket, he wiped off the sweat dripping into his eyes and slowly exhaled his breath he felt he had been holding for what seemed like an hour.

I did it! He thought with amazement, I could be a pilot. He laughed at that. He imagined his father standing there watching and nodding with appreciation at the almost handbook-precise landing, albeit after almost nose-diving to the ground. He could even hear him saying, "That's my boy!"

Then he thought, here I am fighting this war and I still want my father's approval. *Ridiculous. Maddie was right—who was he to criticize me about anything?* His father was giving classroom training sessions and supervising aircraft repairs on the prairie in Canada while he was risking his life. But he reminded himself his father risked his life, flying biplanes solo in the last war.

The plane slowly rolled to a stop. William lifted the glass cover from over the cockpit and jumped out, feeling thankful to have two feet on the ground.

"Hey, William! How are you, buddy? I remember you from the Manor!" A slightly built, amiable fellow around his age, with a brown crew cut and a wide grin, shouted to him as he ran toward the plane.

"Yeah, that was a little rocky but I made it. Good to see you. Sid, right?" William said as he saluted the other man then shook his hand firmly.

"I hate to tell you but I only have a motorcycle—no jeep," Sid nodded toward the motorcycle nearby leaning on an angle on its kickstand. "It was the best we could do—under the circumstances—as we were hit just a few days ago," he shrugged, as if to say, *this is what it's like. Deal with it.*

"Not to worry, mate. That will do just fine," William smiled then jogged toward the motorcycle, jumped onto it, kicked the starter and with a wave to Sid, rode off.

* * *

Chipping Campden, The Cotswolds

Maddie walked the bicycle down High Street, knowing she might be early and that William could still be on his way. Bluebell had told her very little except that he was returning from a mission. She tried to steady herself after the long ride and the excitement she felt at the prospect of finally seeing William. She walked past cottages with thatched roofs, then rows of attached two-story stone houses sitting directly on the cobblestone walkway. Wide wooden doors designed for shorter people of the sixteenth and seventeenth centuries looked at once formidable to strangers and protective of the cottage inhabitants. Very few had any windows facing the street and those that did were concealed by lace curtains occasionally parted to reveal a vase of flowers, a piano, or a sitting room.

Maddie thought for a moment about the lives that were unfolding behind those walls and how many of these houses might have stood here for 400 years.

She could believe that all lives are just dots of light in time. She loved how some of the houses had names inscribed on plaques next to their door—*Molly's Cottage, Twickenham Cottage, Wisteria Terrace* distinguishing them from the rest. She felt somehow reassured that people had lived here long before the war and would hopefully be here long after the war ended.

She walked on toward the medieval market building in the central square— no longer being used but a reminder of the lengthy history of the village. It was a quiet morning with only a few people walking on the street. As she looked ahead, she couldn't believe what she was seeing.

It was the familiar back, the broad shoulders and slim figure she remembered so well. He was standing under one of the arches.

She gasped then began to cry as she broke into a run, shouting, "William! William!"

He turned, a wry grin on his tired face, his bright blue eyes shining. As he held out his arms, Maddie rushed into his embrace murmuring, "I can't believe it. Finally! Oh William, what took you so long?" and she punched his chest lightly, laughing and crying at the same time.

William laughed too, as they kissed passionately, caressing each other's faces. They held each other tightly as they both wondered how long they would be together.

Chapter 29

Chipping Campden, The Cotswolds, England

There was a faint hint of the rosy-golden glow of early dawn through the bowed window framed with sheer curtains and shabby floral damask drapes, as Maddie stirred in the white sheets still fragrant from their lovemaking. She reached out with one hand to the lean, muscular body sleeping beside her. William's closely cropped blond hair was uncharacteristically tousled and his boyish face peaceful, with a small smile just for her.

She was glad he had fallen asleep again after he woke suddenly in the middle of the night shouting, "No! No!" and punching the air. He shouted again something unintelligible and fell back onto the pillows without seeming to know she was there.

Maddie gathered up the threadbare pink chenille robe from the faded chintz chair as she rose from the bed and put it on quickly, hugging it close to her shivering body. The robe had hung like a faithful friend on a hook on the door, perhaps left by a previous guest who had fled in haste or maybe provided by the thoughtful owner of the cottage. There hadn't been time to bring any of her own belongings to the village nor did she care about having them or anything else. Being with William was enough.

She wondered who had been in this room before them. Did they also reunite after a long separation? Or maybe it was a new romance—moments stolen. Or maybe a mother and a child in transit who had escaped from a country strangled by violence and death, who might even have evaded the camps or some other nightmare. She no longer lived in a sheltered world.

Anything was possible in wartime. She had no way of knowing all the terrible things that were happening. But she had heard plenty at the Manor from other agents-in-training.

She left the room and walked down the hall to the tiny bathroom. When she returned, there were only a few embers burning in the small fireplace so

216

she took off the robe and tossed it onto the chair, then eased back into the warm bed, careful not to disturb William as she nestled against him. She felt restless but was comforted watching him sleep.

A soft knock interrupted her thoughts and she jumped up from the bed, enfolding herself again in the shabby robe. She remembered that an early morning breakfast had been promised by the lady of the house the night before—a youngish, brown-haired, congenial widow with bright eyes and flushed cheeks, who carried an air of sadness barely visible beneath her cheerfulness. "I won't disturb you," she had said with a knowing smile. "Just a wee cuppa and toast."

Maddie slowly opened the door to find a thin, long-limbed, pink-cheeked girl who awkwardly held a tray carrying a small pot of tea, china cups and saucers, and toast. The girl handed the tray to her with a small curtsy as if she were serving royalty. Maddie curtsied back, momentarily feeling lighthearted and girlish. She could almost imagine that she and William were here for a week or two on a romantic holiday—and could forget about the rest of the world and all the promises they both had made to others.

Maddie closed the door quietly and placed the tray on the small round mahogany table by the window. She sat on a floral slipcovered chair, poured a cup of tea and focused her gaze on William's body facing away from her. He seemed in many ways to be the same William despite being much thinner than when she had last seen him five months before. He had collapsed into a deep sleep and she wanted him to rest as long as possible.

He had seemed so serious and quiet the day before, even as he kissed her with intense passion saying, "Oh Maddie, I've missed you so much!" When he looked deeply into her eyes, she saw something dark in his gaze that she didn't recognize. He had held her face in his hands and looked at her with a kind of intensity she had never seen before.

"You should never have come," he said. "Why, Maddie? Tell me what you are doing. How did you get here?" But his look made her wonder if he really wanted to hear everything at that moment. She just wanted to be with him and not think about any of the darkness that had entered both their lives.

When she started to answer, he put two fingers on her lips and whispered, "Okay, maybe we should talk about this later." She understood he wanted to forget everything except the two of them. At least for this night.

"Here you are! I can't believe it!" He kissed her again even longer, holding her tightly then threw his head back with a laugh and shook his head. "Incredible!" he said. "You are truly amazing, Maddie. Crazy—absolutely. You astound me, my darling!" He pulled her to him even more closely and studied her face intently.

Maddie had felt so breathless and excited. They were finally together. She didn't want to think about anything else. William rode the bicycle Maddie had thrown aside to run to him, while she sat on the handlebars. They laughed as they swerved recklessly on the stone-walled lane curving through a thicket of neatly trimmed hedges.

She had enlisted Serge's help through his contacts in the village to arrange for an upstairs room in the ivy-covered, thatch-roofed cottage. He was not only a patient coach teaching her everything she needed to know to be an agent but he was resourceful in other ways.

He had winked at her knowingly and said, *"Bien sur, Madeleine! N'importe quoi—pour vous!"* saying he would do anything for her.

Even Bluebell didn't know exactly where they were. Maddie didn't know how much William had been told by Bluebell or how much she could tell him. She was prepared to be careful and play it by ear.

Maddie and William had quickly greeted the owner of the small cottage before racing upstairs to the tiny bedroom knowing they might only have a single night together. As soon as they entered the bedroom, they began to take each other's clothes off in an electric rush to feel their bodies and touch again in all the ways they both remembered during the long separation.

William suddenly interrupted her thoughts, saying in a low, sleepy voice, "Come back to bed, my darling Maddie. We have to make the most of this time." Then he chuckled and said, "Do I have to carry you over here, myself?" William pulled back the thin coverlet and flannel sheets and reached out his arms to her.

The sight of his slim, naked body and sly, inviting smile removed any resolve she might have had for a serious conversation. She smiled as she lowered herself onto him. He pulled her closer wrapping his arms around her. The warmth and smell of him were intoxicating as she lightly stroked his chest and then began to kiss him deeply. As they moved against each other with mounting passion, she thought, there is nothing else to think about but this. Loving each other. He gently caressed her breasts then placed his mouth on each nipple while she moaned into his ear and kissed his neck. He plunged more deeply into her with slow, rhythmic movements that gradually became faster and stronger. The pleasure was unbearable.

Afterward, they laid in each other's arms, breathing quietly in companionable silence, not daring to speak and break the spell.

Before Maddie had a chance to quiet her mind, waves of anxiety rose within her. Unbidden thoughts pushed away the pleasure she had just felt. Her breath became shallower and labored, an unseen force grabbing her throat. The morning light was becoming stronger and they would need to leave before nightfall. She had to persuade him somehow to agree to her plan.

She touched his face then brought his hand to her chest as he rested next to her, his eyes closed.

She leaned over to kiss him, murmuring, "I know you want to rest, darling." She paused, took a deep breath then said, "William, we need to talk."

* * *

New Town, Edinburgh, Scotland

Rachel was back in Hugh's flat, a cup of tea growing cold in front of her as she sat in the drawing room furnished with comfortable leather club chairs and art deco lamps, the Stradivarius violin resting on its stand. A crackling fire in the white brick fireplace below a marble mantle, barely warmed the room against the late autumn chill. She was waiting for him to return from his trip to the Edinburgh branch of the Home Office. She felt practically hysterical with worry.

She had quickly thrown on her coat and followed him as he escorted Mr. Swift out of the pub.

Hugh said to her grimly, "Go back to the flat, Rachel. I'll take care of this bloke."

What had she done? Had she caused another death? Mr. Swift, the erstwhile blackmailer and informer to the Nazis, looked frightened as Hugh abruptly escorted him out of the pub. For the first time, Rachel understood what Hugh was capable of.

But now all she could think about was her daughter and what she was doing with Bluebell at the Manor. She couldn't leave her daughter who was probably in danger or would be soon—and return to New York. She had to find Maddie.

Chipping Campden, England

"What do you mean, Maddie? Tell me what has happened. Whatever it is, we can figure it out," William said as he grasped her hands gently and saw in her dark brown eyes, a new seriousness but also a spark he hadn't seen before. What had happened in the months they had been apart? Something had changed her.

He had changed too and had his own demons. He could still see Sven's body bleeding onto the fishing boat's floor. At that moment, he felt that his world might be coming apart but he needed to know what she was intending to do. He also knew he would have to leave as soon as possible and not put her in further danger.

Chapter 30

The Manor, The Cotswolds

Bluebell gathered up the maps and charts from the dining room table after the briefing and walked toward the small office overlooking the lily pond, next to the white-washed stone kitchen where she would record the plans for the missions that were to take place later that night. More agents were scheduled to be dropped behind enemy lines in France, Belgium, and the Netherlands.

She was worried about Maddie and William, now two of her best agents. They were scheduled to leave for France. Maddie was newly trained but Bluebell saw how driven and focused she was—crucial traits for operatives. She could be emotional but she was much older in so many ways than most young people she had recruited—usually in their early 20s or even younger. But this war aged many well beyond their years. William and Maddie were extraordinary in their discipline and dedication. They could be very valuable.

William called her after he shot Sven and needed a plane out of the Orkneys. He seemed distant and evasive. Maybe he suspected she knew Sven was a double. Right now, she couldn't help that.

William might try something foolish, especially if he knew about Maddie's mission to Paris. He might be pursued by German agents. She wasn't sure whether she could protect him. She had called the RAF contact that morning once she knew what had happened in the Orkneys. They already knew that only part of the mission had been completed but not exactly why. They were thinking of putting William back onto bombing missions.

For now, he was going to work with MI6 to drop agents and supplies behind enemy lines and gather more intel about possible invasions planned by the Nazis.

As Bluebell walked by the drawing room that doubled as her library, she stopped to gaze at the unfinished painting resting on an easel. A narrow beam of early morning light illuminated the large canvas. Even in the corner away from the casement window, it glowed with life. Its colors were clear and warm, yet almost translucent and ethereal. A swathe of golden road curved off into the sage green hills beneath a pale sky streaked with thin ribbons of white clouds. A large, black-trunked tree with an umbrella of abundant and brilliant burnt orange and scarlet autumn foliage cast a long dark shadow across the golden road. Triangles of verdant grass anchored the scene on both sides. A small village with a church spire and cottages in the distance almost seemed to be an afterthought. There was an aura of magic and mystery about it—even more than in his other paintings.

Bluebell, not for the first time, pondered the possibilities for William. What talent he had for someone so young, she thought. If he survives this war, *God help us all*—what great things he will do.

* * *

The Cottage, Chipping Campden

It was late afternoon and William was sitting up against the pillows placed at the headboard of the four-poster bed. His brow furrowed as he looked intently into Maddie's eyes. She lay next to him, touching him gently.

He said with a low voice, "We have to talk before I go. German agents may know where I am. And besides that, I'm not sure we can trust Bluebell."

Maddie looked shocked but said nothing.

He had so many questions. "What is it, Maddie? What has happened? What are you planning to do?"

Maddie told him how she had traveled to England on a troopship with other musicians so they could perform at concerts in London to boost morale and show American support. And that Rachel, her mother had come to England as well. But William could see Maddie was different now. She was single-minded—but not in the same way as before when she performed. She was still Maddie but more serious in a life-or-death kind of way.

Maddie reluctantly pulled away from William, slowly rose from the bed and walked to the other side of the small room, gathering up her clothes that had been thrown on the floor the night before. She quickly glanced at him then began putting on her blouse, tweed skirt, and woolen stockings as she spoke quietly, "William, I thought I was coming to get you. I am here because of you. But some things have changed. I've changed."

"What do you mean, Maddie? You have to go back to London. Your mother is in Edinburgh with Hugh but I'm sure she is planning to take you home. That much we can be sure of." William felt like shouting in frustration. But they had to be careful that they weren't overheard so they spoke in hushed voices. "You know it's not safe. You have to get out of England. Between the bombs and everything that's going on—" he said, feeling more desperate as he studied her face.

Maddie interrupted, meeting his gaze, "I know what I'm doing, Will."

Becoming more insistent, William said, "I'm leaving tonight for another mission and this time, it's been ordered by my flight commander. Bluebell may be a double agent. Or at least betraying us to enemy agents. I can't be sure. We have to get you out of here." He rose out of the bed and began to throw on his clothes.

"William, I'm trying to tell you something. I don't know what you mean about Bluebell but I need to do this." Maddie reached out to him and stroked his face. "I'm different now. You have no idea. There are things I can do. No one is *taking me home*—especially not my mother. I don't want to go back to New York. At least not until the war is over. William, I know you can't believe this, but I've been trained and I'm ready."

"That's crazy, Maddie. You can't be serious," William said but his heart sank. He knew how determined Maddie could be once she made up her mind.

She looked at him more intently. "I don't know why you don't trust Bluebell after working with her all these months. She knows what she's doing. I know she's mysterious and secretive, but she has to be. I think we can trust her."

He looked away and sighed. "There's so much I can't tell you. But believe me, we just can't be too sure about her." He paused and added, "Or much of anything right now." He had an increasing sense of urgency to confront Bluebell and protect Maddie. *How dare she recruit Maddie!* But there was nothing more he could do for now.

"I know you have your reasons, William," Maddie said, determined to follow the plan despite any doubts he might have about Bluebell. She added with a catch in her voice, "I came here for you—as crazy as that seems. Things happened, William." For a moment, her thoughts drifted off and she bit her lip then decided that now was not the time to tell him what happened on *The*

Princess Sofia. "If you won't go back with me, then I won't go back home either," she said firmly.

His face darkened as he held Maddie's hands. "You know I can't go back. I'm an agent now and a bombardier. I could never be a deserter. I'm sick of this war, believe me. The destruction, death everywhere." He sighed and looked away, not wanting to say more.

She pulled a hand away from William's grasp and raised it to interrupt their conversation. A slight smile erupted unexpectedly on her face. An upbeat yet poignant song—heartbreaking in the memories that arose with the rhythms of the familiar swing music—played from a radio in another room of the cottage.

"Listen, William," she said as the familiar strains of Glenn Miller's romantic *Moonlight Serenade* drifted into the room. She didn't want to talk any more about painful things. She wanted him to go home with her, but if not—she had to stay in this part of the world and do what she could. And be with him when it was possible. Agents had been recruited for lesser reasons.

They might even be on missions together. She had met other female agents at the Manor. And now she was one too.

"Remember our song, William? Remember dancing after our wedding?" Her voice quivered as she thought of that night and all the happy times they had together—until the war took him away.

"How could I forget?" he answered, smiling. "You took my breath away. You still do."

Maddie was resplendent and radiant in her beautiful white satin gown, as they danced together to *Moonlight Serenade* in the opulent Crystal Ballroom on the 18th floor of the King Edward Hotel in Toronto with views of the glittering lights of the city through immense walls of glass. Crystal chandeliers sparkled from the ornately decorated ceiling high above them.

In a room half a world away from that night, William pulled Maddie into a close embrace as she struggled to button her blouse. He swung her around the room in graceful movements to the music. She laughed, enjoying the magic of dancing again in William's arms. She thought, despite what might happen next—here we are and maybe we will be all right after all.

He stopped for a moment looking intently into Maddie's eyes and said, hiding his anxiety about the future, "We will be together again after the war. I know we're heading toward a victory. It's coming, Maddie. I'm leaving soon but I'll be back."

She held him tighter, wanting him to understand what she had decided to do. No turning back, she thought. Their night together in this quiet English village had helped her to feel even more sure of what she had to do. *I am a lot like him after all.*

Like stepping onto a stage before a performance, she knew the only way through a frightening thing was to take a deep breath and keep pushing forward.

She pulled away slightly, holding William's hands and looked into his eyes matching the intensity of his gaze. She said in a quiet but strong voice, "William, I am leaving soon too. For France."

Chapter 31

The Cotswolds, England

William swung his rucksack over his shoulder as he left the cottage where he and Maddie had spent the night. He couldn't believe they had actually been together. It felt like a dream he never wanted to leave. He carried paints and rolled-up watercolor landscapes, his pochade box, logbook, and kitbag with a change of clothing and what remained of his food rations of tinned beef, soda crackers, powdered eggs, and a small bar of chocolate—all that he needed for the trip to France. He would be navigator and co-pilot on this flight to drop supplies for French Resistance workers in the woods outside Paris. They might also be carrying agents who would parachute into the area.

He walked toward the shed behind Market Hall where he had hidden the motorcycle when he arrived in the village the previous day, then wheeled it out; pulling one leg over the frame and sat astride the narrow, cracked leather seat. He leaned forward and kick-started the bike with one foot on the ground, turning one handle to rev the motor. The motor coughed, then roared to life spewing black smoke.

He glanced quickly around him to make sure he wasn't being followed, then rode toward the airfield where he had landed the plane just over a short 24 hours before. There would be a larger plane waiting for the next mission. He desperately wanted to stay longer with Maddie but his orders from the base were to meet the other crew members and prepare for the midnight flight. He considered for a few moments whether he could return to the Manor and work on the painting that he had left in the library half-finished, but there was no time.

Hank and the rest of the crew would be waiting at the airfield. The RAF preferred to keep the same crews together. There was less room for error when they knew each other. A mechanic would make sure the plane was fit and fueled. The crew would check and store all their gear, weapons, parachutes, and supply canisters for the trip then review together the charts and flight plan. They would return to the base near Oxford before daylight the following day after the mission.

He looked forward to seeing the other airmen after the weeks of covert operations in Scotland—especially Hank, the English pilot who had hundreds of missions under his belt.

Hank wasn't much older than William and had an air of easy confidence. He was never fazed by anything, including the time they had nearly crashed north of Lincolnshire while on a training flight. Hank had just said, "Hey, Will, that was a close call. Bloody good work, mate! We'll have a pint or two to celebrate," and laughed, barely breaking his concentration as he swiftly and expertly brought their plane safely to the ground.

On a lovely Sunday in early fall, before he went to Scotland, he had visited Hank at his family's estate 20 miles from the Manor. He had felt so calm and at peace as he painted the woods with the sun shimmering through the tall oak trees and the clear stream gently flowing past the large stone house. He remembered the fish pie they had for tea and the concerted effort he and Hank had made to not talk about the war. Instead, they talked about the food at the base and what a welcome change it was to eat real food. The cook's pastry had been flakey and delicate like his mother's. How he loved good pie.

At the base, it was more likely to be a tasteless meal of lamb suet broth with stringy bits of meat and sodden Brussels sprouts that even though boiled almost past the point of recognition, still reeked of a disgusting sulfuric cabbage-like smell he would never forget. He almost gagged at the thought. The real meat was often saved for the infantry and the army or higher-ranking officers. It was thought that the aircrew men were a hardy lot, not physically exerting themselves as much and could survive on less. It was strange how preoccupied he had become about food in this war when it had never mattered to him before, one way or the other.

William rode on toward the airfield, glancing up at the canopy of trees overhead and watching as the shadows lengthened on the road. It felt good to be out in the early evening air.

The fading light cast darkening shadows from the groves of trees and rustic stone walls lining the country road leading away from the village. There were no signs of farmers or inhabitants of the small cottages scattered throughout the countryside and nestled into the hills. Occasional furled cones of white chimney smoke ascending into the sky were the only indication there might be people cooking dinner or warming themselves by a fire. It was quiet except for the sporadic sputtering of his motorcycle and the odd distant squawk of a bird in a tree or flying overhead, swooping down onto some hapless rodent then snatching it with its beak. He thought about how he would capture this mysterious purplish-silver twilight in his next painting.

It was always safer to fly close to midnight once darkness was heavy enough to cloak them for the trip over the channel. They might also be joined by other Allied planes from other airfields. They sometimes charted by the stars on night flights which always made him feel connected to the universe. Flying at a lower altitude enabled the agents to parachute safely to areas where they would be met by French Resistance fighters. There was always a risk of miscalculation. Planes crashed frequently when they had to depend on the stars for navigation. But it was too dangerous to communicate by radio on these flights as messages could be intercepted by the enemy. They could be shot by the guns on the ground or in the air by German fighter planes with much better guns than theirs—making these trips even more perilous. He was grateful every time they returned safely to the base.

The motorcycle's motor coughed again threatening to stop altogether. Then with a sudden burst of power, it propelled him forward on the deserted road toward the airfield.

William's thoughts turned to Maddie. He blamed himself for what she was about to do. How could he stop her from flying to France? He had tried to convince her to remain in England and work with the SOE if she refused to go home. She would be safer there than in France. She could train as a decoder or even work at the War Office in London since she was fluent in French and, like most-accomplished musicians, had a mind for mathematics. There were rumors that the German Enigma coding machine had finally been decrypted. She could fit in well at Bletchley Park.

But he knew how stubborn and strong-willed she could be and her mind was made up.

He always thought she was magnificent and brave when she performed beautiful music in a crowded concert hall. Now she had another type of courage. They had argued most of the afternoon. Despite himself, her determination made him love her even more. Their fighting had only increased the passion they felt for each other. They fell onto the bed, impatiently tearing each other's clothes off. William leaned over Maddie, meeting her gaze as they melted into each other and made love one more time with exquisite tenderness. There was no way of knowing when they would be together again.

Eventually, Maddie rolled away from William and leaned on one elbow, studying his face, "I am doing this, William," she had said firmly. "I am not going to stand by when I can do something important to help. I want to do more than stay in England and work in a stuffy old office. You can't talk me out of it, my darling."

When they parted, she had tears in her eyes but she smiled with an impish grin. She hugged him tightly then whispered in his ear, "I am an agent now too, darling. I'm one of you," and then rode away on her bicycle back to the Manor, with a jaunty wave and a brief ring of the bell on her handlebar.

He couldn't stop her. With any luck, they could be on the same plane leaving the Cotswolds.

* * *

Airfield, Near Cambridge, England

Rachel glanced at Hugh as he walked briskly beside her to the plane waiting on the tarmac in the darkness. She could see he was not happy with her but was willing to help anyway.

She wore a dark wool coat over tailored trousers and a turtleneck, with a broad-brimmed homburg hat borrowed from Hugh that could be helpful if she had to be disguised as a man. The simple ensemble would also attract less attention than her usual expensive clothes and jewelry. She carried only a small leather duffle bag containing a knife wrapped in a silk scarf, a map, cigarettes and lighter, some toiletries, a canister of water, and a few cans of tinned meat and biscuits.

The wind was rising in forceful gusts from the nearby North Sea and she could feel the first drops of cold rain against her face. They were flying together from an airfield a short train trip from London. Hugh had tried to dissuade her from going to Paris but she had made up her mind. She knew the dangers she would face there.

Rachel was determined to find her mother and grandmother who she hoped were safely in hiding there. When she found out Maddie was on her way to France and probably heading to Paris, there was no way she could be stopped.

Her phone call to Bluebell at the Manor had been unsatisfying. Bluebell had just said, "Maddie is very strong-willed. She will be fine."

Rachel thought about how their father was ruthlessly killed just before the last war. She was not going to lose anyone else to violence if there was anything she could do about it.

Hugh had arranged for her to fly with him and some agents he was running with the French Underground in preparation for the invasion that everyone hoped would be soon, which would free France and, possibly, even lead to winning the war.

"You are crazy to be doing this, Rachel. Now, especially," Hugh said with a worried frown. "I wish I could talk you out of going," as he lit another cigarette.

She just shook her head and said, "I *have* to. You know that."

"Right. Well, there are people who can help you get to Paris from Calais. You may need to ride in the back of a truck or on an old bicycle. Are you up for that, Sis?" Hugh chuckled briefly, contemplating the image of his sister in the back of a dirty truck. He inhaled deeply from his cigarette that glowed a fiery red in the darkness and adjusted his fedora as he quickly blew out smoke into the misty air.

"Yes, Hugh," she said and tried to smile reassuringly. "Your little sister is not what she appears to be. I can do this. I know I may have been a wreck back in Edinburgh, but I am up for the job now." She tried to laugh, pretending for a moment that this trip was for a bit of fun. Then more seriously, she said, "I need to know where Mama and Grand-mere are and get them out. And Maddie too, if it's possible. I have to try!" She felt a catch in her throat. Her heart was pounding but there was no turning back.

Hugh flicked his cigarette into the darkness as they boarded the plane.

"Your contacts will help me. Your plan is a good one." She turned to him, the brim of her hat angled over her face concealing the fear she felt and said, "I will do whatever it takes."

Part V

The Cotswolds

"Olivia! Olivia Banks! Over here!" a cheery voice called out.

I turned and saw a middle-aged, gray-haired man with a spry, athletic gait and a rosy nose suggesting competing vices. I had spotted him from the train as it slowly approached the station of Moreton-in-Marsh, walking purposefully from the car *park*—an English term I appreciated, like *boot* for trunk and *pint* for a glass of beer, the declarative *Gordon Bennett* if shocked or amazed, or *Bob's your uncle!* when commenting with satisfaction on a task accomplished.

Charming expressions. I felt at home in England—especially because William had found happiness here.

I walked toward the friendly driver who would be taking me to the inn in the Cotswolds where I would stay for the next few days. He greeted me with a wide grin and a firm handshake.

"I'm Nigel," he said, "Pleased to meet you. You're the American." He chuckled at the implied nuances as he briskly led me to a shiny, black late-model Mercedes Benz sedan parked at an odd angle suggesting a hasty arrival or maybe a sudden interruption of his usual afternoon at the local pub. Judging from his ruddy complexion and bright eyes, he might have already have had a few. I tried not to worry about what this might mean for our trip to the inn as he swung my duffle bag and compact roller-bag stuffed with biking gear, running shoes, journals, camera, travel maps and books, and a few nice outfits for dinners at the inn and if I was lucky, a visit to the Manor, into the trunk of the car.

I had been told that Nigel was the local taxi driver—something he did for visitors like myself—*on the side* he said of a career which seemed a little secretive if not dubious, as suggested by his evasive response when I asked about it.

"Oh, I do a little of this. A little of that."

As Nigel steered the car out of his parking spot into the narrow country road lined with ancient stone walls and tall, graceful trees reaching toward a cloudless blue sky, he gave me a quick glance and said, "I understand that you're here to do some research for a book." He drove with the confidence of someone who had negotiated these narrow, curving roads many times before.

"Yes, I've come to see where my uncle painted on leaves during World War II. He was a bombardier. I'm pretty sure he was stationed not far from here. I'm researching a book that I'm writing about him." I didn't want to say more. I had a superstitious belief that if I talked too much about William, the magic of my search would stop.

But in my excitement, I couldn't help myself and added, "He mentioned a *Manor* in his letters. He apparently stayed there often and painted. It's a bit of a mystery how he could do that when he was an elite member of the RAF.

He nodded. "Well, many strange things happened here during the war. I understand you will be staying at the Green Pond Inn in Waverley. That's where the Manor is. But I expect you know that," he said casually as he quickly turned into the next curve.

I was beginning to feel lightheaded from all the sudden turns on the winding road. It felt like my heart stopped. "What do you mean? The Manor is near the inn?"

Nigel glanced at me incredulously as if to say, "Bloody American."

I murmured under my breath, "Oh my God. This is unbelievable."

"Sally and Joe may be helpful to you. They own the inn where you're staying and they love all that war stuff."

Nigel continued to speed past rolling hills and quaint farms nestled into lush valleys, scattered clusters of sheep grazing in the fields, and distant church spires.

In no time, we entered a picturesque village of golden stone cottages. Nigel casually pointed to an imposing structure rising above tall stone walls as we approached the village.

"That's the Manor, miss," he said casually. "You may want to meet Henry. He's the owner now. Made quite a killing in London on the market in the 1980s and '90s. I hear he travels back and forth to France. He may be there now. You never know with him."

I felt my heart starting to race. *That was the Manor? Would I be able to see inside?* It seemed too good to be true.

Nigel made a hard, swift turn into the car park of the inn, scattering gravel in his wake. As I jumped out of the sedan, he called out, "Hallo!" in the general direction of the yellow stone pub with small Tudor-style paned windows. Sally who owned the inn with her husband would check me into my room in the former coach house across the driveway.

* * *

A few hours later, after I had taken a walk through the village and a long soak in the narrow bathtub in the tiny adjoining bathroom, I sat at a table in a corner of the pub near one of the windows overlooking the pond and facing a large stone fireplace. A few couples quietly chatted over their dinners as classical music played softly and a crackling fire warmed the cozy dining room. I sipped a glass of a robust French Cabernet and nibbled a warm herbal goat cheese mini-soufflé on a bed of spring greens, to be followed by grilled local trout and roasted potatoes.

I felt guilty thinking about how food was rationed here during the war. I wrote notes and typed on my iPad as I thought about William spending his leaves in this village then returning to the base for bombing missions.

Sally, middle-aged and trim with a chic black bob and wearing a black knee-length pencil skirt and crisp blue Oxford-cloth shirt with rolled-up sleeves, approached my table.

"Well then, so you are settled, I trust? Welcome to our little village," she said with a warm smile. "It's so exciting that you're here to work on your book." She had a friendly but authoritative, no-nonsense manner that suggested she might have been a schoolmistress or a business executive in a previous life.

News travels fast, I thought.

Sally spoke with the easy grace of someone who greeted strangers on a nightly basis, "Writers come to Waverley quite often. You would be surprised." Her eyebrows rose and her dark eyes sparkled as she refilled my wine glass. "Something in the air, no doubt. They can be a strange lot, though," she laughed amiably.

"I suppose so," I nodded, not sure if I wanted to continue this conversation.

A bell rang indicating a dish was ready to be served. Sally turned on her heel and walked briskly back to the kitchen.

Before long, only one couple remained in the dining room probably because it was a weeknight and now, later in the evening. I was still on California time—eight hours earlier so I felt like I could go all night. A youngish, conservatively dressed woman with long, curly, brown hair, sat across from an older, tall, balding, angular man who waved his hands in emphatic gestures. She leaned toward him as they argued in lowered voices that chirped occasionally with British civility about renovations of their holiday cottage. It sounded like things were not going well.

Finally, the woman threw down her napkin and shouted, "I do not want a loo off the kitchen. That is so common, Marcus!" then rose and stormed out of the dining room. The man slammed down a wad of cash on the table and rushed out after her.

I tried not to laugh and turned back to my notes that were spread over the table.

Sally returned with a basket of fresh-baked mini-scones and the entree. She said with wry chagrin, "Ah, I forgot these earlier," placing the basket on the table. "Not always at the top of my game," she laughed. "Joe and I moved here from Lincolnshire ten years ago so we're not considered genuine villagers. I think that would require three generations and probably at least 150 years. Maybe more," she chuckled.

I smiled, meeting her dark eyes crinkled with humor and murmured, "I can imagine."

Then her tone changed and she looked serious, clearly wanting to chat, "You know, this is a magical place in many ways. It was quite a bohemian enclave for artists and free-thinkers in the 1920s and 1930s. Then the war hit and things changed. But there were artists—even then. So that's why you're here, right? It's about your uncle? I heard he stayed here during the war." She smiled and laughed amiably. "Ha! Not too many secrets in Waverley."

Since the dining room was now empty, I was eager to hear more. "I had no idea that so much happened in Waverley," I said, thinking about the artist enclave. *Was that why William kept coming back?*

Sally leaned forward and in a conspiratorial tone said, "Olivia—May I call you Olivia?"

I nodded, hoping I would find out more.

"There were many Air Force men here during the war. I expect you know that. We didn't keep the best records. You know—it being a village in the country and all. But they say there were other activities going on here as well. Spy training and such."

I told her that the village records I had searched earlier had not revealed much.

"My uncle spent leaves here quite often in 1943 and 1944—and traveled all over England and Scotland. Even though he was a bombardier. According to his letters, he stayed at the Manor when he was on leave and painted since he was also an artist. He vanished just before D-Day and the reports of what might have happened were contradictory. I'm trying to find out what he might have been doing here for such extended periods of time." I said more than I intended but I sensed Sally understood my obsession.

"Well, you might want to meet Henry Simpson then," she said eagerly. "He lives at the Manor now, you know."

I nodded, feeling rising excitement. "Nigel told me when we drove from the station."

Sally smiled and said, "Ah yes, Nigel has lived here all his life and knows all the juicy tidbits. Henry might be able to help. I think he knew the woman who owned the Manor during the war—he lived in the village then. He was just a boy. And now he owns the Manor," then she stopped. "Oh, I am going on, now aren't I? And you probably want to be left alone."

"Oh no, it is quite all right. Please tell me more." *Could Henry have known William?*

"Well then," Sally began as she sat down across from me, leaning in closer and lowering her voice. "Henry is quite a character. He and his wife have a house in France as well. He mostly keeps to himself when he is here. But you never know. He might be agreeable to meeting you."

Then changing the subject, Sally said, "My father was an airman too in the war. He always said that the Canadians were so well-trained and earnest. Not like some of the Americans who came later. Those poor sods didn't have the proper training, is what my dad says. There was such a rush to get more men and they weren't always ready. Apparently, Canadians sometimes flew with the RAF. They liked to fly with the same crew but often they had to change at the last minute. You know, if someone got sick. But that was always less safe." She paused for a minute then said, "I know you live in America. Was your uncle Canadian or American?"

"Canadian. And yes, he was flying with the RAF. But he loved this area and painted quite a bit when he stayed at the Manor. I would be very grateful if I could meet Henry and see the Manor," I said as calmly as I could.

Sally stood up and said brightly, "All right then, I shall ring him up first thing in the morning. And now, I'll make you some fresh coffee. Stay here as long as you like," she said and strode off to the kitchen.

I returned to writing and finishing the rest of my dinner, although I no longer had much of an appetite.

* * *

The next morning, I heard a light tap on my door.

"Olivia, it's Sally," she said in a cheerful voice. "I couldn't reach Henry. Why don't you come to the pub for some breakfast and maybe we can find him later?"

I quickly showered and dressed, then crossed the gravel driveway to the pub. After coffee, a small bowl of Bircher muesli, and toast while reading *The Guardian* and assuring the solicitous, rosy-cheeked young server that I didn't want a "proper English cooked breakfast," I decided to take a walk around the village. I wandered along the narrow walkways leading from one house to another, appreciating the ubiquitous massive hydrangea bushes laden with perfect globes of periwinkle blue, raspberry red, purple, and white blooms that grew to impressive proportions due to the frequent rains and cool, damp air.

I circled back to the Manor and tried to imagine what it was like behind the high stone walls. The large, imposing house rose imperiously above the nearby cottages built of the same golden stone that glowed with magical luminescence. Although the Manor was a short walk from the pub, William never mentioned in his letters drinking beer there with other airmen.

Instead, he described sipping tea in the evening at the Manor with Lady Braithwaite-Smith. I wondered about that. And what else he might have concealed.

There was a chill in the air but the sunshine was beginning to filter through the rapidly disappearing clouds, suggesting that spring was on its way. Butter yellow daffodils and purple crocuses grew in haphazard clusters scattered along the side of the country roads and in well-tended gardens surrounding some of the cottages in the village. I planned to cycle later in the day through the countryside where William rode his bicycle so many years before.

As I walked toward the Manor, I noticed that the gate was open and a gardener was raking leaves—his back to me.

"Excuse me, sir. Hello?" I called out. The gardener glanced sideways at me with a scowl on his face, clearly not welcoming an interruption in his work to talk with a stranger.

"Is Mr. Simpson home? I would love to speak to him if that is possible."

A spritely voice called out behind me, "I heard you might be looking for me, young lady. I don't have many visitors these days." He chuckled amiably.

I turned and saw a thin, dapper, elderly man in corduroy pants, plaid shirt, red vest, and peaked tweed cap ambling toward me. He looked fit and probably in his late 70s or early 80s.

He walked more briskly when I answered, "Hello, I'm Olivia Banks."

He had a wide grin as he approached me and extended his hand, "Ah yes. I heard you were here. I'm Henry Simpson. I knew your uncle."

"It is so good to meet you, Mr. Simpson," I said, shaking his hand. I suddenly felt shy and emotional.

"Please, call me Henry. Let's go inside and have some tea." He led the way and opened the gate in the stone wall cautioning me to "mind the steps and your head" as two Jack Russell terriers barked and nipped at my ankles. We ducked below the low stone archway and entered the quintessential secret garden.

Tall stone walls enclosed expansive grounds filled with shrubs and flower beds just beginning to bloom. A lily pond bordered by flagstone sparkled in the distance, adjacent to a gazebo with a wrought iron table and chairs inside. Sweeping lawns surrounded the large stone house in the English manor style with casement windows, several chimneys, and a grand front entrance with a massive, ancient oak door. The morning sunshine intensified the glow of the golden stone of the house and the high walls. Beams of light glimmered between the branches of ancient beech and oak trees starting to break out into bright emerald buds soon to unfold into abundant leaves providing canopies of shade as the days lengthened into summer.

I thought about the remarkable events that might have occurred here during the war. In some ways, it seemed like such a long time ago. In other ways, it felt like William might suddenly appear.

As we walked through the house, I glimpsed elegantly furnished rooms. Henry led me into a large drawing room with a grand piano covered with silver-framed photos facing a wall of Tudor-style paned windows overlooking the gardens. I gasped when I saw the huge white fireplace where William had stood in photographs 70 years ago.

Henry invited me to sit down. He must have noticed the tears in my eyes and said kindly, in the charming English manner when confronted with emotion, "I shall make us some tea. My wife is away at our house in Aix-en-Provence but I think I can manage." He chuckled and left the room, giving me time to catch my breath.

I felt shaky and dizzy being in this room, imagining William standing nearby at an easel, painting.

Henry returned a short time later and carefully placed the tray with matching china teapot, cups and saucers, a pitcher of cream, and a tiny bowl of sugar cubes on a table in front of the fireplace. He poured tea into two cups and passed one to me, then sat down on a chintz chair with a colorful pattern of roses and peonies. I was mute and embarrassed, feeling colliding emotions. I took a deep breath and tried to steady myself on the edge of a moss green velvet sofa across from Henry. He looked back at me with a sympathetic expression on his face.

Henry spoke gently, his blue eyes bright with intelligence. "I heard a bit about you from Nigel. He dropped by last night after a few pints. That bloke does like to talk!" He shook his head good-naturedly and I laughed with him, feeling myself beginning to relax.

"News travels fast in Waverley, to be sure. Not much happening—not like in the war." He rested his hands on his knees and leaned forward. "I was just a boy when your uncle stayed at the Manor. I think it was 1943 since I was almost eleven. He painted me, you know. Even though I wasn't a very cooperative model," he laughed. "A bit fidgety—I was. But your uncle was quite the gentleman. Never lost his temper. No matter how much I jumped around." He smiled at the memory. His eyes twinkled, and I could imagine he still had quite a mischievous side just as William had described in his letter to Auntie.

Henry paused and looked thoughtful as he spoke, "He seemed to be somewhere else when he painted. You know, distracted. I remember he liked to listen to music too, often when he was painting. I think he was happy here. Almost as if there wasn't a war. Curious."

I held my breath, grateful to be in this place with someone who had known William. It felt surreal.

Henry's expression became more serious. "People came and went but he stood out. He was different. He was always painting. There was a lot of secrecy about what was going on, of course. You didn't know who you could trust. I didn't really understand any of it until after the war. But even young whippersnappers hear things." He sipped his tea and fell silent for a moment.

I felt overcome with sadness at the significance of being in this room, where William may have felt some solace from the war and being separated from Maddie. I thought about how wars have affected so many—and maybe, especially children like Henry, changing their lives forever.

Before I could ask about what might have happened to his paintings, he said, "But we don't know where all the paintings ended up. There are a few crooks and crannies here but nothing has turned up that I would recognize as William's work. He had a distinctive style."

I nodded but my heart sank. I had so many questions. "Do you know what might have happened to my Uncle William, Henry?" I asked. "We never had conclusive proof that he died when his plane was shot down not far from Paris. He was reported missing but there were contradictory explanations for his disappearance. He was officially declared dead a year later in 1945. But we never knew for sure… he just vanished. I don't think my mother or the rest of the family ever recovered." I quickly wiped away a few tears with a napkin Henry had given me.

Henry poured another cup of tea. The stillness between us was palpable. Then he broke the silence, sadness in his voice. He spoke slowly at first, then more quickly as if he hadn't spoken of those wartime years in a very long time. "There was a lot going on in England and everywhere in Europe, as you know. Especially leading up to Normandy and the French liberation. A lot of confusion and chaos—the war had gone on for so long—things were escalating. There was an air of desperation. We all felt the outcome of the war was going to be decided in the spring of 1944. More and more airmen went on missions into Occupied Europe—disappearing at shocking rates. RAF crews didn't wear dog tags when they flew because we didn't want the Germans to have any information about our blokes if they were captured. Airmen were shot down quite often, of course. The Resistance was very active where your uncle was supposed to have been shot down. Then again, the Germans were swarming all over the countryside in France. Bloody Jerries. The war was such a damn mess. So senseless." He shook his head in disgust and his eyes darkened.

I felt swept up by his words—back into that terrible time. Henry's mood then seemed to shift as he spoke, "Some said the French found a way to get airmen to safety after they parachuted out of their planes and hid from the Germans. I know it sounds crazy, but I heard that there was something called a 'Skyhook'—a contraption like a huge slingshot set up with cables and poles. Very ingenious. A special plane would then pick up the airman. I heard about it after the war—very experimental and developed by the French Resistance and SOE agents to quickly lift airmen to safety. French farmers hid downed airmen for long periods of time—sometimes weeks—until they could return to England, and other times to Paris, then brought them back through Spain. I even heard there was the odd RAF airman hidden at places like the Ritz Hotel in Paris. Isn't that a caution? Such gumption!" He clapped his hands appreciatively. After a moment, he said, "You may already know these things."

I shook my head and murmured, "Please tell me more." I was beginning to realize there were new possibilities of how William might have disappeared.

Henry looked pleased that he might be offering new information. "I don't get a chance to talk like this very often—about the old days," he said with a shy smile.

I thought that maybe it was easier to talk about painful times with a stranger. We chatted more about his experiences during the war—the mysteries of what might have been going on at the Manor, his boyhood pranks with his mates in the village, the war rations, and how his mother would say when he lingered over his food, "You better eat that up, Henry. There's a war going on!" I nodded, captivated as he spoke—as if a dam had suddenly been broken.

Henry told me he had found out the Manor was up for sale when his business was doing *rather well* in London 20 years before, and he had *snapped it up*. He said with a gleeful laugh, "Imagine that! Ha! A lowly village lad living at the Manor! Now that was a strange turn of events." He looked quite pleased with himself. "Lady Braithwaite-Smith was long gone by then, of course. Her daughter left for Scotland soon after the war. You know, she was a nurse—worked near here at a convalescent home for the wounded. Probably saw too much and had to get away. Then there were a few more owners. In fact, Webster worked on a revised edition of his dictionary right over there," he pointed proudly to a corner of the large room. "Then it was up for sale again. So not long after, here I was, moving into the grand Manor!" He grinned impishly, seeming to take great delight in his good fortune. "Yes, the Lady might have had a few things to say about me of all people taking up residence. She just knew me to be a scrappy bit of trouble," he laughed, slapping his knee, obviously amused with living in her home. Then he paused looking thoughtful and said, "You could say she was a bit eccentric."

I wondered what he meant by that.

"Quite educated and very cultured, you know. But she had... what would you say... a tough, reserved, somewhat mysterious way too. A bit of an enigma. But definitely in charge of this place and everybody else, too," Henry smiled, an expression of fondness on his face. "And she had quite a collection of guns. I remember seeing them in a case, but she always kept a shotgun handy too. I don't think she would have hesitated to use it either!" He laughed and shook his head.

"Do you think she was recruiting and maybe training spies here?"

"Who knows? She was definitely not your typical *Lady*, but then it was a time that people did things they never imagined they'd do," he said with a wry smile. "I couldn't tell you all the goings-on here. All I can say is, I had a sense that important things were being planned and decided. Even though I was wet behind the ears. I noticed your uncle and Lady Braithwaite-Smith spent a lot of time together and often behind closed doors," he paused as his eyes met mine and he smiled kindly.

I nodded, thinking about William's letters describing extended leaves here.

"I'm sorry I can't tell you more about your uncle and that you don't know what happened to him. He was a good man. And so young. So many disappeared." Henry looked thoughtful. Then he smiled and said, "But William's story needs to be told. And I'm glad you're doing just that." That's what Charlie had said to me in his house in Toronto, not long ago.

We talked on into the early afternoon until I felt it was time to go. Henry took a photo of me holding one of his Jack Russell terriers by the immense fireplace, standing exactly in the spot where William was photographed holding a small dog in 1943.

I didn't want to leave. But soon after, I reluctantly said good-bye to Henry and walked to the inn to pick up the bicycle I would ride through the countryside where William had traveled.

Chapter 32

Paris, France, May 1944

Maddie sat at a table on the outdoor patio of the café, Le Papillon Bleu et Le Rose Rouge with the faded red awning and the swastika flag flapping in the wind above her, near the Ritz Hotel on Place Vendôme in Paris, sipping a cup of café au lait. How she hated to be reminded of the Nazi occupation in this beautiful city.

She barely noticed the occasional passerby as she held her breath and her hands began to shake. She slowly slid a butter knife under the sealed flap and opened the small envelope that had been slipped earlier that morning under the door of her room above the café where she now sat alone. This was one of the few moments she had these days to be on her own.

It was addressed to her in the familiar handwriting that never failed to make her heart beat faster. How had this letter managed to reach her? The network of agents had expanded in the last few months but many were disappearing or being tortured in the Gestapo headquarters only a few blocks away. Still holding her breath, she read:

Dear Maddie,

My darling, it has been such a long time since I have been able to write.

Please don't take any more chances than you have to. I have heard what you are doing.

Things are even more dangerous than ever. But the situation may change very soon. It could get even more risky for you where you are. Please be careful, dearest Maddie.

We will find a way to be together soon. I promise. I miss you so much.

Much love always,

William

Maddie slowly folded the letter and placed it back in the envelope. She thought this latest cryptic note had probably been written in a rush. She could only guess the dangers William must be facing.

She looked up as a tall German officer approached her table. He was smiling as he walked briskly toward her, the heels of his leather jackboots clicking on the pavement. She quickly slipped the envelope into her handbag resting on the table.

"Well, well, my dear *Fraulein*. I thought I might find you here," he said casually but with a hint of a threat.

"*Enchanté*, Herr Sturmbannfuhrer," she answered, calmly meeting his glance as he leaned over to take her hand and kiss it. She tried not to pull away in revulsion.

She had seen him before at the Ritz Hotel and knew his name was Herr Sturmbannfuhrer Schmidt and that he was a commanding officer in Paris. He spoke English and French with a barely discernible German accent. He had been educated in London before the war but was very loyal to the Wehrmacht machine and was known to be working closely with the Gestapo in Paris.

Maddie hoped he would never discover that her family had Jewish roots in Germany and France.

He was frequently at the nightclub near the Ritz Hotel where she played the piano and sang French café songs. Her cover was that she was just another Parisian who had stayed on after the Occupation. Her fluency in French had improved at the Manor. She had a knack for imitating the Parisian accent, probably due to her musical ear. She had often heard her mother and Ma-mere speaking French together. She also was known to be English-speaking as many educated Parisians were.

Herr Sturmbannfuhrer Schmidt carried a white pastry box bound with string and set it down on the table in front of her with a flourish. He met her gaze and said with cloying sweetness, "I thought you might like some *éclairs de chocolat et petit macarons, Mademoiselle Laurent*. Such a rare treat these days."

Maddie wondered why he had taken time to find her and what it meant.

He sat down opposite her and spoke in a low voice as he leaned toward her, "Perhaps we could share them together. I know how you *femmes Francaise adorent les pâtisseries*. And you might do anything to taste one, *n'est-ce pas?*" he said with a sly grin then raised one eyebrow as he tweaked an upturned end of his mustache which gave him a macabre double smile. Such a caricature of a villain, she thought. This city was full of people who would be laughable if they weren't so dangerous.

Maddie squirmed on her bistro chair and spoke carefully so as not to offend him, "My apologies, Herr Sturmbannfuhrer Schmidt. I must leave soon. I have to prepare for this evening."

"*Mais oui*, we have another party arranged *ce soir*. Many officers are coming. We look forward to you performing for us, *Mademoiselle*"—the last word he emphasized with snide sarcasm. Maddie thought he was probably affronted by her rejection of his thinly veiled seductive overture but she didn't care. He was repugnant and William's letter preoccupied her thoughts.

Schmidt's leering smile revealing large white teeth reminded her of a wolf. His cold green eyes with their tiny black pupils glittered as he spoke. If you didn't look too closely and just noticed his high cheekbones and the way he carried himself, he was almost handsome. Behind his arrogant demeanor, she was sure there was a sharp mind. *He probably doesn't miss much.* She had felt his eyes on her before at the nightclub and managed to avoid him as much as possible. One night, he had sent a bottle of champagne to her dressing room that remained untouched.

Maddie trusted the French and British agents she worked with but kept mostly to herself. She had been in Paris for several months and worked hard to maintain her cover—Hélène Laurent—who had been raised in the 6th Arrondissement near the Luxembourg Gardens.

She hoped Schmidt had no idea of what she was doing and who she really was. He could be pretending to believe her story. She might be trapped in a dangerous cat-and-mouse game and not know it until it was too late.

Countless charades and acts of subterfuge were going on behind the supposedly civilized facade of German officers mingling with French citizens and international guests at The Ritz. The hotel had been established early on in the war as a relatively safe hub for American journalists, French movie stars, and Nazis alike. Well-known celebrities like Coco Chanel and Marlene Dietrich dined and shared drinks there, exchanging social niceties that concealed layers of intrigue. American journalists and writers like Hemingway had departed hastily once the United States entered the war.

Intimate encounters occurred in the hotel while it maintained a pretense of a neutral sanctuary from war and death. Covert operations were conducted between agents and double agents. Occasionally, a black sedan would slide up to the entrance and leather trench coat-clad Gestapo agents would leap out, then leave soon after, hurriedly escorting an unfortunate figure into the darkness. But for the most part, life went on in the bar, dining rooms, and bedrooms on the upper floors without obvious disturbance.

Maddie provided the entertainment in the nightclub near the hotel most evenings, singing in long shimmering evening gowns from the fashion seasons of the mid-1930s, sometimes borrowed from Mademoiselle Chanel who lived at The Ritz. She was still very much an *au courant* designer for those who could afford her elegant designs in wartime Paris, although her *atelier* across the square, Place Vendôme with the monument to Napoleon, was closed at the beginning of the German Occupation.

Maddie played piano French café songs like *Deranger Les Pierves* and popular American songs such as *Full Moon and Empty Arms*—a modern riff on Rachmaninoff. Nobody guessed she was a concert pianist. She found it oddly amusing—liberating in many ways—to be so far from the concert stage.

Could Schmidt know that she was helping to hide RAF airmen at the hotel? Usually one at a time, in a tiny room behind a huge antique armoire in a forgotten corridor under a hidden staircase and in another room behind the pantry adjacent to the hotel kitchen. She had been working with the French Resistance since she left the Manor.

She smiled coyly and nodded, "*Mais oui*, Herr Sturmbannfuhrer Schmidt. I would be so delighted to play for you and your friends. *Très amusant, bien sûr*. Are you celebrating something tonight?"

"We are always celebrating this fine city that has been ours these past years," he paused and smirked as he looked her over closely. Then he said in his clipped accent, "But we are entering a very special time." He smiled with condescension in his voice as he spoke, "I believe greater things are yet to come. You will see. We are the master race after all." He leaned toward her—his sharp eyes boring through her.

His tone quickly reverted back to flirting with threatening undertones, "I will look forward to *ce soir, Mademoiselle Laurent*. And perhaps, a drink later? It would be lovely to chat more. Perhaps in my room at The Ritz," he said, raising an eyebrow.

So obvious what you are up to with your pastries and champagne, she thought. *I might just be able to use this to my advantage.*

Before she had a chance to respond, he rose from his chair, clicked his heels and made the customary Nazi salute exclaiming *"Heil Hitler!"* then turned and marched off.

* * *

Over Ottignies, Belgium

William peered through the glass nose of the Halifax, as he lay on the floor of the plane directly below the pilot, Hank. Although they were situated close to each other in the aircraft, the roar of the engines almost drowned out Hank's voice in his ears. He could barely hear him through headphones that always made his ears ache after eight hours or more in the air. Here he was again, back where he didn't want to be. But at least the killing wasn't up close.

He blinked, trying to clear his mind from the images that frequently woke him in the middle of the night—his near-death in the Orkneys and shooting Sven—blood everywhere. It was something he would never forget. Not for the first time, William wondered what his father experienced as a World War I pilot ace. A highly decorated lieutenant colonel. He knew he had seen his share of combat.

"We've got lots of company up here, Wills," Hank said through the headphones. "Thanks to the moon, we can make out where we're going. The boys in the back are ready for the Jerries. Don't you worry."

"Okay. Just give me the word." William then spoke to Jack, the navigator seated behind him who was attempting to read maps with a flashlight in the darkness illuminated only slightly by the few lights hooked up on the sidewalls of the plane. The small windows allowed him to also navigate using the position of the stars. He was locating the site to drop supplies—mostly espionage equipment in metal containers to resistance fighters in Belgium. The rear gunners were ready to shoot any German planes that came near them.

William tried not to think about Maddie—in Paris working with the Resistance. They had not seen each other for much too long—not since their night together in Chipping Campden.

He had resumed flying to drop supplies and agents into occupied parts of Europe, then more bombing missions to destroy strategic rail lines providing troops and arms to northern France.

But their paths had not crossed as they had hoped.

He had received a message through another agent—that she was safe and using her cover as a pianist at a nightclub to get intel from German agents and hide British agents and airmen before helping them to escape. It was too risky for her to send any letters. He hoped she had received his last letter.

Suddenly, there was a loud explosion behind him.

"We've been hit! Oh my God!" Joe, the rear gunner yelled into William's headphones.

Hank shouted, "I'm rearing up. We're going higher and heading back. We can do it! Just hang tough, mates! Time to get out of here!"

The Halifax suddenly lurched sideways then upward. The heat of a fire in the rear behind one of the wings and the smell of smoke filled the aircraft. They had been hit but the plane was still in flight so they might just make it back to Coventry airfield near the Manor if not the base at York or the one near Oxford. William thought *beggars can't be choosers—what a stupid expression.* They would be happy to land anywhere safe. *If we make it at all.*

The plane shook as they gained altitude away from all the other aircraft and William's teeth chattered as he tried to push away the fear. If he could climb out of his position, he could join Hank in the cockpit to co-pilot them to safety. The Halifax stabilized slightly at the higher altitude but he could hear one of the engines choking and sputtering. *How long could they keep going without losing power altogether?* He stayed in a ready position—prepared to parachute.

It wasn't safe for him to move from where he crouched in the lower half of the plane. But they couldn't parachute while they were still flying over the Channel.

The temperature was dropping. William was glad that his leather flight jacket gave him some warmth and that he was wearing sheepskin-lined leather gloves but he felt numb all over and prayed it would be over soon. He could see his breath swirling in front of him in distinct funnels of gray smoke. He was still alive. Well, that's reassuring, he told himself and laughed, thinking he was probably giddy from sleep deprivation.

He heard the engine that had been hit finally sputter one more time and then it was silent. At any moment another engine could choke and die.

Hank was a good pilot and could land under any circumstances—a star in their squadron of elite airmen. But even he might not be able to get them back.

The plane was losing more altitude. After what seemed like an eternity, William could see a landing field rising up to meet them. Maybe they would be okay after all. Until the next time. But this war had to end soon. He had to believe that. That was what kept him going. He and Maddie would be back in New York where they belonged.

Chapter 33

Northern France

Rachel wrapped her arms around herself as she huddled under musty woolen blankets next to baskets of fruit and vegetables among bundles of straw in the bed of a truck heading toward Paris.

Earlier that night, she and Hugh had landed in a field near Calais. Arrangements had taken longer than expected, especially with increased bombings and she had remained in Edinburgh with Hugh until she could finally leave for France. She guessed from how distracted he had been and the frequency of late-night telephone conversations behind closed doors at his flat that preparations might be in the works for an Allied invasion.

After she was confronted by the blackmailer and probable informant, Mr. Swift, at the church in Edinburgh, she knew Hugh had important connections and was involved with handlers like Bluebell and a network of operatives—with training centers throughout the English countryside and Scotland. He was probably also working with the SOE and the RAF. She had felt safe with Hugh and was reluctant to be on her own. But she had to find Maddie.

He had waved down the prearranged truck at the airfield and said, "You'll be all right, Sis. Go to the Café Le Petit Oiseau Jaune in Montmartre. You will meet Emile. You should not go near The Ritz or Place Vendôme just yet. We can't have you blowing Maddie's cover. We will let you know when you can make contact." With a reassuring smile and an affectionate grasp of her arm with a gloved hand, he added, "Rachel, it is going to be okay. Emile and the others will take care of you. They may have information about our mother and Grand-mere. But you should prepare for the worst," he paused. "People are disappearing all the time. You need to be careful."

Hugh's eyes darkened and a shadow seemed to pass over both of them.

"I will be careful, Hugh. I promise," she said while keeping other thoughts to herself.

Hugh's face brightened as he tried to reassure her, "We are doing everything to end this damn war. Things are going to get better soon. We have to believe it. Just keep your head down, Sis. Maddie is strong. She can take care of herself. She's a lot like you." His warm brown eyes crinkled as he smiled again and squeezed her arm.

Rachel laughed and said, "I'm not so sure that's a good thing."

"And others are watching out for her, believe me. When the time is right, we will get you both back to England." Hugh looked over his shoulder to the jeep waiting for him, next to the truck that would take Rachel to Paris—both with their motors rumbling and the drivers anxious to leave. He said in a rush of words, "We have to go now. My contacts in Paris are good and they will take care of you. But Rachel, please don't take any foolish chances." Hugh gave her another one of those stern older-brother looks she remembered from childhood and said, "And stay hidden as much as possible." He looked as if he wanted to add something more but just said, "Well, right then. See you after the war, Rache."

Rachel felt tears stinging in her eyes and struggled to hide her fear.

Hugh gave her a big hug and a kiss on her cheek then stepped back and saluted smartly. He turned quickly and ran toward the jeep with long-legged strides, then jumped in beside the driver before they drove off into the darkness. The headlights' narrow beams diminishing into the black night filled her with such sadness. Would she see Hugh again? She had a strong sense of foreboding but she couldn't lose faith.

Now alone in the back of the truck, she thought about those last minutes with Hugh and how he had left her with such an emptiness in the pit of her stomach despite his confidence and reassurances. She longed to return to those summer afternoons when they were just kids—on the beach near Cornwall with the sun dancing on the waves—tossing a beach ball and hooting with laughter while Lolly, their black and white spaniel cavorted and barked joyfully. That seemed like such a long time ago.

She didn't think she could be the same after all that had happened. *Am I a better person after all these years? Now that I really have found a purpose?* She wondered. *But that is crazy.*

She had always been right there for Maddie—making sure she practiced and was prepared for her lessons with Madame and the concerts that were so nerve-wracking yet thrilling. Maybe she had been overbearing at times with

Maddie and Charlie, but she had always meant for them to have the best of everything and achieve great things. And not be hurt in the ways she had been hurt.

She so wanted Maddie to be safe and to find her mother and grandmother. She longed to smell her mother's fragrant shortbread baking or taste the wonderful cassoulet she would make on special occasions and to hug her spunky, strong but tiny Grand-mere.

She tried to breathe through panicky thoughts now that she was on her own. *When will this terrible war finally end?* I may be just as foolhardy as Maddie, she thought, but I have no choice. I couldn't stay in London or Edinburgh and do nothing.

She wondered if there would be others following her, trying to blackmail her for what she had done—and who she was. She had to believe that she, Maddie, Hugh, and the rest of her family would be all right. She would not let them down.

* * *

Coventry, England, Near the Manor, The Cotswolds

William braced himself as the Halifax landed on the narrow airstrip, finally resting at a precarious angle with what seemed like a noticeable groan. As he, Hank, and the rest of the crew leaped out of the plane with a smoldering wing and a burned-out tail, they all whooped and slapped each other on the back.

"Whoa, can't believe we made it! That was a close one! Let's not do that again anytime soon, fellas!" they shouted and laughed with the giddy euphoria of having escaped certain death.

The rear and mid-upper gunners who had been overcome the most by the smoke were choking and coughing as they bent over with their hands on their chests. Then they looked at each other and suddenly broke out into raucous hoots of relief.

"That was enough to make a bloke mess in his drawers!" one of them said as he shook his head in disbelief and they all hugged each other, knowing they had narrowly escaped being blown into the abyss.

William and Hank gave each other high-fives and then simultaneously dropped to the ground and kissed it, glancing at each other and laughing.

"Hey, Wills, that was something!" Hank shouted as they both jumped up. "Let's not make a habit of that sort of thing, old man! Damn Nazis! They nearly got us that time. But, hey, they don't know what stuff we're made of! Ha! We're always one step ahead of them. Right, Wills?" and he slapped William on the back.

"No doubt about it, Hank!" William answered with a wide grin. "It's getting crazy up there," he added, still feeling shaken but not wanting to show it.

Hank punched William's arm playfully with a laugh, then unzipped his flight jacket and flamboyantly removed his gloves with what William thought might be forced bravado concealing some real fear. For just a moment, Hank's dark eyes narrowed and he became more serious, "We've got a job to do. We'll be more ready next time."

William nodded and they turned toward the Officers' Mess Hall. It was definitely time for a pint.

* * *

Several hours later, when the lights were out in the officers' quarters and the others were asleep, William began to sketch. He thought about what had happened. They had come very close to dying. He thought about how his life could have been.

His mind turned back to New York in the fall of 1942 before he and Maddie were married, when he had been able to get away from flight school and took the train to see her. She was practicing at the Juilliard piano studio, preparing for a concert. He sat on a straight-backed chair near her, sketching on a small pad, touching her shoulder or wrist gently between pieces to remind her that he was there but not wanting the beautiful music to stop.

"You're a terrible distraction, my darling!" she said and pushed him away laughing and kissing him, then turned back to the piano. "Why don't you go out and see some art?" She smiled. "I know just the place. There are so many beautiful things to see at the Frick. I think you'll like it."

The Frick Collection was in a mansion transformed into an art museum on the Upper East Side that he had heard about at art school. It was one reason that he loved New York even if it was a huge, noisy city. So many art galleries. So much frenetic energy. He could think anything was possible.

She told him that one of the most magnificent private collections of art in the city was there—established by a wealthy businessman and open to the public since the 1930s. "It will be good for you to go, William," Maddie said, then kissed him as she added, "You need to take a break from all your thinking. And I know you're getting antsy listening to me practice."

It was raining hard that day but he enjoyed the walk across Central Park from Rachel and Maddie's apartment on the Upper West Side to 5th Avenue and down to 70th Street. The sidewalks were filled with processions of black umbrellas bobbing above rapidly striding legs and feet. The occasional hapless pedestrian held a pyramid of newspaper over his head as he raced across the street in the downpour, oblivious to traffic lights and weaving his way through a gauntlet of honking yellow taxis. A cluster of shop girls held their handbags over their carefully arranged curls and elaborate pompadours rolled back from their foreheads over the requisite *rats*, as they ran squealing precariously balanced in high-heeled pumps to their posts at the shops on 5th Avenue.

William entered the gates of the mansion feeling a strong sense of anticipation—but not knowing that what he was about to see would change his life forever.

As he walked through the ornately decorated rooms painted various shades of turquoise, rose, and pistachio green bordered by gold filigreed trim and accented with garish gilded mirrors, he noticed the Louis IV furniture, Greek sculptures, and fifteenth-century Raphael's Madonna—all quite beautiful and priceless. Just another rich person's collection. What a bore, he thought. He had never developed a fondness for antiques. He didn't understand what was so special about so many precious old objects being displayed nor how anyone could have amassed such a collection—especially during the Depression when so many others had suffered in relentless poverty.

He read on the plaque at the front entrance that Mr. Frick had instructed the famous architect, Thomas Hastings, to design a "small, unpretentious mansion"—"nothing ostentatious." William thought this was a bit ironic given all the antiques and priceless objects. But he knew that Mr. Frick had humble roots. Later, he had fled Pittsburgh after dubious dealings with Andrew Carnegie and a scandal involving his company's violent attack on striking steelworkers and coal miners. He wanted an estate near Central Park with sufficient space to hold his impressive collection that would eventually become a museum for others to enjoy.

William strolled quickly through the rooms wondering why Maddie would have recommended this place. She knew he didn't care for material things. All this wealth and opulence left him cold, especially in the midst of war.

He had started to do a little sculpting before he left for England, even creating a double bust of Maddie and himself. But ancient Greek statues didn't interest him in the way Rodins or the fairly new Henry Moores had, when he was still at art school. He loved the abstract landscapes painted by Lawren Harris of the Group of Seven artists painted in the 1920s and 1930s— sometimes cold and bleak in their starkness depicting scenes of the Canadian north, but also magnificent and architectural with sharp edges and glacial peaks of striated blues and grays. An artist who broke all the rules. He wished he had that kind of courage to break loose from the more traditional landscapes and still lifes he had painted so far. But there was time.

He felt growing impatience as he strolled quickly from one room to the next, thinking he would leave soon. Then, in the ornately decorated drawing room, he stopped short as a luminescent Vermeer, *Officer and Laughing Girl* caught his gaze, hung over the fireplace. It was still vibrant and alive after three hundred years. This was more like it. The ethereal light and joy in the face of the young woman held him captive as a few people chatting in low voices strolled by. He pulled himself away and walked further out into the main hallway—so much stone and marble gave the place a cold but grand feeling like a damp English country manor. He glanced into an alcove roped off from the rest of the museum and tucked away by the wide stone staircase rising to the private quarters on the second floor.

A painting illuminated by a Victorian lamp stopped him in his tracks. The sheer intensity of the colors and penetrating blue eyes of the subjects were otherworldly. He had heard of the Renoir's *Mother and Children* but to actually see it was to be immersed in another time and place—a glorious dream. The bright azure eyes of the fashionably dressed young woman and her two small daughters pierced through him as he was transported to the lush gardens of a park in Paris on a spring day. He finally turned away, feeling breathless and overwhelmed, questioning whether he could ever become a real painter.

He passed the Garden Court and found himself in the vast West Gallery. It was a massive hall filled with more priceless art. He imagined Mr. Frick spending evenings strolling from painting to painting, absorbing their beauty.

William gazed first at the Gainsborough as he entered the room—then gasped audibly.

The huge painting on the other side of the spacious gallery was like nothing he had ever seen before. J.M.W. Turner's *The Harbor of Dieppe* was painted between 1825 and 1826. The intense radiance of the sky and light on the water seemed surreal—a true harbinger of the Impressionist style to come. William knew then that he had found a painter who spoke to his soul. He sat down on the antique velvet-covered bench and drank in the scene, spellbound.

He had never seen anything like it. As he finally rose to leave, he looked at the wall above the upholstered bench where he had been sitting. There, unbelievably, was another equally immense and luminescent Turner—another seascape entitled, *Antwerp, Van Goyen Looking Out for a Subject*. Suddenly, he felt swept up in the vortex of beautiful light emanating between the two paintings. He would never fully understand what he just experienced but he knew he would never paint the same way again.

Now, here he was—in England, the very place where Turner had created so many amazing works. He was in the middle of a horrible war not knowing if he would live another day. But he felt the magic of Turner's paintings all over again. He thought of his own painting back at the Manor and suddenly felt an urgency to return there and finish it.

Chapter 34

Paris, France

On the Place Vendôme in the 1st Arrondissement near the Ritz Hotel, Maddie dressed quickly in the small attic room, slipping a flowing garnet red silk gown over her head onto her shivering body. The elegant dress barely concealed the sharp edges of her slight frame that had become even thinner during the past few months. She stepped into black velvet pumps borrowed along with the gown from another Resistance fighter, one of the last surviving members of a wealthy Jewish Parisian family. She firmly clasped the rhinestone necklace and bracelet around her neck and wrist—given to her by the boyish, self-described bourgeois Genevieve, another agent displaced from a comfortable life when the Occupation began.

Maddie's wardrobe except the most essential pieces had been left behind in London. She sighed and said to herself, *I can do this* as she left the room and began her descent to the street three floors below.

Meanwhile, across the City of Light, in Montmartre in the 18th Arrondissement, an artists' enclave and a medieval neighborhood filled with narrow stone-walled alleys and steep cobbled stone streets, Rachel sipped a café au lait at a table on the patio of a tiny cafe near Sacré-Cœur. She gazed at the rosy sunset and the gathering clouds while she contemplated how to see her daughter at the nightclub near the Ritz Hotel. She had stayed in the small flat until she could wait no longer.

Hugh had briefed her about what was happening at the hotel—German officers, American celebrities, French movie stars, and spies all mingling on ostensibly neutral ground. He had been adamant that she not blow Maddie's cover. He had given her contact information and she was to wait at her hotel for an envelope to arrive.

But she had come so far. She had to do something. As the war and the Occupation dragged on, things were becoming more desperate on both sides.

She needed to see Maddie before something happened to her—before she was picked up by the Gestapo—or she disappeared. She was not going to sit by and wait until Maddie was hurt again.

* * *

RAF Base Near Oxford, England

William suddenly woke from a fitful sleep that brought more vivid nightmares of the struggle with Sven—the wrestling with the gun, then two loud shots. He was filled with dread as he thought about how he and the crew had almost crashed to their deaths. He rose up from the meager square of unyielding foam that barely served as a pillow, feeling beads of sweat on his forehead and the emphatic pounding of his heart. He hadn't taken off his clothes and fell asleep while he was sketching.

As if he knew exactly what would help, he heard the opening bars of the romantic, haunting music of the Rachmaninoff *Vocalise* and saw Maddie bent over the keyboard, her hands rising and falling with passion but also sadness.

A wave of emotion flowed over him. He had to return to the Manor, find out what Bluebell knew and finish the painting that lured him back like a powerful magnet. He had to talk to Bluebell. He might not have another chance. He had to go to the Manor one last time.

Exhaustion swept over him and he drifted back into another dream.

* * *

A few hours later, he woke again and prepared to leave the officers' quarters before the others rose for breakfast. He splashed some water on his face and walked briskly to an adjacent building and then to the office of the Lieutenant in charge of equipment at the base. Lieutenant Cooper was up as well despite the early hour, typing a report at his desk.

William knocked on the open door and said, "Excuse me, Lieutenant Cooper, but I have an urgent request. We're not scheduled to leave on another mission for 48 hours. Our plane needs some repairs, as you know. Would it be possible to take one of the jeeps to the Manor in Waverley? You know about the Manor, right?"

William knew that others at the base aside from his commanding officer were aware that he was part of the joint SOE/RAF and MI5/MI6 operations. He also knew there was often jealousy from mainstream RAF officers not recruited as agents, especially if they were stuck behind a desk and not involved in the supposed adventures in the field. Even though lives were being lost on those high-stakes missions.

Lieutenant Cooper stared at him with an inscrutable, blank expression—his bushy eyebrows furrowed together, threatening to meet over his flat gray eyes. He didn't look very encouraging. After a moment, Cooper shrugged and pulled out a set of keys from a drawer in his desk then flung them at William.

"What the hell," Cooper muttered. "Somebody might have a problem. But I've heard what you've been up to. You're a mate in my book. The first one on the left." He pointed in the direction of the designated jeep then turned back to his typing.

This might be a bit too easy, William thought. But he wasn't going to question his good luck and ran out of the office to the area where the jeeps were parked behind the barracks. He jumped into the one he had been assigned and drove off.

As William wound his way on the narrow curving road through the quiet countryside cloaked by a morning mist rising from the verdant hills, he rehearsed what he wanted to say to Bluebell. Despite all the time he had spent at the Manor painting, he was nervous about seeing her. He could be on his own in what he planned to do next. He had to try to find a way to get to Maddie. Confronting Bluebell was not something he or other agents ever relished.

He briefly touched the pistol in his waistband. A recently sharpened commando knife was strapped to his ankle. As he pulled into the driveway in front of the Manor, he muttered under his breath repeating what he wanted to say. He jumped out of the jeep and saw her standing in the doorway, dressed in a gray wool suit and crisp white shirt.

Bluebell did not look surprised to see him. "Well then, there you are. Come in and we'll have some tea, William," she said with a slight smile.

He stood in the driveway not wanting to lose his momentum and glared at her, "What are you doing with Maddie? And what about Sven? Did you know he was a double? I thought I could trust you." His voice rose as all the pent-up feelings of the past months were released in a rush of rage.

She nodded curtly and said without emotion, "I can imagine you have many questions, William. We have much to discuss. But not out here." She beckoned him inside.

He entered the darkened foyer, threw down his haversack filled with paints, charcoal pencils, and sketch pad and followed her into the kitchen. He would have to rein in his anger if he was going to find out anything about Sven or Maddie.

No one else seemed to be around, which he thought was strange given all the increased activity propelling the Allies toward an invasion. Agents were not only trained at the Manor but were also sent from there on missions into Occupied Europe. Bluebell might have arranged to be alone if she had been warned of his arrival.

He stood by the Tudor-style paned casement windows overlooking the beautiful back garden that had awakened from the long damp, gray winter. Massive hydrangea bushes laden with globes of blue, deep pink, and white blossoms, and colorful flowerbeds of primroses and daylilies announced the return of spring despite the foreboding dark clouds that filled the sky.

He thought, okay, now or never. *No more Mister Nice Guy.* As his father would say. He had been trained to fight back—especially if he felt as trapped as he did right now. He had to get some answers.

"Bluebell, *Lady Braithwaite-Smith*, whichever you prefer—you have put Maddie in great danger. I know she is in Paris. And in the thick of it!" He paused as he clenched his fists, trying to contain his anger. "Is it not enough to be running agents from here who aren't brilliant concert pianists? How could you do that? I haven't heard from her since she left. How do I know she's even alive?" he said as his voice started to shake. He was not going to lose his temper.

Bluebell was surprised at William's anger but remained calm—something she had learned a long time ago. She continued with the task of filling a kettle with water and placed it on the large cast-iron, pot-bellied stove, then said quietly, "William, Maddie is fine. I would have told you if that wasn't the case. You must know that."

William said, "Actually, I'm not sure of anything, but thank you." Then his tone changed and he said, "Bluebell, I need to know if you are a double too. How could you not know about Sven? Were you running him for the other side as well? I could have been killed. Right, you know that." He shook his head in disgust. He felt his color rising and his heart pounding. He held his fists tightly by his sides but he was well aware of his knife and pistol. The skin at the outside corners of his eyes was streaked with redness revealing his anger and sleeplessness. He would shoot Bluebell if he had to, his emotions fueled further by the knowledge that he had led Maddie here and she could be in grave danger.

Bluebell turned away from him and poured the hot water from the tea kettle into the violet and larkspur porcelain teapot he remembered from his stays at the Manor. She placed matching cups and saucers, cream pitcher, and dainty sugar bowl onto a tray and led him into the large sitting room where the grand piano dominated one corner. His unfinished painting he had entitled *The Golden Road* sat on a large easel in the opposite corner.

Bluebell sat near the hearth of the massive, centuries-old open fireplace, poured a cup of tea and handed it to him as he sat opposite her on a floral slip-covered chair. She thought of their times together months ago when they had sat in the evening talking about art and music. *Did I do the right thing, recruiting William into the SOE?* She hoped so.

"All right, William," she said. "You deserve an explanation. I can assure you I am not a double nor did I know that Sven was one. I had my suspicions so I had to force him out in the open. We had to know more about what the Germans were planning." She held up a hand when he tried to interrupt her as she continued, "Let me tell you what happened. Sven was a Norwegian so obviously, he was invaluable in terms of what we wanted to accomplish in the Orkneys. You have to understand, since the Nazi occupation in Norway in 1940, the Germans have been everywhere in the North Sea and still are. We had to do everything possible to stop an invasion. And there is still that threat. We know there is at least one German battleship hidden in the Norwegian fjords. Your work has helped tremendously, and for that, we are very grateful." She glanced at him hoping he could believe what she was telling him.

William nodded but did not feel reassured. He was anxious to know more about Maddie and where to find her in Paris. But he knew it wasn't wise to push Bluebell. She might clam up completely.

She slowly sipped her tea and wondered whether she should tell him more. She had missed William and impulsively decided to continue. "We are still on a regular basis intercepting Germans who are stealing Norwegian fishing boats and recruiting agents like Sven. We have to work with the Norwegians and we don't always know who are sympathetic to the Nazis and who we can trust. Believe me, many of them are very much against the Nazis. They too have their Underground and have been trained by our people. We thought Sven was someone we could trust. That was our mistake." Bluebell paused, took another sip of tea then placed her cup and saucer on the table by her chair.

"Yes, well, I was very nearly killed. No thanks to you."

Ignoring his remark, she said, "I think it's time for a bit of sherry." She stood and turned toward a cabinet in the corner where she picked up a crystal decanter and poured two glasses, passing one to William.

He remained quiet, remembering the Orkneys, lost in his thoughts and wanting to believe her.

Bluebell sipped her sherry and sat more upright on a velvet upholstered chair, then said, "It happens, unfortunately. And for that, I am truly sorry. I know that you could have been killed, William. And that would have been terrible." As she spoke, there was a brief catch in her voice and she felt her face soften.

William listened and felt some of his old trust of Bluebell return, although his mind wandered back to Maddie. He was still angry and only slightly less worried about her.

She continued to speak firmly in a quiet voice and without rancor, "We have so much to do, William or we will surely lose this war. I know how you feel about Maddie. She is your wife, after all. But believe me, she is strong and very well trained." She paused and narrowed her eyes as she said confidently, "Maddie is one of our best agents. No one suspects her. She is excellent at what she does. There is nothing more you can do. Maddie is about to be involved in a very important operation."

William saw that he had no choice for now. But maybe there would be a way to get Maddie out of France.

Bluebell took a deep breath and placed her sherry glass gently on the side table. She glanced at him and said softly, "You are here now. Perhaps you could finish *The Golden Road*. You have some time before you have to return to the base."

She looked over her shoulder to the corner where the painting waited for him.

Chapter 35

Place Vendôme, Paris, France

J'attendrai
le jour et la nuit
J'attendrai toujours
Ton retour

    I shall wait
    Day and night
    I shall wait for your return

J'attendrai
Car l'oiseau qui s'enfuit
Vient chercher l'ousie

    Because the bird that flees comes back to find lost
    memories
    In its nest
    Time passes and runs, beating sadly
    In my heart so heavy
    And yet, I shall await your return.

The chatter and muted laughter ended abruptly as the slender figure of Maddie in a garnet silk gown, her glossy black hair curling over her shoulders, suddenly appeared on the stage in a beam of light. She sat at the piano in the nightclub adjacent to the Ritz Hotel while guests in elegant evening attire and German officers engaged in murmured conversations at small lamplit tables and sipped cocktails served by waiters in white jackets circulating through the smoke-filled room.

She was a stunning sight as her graceful hands began a hypnotic dance over the keyboard.

She sang in a deep, throaty voice with the emotion of Edith Piaf, the haunting lyrics of *J'attendrai,* a popular song of the war, alternatively in French and English.

Uniformed Germans, Parisians, agents with the Underground, and collaborators alike filled the room—most spoke several languages. Many of the nightclub and hotel staff were French Resistance agents who risked their lives every day passing information and hiding Allied airmen shot down in the nearby countryside who came to Paris with help from local farmers and agents.

Maddie felt at home at the piano as she played and sang the melancholy song, thinking of William. He was always with her but she missed him more than ever. She pictured his handsome face—his crooked wry grin and bright blue eyes that were often so serious and intense then sparkled when he made a joke or teased her. His neatly groomed, close-cropped blond hair—every strand in place except the small, obstinate cowlick that stood up on the crown of his head. She loved to touch it and tease him that even he was not completely perfect.

As she and the small band ended *J'attendrai,* she knew she had to switch to something more cheerful or the Germans would start to grow restless. And that never meant anything good.

She played the opening chords and began singing the classic, upbeat pre-World War I French song, *La Valse Brune*—but this time singing only in French—a small act of defiance. She knew the words in English and thought of them as she sang.

They are not ones to dance a slow waltz/Good roamers who slip into the night/They prefer the lively waltz/ Flexible, fast, where one turns without noise/Silently they entwine their beauties/Merging with the group/Lightly, lightly they leave with them/in a joyful whirl.

A trio of musicians performed with her every night—a sad but dignified, middle-aged woman who played a soulful violin, a tall male bassist with hunched shoulders who always wore a threadbare black suit and white shirt with a frayed collar and cuffs, and a short, wiry, older man of an indeterminate age who chain-smoked and wore a black beret. He played a harmonica when he didn't have a *Gauloise* hanging out of a corner of his mouth and for more traditional French songs, the accordion. She almost felt like dancing, momentarily forgetting where she was and the horrors that were happening in the streets of Paris even now, as she sang with bittersweet joy.

She remembered afternoons with her brother Charlie in their Toronto home when they were kids and she was having a school break from her music studies in New York—jitterbugging, waltzing dramatically, and swing-dancing frenetically, then finally falling onto the floor giggling just as their mother entered the room and clapped her hands saying firmly but with a happy smile, "Bedtime now, you two!"

In the dark, smoky room of the Paris nightclub, Maddie played the piano with a light touch instead of her usual intense passion. She felt almost a brief escape as she sang the words reminiscent of happier times. She glanced around the crowded room, scanning for the Nazi officer who had spoken to her at the café that morning. Some of the patrons joined her in the refrain while others sipped their drinks.

As her eyes glanced over the crowd, she felt a sudden jolt of shock.

Partially hidden by a black net veil below a cloche hat covering her hair, a familiar face appeared. The deep red lips formed into a slight smile then casually blew smoke from a cigarette held aloft in a distinctive silver holder. Blue-gray eyes met Maddie's dark-eyed gaze. Then the veiled face signaled with an almost indiscernible shake, warning her.

It was her mother, Rachel.

No, I don't believe this! Am I hallucinating? How is this possible?

She kept playing and singing, then stood up from the piano amidst the applause and walked to the standing microphone. She began singing the more upbeat *Au jour le jour*, a song from the year before that all of France had embraced, wanting her mother to see how she had changed. She was now much more than a concert pianist. When the song ended, she nodded to the other musicians to continue playing and left the stage.

* * *

A few minutes later, Maddie was seated at the cigarette-scarred table in front of a mirror reflecting her anxious face. She tried to gather her thoughts and decide whether she should leave the small dressing room that was more like a closet and look for her mother.

But she couldn't blow her cover or endanger Rachel. She thought it was probably best to stay where she was for now and try to find her mother later. *Or will she try to find me backstage?* Maddie rarely smoked but she was so nervous that she quickly lit a cigarette, immediately feeling herself calming down. So that's why people smoke, she thought.

A sudden knock on the dressing room door interrupted any plan she could have made.

She rose to see who was there. Her sharpened commando knife in its sheath was concealed in her bra under her gown. She was prepared to use it. Maddie had been in some tight situations the past few months and had been forced to use her knife to defend herself. She also kept a British OSS revolver in the pocket of her jacket hanging on the nearby coat tree.

She thought it might be Jean-Pierre who often brought instructions for her next mission. He also picked up intel she heard in the nightclub over drinks at the late-night post-performance parties with Nazi officers—one of the things she had to do as an agent that made her cringe the most. It was surprising what they would share over their third bottle of champagne when they thought they might seduce her into their bed.

She opened the door to find Herr Sturmbannfuhrer Schmidt.

He was in uniform and held a bottle of Moet and Chandon champagne reserved only for the elite—primarily Nazi officers and their guests. He smirked as he said, "*Bon soir, Fraulein*" and pressed the other hand on the door jamb making it clear she had no choice but to invite him into the tiny dressing room. "Well, *ma chérie, très belle Mademoiselle Laurent*, your performance was brilliant tonight as always. *Très magnifique. Et maintenant*, we shall celebrate your triumph," he said barely concealing a coldness in his odd, clipped, yet anglicized Germanic-Gallic accent.

His green eyes glittered like a snake eyeing its prey. He removed the foil from the bottle of champagne then expertly twisted the cork several times until it popped with cheerful alacrity and landed on the floor at her feet.

She looked down at the cork, mesmerized for a moment by how it spun for a few seconds then rolled to a corner of the room. *What is the matter with me? Stay focused.*

Maybe this was an opportunity she could use to her advantage. She felt her pulse quicken as she thought of how she might use Schmidt to get to the

General who was one of the Resistance targets, responsible for so many French Jews being sent to the death camps.

Maddie watched as Herr Sturmbannfuhrer Schmidt pulled two vintage champagne glasses with a dramatic flourish out of his pants pocket—no doubt snatched from the bar. He set them down on the table as he began to pour their drinks.

"There we are. Now let's toast tonight—your crowning glory, *ma chérie.*"

They each raised their glass for a toast. "To a great performance!" he said and clinked her glass with a Cheshire cat grin and a theatrical wink.

Then something changed. His face suddenly transformed into a distorted mask as he put down his glass then picked up the bottle of champagne and suddenly smashed it against the table. Shards of glass flew in the air narrowly missing Maddie's face, the rest of the precious liquid flowing onto the wooden floor.

"*Mais, peut-être votre dernier*—maybe your last, *Mademoiselle,*" he said as he leaned in closer holding the broken bottle over her, his green eyes widening then piercing through her.

Before Maddie could act, he grabbed her right hand and slammed it onto the dressing table as he raised the broken bottle over his head, his face now beet red and twisted in rage.

"I know what you've been doing, whore," he sneered. "You're not an innocent French singer. As if you could fool us," he laughed humorlessly as he leaned into her face. "I've been watching you for a long time. You're working for the enemy. I had hoped for something else. But alas...," he sighed dramatically, then grunted and shook his head in disgust. "In any event, it ends here. I'm going to destroy those precious hands of yours," he paused for a moment, his eyes cold and dead staring at her menacingly.

Maddie gasped, her mind racing as she tried to stay calm and said to him in her most seductive, cajoling voice, "But Herr Sturmbannfuhrer Schmidt, perhaps we can work something out." He slowly lowered his hand holding the broken bottle.

"Well, if you tell me who else is working with you in this damned hell-hole, I might spare you for some fun and games. And then if you're lucky, off to a special camp—just for Jew-trash like you." He spat out the words then leaned in closer, bringing his hand with the broken bottle closer to her right hand that he held roughly on the table. His eyes were bloodshot and glittering like shards of glass in a snake's head. She could see he was quite drunk.

Then he seemed to calm himself. His voice lowered and he spoke as if he were asking her what she would like to order from a menu. "Should I cut off some fingers or maybe just break your lovely hands? A tough decision, indeed. But either way, you will never play again." A look of pity crossed his face.

Maddie held his gaze and spoke softly, "But then I won't be able to play for you and your friends, Herr Sturmbannfuhrer Schmidt." She tried to reach behind her with her other hand without him noticing, toward the jacket hanging on the coat rack to pull out her gun. But it was too far away.

The Nazi grabbed her more tightly, holding down her hand. Even though he seemed thoroughly drunk. His grasp was unyielding as he squeezed her fingers so hard, she gasped in pain. Her vision blurred with tears filling her eyes. She was having difficulty breathing. She had to do something.

The thought of never playing the piano again was almost worse than the thought of dying. It was not going to end here. She struggled against his grip with all her strength. She had to keep him from hurting her hands. She couldn't live if she couldn't play again. Maybe she could distract him so she could reach the knife hidden under her gown.

"Please don't do this, Herr Sturmbannfuhrer Schmidt! I'm sure we can work something out," she pleaded, hating how her voice rose to a higher register. But her hands were everything to her.

Herr Schmidt raised his weapon again over his head, nostrils flaring and his face fixed in an ugly grimace of anger. Just as the broken bottle was about to crash down on her hand, the door flew open.

Two rapid shots rang out and the Nazi officer fell backward onto the floor, releasing Maddie from his grip. The jagged half of the bottle flew out of his hand as he grabbed his chest where bullets had ripped a gaping hole, blood gushing out of the wound.

"You bi…" The words were unintelligible but clear in their hostility. Then his head lolled to the side and his eyes became lifeless. Maddie gasped, still shaking, then turned.

Her mother stood in the doorway holding a mother-of-pearl handled pistol—a strand of smoke rising from the short barrel.

"You're not the only one who learned to shoot," Rachel said in a steady voice, her eyes dark in her ashen face.

Rachel's hand holding the gun lowered to her side. Her small, sequined evening bag where the gun had been hidden hung open on her wrist. She dropped the gun back into it and firmly snapped the clasp. She felt calmer than she had for weeks and straightened her back with a new confidence. It was as if a huge weight had been lifted. *Maybe, just maybe, some injustices have now been rectified.*

Then she smiled and stretched her arms out toward her daughter. Maddie ran into her mother's embrace, sobbing.

"I will never let you go, dear daughter," Rachel said quietly as they hugged each other tightly.

Chapter 36

Northern France, Near Paris, June 1944

The plane shifted in the wind as it began to drop steadily to a lower altitude. They were flying in full moonlight to drop more bombs on the rail line north of Paris that served as a main artery for transporting German troops and supplies to the Normandy coastline. The success of the Allied invasion depended on bombing missions like this one.

"Wills, are you there? Are you dozing off, mate?" Hank shouted over the engine noise to William who lay at the bottom of the glass nose of the Halifax below the cockpit. William was dressed for the bracing cold in his RAF uniform, thick woolen sweater, fur-lined leather flight jacket, and leather helmet. When the pilot and crew members left the base, they were always given a thermos of hot tea and a small bar of chocolate that was frozen hard until you put a piece in your mouth and it slowly melted—to sustain them on the eight-hour and even longer flights—or as long as their petrol would last.

Some airmen took amphetamines to stay alert but William never had a problem staying awake. There was no chance he would close his eyes for even a moment. The pressure was too great. They had to hit their targets as precisely as possible without being hit from the ground or the air. Over 30 allied planes were flying with them in preparation for the invasion in France.

But the Germans were also sharing the air space and they had to count on the mid-upper and tail gunners to keep them from being hit by enemy planes. When they were flying at less than 10,000 feet, they ran the risk of getting caught in the explosions once the bombs hit the ground. Staying alive and in the air was always the goal.

His father told him when he shipped off to England, "Remember, son, kill or be killed. That's what counts. Keep that in mind and you will come back," with the steely-eyed, grim expression William had seen many times before. Then, his dad shook his hand firmly and patted him on the back. That was as close to any sign of affection he had ever felt from his father. He heard the same advice from his training officers—"No time for sentiment, boys! Kill or be killed. Don't ever forget—the Jerries are saying the same thing."

He thought of the incredible human will to live, no matter what. Flashes of the struggle with Sven appeared. *What more will I have to do to stay alive?*

"Don't get your knickers in a twist, flyboy!" William shouted back at Hank, trying to keep things light, despite the noise, the cold, and the constant dodging of enemy planes. "The boys in the back have us covered. No flak for us if you just keep this bird in the air and dodge the Jerries, old man!"

The best way to keep focused in the midst of the imminent dangers in the air, was to keep up a lively banter with Hank. Since he had often acted as co-pilot with landings and takeoffs, they had become close partners. Their camaraderie had developed even more over the past few months as their missions became more frequent—dropping agents and supplies behind enemy lines and more recently, reconnaissance ops collecting from the air location information and photographs of German submarines off the coast of England and Scotland. He and Hank shared similar instincts and more than once had seemed to read each other's minds which had helped them through some tight spots. In fact, he felt good about the entire crew. William missed the missions as an SOE agent on the ground and the opportunities he had to paint. But as the Allied invasion was imminent, trained airmen were needed even more.

The navigator behind him exclaimed occasionally with excitement, "That was a close one, boys! Rear up now!" Mostly, though, he was a quiet chap from the Lake District of northern England, who communicated only critical information to keep them on course—such as key coordinates from his charts and orientation details from the sextant when the stars were visible.

William and Hank kept up their good-natured banter to handle their jitters and distract them from the constant nerve-rattling noise of the engines and cramped space. William felt his adrenalin kicking in.

This mission was even more dangerous than others. There was a greater chance these days of being shot down or blown up in the sky. He knew fewer crews were returning to the base from bombing missions, signified by the silent and unceremonious erasure of a pilot's name from the blackboard in the Officers' Mess. It was never discussed just how many crews had been lost—but William knew it was close to 50 from their base in just the last few weeks.

He heard Hank laughing into his headphones after his teasing answer. William released one bomb, then another and then another—trying not to think about what he was doing. The contrast of the joking and the devastation below was never lost on him. He kept focused on the targets, checking his chart in front of him and verifying coordinates with the navigator. He lay on the floor of the vibrating plane, hearing arias from Verde's Tosca in his head. He sang some of the lyrics in Italian, reminding him of Saturday afternoons at home listening to opera on the radio. How he longed for those days.

William tried not to think of the German troops that were being blown up below—some of whom may not have chosen to be where they were—just as he hadn't chosen to be where he was now.

He thought about how he had to find a way to get Maddie out of Paris. He was so close. But they would be on this mission for several more hours then return to the base near York. He would have to find another way to get to Paris—maybe after the Allied invasion that was to occur in a few days.

As William began to plan how he might get to Maddie, he heard a loud explosion and yelling from the back of the plane as it suddenly dropped and lurched sideways. He grabbed onto a loop of canvas hanging from the low ceiling above him as his body slid backward.

"Mayday! Mayday!" Hank shouted, which was followed by more screaming from the rear.

Then the fateful words no one wanted to hear, "Every man out! Now!"

There was a frenzy of chaotic activity and shouting behind him and smoke was quickly filling the plane. William scrambled to grab a parachute stored nearby and attach it to his harness, then rushed past the navigator to the tail and turret gunners to make sure they were okay and ready to jump. The tail gunner had been hit and was gasping for air. William tried to pull the parachute pack over the gunner's head and push him toward the hatch, but he could see that he was unconscious and maybe even dead.

The other gunner yelled something that was lost in the noise and shook his head, pointing at the escape hatch and motioned to William to jump. He could see the navigator in front of him also shouting at him and madly gesturing to him to follow. But William was worried about Hank and shouted back that he needed to get to him and they'd get out together. He scrambled up the short ladder to the cockpit. There was another explosion and the plane dropped suddenly. They were descending too fast.

"Get out, Will!" Hank yelled as he unbuckled himself and leapt out of his seat, pushing William toward his designated escape hatch.

"Not without you!" William shouted. Hank slapped William on the back and pushed him out of the plane, shouting, "Safe landing, Wills!"

William desperately hoped Hank was right behind him. He knew that the navigator had jumped already but he didn't know about the rest of the crew. He thought the worst as he pulled his rip cord and looked back to see the back half of the plane explode and what was left of it plummet toward the ground below or into another plane—whichever came first.

* * *

William woke up in a tangle of ropes and parachute silk in the French countryside. He thought he must have landed in a tree, knocked himself out then fell to the ground where he had remained unconscious for a short time. He felt his body for broken bones but found none—to his relief—because he knew he would have to get out of there in a hurry. His head hurt and he felt a little dizzy but otherwise seemed to be okay. He had a sore wrist and one of his ankles felt like it might have been twisted in the fall. As he stood up and took a few steps, it didn't seem to be sprained. He knelt down and grabbed his parachute off the ground, rolling it up as he unhooked the harness and pulled it over his head then quickly buried them with his life jacket under dead branches and leaves, grateful for the darkness. He carried another pack with his kit bag, rolled up maps printed on silk, pistol, and combat knife.

It was still the middle of the night but he could see more clearly as he looked around in the moonlight, his eyes gradually adjusting to the darkness.

There was no sign of Hank. William hoped he had landed safely but he couldn't take the time to look for him. He had to get to the nearby woods or a farmhouse where he could hide. He knew from their briefings at the base that Nazi soldiers were likely to be patrolling the area. As he tried to get his bearings, he still felt lightheaded and dizzy but figured he couldn't stay here. He heard voices in the distance. And they weren't speaking French.

William started off in the direction of a barn that was leaning to one side, less than a mile or so in the distance. Where there was a barn, there was likely to be a farmhouse and people. He hoped they would be farmers who were working with the Resistance and could hide him for a few days until he could figure out what to do next. He broke into an awkward run as he heard the voices getting closer.

He stopped when he saw a grove of large trees abutted by dense thickets and tall hedges covered in lush green foliage. He crouched in the darkness and held his breath as the German soldiers marched by, shouting, and searching for survivors of the plane crash. After their footsteps faded, he stood up and started running again in the opposite direction—to the barn.

* * *

The next morning, William's luck changed for the better. After he had slept fitfully for a few hours, waking each time he heard a noise only to discover it was a rat skittering across the floor or a horse snorting, a farmer entered the barn and started cleaning out a stall.

William took a chance and emerged from behind a stack of bales of hay with his hands in the air. With a few words in his high school French and some hand signals, he explained to the farmer that he was an Allied airman whose plane had been shot down. The farmer nodded and gestured to William to stay hidden in the barn.

Later, a woman he assumed was the farmer's wife or maybe a sister, returned with a basket of bread, apples, a sausage, a small round of soft cheese, and a cup of cold milk. He ate ravenously as he tried to think about what he would do next. She also brought country clothes—trousers, shirt, and jacket— that he threw on then hid his flight clothes behind a bale of hay.

It wasn't long before three men and a woman entered the barn as the sun rose higher in the sky. The air in the barn became warmer and fragrant with the strong smell of fresh-mowed hay. The newcomers were rail-thin and dressed in shabby shirts, baggy pants, boots, and caps—and carried guns and haversacks. Their world-weary but proud faces showed years of suffering but warmth for William and his situation.

Fortunately, they spoke some English since William had used up his meager French when they appeared, saying, "*Bonjour, Je m'appelle* William. *Je veux aller* à *Paris, s'il vous plait,*" to which they all nodded and began to speak to each other rapidly in French.

One of the men with hollow cheeks and haunted eyes said, "We have a way—*très dangereuse, mais*—how do you say? It could *do the trick—Faire l'affaire*." He smiled as he spoke around a lit cigarette in a corner of his mouth. "We leave now—to prepare," was his next enigmatic comment and they left.

William waited through the afternoon in the barn not daring to venture outside. He found a pencil and blank paper inside his logbook and sketched the horses and few cows who were his only company.

At dusk, when they returned, he discovered the three French men and one woman were agents with the Resistance and working with the RAF to extract agents and aircrew. They carried equipment that William had never seen or heard of before.

He had heard rumors of a human slingshot, the "Skyhook," and knew that only the British and French were using it. It was the best way to get him out—especially with so many Germans in the area.

"*Allons-y*, William," the agent who seemed to be in charge, said to William who followed close behind out of the barn. He was excited to be picked up by a plane that would take him closer to Paris. And somehow, he would get to Maddie.

They stopped in an open field. It was getting dark enough that they were less afraid of being seen by any of the Germans who might be in the area. Everything had been timed carefully so they wouldn't be waiting long. Two long steel poles were set upright some distance apart, with a transfer line strung between them. William lay on the ground as the agents pulled the harness attached to the line over his head and snapped the belt closed around his waist. He waited, feeling some impatience to get on with the operation.

Before long, he heard the unmistakable rumble of an approaching plane. It was flying low as a 50-foot steel cable unfurled out from it, swinging wildly in the air then descended to the spot where the agents on the ground hooked it to the line attached to William. The plane then rose steadily as he flew upward and disappeared.

* * *

He felt himself soaring higher, then entering and moving through a long, dark tunnel. He emerged to light and expanse. Ahead he saw the familiar hills, amber and burnt orange trees, and the winding road in front of him. *The Golden Road.* It engulfed him and filled him with peace but also uncertainty as to what it meant or what may be ahead.

He didn't feel afraid. It was like the times he felt immersed in the scenes he painted—the villages, winding roads, and countryside of the Cotswolds, the imposing majestic stone colleges of Oxford, lone figures wandering in windswept ancient Celtic cemeteries. In northern Scotland, he had been a part of the rugged hills of the Highlands and the scenes he painted of whitewashed cottages on rocky cliffs above churning seas and foamy waves crashing against the gray rocks. He had been absorbed in—and by—so many beautiful places.

As wisps of white clouds drifted across the pale blue sky in a light breeze, the hills and trees of the countryside he had loved so much were all around him. The golden road curved ahead, leading him further into the distant hills. He began to follow it past the majestic trees that arched over the road, their colorful umbrellas of amber and orange foliage catching his breath as beams of sunlight transformed the bright leaves into translucent jewels.

The sweet, melancholic notes of Chopin's Piano Nocturne #1 in B Flat Minor filled his ears. Then the music changed and became the music that had always soothed him when he was missing Maddie.

Chopin's Piano Concerto #1 swept over him, filling him with joy and wonder. An image of Maddie leaning over the keyboard, her dark hair sweeping forward as she played with deep emotion, appeared in a sudden flash of memory. The music continued as he returned to the scene he had painted at the Manor not long before—the one he had finally finished and maybe had loved the most. *Was he in the painting or just seeing it before him?*

It didn't matter. Peace and calm filled him as he thought, I am all right. This is a good place to be.

And then, he and Maddie were in his canoe, the soft sound of his paddle dipping quietly into the still water of the lake creating a gentle wake in the still black water. He closed his eyes as he imagined his next painting of the waterfalls and the rocky cliffs surrounding Kahshe Lake.

Where it all began.

Chapter 37

Paris, France, Late August 1944

Rachel and Maddie walked arm in arm toward the brasserie in the Saint-Germain-des-Prés district on the Left Bank—a well-known café and meeting place for writers, artists, and intellectuals alike, in the 1920s and 1930s and even during the Occupation. Sartre, Simone de Beauvoir, and Camus were known to have long discussions of philosophy, literature, and politics here. Many romantic liaisons had begun and ended in this bustling, smoky mecca. The atmosphere was lighter now that the city had been liberated a short time before, but a pall of sadness still hung in the air after all the deaths and disappearances during the past four years.

The bottle green awnings over tables and chairs on the stone patio were faded and tattered on the edges, but the distinct gold letters proclaimed the café's name *Les Deux Magots,* cheering Maddie even as she was preoccupied with worries for William.

More and more people were venturing out on the streets. For many, there was almost an air of euphoria although it was still a time of overwhelming trauma, loss, and mourning after years of enemy occupation. Others grieved for their lost or missing loved ones. Paris was liberated earlier in August after the invasion of France on D-Day—June 6—turning the war in favor of the Allies. The streets had finally emptied of visible German occupiers and the huge red swastika banners and flags had disappeared from the city.

Crowds lined the streets at times, shouting and cheering as women with shorn heads, accused of collaborating with the Nazis were paraded in the street. Some had been subjected to swastikas branded on their foreheads. Maddie could only guess the circumstances of their alleged *collaboration* and the citizens' zeal for revenge. French women had often been forced by the Nazis to do things to survive and now they were being brutalized by their own people. She felt horrified and saddened. *Would the cruelties never end?*

The morning sunshine had quickly transformed the coolness of the previous night and dried the wet streets after the early morning thunderstorm. It would soon be another hot, sultry late summer day.

Food was still scarce in the city. Rachel and Maddie had saved their ration cards for days, in order to enjoy café au laits and share a breakfast. They murmured to each other how it felt good after so many weeks of hiding, to be mingling with other Parisians even if they were still wary of anyone following them. Each of them always carried a weapon when they left Maddie's small flat. The war waged on elsewhere in the world and there was still considerable danger—especially for an agent and someone who had shot a Nazi officer. Enemy agents still operated in the city. And Maddie's cover had been broken.

It hadn't been safe for them after Rachel shot the Nazi officer in Maddie's dressing room. They managed to escape from the nightclub before they were found and tortured or killed. Two of the waiters working for the Underground carried out the bloody body rolled into a carpet from one of the rooms at The Ritz. Maddie was directed to lay low after that night and was not summoned to any more missions other than passing occasional messages to other agents, usually under the cover of darkness.

She no longer performed at the nightclub adjacent to the Ritz Hotel since collaborators were still reporting agents working there with the French Resistance. She missed those nights of performing at the club. It had been a good cover and she had felt useful. But now it was too dangerous to even find a piano to play in a hidden bar or at one of the music rooms at the Sorbonne or another university in the city. She had felt lost the last few months not being able to play anywhere and filled her days with writing letters to William even if she couldn't send them.

A letter had arrived in early July. It was delivered by an earnest young man who appeared unaccustomed to the gendarme uniform that was too large for his lanky frame, pulling at his collar nervously as he extended the envelope and said, "*Bonjour, Madame. Cette enveloppe est arrivée pour vous aujourd'hui.*" He quickly turned on his heel and left her standing in the doorway.

The agents are getting younger every day. I guess I'm back on the job, she thought. She closed the door still in a daze and sat on the edge of the bed covered with the pale pink chenille bedspread that reminded her of the night with William in the cottage in the Cotswolds.

She ripped open the envelope with shaking hands and gasped when she read the first sentence.

July 5, 1944

Dear Madam,

It is with regret that I must inform you that your husband, Flight Officer William Craig, is reportedly missing in action. His last flight occurred on June 2. We have no further information at this time. You will most certainly be notified if further details regarding F.O. Craig's disappearance from active duty become available. On behalf of the Royal Air Force of the United Kingdom, I wish to convey that we will make every effort possible to determine F.O. Craig's whereabouts. However, at this time, he is declared missing in action.

Sincerely,

Flight Commander Gerald G. Fitzpatrick
Royal Air Force

She flung the letter on the floor with rage, then threw on a sweater—suddenly feeling cold—and ran out of the room and down the stairs, choking back tears and trying not to scream.

She thought she might stop breathing if she stopped moving. She raced through the streets as if she believed she could find him—he might appear in an alley somewhere or be sitting on a bench in a park sketching, then look up with that sly, teasing smile and say to her, "Maddie, I'm not gone. I'm never gone."

Maddie and Rachel had stayed in Paris after the letter came, not wanting to go back to England. Maddie hoped desperately that they would receive word that William had somehow survived his last mission. She had not given up hope. She had heard of many miraculous, unexpected reunions. He might show up at The Ritz where other aircrew men had managed to escape after their planes were shot down. And William was so clever and resourceful. She felt he was still alive. How could she feel this, if it wasn't true?

And now, over a month later, as Maddie and Rachel turned the corner of Rue de Bonaparte, they spoke in low voices still in shock with the latest news they had just heard.

With Hugh's help and others from the network of agents in Paris, they had finally been able to find the small flat in the 10th Arrondissement where Ma-mere and Grand-mere hid during the Occupation. The few neighbors who would talk to them and who they felt they could trust enough to ask questions, told them they had occasionally seen an older woman who wore a faded but still elegant coat and bright silk scarf over her head, walking with a frail, dignified elderly woman who leaned on a cane. They were told the two women had kept to themselves, making weekly trips together to the local market and the *boulangerie*. Collaborators were everywhere and would report Jews or those thought to be suspicious for any reason, for food or cash. The two women believed to be Ma-mere and Grand-mere had disappeared without a trace several months before the Liberation.

"Mother, maybe they went somewhere else and are still hiding," Maddie said hopefully.

She couldn't imagine losing William, her grandmother, and great-grandmother all in such a short time. It was too cruel. *William had to be alive.* She had to believe Ma-mere and Grand-mere had somehow survived too. But people were disappearing every day from Paris—some said at a horrifyingly accelerated rate as the Germans became more enraged that the Allies and the Russians were gaining more ground. With the Americans returning to the City, victory seemed imminent. But war still raged on with mounting casualties on both sides.

"I know you want to believe that," Rachel said with a sigh. She felt too sad to say more and especially since she was about to give Maddie something she knew would upset her. After they entered the café and sat down, she placed an envelope in front of Maddie who looked down at her name written in a familiar hand and gasped.

"This came this morning, Madeleine," Rachel said. She called her Madeleine when she had something difficult to tell her. Maddie felt her chest would burst. *Could this be the good news she had been so desperately hoping for?*

"Hugh managed to get it to me," Rachel said carefully, studying Maddie's face. "It was found in William's things at the Manor. He must not have had a chance to send it."

Maddie's heart jumped. Rachel placed her hand on Maddie's hand, wanting to take care of her daughter. She motioned to a waiter wearing a long white apron and holding a small white pad, to take their order which she quickly gave before sending him away.

Maddie glanced at her mother as she removed the letter from the envelope with a shaking hand, took a deep breath and began to read, noticing the date:

May 28, 1944

Dearest Maddie,

I am writing a few words at the Manor before I leave again. By the time you read this, the war may be turning our way and maybe you can get out soon. I so hope that you are safe, my darling. Please be careful. As if I could tell you what to do. I have talked to Bluebell and she seems to think you can handle yourself. But it's not right, Maddie. You should leave Paris as soon as you can. I will find you wherever you are, just as you found me.

We will be together again soon, I promise. But there is more I have to do. We have to believe we will win this bloody war. A very apt description. Yes, I have picked up a bit of the local color. It's all about fitting in, as you know.

So much has happened to both of us and things have changed, but not my love for you. We will have so much to talk about when this is over. But just being with you will be enough.

Please listen to me and go home or at least back to England. I am so worried that something will happen to you. Hugh can take care of you. We will find each other. No matter what happens, I will be all right.

Until we are together again, all my love to you always,

William

Maddie looked up from the letter then read it aloud to her mother. Her eyes were brimming with tears as she carefully folded the small piece of paper, returned it carefully into the envelope and put it back in her handbag resting on the table. Rachel took her hand again as her eyes also filled with tears. They sat in silence as Rachel touched Maddie's cheek tenderly and squeezed her hand.

It seemed that only a few moments had passed when the waiter hurried back to their table holding a tray above his head. He briskly set down a steaming plate with a golden *omelette au fromage* and incongruously, a cheerful sprig of bright green parsley beside it.

Where did he find that? Maddie wondered. *And what is the point?* She felt she was suffocating with anger and hopelessness.

The waiter then placed a wicker basket containing a small warm baguette with a minuscule pat of precious butter, two plates, and two cups of café au lait on the table. He nodded to them with a vague smile and said, *"Bon appétit,"* before rushing back to the kitchen for another order.

Maddie wondered how she was going to eat anything. She thought the waiter had probably noticed the sadness that hung in the air between her and Rachel and didn't want to linger to see any more. *How many similar scenes like this had he witnessed during the last four years since the Occupation began?*

Rachel sipped her coffee and spread butter onto a piece of baguette then chose her words carefully. "Maddie, darling, it might be time to go back to England. Hugh can help us to get home. Think about it."

Maddie looked at her mother and spoke firmly, "This feels like my home now. I need to stay at least until this horrible war is over. Maybe William will find his way back to me. I can't leave yet. People are reported missing and then they suddenly appear!" She said defiantly as her eyes filled with tears again.

"But sooner or later, Maddie, you need to return to your music. It will help," Rachel said with emotion tightening her throat. "You could even perform again in London, I'm sure—if you wish. Before we return to New York." She felt desperate to give her daughter something to look forward to— something to hold on to.

"Maybe you're right. We'll see, Mother. But my heart isn't in it, right now. I'm not ready yet," Maddie said as she pushed her plate with the untouched half of the omelet and the coffee cup away from her.

Rachel put her fork down on her plate, wiped her mouth with her napkin then folded it carefully and placed it next to her plate. She sighed and said emphatically but with love, "Think about it, Maddie. We can talk later." Then she rose slowly.

Maddie saw the same strength in her mother she had seen the night she shot the Nazi officer.

Rachel placed a hand gently on Maddie's shoulder. "I will see you back at the flat. You probably need some time to yourself." She leaned down to kiss Maddie on both cheeks and without another word, turned and left the café.

* * *

An hour later, Maddie still sat frozen in place, feeling incensed at the officers and civilians cheerfully chatting at other tables in the crowded café—an annoying blur of swirling voices. *How dare they laugh and enjoy themselves.* She caught the odd word or phrase spoken with an American accent, then a Parisian, *"mon dieu..."*, *"ce soir, je pense que..."*, *"ou nous allons..."* She felt no curiosity to listen to more fragments of conversation and quickly picked up her small leather handbag containing William's letter, clutching it to her chest.

Maddie left the café, walking away from Boulevard St. Germain toward the Seine and Notre Dame Cathedral with a vague plan to sit in a pew of the immense church. She knew she was like her mother in so many ways—she also found solace in the quiet majestic beauty of churches and chapels. She passed a small market with a few buckets of flowers on the sidewalk and a sign in the window, *"Du Poisson Frais Ici,"* then a pastry shop—one of so many that were springing up in the streets of Paris, exuding small bursts of optimism that were growing in the city with each day.

As Maddie walked further on La Rue Bonaparte and then turned toward the Seine, she felt dazed and disconnected from her body. She looked up to see Notre Dame. Just as she considered crossing the street and entering the huge awe-inspiring cathedral with its gargoyles and flying buttresses, she changed her mind and continued walking toward the Louvre. She knew that although the Nazis had re-opened the Louvre during the Occupation, the most valuable artworks had been taken away for safe-keeping in 1939 and were not yet returned. But she thought, if I can see even a few pieces of art, I will feel close to William and then I can breathe.

Suddenly, on the opposite side of the street, she noticed an art gallery with a sign hanging in the window written in English—"By appointment only" with the same phrase in French underneath, *"Surrendez-vous uniquement."* This is odd, she thought. Who would they expect with the war still going on? And why a sign written in English? Maybe for the American soldiers who were arriving in Paris every day?

She tapped lightly on the door and saw through the small beveled glass window, a tall, thin man wearing a burgundy silk vest and a monocle approaching. He didn't look particularly welcoming. She thought, if I can coax him to let me in and see even a few paintings, I won't feel like my life is over.

"*Oui, Mademoiselle?*" he said with a scowl then reluctantly opened the door. He stood in the doorway, glowering at her with his arms crossed. Squinting through his monocle with one eyebrow raised, he peered at her with polite disdain then seemed to change his opinion and asked gruffly, "*Comment puis-je vous aider?*"

"*Est-il possible de voir certaines de vos oeuvres?*" Maddie asked with a smile, thinking if she looked friendly, she might thaw his iciness and see some of the paintings she had glimpsed behind him.

He looked her over with an appraising eye and seemed to decide she wasn't French. He switched to lightly accented English but continued peering at her sternly, "Well, *typiquement*, I take appointments *seulement*." Then his expression appeared to soften. Maddie thought he might have noticed the tears in her eyes that she quickly wiped away.

"I suppose I can make an *exception. Enterprise est très lente. Bien sur*," he said, then motioned her inside.

As Maddie passed through the narrow hallway and entered the converted stone 18th century Neoclassical town house, a large beautiful gallery appeared with one wood-paneled wall and small copper sconces providing scant fans of light that cast triangular ghostly shadows throughout the room. The other walls were painted in a contrasting eggshell white.

The center of the room was brightened by narrow beams of sunshine bursting through an arched skylight in the ceiling high above, that illuminated a collection of paintings of different sizes hung on the walls with ample space around them. All the artwork had been placed so that they could each be fully appreciated.

There was a variety of styles—in the Impressionist tradition and some more abstract in the current modern fashion including some Cubist-style still-lifes, landscapes, and portraits, and some even more dramatically representational pieces painted with odd shapes in vivid colors. Most were labeled as completed in the 1930s and 1940s.

She began walking slowly from one painting to another, silently absorbing each work as she imagined each painter's life and circumstances.

The gallery owner watched her curiously and asked, "*Puis-je vous aider?*" She felt him studying her closely as she moved through the gallery. He seemed almost respectful and may have noticed the melancholy mix of impatience and sadness she felt.

As he followed Maddie, he told her she could take her time as there was no hurry, "*Pas de precipitation.*" He easily switched back to a few words in English, almost kindly, then a French phrase, "*Est-ce que vous regardes,*" his eyebrows raised, "*pour quelque chose extraordinaire—par chance?*" He was asking if she was looking for something in particular.

Maddie shook her head and murmured, "*Je ne suis pas sur,*" as she turned toward another wall of framed landscapes and portraits. Just then as if a spotlight was shining upon it, a large painting vibrated with life and dominated the wall, drawing her to it.

She stepped closer and gasped, then stopped short in front of it—not believing what she was seeing.

It was *The Golden Road*, signed in distinctive block letters, *CRAIG*. But something had changed. A familiar figure was walking away from her. On the road winding into the hills.

CPSIA information can be obtained
at www.ICGtesting.com
Printed in the USA
LVHW052226140723
752120LV00005B/76